The Second Profile

Robert Buuck

All characters and events in this publication, other than those clearly in the public domain, are fictitious and any resemblance to real persons, living or dead, is purely coincidental.

Cover designed by Debbi Stocco, illustration by Blair Harrington. Edited by Marianne Morris.

First published in 2013.
This edition published in 2014.
ISBN 978-0-9893890-8-2 (Paperback)

Copyright © Robert Buuck, 2013. All rights reserved.

CONTENTS

CHAPTER ONE, The First Hit...p.7

CHAPTER TWO, The Raid..p.13

CHAPTER THREE, The Database..p.22

CHAPTER FOUR, The Accident p.30

CHAPTER FIVE, The Eagle p.39

CHAPTER SIX, The Player p.48

CHAPTER SEVEN, The Boat p.54

CHAPTER EIGHT, The Nurse...p.66

CHAPTER NINE, The Board p.81

CHAPTER TEN, The Executive p.94

CHAPTER ELEVEN, The Metamorphosis p.104

CHAPTER TWELVE, The No-Show p.121

CHAPTER THIRTEEN, The Profiler p.135

CHAPTER FOURTEEN, The Profile p.147

CHAPTER FIFTEEN, The IPO p.160

CHAPTER SIXTEEN, The Farm p.173

CHAPTER SEVENTEEN, The Queen p.190

CHAPTER EIGHTEEN, The Reporter p.207

CHAPTER NINETEEN, The Connection p.219

CHAPTER TWENTY, The Deadline..p.235

CHAPTER TWENTY-ONE, Day One p.246

CHAPTER TWENTY-TWO, Day Two …...............................p.265

CHAPTER TWENTY-THREE, Day Three p.282

CHAPTER TWENTY-FOUR, Day Four p.297

CHAPTER TWENTY-FIVE, Day Five ….....……………..…....p.310

CHAPTER TWENTY-SIX, Day Six p.322

CHAPTER TWENTY-SEVEN, Day Seven p.334

CHAPTER TWENTY-EIGHT, Day Eight ....…...............p.348

CHAPTER TWENTY-NINE, Day Nine p.364

CHAPTER THIRTY, Day Ten ....…p.382

*To my wife Gail
who suffered with only moderate complaints
all the late night typing, and provided
positive feedback to the first draft at a time
when it was really needed.*

CHAPTER ONE
The First Hit

The larger of the two men tapped the onyx ring on his right hand rhythmically against the steering wheel as he glanced one more time into the mirror. They were parked in a tow-away zone on the side street facing the restaurant, but the presence of numerous other cars in a similar situation suggested that they were not likely to get any special attention. Dressed in a navy blue sport coat and gray slacks, Jack Shafer could have easily blended into the after-dinner flow of people filtering into the nearby hotel, although his rugged physique and chiseled features might have drawn a few glances from some of the nurses coming back to their rooms after a post-convention party.

Shaffer's companion in the front seat was wearing the best suit that Sears had to offer, along with a gray patterned tie that almost, but not quite, appeared to be a good match with the brown tone of the suit. A second tie was in the gym bag in the trunk and would be thrown away the next morning with the rest of the outfit. The one item that most differentiated his attire from that of his partner was the name badge pinned to the right lapel of his suit coat.

NORTH AMERICAN ASSOCIATION FOR GYNECOLOGY
1985 ANNUAL MEETING
DR. BRUCE R. OLSON
CHICAGO, ILLINOIS

The name badges provided at most medical conventions are not designed with subtlety in mind. Three by four inches at a minimum. Blue background for physicians, red for exhibitors, and green for visitors. Lloyd Barnett's was blue.

Barnett had been wearing the blue Dr. Olson badge that afternoon at the convention as he observed the Telmark Corporation exhibit booth and made the ID on John Levard. It had been several years since he had seen Levard, but the image was still burned in his mind and he had no difficulty in picking him out again. While standing in the aisle with his back to the booth, Barnett had overheard Levard invite one of the salesmen to join him for dinner at Murray's Steak House, and a subsequent check of the address had brought 'Dr. Olson' and his partner to their King Street location in time to see Levard and three others enter the restaurant a little before seven. The two hours of waiting since then had done little to improve either Barnett's or Shaffer's disposition.

"I wish to hell you'd ditch the cigarettes," Shaffer said when Barnett lit up his third one of the hour. "The light's gonna attract attention, and the smoke is driving me nuts."

"Well I can't hand it out the window when I'm wearing this badge. I'm a doctor. Remember?"

"Yeah. You're a doctor and I'm a priest. You're gonna need a doctor if you keep up with that smoking." Shaffer was not going to quit. "I don't know why you don't take better care of your body."

"Lighten up, Jack. You've got to have some fun while you're living. You're a long time dead."

In what might have been viewed as a small act of contrition, Barnett rolled his window down another inch, but the cigarette stayed in the car, and so did most of the smoke. "What time is it now?" he asked. "We've got to get this thing moving."

"It's a little after nine," Shaffer said, without looking at his watch. If he was at all nervous about their plans, it would not have been obvious to the casual observer. "He's gotta be coming out pretty soon."

Inside the restaurant, John Levard was deciding whether or not to have one more after-dinner drink. A small man in his early fifties with a slight facial tic that seemed to intensify as the evening wore on, Levard had not stopped complaining since he sat down for drinks and dinner two hours before.

"I'm going back early," he said to the others at the table. "You guys don't need me here and I sure as hell have better ways to spend my time." After walking the concrete floors at the convention center in Toronto for a day and a half, Levard had made his decision. He was now booked on American Airlines Flight 361 to Boston at 1 p.m. the next day.

"Your know John, you're not going to get a lot of sympathy from us when you start bitching about spending a couple of days at one convention. We go to four or five of these a year and work the booth all week." Steve Kyle, the most senior of the three salesmen at the advanced age of 32, was trying to provide some element of balance to the conversation. "You engineering types fly in first class," he said, "spend two days at the show, stay in a nice hotel, eat at great restaurants, and then you talk like you're pulling the tough duty. Try spending five days straight at one of these things."

"I've been there, Steve. All these meetings start to look alike when you've gone to as many as I have."

Although product promotion at conventions was the responsibility of the Telmark sales and marketing staff, Levard knew that, as the company's vice president of catheter engineering, he needed to go to a few of the meetings each year to see what the competition was doing. On this night, keeping up with the competition did not require a great deal of effort, since most of them seemed to be eating in the same restaurant, half a block down and across the street from the Holiday Inn where the Telmark personnel were staying.

Turnover of personnel in the sales side of the industry was a relatively common occurrence in the eighties, and it was not unusual at these meetings to see two or three people who had once worked for your company now sporting the name badge for some other outfit and vice versa. One of the Telmark alums, who had been a district manager when Levard first joined the company four years before, stopped by to say hello as the check was being paid.

"You guys didn't let John talk to any customers today, did you?" asked the alum. "When I was with the company we assigned one of the rookie salesmen to stick with him all day so he wouldn't screw up any big accounts."

"Yeah, yeah," Levard said, the tic firing off again, distorting what was to have been a friendly grin. "Talk it up. My products saved your ass when you were with Telmark."

In the white Toyota parked on King Street, Barnett and Shaffer were watching the door of the restaurant and making periodic glances into their respective rear view mirrors. The rental sticker on the back bumper of their car had been covered with silver duct tape, a fact that could have been noticed by a careful observer, of which, as they anticipated, there were none. The exchange of license plates made at the airport parking lot two days earlier when they picked up the car was the only other effort made at subterfuge.

As Barnett was lighting yet another cigarette, Steve Kyle was asking John Levard if he wanted to join the group for some drinks at a bar on Yonge Street. The invitation was proffered in a tone and with a lack of eye contact sufficient to leave the clear inference that the group would not be disappointed if Levard went back to the hotel, took a warm bath, and crawled in bed early so as not to cramp their style.

"Thanks, but I'll pass," Levard responded, to no one's surprise. "I'm going to walk once around the block to get the kinks out and then call it a night."

The last mistake of John Levard's life was to turn left at the end of the block onto Spadina Avenue and then walk along a darkened section of the street where former store owners had long since recognized the lack of pedestrian traffic. The front passenger door of the Toyota sedan had opened almost immediately when Levard came out of the restaurant. Barnett had gone five steps toward the hotel before remembering to drop the cigarette and button his suit coat over the slight bulge on the left side of his waistline. When Levard split off from the other three men and turned at the corner, Shaffer started the car and slowly pulled out onto King Street as Barnett crossed against the light to close the gap between himself and the target.

"Mr. Levard! Mr. Levard!"

Levard stopped walking and turned around, peering into the dim light in an effort to see who was calling.

"Mr. Levard, I'm Dr. Bruce Olson from Chicago. I was talking to one of your associates today about a new product concept I'd like your company to look at. I know this is a strange time, but I'm leaving the meeting tomorrow and when I saw you come out of the restaurant I thought I'd better catch you while I had a chance."

As he spoke, Barnett casually took Levard's right arm with his left hand and began walking with him on a slight angle toward the darkened buildings bordering the wide sidewalk. The Toyota had turned left onto Spadina and was now stopped by the curb, 50 feet behind the two men walking on the opposite side of the street.

"Maybe we could discuss this at breakfast tomorrow," Levard said as he tried desperately to remember where he had seen this man before.

"That's not going to work for my schedule." Now the grip on Levard's arm was starting to tighten as Barnett spotted the alley 20 feet ahead on the left. As he glanced back he saw Shaffer crossing the street to take up a position behind them.

"If I could just show you this prototype."

Levard looked down one more time at the blue badge, straining to reconcile the name with the face, and watching as the man, in slow-motion horror, unbuttoned his coat, and with a smooth, fluid motion pulled a black revolver from a shoulder holster. In an instant the gun was jammed against Levard's rib cage, and now there were two men, each gripping one arm and pushing him into the alley, the taller of the two looking back at the street one more time.

"Give me your wallet!"

"I don't understand. Who are you?"

"Shut up – now the watch!"

"You're not a doctor – I know you!"

The gun was jammed harder into the ribs on the left side of Levard's body. As a look of recognition came to his face, he was pushed backwards by the explosive force of the hollow point lead bullet as it formed a small hole in the front of his chest and, a microsecond later, made a ragged and bloody exit out of his back, interrupted only by the massive rupture of the left ventricular chamber of the heart which had stopped beating by the time Levard's body hit the ground.

*

At exactly 9:35 on Tuesday morning, Barnett, dressed in brown slacks and a blue sweater, was feeding coins into a pay phone next to the rest rooms in the lower level of the Holiday Inn. "The assignment has been completed," he said to the disaffected voice on the other end of the line.

"Any difficulties?"

"None whatsoever."

"Thank you for the report. The remainder of your fee will be forwarded tomorrow. Enjoy your vacation."

"I will," Barnett responded, but the line was already dead.

As Barnett was hanging up the phone, Jack Shaffer was dropping a weighted gym bag off the stern deck of the Misty Gale as she turned into the wind to start back to the dock after an early morning tour of the Toronto harbor. Inside the bag were the Sears suit and ties, a billfold, watch, and gun, along with a blue badge for Dr. Bruce R. Olson, Chicago, Illinois.

CHAPTER TWO
The Raid

Under ordinary circumstances it might have been humorous, but on this night it did not even raise a chuckle. "Why are you whispering?" David asked. "We're still two blocks from the lab and there's not a soul within five hundred feet. And now I'm whispering myself."

The incongruity of four people whispering to each other as they slowly drove along the dark service road leading to the faculty parking lot at the school of veterinary medicine was not lost on David VanTassel. As the youngest of the group, and with the look of someone who seemed intent on being in a perpetually good mood, David had previously upset the others when he tried to lighten the atmosphere with a little humor, and so was not terribly surprised to see how seriously they were now taking themselves.

"David, you may think of this as a lark, but I assure you it's not." Carol Osterling was the leader of the evening's activities, and not in the mood for levity. "What we're going to be doing is technically considered breaking and entering and will qualify all of us for some time in jail if we're caught. Even though you'll be staying in the van, you'd still be considered an accessory."

It was 1:20 in the morning and they had ten minutes to go before David would pull the van into the parking lot. Osterling had been active in the US version of the Animal Rescue Band for several years and had organized this night's raid on the animal lab in the Gresham Hall sub-basement at the University of Northern Wisconsin's School of Veterinary Medicine. She was a woman who gave no visible indication of being in any way bothered by her appearance, despite the complete absence of makeup and hair styling. When Osterling had first visited the University ten days before to learn more about the conditions of the Gresham Hall lab, she felt very comfortable walking around and talking to the people she met, reliving for a short time her heady days as a radical student leader on the main campus in Madison some twelve years before. Now, with the heightened level of tension in the van, she was once again feeling the rush that came from being in command. On this night she was not just a systems analyst in the computer department of the First National Bank of Wisconsin, but the woman in charge of the raid that would wake up this state's social consciousness once and for all. So it was with an edge of authority in her voice that she asked Brian to review the layout of the lab one more time.

"I know we discussed it before," she said, "but I want to hear it again. We are not about to make any mistakes on my shift! Can we get into the main lab if we have time?"

Brian McKnight, a 23-year-old graduate student from Shawno, Wisconsin, was about as nervous as he had ever been in his life. After debating with himself for months about acting on what he had seen in the lab, he was convinced he had made the right decision, but was still scared about how he would handle himself over the next few hours.

"Not without setting off the alarm," he said. "The only key I could copy gets us in the service entrance and that connects to the stairwell. The big labs are in the main basement, but we'll miss them since we'll be taking the back steps down to the sub-basement. There are some utility rooms down there that aren't locked, and Kline's lab, which will be locked. On weekends the cleaning crew finishes at midnight and the first vet student comes in to feed the animals in the main lab at six a.m. We should have four hours by ourselves."

"I want us in and out in one hour,' Osterling said. "If any alarm goes off you're all gonna be on your own. David can't stay in the lot with the van. He'll come back at two thirty and every half hour after that unless there's trouble. If there is, we'll try and meet him over by the stadium."

Carol Osterling had been uncomfortable with this assignment ever since she started planning it two weeks before. Brian McKnight had contacted PMTA with a report about some experiments that were being conducted under conditions that he described as atrocious. Although the organization known as People for the Moral Treatment of Animals, or PMTA, did not condone violence, some of their staffers would occasionally pass on information to members of the Animal Rescue Band, and the ARB would take action if they could find a way to pull off a raid with a maximum public relations impact and a minimum chance of getting caught. When the ARB had gotten this call from their contact at PMTA, the message was transferred to Carol who in turn made the connection back to Brian and convinced him to help her gain access to the lab. As a potential target, the University vet school was not considered to be ideal. Most schools of veterinary medicine maintain an animal lab, but such labs are primarily intended as a means for the students to get surgical and medical training by treating a cross section of the local pet or stray population, usually on a gratis basis. As such, it is tough to make a charge of animal cruelty unless the lab conditions are substandard, which Brian did not think was the case at Northern Wisconsin. Dr. Kline's lab was another matter.

"This is a guy we wanted to shut down years ago," Carol had told Brian when they first met at a McDonalds restaurant three blocks from campus. "We had someone else send us an unsigned letter describing what he does to those dogs, but we had no way of getting into his lab. Tell me what he's doing in there now."

"I couldn't believe it the first time I saw it," Brian said. "He's got six dogs in there under conditions that'll just make you sick. What he's doing is trying to show what happens when the dogs can't sleep for more than a few minutes a day, so he's got three of the cages rigged up to get blasted by noise every few minutes and also to tip sideways in between sound blasts."

"What's being done to the other three dogs?"

"I think he switches the groups every one or two weeks so he can compare measurements of weight and body characteristics between dogs that sleep and those that don't. The three that aren't being blasted are in another section of the lab that has some sound baffling, but their cages don't look much better and the dogs I saw were all bruised from getting thrown around when they were in the first group. I don't think any dog gets out of there alive."

"Isn't science wonderful?" Carol said, slowly mouthing each of the three words as if speaking to an audience of lip readers.

"I just can't understand it. I don't know why the University lets him operate this way."

"It happens all the time, Brian, you'd be surprised at what we find. You did the right thing telling us about this and you're doing the right thing to help us get in the lab and rescue these dogs."

"What are we gonna do with the dogs if we get 'em out?" asked Brian.

"We'll get them out, don't worry. And when we do, Mary Devlin and I will take them to a vet I know near Milwaukee for examination and treatment. Later on, they'll go to some of our supporters. You don't need to know any more than that, but I can assure you they'll get the best possible treatment from these people."

The phone call two days earlier had been the first introduction to Mary Devlin. The ARB contact in Chicago had passed on instructions and the new name to a less than eager Carol Osterling, never one to be excited about getting outside advice under even the best of circumstances.

"For your job in Kline's lab, I want you to use somebody new. She'll be flying to Milwaukee on Northwest Flight 563 from Boston Saturday morning. Pull your van up in the arrival lane at exactly eleven forty-five and she'll get in."

"How will I know it's her?"

"She'll find you. I've given her the number on the dummy set of license plates. For the record, she's in her early thirties, about five foot two, a hundred and ten pounds, attractive. And she's English."

"English?"

"Yes. She's a nurse who just moved to Boston from London about twelve months ago. My British friends tell me she was active over there in the ARB for about seven or eight years. She's done the whole bit including helping out on the activity last year at Oxford where they burned a new dog lab on the day before it was scheduled to open.

"She's not too radical, is she? Some of the Brits have a reputation for violence that goes a lot farther than anything we've been doing over here. I'm going to have two rookies with me Saturday night and I don't want to have to worry about some wild woman going ballistic."

"I haven't met her but from what I've heard I can almost guarantee she won't be going ballistic on you, Carol. I was told that she's a woman with access to a lot of money who's very organized and methodical and about as committed as they come."

"We hope!"

"When you get inside the dog lab, have her take the pictures and check out the files. She's not going to be bringing any equipment along so you'll need to supply the camera and film, plus any tools you need. Questions?"

"No, I guess not."

"Okay, then drop the film in the mail to me as soon as you leave the campus and I'll arrange for publicity with PMTA."

*

When the ARB went into an animal lab, they always had several objectives in mind. Free the animals, destroy equipment that might be used for other tests, steal any records or files that could be used to incriminate the research process, and finally, take pictures. If possible, dozens of pictures, and not actually as the final step, but rather both before and after, so that hopefully the record would be clear about how the animals were being tortured in the name of science before being liberated by the good guys. It was not always possible to free the animals if you were in a lab that held a hundred rabbits or a few large chimps that are too strong or too diseased to handle safely. But it was possible to take photos, and the old adage about the worth of a picture is never truer than when getting front-page coverage in the local newspaper. Rule number one was to take pictures, everything else came second. If you had to leave in a hurry, you would at least have proof of what was going on in the lab.

As David pulled into the parking lot and turned off the lights, the drizzle that had started to fall 15 minutes before was beginning to turn into light rain. In the back of the van were two wire cages in which they hoped to be putting the dogs within the next hour. Carol would have liked to have six individual cages, but the van was not large enough and there had not been an opportunity to custom-build some other types of holding pen. The irony of jamming six dogs into the two small cages had not been lost on the group. When David first saw the van he said, "It'll be our luck to get past the cops and then get stopped by the Humane Society and cited for poor transportation conditions."

The rain was starting to move in sheets across the empty parking lot when they got out of the van and moved quickly over to a large pine tree near the back of the building. They watched without saying a word as David drove out of the lot and turned back on to East Campus Drive.

"Okay we've got one hour before he returns. Lead the way, Brian." Carol was whispering again.

A few minutes later, after they had left the van and walked quietly past the loading dock to the rear service entrance, Brian took out his key and opened the door several inches. They could see the faint glow from the EXIT sign inside the back hall but no other lights were visible in that part of the building.

"Okay, let's go in."

"Should I lock the door behind us?" Brian asked.

"Yes, lock it," Carol said. "It'll take us another few seconds to get out, but if they have anybody checking doors we'll be in deep trouble if they find it open. Nixon would probably still be in the White House if those bozos had locked the door behind them in Watergate."

Mary shielded her flashlight to allow enough light so Brian could see to lock the door and then pointed it to the floor as they walked along the inside hallway toward the steps. There was an open stairwell descending to the two lower levels with a door at the basement level leading into the main animal lab used by the vet school. As they started down the first flight of steps they could see the light from the lab.

"There are windows in the door to the main lab," Brian said quietly, "and they always leave some lights on. But there won't be anybody in there this time of night."

"All right, let's go," Carol said. "Stay low until we get past the door."

As they moved down the second flight of stairs, the noise that Brian had told them about became obvious. Every minute a series of blasts from some type of horn could be heard. This would last for about fifteen seconds, followed by the sound of metal rattling and the barking of dogs.

"Listen to that barking," Carol said. "It's not real barking from healthy dogs, it's almost a wail, a cry for help. That's why we're here!"

"This goes on all the time," Brian said, his confidence returning now that he was back on familiar ground. "The horns making noise and then the cages rattling. Twenty-four hours a day – seven days a week. Welcome to Science City!"

Mary had moved over by the door to the lab and was looking closely at the hinges and doorframe. The noise had stopped but light flashes could be seen under the door, the contrast with the dark hallway producing an eerie strobe light effect in the period of momentary silence between the horns and the rattling. "What's the light?" she asked.

"I forgot to mention that he also uses flashing lights on some kind of a cycle in between the other stuff. I guess he figures the dogs will get used to the noise if he doesn't mix it up a little." Brian was glancing nervously at Mary as if anticipating another put-down for the latest surprise, but she seemed more interested in the door as she pointed her flashlight at the hinges.

"Just how do you plan on us getting in here, Carol?"

"Well, I'm not sure, since I haven't done it before. I think we might have to pry it open with the crowbar. You have any ideas?"

"Well, I looked at your tool bag and saw that you didn't bring a pick kit for the lock, so we're going to have to take the door off. It's steel-jacketed and you don't have a drill, so it's got to come out of the frame. At least we won't have to worry about the noise, but once the door is out, it stays out. We'll have to work fast after we're inside."

As they pulled the door out of the frame and slid it against the wall, the first thing that hit them was the stench. Although probably always dirty, it seemed obvious that no one had been in to clean during the weekend.

Mary had taken one roll of film and was loading another. "You Yanks might win the prize. I never saw anything this bad in England!"

For the next twenty minutes, Carol and Mary raced through the lab taking pictures and looking for records. Records that could be taken with them if they seemed of value for display or publicity, or records that could be destroyed if they appeared to be of use for Kline's research. In the side room they found two other dogs, not the three they had expected. Both of them appeared in poor health, but at least not as bad off as the ones in the main section of the lab. Brian managed to find a hose which he hooked up to a sink faucet, and after getting all of the electrical connections unplugged, washed down the dogs with warm water. As he gently took them out of the cages and put on the collars and leashes, Mary and Carol spray-painted the walls with a variety of ARB slogans and miscellaneous words of wisdom for Dr. Kline.

"Are we ready?" Carol asked. "It's three fifteen now and David should be coming back again at three thirty. I think we're going to have to carry three of the dogs. I doubt that the ones from the rocker cages can make it up the two flights of steps. Brian, this time you can leave the tools here. They can't be traced."

One hour later, Carol and Mary were on their way back to Milwaukee after having taken Brian and David to an all-night restaurant near campus where Brian had parked his car. The next stop was going to be in a northern suburb of Milwaukee, where Carol would drop off the dogs at the friendly vet's office for examination and treatment before they went on to homes of ARB supporters. The film would go into the mailbox at the airport when she dropped Mary off for the return flight to Boston. Carol was starting to relax for the first time in several hours.

"Well, Mary, we had a few tight spots but I guess all's well that ends well. You did a great job and I'm glad you were along. How'd this compare to what you've done in England?" Carol kept an eye firmly glued to the speedometer to confirm their speed at exactly 55 miles per hour.

"I'm not sure you really want to hear how this compares to my other experiences," Devlin said softly, in a voice that did not suggest a desire for extended conversation. "Each of us has our own direction to take and it's unlikely we'll be together again. Those pictures should put Kline out of business, so I doubt that I'll be back in Wisconsin."

"Look, Mary, if there's something you think I could have done better I'd like you to tell me. You people started the ARB so I presume you've learned a thing or two along the way. I've got a thick skin and I'm happy to take a suggestion if you think I missed something."

"Just for the record, I didn't start the ARB, though I've been involved about eight years. I'd like to be doing this another eight years, but quite frankly, not with you. It's not one bloody thing you missed, but about six or seven." The stridency in Mary's voice seemed to be strangely out of keeping with the accent. "You had two rookies with us tonight, which is at least one too many. We had no way to communicate with the van. We should've had some type of walkie-talkie system along. We needed pictures in advance showing what the lab looked like, along with each of the doors. Brian could have taken them with a small camera when he was in there the last time. But the biggest mistake you made was not having video. Kline's lab would have been a gift from heaven for our cause if you had brought a video camera. This is 1986. Video cameras aren't that bloody expensive anymore. If you can't afford to buy one then I'll buy it for you. Two minutes of video on the telly with the sights and sounds from that lab could have doubled our membership and slowed down all of this bogus research that your government supports."

"Well, I'm sorry. I've never used video."

"You'd better learn! We move our mission by moving people, and in your country, people are moved by what they see on TV. Why do you think America finally got out of Vietnam? It was the pictures on the telly, bringing the war into the living room. Nobody wants to see the neighbor's kid get his leg blown off in living color, and nobody wants to watch dogs getting bounced around." Mary was looking straight ahead, staring into the dark Wisconsin night. "You know, in England the animal rights movement got started, in part, because some people liked to torture cats. Set 'em on fire and hear them scream. What Kline does is worse. We need to find ways to be sure men like him never have a chance to torture more animals in the name of science. Do you know what I mean, Carol? Do you know what I mean?"

Carol Osterling drove on to Milwaukee in silence, the dogs sound asleep in the back of the quiet van.

CHAPTER THREE
The Database

Martha Laudner pushed back from the computer terminal and turned around to face the print station. Even after seeing the information on the monitor, it was still a kick for her to watch the data spit out onto paper, the cog wheels on the printer spool moving in an episodic rhythm as the program software adjusted for the spaces between paragraphs and sections of the three-page report. She picked up the phone and dialed Morkin's number.

"Is he there? I've got something for him."

As she waited for David Morkin to come on the line, she broke apart the printout on the serrated lines, carefully pulled off the tractor feeds on each side of the three pages, and pushed the barely visible white confetti from the serrations off the counter and into the smaller of the two waste baskets that were within arm's reach.

"I found him! I found him, David, and I did it in less than two hours! The system's working even better than I expected. I knew it was looking good when I found Jacobs at GE and Martin from that little outfit in California, but this one really shows the power of the model now that I'm finally getting it loaded. Listen to this. Bachelor's in mechanical engineering from Michigan, two years work experience at a local company, then back for a masters degree in engineering with his thesis on Advances in Biomaterials. Four years experience with Dow then off to Stanford for an MBA. Worked as a plant manager for Baxter on the coast with several promotions along the way, and get this! Two years at one of their operations in Belgium and he speaks French!"

"Look, Martha, it does sound like a fit, but they all do at first," Morkin said when he was finally granted enough of a pause in Martha's staccato delivery to slip in a response. "It'll take awhile before we can put him on the short list."

"Bullshit, David! This guy's a fit and you know it! He fits at least six out of the nine spec points and that's only because I haven't checked out the other three yet. He's an Eagle!"

"What about a contact list?"

"I'm working on that. I should be able to pull up at least three of the organizational charts on his last assignments. I'm sure

I'll have the names and backgrounds of ten or twelve of his bosses and subordinates in the computer, given the companies he's worked for. This is working, David – just like I said it would!"

"I hope you're right, Martha. We've sunk a ton of money into this system of yours over the past six months."

"Do you want this sent over by messenger?" Martha asked, ignoring the remaining note of skepticism.

"No – I can't contact the client this soon after starting or he'll wonder how we earn our fee. Besides, you're going to need to give me three or four more names for the short list in case your Mr. Right doesn't pass the background checks."

As it proved out, David's skepticism was well placed. Martha's initial efforts to obtain a contact list off the database fizzled when she could develop only one of the organizational charts. When David made some calls to a few of his own contacts, it was soon apparent that "Mr. Right" was certainly not an Eagle, and indeed was unlikely to fly again at any altitude. One of David's sources was so eager to document Right's fall from grace that he Fed Ex'd a copy of the clipping from a trade journal referencing the lateral transfer of Mr. Right back to the States a year early from the Brussels position after his second arrest on a DWI. Martha had taken the setback in good form.

"It just shows that I've got to get more background information loaded, and keep the system up to date," she told Morkin. "I've just sent for a subscription to the journal that had the lateral transfer information, plus I've ordered two years of back issues. I've also ordered back issues on the other eight subscriptions I'm getting. I should have done that before, rather than just starting from my first copy. And, David–"

"Yes."

"I'm going to need some contract help again to load the new data."

"I thought you might."

In actuality, Martha preferred not to use contract help if it could be avoided. While she could argue that sitting at a keyboard entering information for two or three hours a day was not the best use of her talents, in fact she derived an almost palpable satisfaction from watching the files take shape. "Maybe in later years," she thought, "I can delegate all the data entry to an assistant." But at this stage she felt a need to touch each one of the files, if only electronically.

It had been a week since her overenthusiastic call to David, and she was now back to her normal Tuesday morning routine. She had been picked up by cab at 7:30 a.m. for the ten-minute ride to the Westview Tennis and Fitness Center for the 8:30 aquatics class in which she participated three days a week. There had been a new cabdriver this morning who could barely conceal his displeasure when given the address of the fitness center, realizing that he had just spent five minutes helping Martha into the cab with her walker so he could drive 11 blocks and run up a $3.20 tab. Martha's five-dollar tip partially restored his civility, and he promised to be back at the Center to pick her up at 10 if Martha's usual driver, a thick-necked Ukrainian woman with an almost impenetrable accent, was not back on duty.

Even though her recovery had gone better than the doctors had predicted, Martha was still frustrated about the amount of time it took her to do basic tasks. Getting into a dry swimsuit and later out of a wet one were the two items on this day that reminded her how far she had to go. Later, when she returned to her apartment and made her way slowly into the kitchen for coffee and a late breakfast, she couldn't help but think of the amount of effort she had put into the place over the past few months.

The apartment was of an architectural style and standard typical of those built in the upscale Delwood section of Baltimore during the late 1970s. Two bedrooms, 1-1/2 baths, a kitchen with a breakfast bar, and a small dining room where Martha had chosen to hang three neatly framed art posters – two Miros and a rather striking blue and gold Matisse. A careful observer would notice during a walk around the apartment that there were no family photos on any walls or counter-tops. No cute little framed slogans, no stuffed toys on dressers, no family heirlooms or mementos.

"Not yet," Martha had decided, "not just yet."

Martha had taken the larger of the two bedrooms for use as an office, and when the apartment was being remodeled, gave instructions that the full bathroom should connect to the smaller bedroom for her use and that both rooms should be tiled in a style compatible with the kitchen to make it easier for her to move around with the walker.

The final change was the addition of a Schlage two-tumbler lock on the office door. Although this was not intended to keep out the committed, it did deter the curious during those few times that Martha had a visitor. It's a storage area, mother," Martha had said during one of those rare visits. "A lot of stuff from the house and Harry's office."

On this day her first emotion upon entering the room was a sense of pride, followed quickly by concern that the project she had embarked upon was not progressing at a rate that could sustain itself. Her premature gloating to David on the French-speaking washout was not the prime issue. The bigger question was her ability to develop a deep enough database with cross-tabular scan capabilities to allow for searches that meant something. To fine-tune the system she needed to do more searches, but Morkin wouldn't trust her with more searches until she fined-tuned the system, and so it went. At least the Tuesday schedule offered Martha the comfort of a routine that had been developing over the past 20 weeks. This day was scan-clip-and-enter day. Six or seven hours broken up only by a late lunch and a trip down to the first floor to get the mail.

The room still had that smell you get when you turn on a new electric appliance for the first few times. The sort of smell that makes you think for an instant that something is burning, and then you remember that you just switched on the TV five minutes before. In this case it was not a TV, but rather a computer, and not one computer but two. Martha had a pair of the second generation Wang units that together functioned as a crude type of network in the days when the term networking was not yet part of the common vernacular. When she had asked the Wang salesman to bring the multiplex cabling and connect the two computers to the compiler, he thought she was nuts.

"Why don't you just get yourself a mainframe like an IBM System II and skip all this network hocus pocus?"

"You convince my partner to spend eighty-five thousand dollars, and I'll order the IBM this afternoon. In the meantime, I'm happy to have this setup."

And indeed she was. Her latest calculations had shown that she was now at about 15% of capacity and using an additional 5% of memory each month, so she had at least a year before the system would near the capacity level when sorts and outputs would start getting sluggish. By then she thought, if she couldn't convince David of the value of a mainframe, she should wrap it up.

In Monday's mail, Martha had received the Sunday editions of *The Boston Globe* and *The Philadelphia Inquirer*. *The New York Times* was delivered direct along with *The Baltimore Sun*. In this day's mail she should get four or five more Sunday editions from Detroit, Minneapolis/St. Paul, Atlanta, Miami and maybe Denver. On Wednesday, the California Sunday papers usually arrived. She had dropped the DC papers after going seven straight weeks without a hit.

She started as always with *The New York Times* business section. Her practiced eye quickly skimmed the lead lines on any articles that covered hirings, firings, promotions or transfers of execs in the biotech, medical device or medical service industry. She was also looking for information on new company formations and mergers. When she had first started entering data, she circled the article and then went straight to the computer to set up a file if it was a new name, or add to the file of an existing name. Now she clipped the articles of interest and waited to go through all of the publications available on that date before starting to load files. While this was only marginally more efficient, Martha focused on the goal of getting rid of big stacks of paper – reducing them to small clip piles – and then disposing of those piles when the data entry was completed. Papers and magazines into the big industrial wastebasket. If Martha was task driven, and indeed she was, one of the things that drove her was her goal of ridding herself of as many pieces of paper as possible in the shortest amount of time.

"Dennis Lathan promoted to VP of Sales at Southwest Bio-Tech" – *clip* – *new name for exec files* – *add to organization section of existing company file. Good article for biography on exec. Also lists prior boss for contact list.*

"Northern Cal-Bio announces Initial Public Offering to be co-managed by Hambrecht & Quist" – *clip* – *add to company file and send form letter to H&Q requesting prospectus for additional info on company and senior execs.*

> *"Company president killed in crash of private plane"* – clip – *delete exec file, update company organizational file.*

> *"Denver-based medical company, Remote Monitoring Inc. granted patent for novel technology on patient monitoring system"* – clip – *new name for company file, no execs mentioned. Send for D&B report and mail form letter to company asking for product literature and financials.*

Since Martha knew that Remote Monitoring was not in her company file as yet, the odds that it was still private were high, and therefore it was not likely that the company would send financial statements. Still, she was continually amazed by the type of apparently privileged information that companies sent out to anyone with a first class stamp and the chutzpah to use it.

Based on a variety of sources that she had tapped over the past few months, Martha estimated that there were somewhere between 450 and 500 medical device and service companies in the US of a size that would be of interest to her. In the biotech area, there were only about 40 companies, but the number was starting to grow rapidly. If a total of 500 companies currently existed in the universe that Martha was covering, and if she was hoping to identify the top eight to ten execs in each company, then she knew she had to obtain 4,000 to 5,000 names and files for the exec portion of her database. At this stage she had 360 companies but only 1,800 names, and many of those had only the barest detail in their files. Still, she had been adding about ten companies a week and about 40 new names, plus a lot of detail on the existing files.

"One new company name so far," she thought, "but a net of zero on the execs." The hit rate from the pile of trade journals turned out to be much better.

> *David Stockton promoted to VP of Marketing at Pharmaseal Division of Baxter* – clip – *lots of good bio information. Age, education, marital status, prior experience.*

> *University of Utah has unusually good record in helping start high tech companies in Salt Lake area* – clip

> – *four medical company names on list of which three are new files. Five exec names, all new. Send for more info from companies.*
>
> ***Remote Monitoring strengthens foothold in patient monitoring business with issues of new patents*** – *clip – more info on background of company and mention of Jerry Fenton as founder and CEO. New exec file.*
>
> ***Medelectro employee asked to testify before congressional panel on pacemaker lead issue*** – *clip – "company says Tim Foster is the in-house expert on subject although he is only 28 and an assistant product manager in the marketing department" – clip – pretty junior guy for the exec file but great bio info and a picture!*

God love the trade journals! When editors had pages to fill between the ads, no level of background was too trivial. Martha's general rule was to set up exec files only on people at the director, vice president, chief operating or chief executive officer levels, plus those with more nebulous senior titles such as group product manager, lead engineer, project manager, etc. She made exceptions in cases like Foster's where there was some evidence to suggest that the individual was destined for greater things and there was enough background information available to warrant establishing a file. In this situation, both criteria were met. Foster sounded like he had potential and there was a ton of information available, thanks to an editor with space to fill.

> Donald Rocke, Medelectro VP for Regulatory Affairs, acknowledges that it is unusual for the company to have someone as junior as Foster provide the primary testimony to a congressional inquiry, "but Tim was the guy who set up the study, worked directly with the surgeons to collect the data, did the statistical analysis, and prepared the in-house report. When he was briefing our senior executives, it became obvious that he should be the one to testify. He had the firsthand knowledge and conveyed an unusually high level of integrity and competence for someone his age."

The article went on to provide much of the biographical data that Martha wanted to have as a key part of any file. She had set up her system so that she could do sorts and cross-tabs on a number of data sets. As she read the article on Foster, she circled the items for entry.

Age:	28
Married:	wife's name Britta
Children:	no mention, code 22 for unknown
Sex:	male
Race:	code 3
Education:	BS mechanical engineering, Notre Dame
	MBA from Stanford – dates unknown
Career Path:	2 years at Zimmer as mechanical engineer
	Currently at Medelectro as asst. product manager
Specialty:	Orthopedics, two years
	Cardiovascular, one and one-half years

Martha had twelve different sort tabs established in her database structure, of which she was able to make entries for Foster in nine, an unusually high number for a first contact. The picture had allowed her to code in the number three for Caucasian. Martha always had a little twinge of guilt when she coded race, since she knew that it was technically illegal to use that information on searches for clients. She had successfully rationalized that issue in her mind with the statement that "this works to the advantage of black or Hispanic candidates when clients look for a minority to help them fill an EEO quota."

The picture also allowed Martha to fill in one of the other sorts – appearance. Although not something that was usually mentioned on a client's spec sheet, both David and Martha knew that the good-looking candidates had major advantages over the less attractive ones, and she had developed a one through four rating on appearance, with four being the top. She looked at the picture for the second time. "Foster is a four, definitely a four!"

The next two trade journals yielded three more company names and four more execs, although none with as much detail as Foster. Still, "not a bad morning's work," Martha thought, as she pushed over to the door for the walk into the kitchen. The bell would be ringing shortly to indicate that the mail was there, so she had 20 minutes for a quick snack before starting the afternoon routine.

*

CHAPTER FOUR
The Accident

Martha's routine had been very different before the accident. Before the accident Martha was always laughing, always finding something to smile about when she talked to Harry. Before the accident, she had been viewed as someone who was impetuous and stimulating, perhaps even provocative.

When she met the young Harry Laudner during their second hour economics seminar at Cornell University in 1968, they were both majoring in Industrial Relations. Martha did not become aware of the tall student from Chicago until he sat next to her in class, when it resumed after the semester break. The same lack of awareness did not hold true for Harry, who had noticed Martha in the very first week of class, aided in no small part by the fact that she was one of only three women in the class of 24. In 1968, women pursuing a degree in what was generally perceived as a male occupational path were clearly the exception, and even more so if they looked like Martha.

"What do you know about Kramer?" Harry had asked in a voice that was not filled with an obvious level of self-confidence. "I hear he's one of the toughest graders in the economics department," he continued, not waiting for a response. Years later Harry had confessed that he had agonized for days over what his first line of conversation should be after he had seen the class list and realized that he might have a chance to get to know the bright and attractive coed who had caught his eye the previous year. From the beginning, Martha had been aware that if anything was to come from their relationship, she would be the one to move it forward, and despite several thinly veiled suggestions from her mother that she was pursuing someone out of her league, she and Harry dated during the remainder of their time at Cornell and were married the day after graduation.

They had both sought out interviews during their last semester on campus. Although Martha received the better job offer from Prudential in Hartford, they decided to move to Baltimore, where Harry took a job as a recruiter at the regional office of Arlington Capital Corporation, a large investment banking firm headquartered in New York. Martha accepted a junior position in the personnel department of Lynncor Fabric, a small clothing manufacturer, working for a boss who was perceptive enough to quickly delegate numerous duties to the young graduate who seemed to find ways to improve on policies and procedures that had been in place for the past 20 years. One of those policies related to maternity leave, which Martha used twice during the next seven years when Jennifer and Thomas were born.

Although the day-to-day aspects of her job were not overly challenging, Martha still enjoyed the mix of responsibilities associated with being a new mother while at the same time covering an increased departmental load at the company. One of her interests was in reading about the advances in technology that were then becoming increasingly available with midsize computers, and she jumped at the chance to obtain a system from the accounting department when they upgraded to newer equipment.

"I don't know how you're going to use the damn thing," her boss had said, "but if anyone can figure it out, it's probably you."

Martha had first loaded the company's compensation data into the system with modest payoffs in information flow and efficiency. She quickly progressed to more creative applications as she learned some basic programming skills and began to realize the potential of the data storage and retrieval power inherent in computer systems. Within a few months she had a process in place which allowed her to load and store applicant information, and then call up and cross-match that data when there was a job opening in any of the different company departments.

When Arlington Capital decided to consolidate the divisional personnel functions into their New York office, Harry was offered a transfer, which after a remarkably short discussion, he and Martha decided to turn down. A recent purchase of a new home in one of the wooded suburban areas outside of Baltimore, and the increasing involvement of the kids in neighborhood activities, caused Martha and Harry to realize that, for better or for worse, they were going to be Maryland residents for a long time to come.

With the security of Martha's second income, Harry took what for him was a rather bold career move. He accepted a job with a small executive search firm specializing in the recruitment of executives for healthcare companies.

"David Morkin and Associates is the type of firm that is in the perfect spot to capitalize on the explosion in healthcare that's going to take place over the next several years," Harry explained to Martha as they drove to meet Mr. and Mrs. Morkin for dinner on a wet Friday evening. "The aging of the population and America's preoccupation with health at any cost means that dozens of new companies will start up or spin off of older firms, and they'll need CEOs and VPs of marketing and finance. The new outfits won't have the experienced personnel staff to recruit these people, so they'll have to turn to pros like Morkin and Associates to fill their top positions."

"Sounds like you're the one being recruited," Martha responded as Harry turned into the restaurant parking lot.

"Maybe so. I realize that I'm susceptible to a hot story right now. I'm tired of working for a big organization and I like the idea of being part of a smaller group where I can make an impact, not only in the firm, but also on my own income."

"Just how small is this group? How many associates are there in David Morkin and Associates?"

"Well – right now I would be the first associate. It would be me, David, one secretary, and one assistant that does some of the resume shuffling and contact work with candidates and references. But David worked for ten years at one of the big search firms in DC, and has some clients who'll stay with him, plus some great contacts with the venture capital groups who finance a lot of these new healthcare companies."

Harry had turned off the ignition but was reluctant to end the conversation. "Look – I haven't officially accepted yet. I told David that I wanted you to meet him and have you hear more about the firm. And I'm sure he wants to meet you, although he didn't make that a requirement of the offer. If after tonight you think it's a bum idea, I'll tell him to take a hike."

In hindsight, it was not really a tough decision. Martha had more confidence in Harry's abilities than he did, and when she saw that Morkin was well connected, and certainly competent, she encouraged Harry to take the position. But not before she coached him through a negotiation strategy where he was able to secure a ten percent partnership interest up front and the assurance of additional step-ups to 20 and 30 percent positions after two and four year intervals, assuming that he was still in good graces with the firm. It was three years later almost to the day, in July of 1982, that the accident happened.

The progress of David Morkin and Associates had gone surprisingly close to plan after Harry joined the firm. There had been a significant increase in the commercial side of the healthcare business in the late 1970s, and the firm was increasingly being hired to recruit one or more of the key executives at various new companies. Harry had gotten the call on the International MedTech CEO job in May from a client he had worked for the previous year. With the prime prospect located in Orlando, Harry decided to combine his interview trip with some vacation time, so he and Martha packed the kids and assorted paraphernalia into the station wagon for the first true family vacation they had ever taken outside of Maryland and away from the relatives.

The Georgia state trooper who investigated the accident said later that he had not seen such a destructive head-on collision since his days patrolling the old two-lane mountain roads. The truck had crossed the median strip and plowed half way into the front seat of the station wagon, continued on up a sharp embankment, rolled over, and burst into the flames. The fire complicated the subsequent autopsy of the truck driver who, the trooper guessed, must have had some type of seizure or heart attack since "– he never had no driving troubles before."

Although the dashboard clock was stopped at 2:17, it was 10:45 p.m. at the home on Gatewood Avenue in suburban Baltimore when the phone rang.

"Mr. Morkin?"

"Yes."

"Sorry to bother you so late, but I just tracked down your home number. I'm Sergeant Daniel Blomley of the Georgia State Highway Patrol. Did – do you know a Mr. Harry Laudner?"

"Yes – what is this about?"

"Mr. Morkin, I found your card in Mr. Laudner's briefcase. I regret to inform you that he was killed in a traffic accident this afternoon on Highway 301, about twelve miles south of Jesup."

"My God!"

"Sir – I must also tell you that a young boy in the car was also killed and a girl is hospitalized in critical condition and not expected to live. There was also a woman in the back seat who was badly injured. Do you know, would that be Mrs. Laudner?"

"Of course!"

"Well, sir, if it wouldn't be too much of an imposition, I wonder if you could assist us in contacting the next of kin."

It was 28 days before Martha came out of the coma, and another 40 days before she was stable enough to be moved back to Baltimore to start rehabilitation. Her mother told her she was fortunate to have been in a coma when Jennifer died, six days after the accident. "I don't think you could have handled three funerals so close together, my dear," her mother had said. "I seriously doubt your father would have made it through the ordeal if it hadn't been for me."

Of the several vows Martha made to herself over the months of recovery that followed, the first was never to exhibit any behavior that would signify, in any remote way, that she might one day be like her mother. Martha realized that with the absence of grandchildren in the family she no longer had any reason to pursue a relationship with her mother. The distance between the two could now be even greater than before, providing Martha with a barrier to insulate her from the almost constant disparagement that seemed to be an immutable feature of her mother's relationship with others.

Another pledge that Martha made to herself was that she would recover fully, and restart what might have been a promising career. With her severely limited mobility and the need to use a walker and possibly a wheelchair, she knew the house in the suburbs was out of the question. And so, while still at Methodist Hospital Rehabilitation Center, she sold the house and bought a two-bedroom unit in a co-op building that was part of a stylish development within six blocks of the inner harbor.

Although the disability income coverage from Lynncor had ended after six months, Martha was not concerned about her finances. Harry had been covered by a $250,000 life insurance policy that paid double on accidental death. In addition, the firm had a travel policy which paid $500,000 for death while on company business. Since the trip down to Florida was considered a recruiting trip, Martha was now looking at a total of $1 million in insurance proceeds, plus the possibility of some other settlement if a successful suit could be brought against the trucking company.

As the months away from work increased, Martha began to consider the possibility of not going back to Lynncor when she finished rehabilitation. Her days at Methodist had helped strengthen a nagging conviction that she was capable of bigger and better things, if not at Lynncor, then somewhere else. So when David Morkin called on a Friday afternoon and mentioned in a vague way that he would like to stop by Saturday morning to discuss something relating to the business, Martha wasted no time in telling him that a visit would be an excellent idea and that he should be there at 9:30, after her hydrotherapy session.

The routine at Methodist had become very predictable, and not entirely unpleasant. Every day Martha would have breakfast in her room at 7:30 and then be taken by wheelchair for hydrotherapy from 8 to 9:15. At 10:30 she was scheduled to start her exercise in the long hallway running past the library and TV room, where she was expected to walk six lengths of the hall, one slow step at a time. All of this while leaning on her walker and then raising it up a few inches and throwing it forward for the next step.

The atrophy of her muscles that had followed the months in a body cast meant that her first short walks in the hall had been filled with intense pain and frustration. Even now, several months later, she still had pain, but pushed herself, sometimes doing seven or eight lengths if the attendant lost count or slipped into the TV room to watch the soaps as Martha went down the hall. This was not a likely occurrence on weekends, when Ruby Washington, a square-boned black woman somewhere between 35 and 60 with a disposition that said, "Don't give me any shit!", was on duty. With Ruby it was four lengths when the chart said four, six when it said six – no more, no less. Pain or no pain.

Martha had told David to meet her in the library where he had visited with her several times before, usually with his wife in tow. Mrs. Morkin was a rather plain looking woman apparently embarrassed by her height and always visibly uncomfortable about being in the presence of sick people. On this day David was coming alone, a clear indication to Martha that this was not going to be a social call. David was many things, but he was not duplicitous. He was late however, and Martha was looking at her watch when David finally seated himself across from her at the corner table in the library at 10:05.

"I'm sorry I'm late, Martha, there was a traffic tie-up on 695," David said. "I'll get straight to the point. I've been thinking about something for the past few weeks and it's time I talked to you about it."

"David," Martha said, "if you've thought about it that long it must be important, so let's get started before Ruby gets on my case."

"Look Martha, as you know, Harry was a twenty percent partner in the firm, going to thirty percent next year. Our business has continued to make strides, and I'm trying to make a decision about bringing in another partner. Frankly, I'm not crazy about doing that. I don't think I work well with other people on an equal basis – Harry was an exception – and I really don't want to split the pie three ways."

"Where does the three come from?"

"Me, the new partner, and you. You now own Harry's twenty percent interest. Surely you remember the deal. I always thought you laid out the negotiation strategy for Harry. Our deal was that if one of us died, then that partner's ownership would go to his family, with the buyout formula to kick in after one year at the remaining partner's option."

"I do recall."

"I thought you would! In any event, I don't want to buy you out and I don't have the cash even if I did. I want you to work for the firm. You've had seven years experience in personnel and you've set up tracking systems. With your help I can handle our current clientele, maybe add a few more, take on a staff assistant if necessary, and avoid having to bring in another partner."

"You're crazy! I can't take interview trips. I won't be able to drive a car for months – if ever. I don't know how I'd get to the office each morning. I'm not even sure how I'm going to get around my apartment when I move in next month."

"Look, Harry told me about the system you set up at your old job. He boasted that you were not only some kind of a whiz with computers, but you also knew how to integrate that technology with recruiting needs. That's exactly what we need, even more so."

David paused for a moment as Ruby brought Martha her morning medication and reminded her about the need to push the walker down the hall again. When Ruby left, David continued his pitch. "I've got hundreds of resumes gathering dust in my files at the office. Ninety-five percent of them are worthless, as you know, since we fill most of the positions with people who aren't out looking for a job. But some of them may be valuable for contacts in the future. Then I've got a completely unorganized batch of clippings – who's who in the industry – who might be who some day, who just got promoted, passed over, passed by, or whatever. All of this would be a virtual gold mine for me if I could access it worth a damn. Will you do it for me?"

"Do what?"

"Computerize it! With the new software and hardware that's coming on the market, plus your knowledge and experience in setting up systems, you could do it. I know you could."

"Where, David? Just where do you think I could do this, assuming I even wanted to try?"

"Wherever you want. That's the beauty of it. Once the files are transferred you can be sitting six miles away or six hundred. Enter data, dig out the stuff I need, transmit it to me by mail or modem, and I'd be off and running on a search."

"I'd need a decent budget for equipment and software."

"I know."

"I couldn't do this with the castoff equipment I had at Lynncor. I'd need tons of memory and a central processor fast enough to do sorts on five variables at once. The hardware would have to be top of the line, David. I won't do this with junk!"

"I know."

"Miss Laudner – five minutes to walk time. You're not gonna try and wimp out on me today are you?"

"No, Ruby. I'll be there."

Martha lowered her voice and continued as if she hadn't been interrupted, talking faster with each sentence. "And David, I would need to buy access to different databases and services. I'd want subscriptions to all of the industry trade journals, and I'd have to monitor the local papers in 10 or 15 cities where the top companies are located, either directly or using clip services. None of this comes cheap, David."

"I know."

"Since I've been here at Methodist I've checked on some of these different databases. I've thought about how to set up a system to do searches, but it would be overkill at Lynncor where I'm hiring

20 secretaries and machinists for every senior exec. With the kind of searches you're doing, David, after six months of set up and loading data, I could pull up names on a screen before you've done signing the contract."

David broke eye contact long enough to cast a quick glance at Ruby, who was standing in the library door looking at her watch. "Look, Martha, I'm sure you can do it. To be honest, I don't know what kind of a system you'd have to set up, but I'm sure you could figure it out and make it work. I'm prepared to invest the bucks, and I'm prepared to pay you $30,000 per year just as soon as you can get started."

"Harry was making $47,000 plus his partnership profits. What about the partnership interest?"

"Well, Harry would have gone to thirty percent in another year. I'm prepared to move you up to twenty-five in a year if this works out."

"David, this will work out, and so I expect to go up to thirty percent in one year." Out of the corner of her eye, Martha saw that Ruby was starting to make a move. "And David, Harry was a partner and making $47,000. I'll be a partner and I expect to be paid $47,000."

Ruby pounced, "Watch out Mister, it's time for Miss Laudner and me to take our little stroll. We're gonna do eight lengths today. This is one tough lady you've been talking to."

"I know… I know."

CHAPTER FIVE
The Eagle

In the first few years following the accident, Martha continued to gain confidence in her professional abilities as well as her physical recovery. The emotional loss she had suffered would not have been apparent to the outside observer, and on those rare days when she allowed herself to grieve, it was not so much for herself, but for her father. Martha was aware that the anger she harbored about the loss of her family was secondary to the rage she felt about how the tragedy had deprived her father of what modest joy he might have had remaining in his life. On this day in July of 1985, during their weekly phone call, it was all he could do to speak, his prior exuberance supplanted by a melancholy that he could not disguise some three years after the event.

Before the accident, Mr. Baumgardner had been absolutely captivated by the children. In his grandson Thomas, he had seen the son that he never had, and in Jennifer, he once again captured the love and excitement of youth that he had seen in Martha as a child when she had been growing up in the small frame house, three doors down the street from the Baptist Church in Davenport, Iowa. As an only child, Martha had spent more than the usual amount of time in the presence of adults. Mr. Baumgardner was the manager of the city water works in Davenport and frequently took his daughter along on weekends when he went to check the valves and gauges at the pumping station. Mrs. Baumgartner was the consummate joiner who worked diligently to glean every ounce of marginal value to which she might conceivably be entitled in view of the modest social edge her husband's municipal position provided in this small city.

Martha's mother had not wanted to have children, and after Martha was born in 1949, Mrs. Baumgardner made it clear to her husband that her suffering in the name of the nuclear family was over. However, if Marcus was ever disappointed in having a girl as his only child, he disguised it well. There was nothing that he would not have done for her, and from the time Martha could walk, she was showered with her father's love and attention.

In October of 1964, when she was 15 years old, Martha and her father went to Duluth to visit her Uncle Jim and his family. "I don't plan on going along you know," Mrs. Baumgardner had told Marcus when he was planning the trip. "We have the Library Guild meeting on Thursday and I expect to be elected treasurer for the coming year."

"Well, Martha and I will be back Sunday evening. I haven't seen my brother in three years and it's time Martha got to know her cousins better."

It was in Duluth the next Friday morning that Martha had an experience that helped change her life forever. Uncle Jim had taken Martha and her father to a place called Hawk Ridge, located on a windswept hill off Skyline Parkway on the north side of the city. From this spot, on certain days in September and October if the temperature and winds were just right, hundreds or even thousands of hawks could be spotted flying south on their winter migration. Martha was mesmerized.

"Uncle Jim, why do they all fly over this spot?"

"Well, they don't all fly over here, Martha, but a lot of them sure do. This place apparently has the right wind patterns, and if the hawks fly over this ridge they don't have to fly over Lake Superior. And now, Martha, I want to see if you can tell the different types of hawks apart."

On this first day at Hawk Ridge, Uncle Jim had Martha stand next to Percy Hargess, an elderly black man with a carefully trimmed white beard. Percy had retired as a cook off one of the ore boats in the Duluth Harbor, and was now the acknowledged champion when it came to total counts on the Ridge. One day the previous year, when the conditions had been just right, Percy had spotted 467 hawks and been able to identify all but five. Today as Martha stood next to him, Percy peered through an old set of binoculars and shouted out to the others.

"Northern Harrier – male."

"Osprey."

"Goshawk – female."

Martha and her father came back to Hawk Ridge again the next two days, and by the time they left to drive back to Davenport on Sunday afternoon she was able to identify most of the species of hawks as well as some of the falcons.

Each fall, for the next several years, they came back to that windswept hill in Duluth. Martha's skill grew to rival that of Hargess as the two of them would stand next to each other in a friendly rivalry and peer through their binoculars at the speck in the distance, looking initially at the flight pattern of the flaps and glides as the first indication of species, then at the silhouette showing wing and tail shapes, and finally, as the bird came closer, looking at the plumage and coloring.

"Sharp-shin hawk, male, immature," Martha shouted out a second before Percy.

"You're right," he grinned. "I'll beat you on the next one."

But the thrill of identifying even some of the lesser-known hawk species was surpassed on those days when the crowd of watchers spotted a golden eagle. The majestic bearing of the bird never ceased to amaze and intrigue Martha. And on the day that she saw an eagle take a seagull out of the air, Martha knew that this bird represented the ultimate in its domain, the very pinnacle of its order.

"You know Martha, you can be an eagle," her father had said on their last drive back to Davenport.

"What do you mean, Dad?"

"You have what it takes to fly the highest, Martha, and there's nothing you won't be able to do if you put your mind to it. You're going to be going off to college this next year and then probably on to some career in another city."

Mr. Baumgardner had both hands on the steering wheel, staring through the windshield, aware that this was one of those father-daughter talks that might be remembered for a long time. "I doubt if you'll be back in Davenport very often, but wherever you go, you're going to be at the top, I just know you will." And for the first time in her life Martha had really believed that her potential was unlimited. Her father was right! She could fly!

When Martha began her freshman year in college, she and her father loaded up the car and drove the 785 miles from Davenport to Ithaca, New York. Before he left to drive back, her father held her tightly and said, "I don't think you can possibly know how proud I am of you, Martha, you're the best thing that's ever happened to me. You're going to have a great experience here at Cornell and a great life ahead of you. Be an eagle, Martha. Be an eagle!"

*

Now, some 20 years later, Martha could still recall that conversation. On this day, as on the other days when she spoke with her father, Martha made a conscious effort to return to her work, doing so with a vigor that she knew would shortly engage her mind and emotion. Any initial doubts she might have had about the value of the system had long since been erased, and David had recently become enough of a believer that he cautioned Martha to keep the project confidential lest any of the other competitors attempt to duplicate the system and imperil the advantage that David Morkin and Associates seemed to be attaining within this segment of the recruiting industry.

Over the preceding year, Martha had finally completed the massive task of converting David's stack of resumes from a useless pile of paper to a potentially valuable resource. After successfully fighting her impulse to set up each file herself, Martha had hired some part-time data entry personnel to key the resume information onto a separate tape that she could subsequently integrate into the master file. The structure of this sub-file was based on the premise that the individuals sending in resumes were not likely to be considered as candidates for the senior level positions that David Morkin and Associates were hired to fill, but rather as potential sources of information.

"The kind of candidates that we want to identify for the vice president's job at your company are not reading the help wanted ads in the local paper," David had told more than one prospective client. "We're looking for the individual who is successfully employed and progressing within his present firm, not someone who is sending his resume all over the country." Notwithstanding this bit of self-serving logic, most well-known search firms receive five to ten unsolicited resumes each day, and are not above occasionally running a blind ad to bring in some additional paper if they need more contacts in a specific industry segment.

This day's agenda was read-clip-enter, from several papers and trade journals. Over the previous two years Martha had identified three news clipping services that she felt comfortable using for some of the smaller regional publications. David had wondered why she did not use these sources for all the clips. "When the day comes that you can perfectly define this industry and the types of candidates that we may need to dig out in the future for some job that doesn't even exist today, then I'll turn it all over to a clip service. In the meantime, David, I'll do it the way that works best."

The *New York Times* led off this day's list again, followed by *The Boston Globe* and the trade journals.

> **Richard Colodny joins board of directors for Delaware Medical** – *clip* – *add to company file and update exec file.*

> **Dr. Theodore J. Wescoe leaving senior position at N.I.H. to join New England Biotics, as VP of Technology Transfer** – *clip* – *update company file, start new exec file. Some bio on Wescoe in article. Check with N.I.H. for more background info.*

This was one of the few gaps still remaining in Martha's system. Although most senior positions in the industry were filled by people working at related companies, an increasing number, particularly in the bio-tech segment, were coming from government agencies or university faculties. Martha made a note to check out sources of names from those two areas.

> **"Pfizer acquires Boulder, Colorado manufacturer of electrosurgical equipment"** – *clip* – **"Valleylab to operate as wholly-owned subsidiary."** *Update co. file. Leave as separate unit but cross-reference parent co.*

> **"Boston executive killed while at medical meeting in Toronto"** – *clip* – **"John Levard VP at Telmark Catheter Company victim of apparent mugging"** – *clip* – *update co. file. Delete exec file and advise David of possible client opportunity.*

> **"Medelectro gives increased emphasis to Neuro Division by establishing Group Product Manager position."** – *clip* – **"Tim Foster promoted from Marketing**

job in Pacing Group" – *clip* – *update exec and co. organization file. Set up separate sub-file on Neuro Division.*

Later, when Martha was making the data entries, she noted that her input to Foster's file would be the third one she had made since the file was established. In addition to the initial reference concerning his testimony at the congressional hearing, Foster's promotion in January of 1984 was also included.

"Someone to watch," Martha said out loud over the background hum of her computer, "someone to watch."

*

Tim Foster was indeed someone to watch, a fact that had not escaped the attention of Coleen Jacobson, Senior Personnel Administrator, at Medelectro's headquarters in the northern suburbs of Minneapolis. As with most rapidly growing companies, Medelectro attempted to maintain a list of high potential personnel who could be groomed to assume progressively higher levels of management responsibility as corporate needs dictated. Such a policy was not without its critics, and Coleen was frequently at the center of the discussion when the topic was raised at Medelectro.

"This company has always had an egalitarian approach with regard to personnel policies. To put together a list of fast track people and single them out for special attention, flies in the face of that policy." The speaker was Glen Rosburg, Senior Vice President for Finance and Administrative and Coleen's boss's boss. "All of our people are important to us and deserve the same special attention.

End of discussion. Rosburg did not have a reputation for making a lot of decisions, but when he made one it was unambiguous. Coleen had her marching orders, and having a separate management development program for high potential personnel was not part of the picture. But she did retain her private register of fast track candidates, and Tim Foster was on that list.

Daniel and Louise Foster of Portage, Indiana would not have been surprised to learn that their son's name was on somebody's list of top talent. From junior high on, Tim's performance in everything he tackled set him apart from his friends and classmates. Daniel and Louise could never quite understand where Tim, the youngest of their two children, got the drive to excel, but it was obvious at an early age that he was setting his own standards, and doing so at a level higher than those set by his parents. Tim's father was a lineman for the local utility company, with a limited formal education, but a passion for things electronic. When Tim – never Timmy – was still in high school, he and his older brother, Brian, went with their parents to visit the Museum of Science and Industry in Chicago. From that day on, Tim knew that he could never spend time stringing cable for the power company.

"I'm going to college to study science, Dad," he said on their way home to Portage. "I don't know yet just what I'll be when I grow up, but I know I'm going to be working with new things, new technology."

"If the boys want to go to college, we'll find a way," Tim's mother interjected when Mr. Foster began to talk about the cost of higher education. Louise Foster had a positive attitude that was so ingrained and so natural that it was years later before Tim realized that this approach to life was the exception rather than the rule.

Although Tim never wavered in his college plans, his brother Brain decided to enlist in the Army when he graduated from high school in 1967, and four months later was starting a tour of duty in Vietnam during the troop build up following the Tet Offensive. The family had lived on the raw edge of pride and fear as they watched the news reports over the next few months.

Tim was home by himself on the Saturday morning in May of 1968 when he saw the car with military markings park in front of the house. He recalled later his thoughts about not answering the door, as if by refusing to accept the message he could alter the sequence of events. As it was, he was forced to sit patiently with the messengers of gloom for an hour, as they politely but firmly refused to discuss their tragic news with a fourteen-year-old boy. When his parents returned, they accepted the news of Brian's death with an almost resigned affectation, as if this now confirmed an event they had long been expecting.

Later, as Mr. Foster walked the two men back to their car, the postman arrived, and the mail, as was the case for the next nine days, included a letter from Brian. For each of those nine days Tim and his parents would read the letter aloud, holding on to every word as if it were the thread that still connected them to their brother and son, praying that the letters would keep coming – knowing they would not. On the day when no letter arrived, Tim's mother finally began her grief, and did so with a passion so intense that it challenged even her indefatigable spirit.

In the years that followed, Tim went on to pursue an engineering degree from Notre Dame followed by an MBA degree at Stanford, during which time he met and married Britta Lindquist from San Diego. Britta had been captivated by this handsome engineer from Indiana, but less than enthralled when he later accepted a position in Minneapolis. Their house hunting trip in February of 1983 was an exposure to weather she had only read about previously. But Tim's opportunity to move into a marketing position where he could use his engineering background and be actively involved in the introduction of new medical technology was a situation too good for them to ignore.

When Tim had first visited with Medelectro, Coleen Jacobson had been the recruiter conducting the initial interview. Tim's appearance had almost worked to his disadvantage, since Coleen had a difficult time believing anyone with Foster's anchorman looks could really be that competent. But competent he was, and now in July of 1985 Tim was addressing the first meeting of his new department after receiving his second promotion in 29 months.

"I had a chance to meet some of you last week when I sat in on the regional sales meeting, and I look forward to meeting with the rest of you individually this week. As you know, I came from the pacing division, so this is my first exposure to the neuro product line. From what I've had a chance to find out so far, we have some great opportunities ahead of us when you look at the products in development plus those that are close to introduction." As Tim was well aware, the vast majority of Medelectro's sales and earnings came from the sale of heart pacemakers, and the neuro division was a distant second fiddle in the corporate pecking order. But he was honest in his pep talk about the increased attention this group was receiving as the company looked for ways to increase revenues outside of the cardiovascular market.

There were indeed several new products in development that appeared to have significant technical advantages over the then currently available treatment modalities, and the company thought that one of them, the Contistim 900 simulator for control of the muscles at the base of the bladder, had a huge commercial potential. The next morning, as Tim started his first full day on the new job, he asked Mark Lipkan, the product manager on the Contistim line, for a status report on the 900.

"Initial results look great so far," Mark said, "but we still have a long way to go before we understand some of the critical factors on muscle fatigue."

"How many patients have we done?"

"Patients?" Mark responded with a note of disbelief. "We should be so lucky! We're still in animals. We have seven dogs at around six months post-op, another eight at three months, and we're scheduled to implant six more over the next few weeks. You oughta sit in on one of the procedures. It'd really help you understand how the product works."

"No thanks," Tim said, without hesitation. "I'll read the reports."

CHAPTER SIX
The Player

It was 11:30 at night and the temperature was still 94 degrees. Barnett had been living in Las Vegas for the past five years and still could not believe the heat. "How in the hell can your company send cabs out on the streets in the middle of July with no air conditioning?" he asked the driver as they left the downtown area.

"We got air conditioning. The company won't let us use it when we're in the cab by ourselves. The compressors burn out too fast."

"Well, you're not by yourself any more. Put on some cool air and get me out to the Hilton. I'm on a streak tonight and I wanna keep it going."

Lloyd Barnett was a big believer in streaks. He had once won $16,000 in five hours at the Golden Nugget and told anyone who would listen that he won that much because he knew he was hot and he was smart enough to raise his bets while the streak lasted. He also liked to believe that he could recognize losing streaks and walk away from the table when the cards were cold. This bit of gambling lore meant that Barnett was part of the ninety percent of players who felt they were smart enough to beat the system if they could just tie together a couple of hot streaks. Tonight might be the night. Tonight Barnett had started one hot streak and was ready to start another.

It had been over two years since Barnett had done the job in Toronto, and he was not exactly flush with cash. There had been two other jobs since then with the same client, but one turned out to be a false start and Barnett and the client had agreed to stop when the setup turned out to be too risky. Lloyd had talked his way into keeping the ten grand upfront payment, but that had long since gone to pay for a cold streak that had snuck up on him.

As a part-time gambler, part-time hit man, and full-time hustler, Barnett kept more than busy trying to maintain what little semblance of lifestyle he had left. At his apartment, buried under a pile of golf shirts in the second drawer of his dresser, was a plaque recognizing Mr. Lloyd P. Barnett as salesman of the year, 1977 and 1978, Landmark Realty Company, Cincinnati, Ohio. Barnett had been a big ticket residential real estate salesman for Landmark in the mid 70s with a style and ego to match. When his wife died suddenly in 1979, even his closest friends were surprised at the complete reversal in fortunes which followed.

A failed lawsuit following his wife's death seemed to start the slide, and a penchant for daytime martinis made the slope a little steeper. When he finally lost his job with Landmark, Lloyd loaded what he could into his car, dropped the house keys off at the bank along with a cryptic note discussing what they could do with the mortgage, and drove to Nevada. With a lack of solid connections, Barnett fell in with some small time con men in Las Vegas and managed to pay the rent with a variety of hustles on visiting tourists, supplemented by the occasional hotel room theft. One of his later contacts, Angelo Cammarta, since deceased, introduced him to other part-time employment that paid well but required some rather persuasive forms of enforcement tactics. All of this plus a real estate listing that came his way periodically, kept Lloyd Barnett liquid enough to engage in his primary passion in life – blackjack.

On this night he had managed to work his cash position up to $1,600, playing ten and twenty dollar bets at a couple of the smaller casinos in downtown Vegas. At the Hilton, Barnett was a rated player with a line of credit, and his personal streak rules said that now was the time to start making fifty dollar bets with a big enough stack of chips to absorb the minor ebbs and flows that occur in even the best of streaks. The advantages of the credit line were obvious, and being rated also meant that he could tap the hotel for free meals, show tickets, and a complimentary room depending on his level of play.

But the main disadvantage of being rated was that Barnett had to use his own name when setting up the account. He also had to give them the number of his one remaining clean Visa card, the only one that would not bounce, along with the name of a friendly secretary at the realty company who was persuaded to say that Lloyd Barnett was one of their top salesmen with an annual income exceeding $100,000. All of this had gotten Barnett his credit line, and tonight was the night it was going to pay dividends.

"Good evening, Mr. Barnett, how are you tonight? I understand you want to pay off your marker."

This was another disadvantage, they knew his name and their omnipresent computer tracked every time he played at the hotel, how long he played, what level of bets, and the general level of gains or losses. Tonight he was using $1,200 of his cash to pay off the line so he could draw down on a clean account and keep the computer happy.

Barnett made his way to a table posted with a $25 minimum and handed his Hilton gaming card to Sid Kasten, the pit boss covering the table. He liked the $25-minimum tables. He could still bet $50 and $100, but the $25 minimum kept away the walk-in tourists who agonized over every $2 bet. Pace was important to him when he was on a streak.

"Keep it moving – keep it moving. When you're winning you can't play fast enough, and any sucker who can't decide whether to stay at 15 when the dealer has a 6 showing shouldn't be sitting at my table."

A few hours later, the pit boss reached for his rating cards and made an entry indicating that Barnett was at the $100 level as of 1:30 a.m. A half hour at $25, about an hour at $50, and now at the $100 level. Each major casino had its own standard about the level of play expected before complimentary rooms or other perks were provided. At the Hilton, four hours' play at the $50 level was about the minimum expected if the player was going to get comped on rooms and meals. Barnett's computer record showed that he usually met the minimums. It also showed that he usually lost.

At 1:30 a.m. on a Friday night, now Saturday morning, the Hilton main casino looked as busy as Grand Central Station may have looked during the heyday of the big trains in the 40s. There was one major difference. Grand Central had clocks – the casino did not. Nothing to remind the player what time it was, what day it was, what year it was. Move them through and work the odds. Seven percent on slots, six on roulette, four on blackjack, and two percent on craps. Let some win, hopefully the loud ones. Everyone loved to see and hear winners, including the House. The odds were relentless. Sooner or later they got to everyone, regardless of what time or what day it was.

Lloyd Barnett knew what day it was. Even with his love of blackjack peaking dangerously close to the climax level, Lloyd Barnett knew that this Saturday was the first Saturday of the month. This Saturday was *LA Times* day. He had a strong feeling that this *LA Times* day was going to put him back on the path towards financial comfort.

The agreed-upon method of communication that Barnett had with his client was to use the personal section of *The LA Times* on the first Saturday of each month. If the client wanted to make contact, an ad would be placed reading along the following lines:

> *To Mom and Dad, Happy 40th Anniversary*
> *from Brad, George, Mary, and the Grand Kids.*

The key words were "40th Anniversary" followed by three names. Barnett's instructions were to then run an ad in the following Monday's paper using the second of the three names as an indication that he was available.

> *George is available for trip to Europe.*

Barnett had rented a post office box in Las Vegas that had been used only seven times in the last three years, twice with each of the first three jobs and once on the false start. At the time of the last payment there had been an indication that the number of contacts would be increasing in the future. However, the client was smart enough to realize that someone with Barnett's personal habits might not always be around to check the mail, so no instructions or up front payments were sent to the PO Box unless Barnett responded to the message in the paper.

At 2:30 Barnett was doing his best to project an image of a skilled and smooth blackjack player while at the same time listening to a stream of small talk from the tipsy dentist's wife from Chicago now sitting next to him. Sharon Weisberg knew almost nothing about the odds of various card combinations, but had the beginner's luck that drove skilled players like Barnett crazy.

"Look, Lloyd," she said to her new presumed friend, "I've got $775 and I started with $150 so I'm up over $500. Max will never believe I could win this much. How much are you ahead?"

"About three grand." Actually Barnett knew he was up exactly twenty-two hundred for the night. He was not given to understatement when it came to his gambling prowess. "I was up over five grand but the last half hour's killed me. This happens even when you're on a win streak. You get a soft spot, but you gotta hang in there cause it'll turn again."

By 3:15 a.m. Barnett's soft spot had turned into a major swamp. He had signed three more slips for $500 each and was now down almost $2,000 at the Hilton but still playing with the black chips. Normally he would have cut back to $25 or $50 bets, but his male ego did not have a lot of latitude when it came to backing off in front of a fan club. Right now Lloyd's fan club was pressing a leg against his. Lloyd's fan club was $2,400 ahead, and Lloyd's fan club was drunk.

At the next shuffle, Barnett lit another cigarette and said, "I don't know how in the hell you're doing it, Sharon, but you're about the luckiest rookie I've ever seen."

"You're my good luck charm," the leg was pushing harder this time. "You've gotta start winning again, okay? How many of those slips can you sign?"

"I've got a twenty grand line here," Barnett lied with absolute ease. "This is nothing. I have streaks like this all the time."

The leg moved. "I got to pee. I got to pee bad. Watch my chips, Lloyd, and don't go away. Don't go away."

Mrs. Sharon J. Weisberg, wife of Dr. Max L. Weisberg, mother of David and Karrie, slid off her stool and moved cautiously along the pitching deck of the cruise ship Hilton as the far horizon rose and fell in her peripheral vision. One step back as the floor tipped upward and three or four steps forward when the nose of the ship dropped between the troughs of the surging sea. As she entered the restroom she was struck by the fact that the other occupants had no difficulty handling the rolling motion of the floor, especially the black woman with the Hilton nametag moving towards her in slow motion.

By the time the good Mrs. Weisberg made it back to the table twenty minutes later, Barnett had signed for yet another $1,000, of which only three $25 chips were left. "I got to go Lloyd, I'm dying." Sharon's skin was now a rather strange shade of Illinois pale, even under the perpetual white light of the Hilton sky. "Can you carry my chips for me? I've gotta sit down."

Barnett motioned for the dealer to change Sharon's big pile of quarters into larger chips.

"Color coming in."

"Go ahead." The pit boss watched passively as Barnett put Sharon's four $500 and four $100 chips in his pocket and took her by the arm. Sid had two hours left on his shift and his interest in the human drama of Las Vegas was waning.

"Sharon, you can't go back to Caesar's looking like this. You gotta wash your face and lie down for an hour. I got a suite upstairs and you can use one of the rooms." The ship seemed to be rolling less now that Lloyd was holding on to her arm.

"How much did I win?"

"I don't know. We'll count it when we get upstairs. Sit here for a minute while I get my key." Barnett found a chair for the mother of David and Karrie and went over to the VIP desk to sign for a room. Any thoughts that Barnett might have had as they went up in the elevator about other forms of excitement that night came to a quick halt when the good ship Weisberg sailed into the room, threw up in the bathtub, and then fell across the bed sound asleep.

Barnett put his $25 chips in Sharon's purse and took out two $100 bills from the assortment of cash she had remaining. As he was leaving the room, he walked over to the bed, removed Sharon's shoes, and rolled her under the covers. He also reached up under her dress and pulled off her panties. He would throw them away when he got downstairs. She could find out his name from hotel security, but no dentist's wife from Skokie was going to tell her husband she ended up drunk in some guy's room at the Hilton without her underwear. By the time she got back to Caesar's at 11 a.m. her story about playing blackjack all night and winning $75 would be almost bulletproof. And by then, Lloyd Barnett would have seen the ad in the Saturday *LA Times*.

Happy 40th Anniversary Joe and Kathy from your friends Eileen, Ron, and Patty.

Ron was available. Ron was definitely available.

CHAPTER SEVEN
The Boat

The mail arrived on the Friday after his response ad appeared in *The LA Times*. Barnett had been contemplating how he was going to use the ten grand advance. He now owed $4,500 at the Hilton plus another $1,500 in rent and Visa bills. The Hilton could wait for awhile if necessary, but the magic plastic was his lifeline if he ever needed to bail out of a bad situation. So, one way or another, Visa had to get paid. The ten grand down payment was intended to cover expenses, with another $25,000 coming after the job was done. The first time Barnett had been contacted by the client he had thought this was a great deal, but that was before he developed an affection for the black chips. Depending upon the assignment, he might be able to get by with a lot less than $10,000 in expenses, and with any luck, he could use the excess cash to play Blackjack at some place other than the Hilton and get himself back up to even.

It had taken a self-issued mental restraining order for Barnett to hold off opening the package until he was back at his apartment. He knew that showing up at the post office on three straight days with an anxious look may already have been logged in someone's memory, so ripping open a package to count the $100 bills would have to wait. As was the case on the other assignments, the package contained two envelopes. Barnett immediately opened the smaller of the two, which he knew held the money. Although he could almost tell exactly by feel, he did count the money to confirm that there was $10,000 in cash, all in used $100 bills, all the bills turned the same way in the small stack.

After Barnett had put the money away, he cleared a spot on the kitchen table under the overhead light and slid open the sealed end of the manila envelope containing the instructions for the next assignment. He had already gotten his road atlas from the cabinet, along with a calendar, and had placed them on the chair next to the table. Barnett realized that he took a rather perverse sense of pride in the way he approached these jobs. When he took the first assignment, he had experienced some mixed emotions about the process of planning for someone's death. At that time he had never killed, and had been somewhat dubious about his ability to complete the job with the level of professional detachment that he knew would be required if he was to remain in business. Since then, he had come to realize that not only could he remain detached, but he could also bring an expertise to bear that surprised even him.

Barnett emptied out the contents of the envelope and looked inside to see that nothing had been missed. There were two rather poor reproductions of some old pictures of the target, which had been printed on a single sheet of paper. The photos looked like they might have come from an annual report or perhaps a newspaper article. The subject was a man who appeared to be in his late forties or early fifties. The typed pages which were attached gave the man's name along with the following details.

> "Randy Pellegrino is an executive with a medical products company based in Dallas, Texas. As noted by the enclosed reproduced pictures, he does wear glasses and may also wear prescription sunglasses when outside. In approximately five weeks, he will be attending the annual meeting of the American Medical Manufacturers Association, which will take place at the Fountain Plaza Hotel in Boca Raton, Florida from September 7 through September 12. Subject is on the Board of AMMA and may arrive on September 5 or 6 for organizational planning meetings. It is imperative that his death should appear to be accidental. Since he is known to be an avid sport fisherman, and since AMMA always has social events planned for meeting participants, it is suggested that some type of boating accident may be in order. Final payment will be made when job is completed. Another assignment may follow shortly depending upon successful completion of this contract."

"Boats, what the hell do I know about boats?" Barnett asked himself. He read the typed instructions two more times and then looked at the small card that was attached.

11/16
684-3595

His instructions from the client were that he should subtract two from each number in any date or phone number which was used in an ad or note. Thus, 11/16 became September 14 and the correct phone number was 462-1373. Barnett knew the area code did not change even though a different phone number was used. He was then expected to destroy the detailed assignment sheet but retain the card with date and number, apparently on the presumption that he would make some note to himself in any event, and therefore it might as well be in code. He had met the client only once and that was for twenty minutes. In truth, he did not know if that person was really the customer, or only someone representing a larger client organization. He strongly suspected the latter, given the money involved and what apparently was going to be a lengthy list of targets. He was also aware that there was a common theme to these assignments, not that it really made any difference to him anymore. Three guys from different medical companies and one from a university research lab.

*

"This boat thing is going to be tricky," Shaffer said when they met the next night in the bar at the Dunes Hotel. Barnett had decided to contact Jack for assistance, though it pained him greatly to think of paying out money to someone else. He had at least managed to cut back the split, aided in no small part by the fact that Shaffer was in deep hock with a rather unfriendly local lender.

"I'm not getting as much on this job, and there's going to be some big expenses." Barnett had lied with his usual aplomb. "You're gonna have to settle for $7,500."

"There isn't any more, Jack, and I'll be the one taking all the risks. Probably the only thing you'll have to do is drive. I'd do it all myself but it's a little safer having a second set of eyes. Besides, I know you need the money and where else are you gonna get $7,500 for three or four days' work?"

"You're a prince, Lloyd. Why are you so damn good to me? Look – at least I gotta have $2,000 up front. I got some people here I need to keep happy. Two grand up front and the rest later. Deal?"

"Deal – now how in the hell are we gonna blow up a boat?"

Over the next two weeks, Barnett managed to work the local network of low lifes until he eventually made contact with one Rodney Lapedis. Rodney was best known among his limited followers as a shill for serious card counters. For twenty dollars an hour and ten percent of the take, Rodney would play blackjack for a counter who would sit next to him acting tourist and signaling Rodney on how to bet and when to take a hit. The fact that Rodney acted dumb, looked dumb, and probably was dumb, allowed him to practice his trade with enough frequency to pay the rent and still support a strong affection for the horses. Barnett had worked with Lapedis one time before on an enforcement job for Angelo Cammarata and knew that Rodney had a working knowledge of explosives from some prior life.

"What the hell do you wanna blow up a boat for?" Rodney asked Barnett when they were sitting in the bar at the Golden Nugget.

"It's some insurance scam this guy is working on. He's got a big ass cruiser up on Lake Mead that he doesn't want, and he's up to his eyeballs in debt. Wants me to fake an on-board explosion and sink the sucker."

"How's he gonna get off?"

"That's his problem. Says he's a good swimmer. He wants me to do it remotely when other boats are around to pick him up. What's the best way to do it?"

"What the hell am I, the public library? Look at this hand!" Lapedis pushed the three remaining fingers of his right hand in Barnett's face. "I lost two fingers getting my education and you want me to give you the whole course for a free drink. Bullshit! It's gonna cost you!"

"I'll give you two hundred bucks if you set up a package for me."

"First of all, I'm not setting up anything. I don't touch that shit any more. I might – I just might – tell you how to do it, but not for two hundred. It's gonna cost you five hundred."

It turned out to be less of an engineering project than Barnett had anticipated. Lapedis sketched out a diagram on a cocktail napkin showing how to wire a block of C-5 plastic explosive using a model airplane control box to activate a small servomechanism that would move the contact wires together and complete the circuit. With the right control box, Barnett could be up to half a mile away when he set it off. The key was to find a source for the C-5, and Rodney managed to recall a name after getting another $150 out of Barnett.

"This guy lives over in Barstow, if he's not in jail. He used to be an enforcer for a biker gang until he left a knee and part of his face on a gravel road. He had a big supply of plastic and he's been selling it off bit by bit but he still should have some left, especially for a generous guy like you."

*

The lobby of the Fountain Plaza hotel was a zoo at one o'clock on Sunday afternoon, September the 6th. The National Association of Landscape Designers was checking out and the American Medical Manufacturers Association was checking in – or at least trying to. In the portico area outside the front door there must have been a hundred golf bags coming in and a hundred going out, all being staged by a platoon of bronzed bellboys in khaki shorts as the rental cars edged their way around the circular driveway. As Barnett entered the lobby, he had a brief flashback to a time ten years before when he and his wife had gone to a resort hotel in Palm Springs as part of an awards package he had won selling real estate.

His goal on this day was to get a basic understanding of the layout of the hotel grounds and the schedule of events for the AMMA meeting. If he got lucky and spotted his target, so much the better, but the main thing was to find out if and when his guy was going to go fishing.

The docks that served the Fountain Plaza were about 200 yards away from the rear of the hotel. The Fountain Plaza itself was situated on acreage that backed up to the inland waterway system, which in turn connected to the Atlantic Ocean via a channel located about a half mile from the hotel. As he walked out the back entrance of the hotel toward the docks, he noted that most of the 15 or 20 slips were occupied, as apparently Sunday was an off day for the charters with most hotel guests in transition. A few of the captains were working on their boats as Barnett walked along the dock. He stopped by the stern of the Florida Belle, where two people were busy hosing off the deck.

"You going out this week?" the older of the two men asked Barnett.

"Well, I'm thinking about it. How far out you go?"

"It depends on if it's a half-day or full day charter. You with the AMMA group?"

"Yeah."

"Well, a bunch of us are booked to do the AMMA charters on Tuesday and Wednesday. They're just gonna be half-day charters in the afternoon, so we'll only go out three or four miles depending on the winds and how the fish are running."

"How deep's the water out there?"

"Well, we usually try to get on the edge of one of the shelves where it drops off to around three hundred feet. Have you done much fishing before?"

"Not much. I'm from Oklahoma, and we don't exactly have a lot of water around there. If I sign up to go out, how do I know what boat I'm gonna be on?"

"Most groups have a sign up desk where they post the names of the people and the boats they're on. I'm sure AMMA is probably doing the same thing."

Barnett walked back up the winding sidewalk past the putting green and into the hotel. The original sections of the Fountain Plaza had been built in the 1930s with twelve-foot wide hallways and high ceilings in the public areas. Small shops with ornate wooden archways were located off some of the main corridors on the first floor level. Several open stairways led up to the second level meeting rooms with large atrium areas at the base of the stairs. In one of these areas Barnett came upon the hospitality desk for the AMMA meeting. Two long tables were set up and staffed by some part-time hotel employees handing out registration materials. What immediately caught Barnett's eye were several bulletin boards placed near the registration tables. The first board he checked had the names and court times for the mixed-doubles tennis matches. The next board had the fishing information, and after a quick skimming of several sheets of paper attached to the cork board, Barnett found the information he needed.

<u>Tuesday afternoon – September 8 at 1:00 p.m.</u>
<u>The Princess Cay</u>   Captain Don Mettler

Ed Whittaker   Foster Wakefield, Inc.
Lawrence Powell   Texas Suture Company
Randall Pellegrino   Hoffman Diagnostics Inc.

His guy was on the list! Now Barnett had a boat name and time. Shaffer would be arriving Sunday evening, giving them one day to get their package on board the Princess Cay and figure out how in the hell they could stay within a half-mile when the boat was out in open water.

Barnett wasted little time trying to rationalize the fact that he could kill people with limited expenditure of his emotional capital. On the rare occasion that he did reflect on this aspect of his persona, he inevitably came to the rapid conclusion that life had crapped all over his parade, and now it was too damn bad if somebody else got crapped on for a change.

Shaffer and Barnett spent most of Monday morning finding a mid-sized fishing boat that they could operate by themselves. Later in the day while Shaffer watched the dock at the hotel, Barnett bought some cheap fishing gear that they could take on their boat, plus a good set of binoculars. One additional purchase was a small styrofoam cooler, which according to the label would hold a "6-pack of your favorite beverage." By the time the afternoon was over, the cooler held a six-ounce block of C-5 explosive, four nine volt batteries, and a wiring harness incorporating a receiving antenna and a left rudder control gear for the Harrer model airplane kit, number 16B. Getting the cooler on board the Princess Cay turned out to be easier than either of them had expected. On the warm Florida evening, several of the hotel guests were strolling out on the docks looking at the various boats, which now included a number of large cabin cruisers and yachts. Shaffer featured himself as somewhat knowledgeable about boats, and had little difficulty slipping aboard the Princess Cay and finding a spot by the fuel tank to place the package.

The plan for Tuesday was to hang around the putting green and dock area to watch and be sure the target got on board, and then jump in a rental car and drive over to the marina where they had arranged for a fishing boat. The marina was located next to the outlet on the intercostal waterway, so they would be able to be in their boat by the time the Princess Cay was moving past the breakwater and out in to the open water. Barnett had spent an hour walking around near the meeting rooms in the hotel before joining up with Shaffer at the sandwich shop in the lower lobby for an early lunch.

"Have you figured out what our guy looks like yet?" Shaffer asked.

"No, only about half the guys are wearing name tags and I can't exactly ask for him without making a big deal of it. The old pictures aren't much use."

"How're we gonna know he's on the boat?"

"I checked the sign-up list again and he's still on it together with the other two guys. As long as they get on the boat we know he's not going any place."

By 12:30 Shaffer and Barnett were walking along the deck that ran parallel to the one at which the Princess Cay was moored. From their vantage point they had a clear view of the area and were able to observe the people starting to come down from the hotel. Barnett had stopped to light a cigarette behind the stern of a well-weathered boat on which the mate was cleaning some fish that had been caught on the morning charter.

"Three guys and a woman are walking towards our boat," Shaffer said softly. "Maybe one of the wives is going along. I don't want to do anything if there's a woman on board."

"Relax, Jack, she's probably walking down here to see them off. No wife in her right mind is going to go out on a fishing boat with three guys smoking and drinking beer all afternoon when she can lie by the pool. Where are they now?"

Barnett was consciously looking the other way so as not to draw any extra attention to the two of them. He flipped his cigarette into the water next to a big pelican that was diving for scraps from the fish cleaning.

"They walked right by. They're heading for another boat. But here come two other guys. They're getting on our boat and they're shaking hands with the captain."

"Okay – we've got two down and one to go."

At 1:15 they still had one to go. The captain had looked at his watch several times and was talking to the two men who were standing in the arms-out, shoulder-shrugging post that sent the unambiguous signal to Barnett some seventy-five feet away that they sure as hell didn't know where the third guy was. After another five minutes the captain got off the boat and walked over to a woman with a clipboard who apparently was coordinating the afternoon social events for AMMA.

"Jack, get over there fast and see if you can hear what they're saying. We've got to find out if our man's on the boat or if he's the third guy."

Before Shaffer was half way over to the other dock the captain had finished his conversation and was heading back to the boat. Jack stopped walking and turned towards Barnett as if to ask what he should do next. After a moment's hesitation, Barnett motioned for Shaffer to come back and then moved to meet him near the base section of the dock.

"I didn't hear anything. They stopped talking before I got close enough," Shaffer said.

"Yeah, I figured that. We don't dare ask that dame who they're missing. She'd remember that later." They both watched as the Princess Cay began to move slowly away from the dock.

"What the hell we gonna do, Lloyd? How do we know who's on there?"

"I don't know. Let's get to the car while I'm thinking."

As they arrived at the hotel parking lot, Barnett said, "We've got to do it! There's two chances out of three that he's on board. This guy's supposed to be nuts about fishing. He wouldn't miss the chance to go out this afternoon."

By the time the Princess Cay cleared the breakwater twenty minutes later, Barnett and Shaffer were in their boat and starting to move out into the channel. Shaffer was at the wheel of their eighteen-foot Day-Fisher, and Barnett was looking through the glasses as they followed at a distance. "Can you see who they are?"

"How in the hell am I supposed to tell that, Jack? They haven't got a sign around their neck. They're just two guys smoking cigars and bullshitting with the mate. Boy she's a looker!"

"Whaddya mean?"

"The mate's a girl. She must have been below when they were at the dock. Now she's in back rigging the lines. Good-looking, young blonde. Might be the captain's daughter."

"Lloyd, I don't want to do this. I didn't sign on to blow up some girl."

"Look, unless you want to walk to shore and give me back my two grand, we're going to finish this job. You don't have to blow nothing. You're here to run the boat and hold a fishing rod if anybody looks. I'll be the guy setting it off." Shaffer stared back at Jack as the boat moved into the oncoming waves. "If it'll make you feel better, I'll wait until she's on the bridge before I blow it. That way she'll probably get dumped in the water and get picked up by another boat."

One hour later both boats were approximately three miles off shore and the Princess Cay had her outrigger lines set to begin a pass over the shelf. "This is going to be it, Jack. Move us off to the side a little and take the glasses 'cuz I'll need both hands on the remote. Tell me what they're doing on the boat." Barnett had estimated earlier that they were about a half-mile apart, but it was difficult to gauge distance with any accuracy on open water.

"The two guys are in the chairs and the captain is showing them how to hold the rods. She's starting to go up the ladder to the bridge. If you're going to do it, Lloyd, now is the time."

Barnett turned on the power switch for the Bolin Top Flight control box and extended the antenna up to the maximum thirty-inch height. By pushing the left thumb switch a signal would be sent which would move the rudder control gear forward by the six-tenths of an inch necessary for the contact to be made and the circuit completed. "Where is she?"

"Up on top."

"Okay, here it goes. This will take about eight seconds. – Four – three – two – one – nothing. We must be too far away. Move us in another hundred yards. What's happening now?"

"The two guys are going down below."

"Good! There's no way they're gonna miss it from down there."

Randy Pellegrino, vice president of regulatory affairs for Hoffman Diagnostics and Larry Powell, president of Texas Suture Company stepped slowly off the stern deck and into the lower cabin as the boat rose and fell with the four-foot swells.

Barnett had managed to light another cigarette despite the wind in his face as Shaffer moved the boat in closer. "They still down there, Jack?"

"Yeah."

"Okay, I'm gonna try it again. Eight – seven – "

Shaffer picked up the glasses again to look at the boat and immediately yelled, "Stop, Lloyd! Stop! She's coming down!"

"I can't stop it now," Barnett said as he turned his body slightly to the left to block Jack's view of the control box. "Six – five – "

"I'm going to pull away, Lloyd!" Shaffer shouted as he turned the wheel sharply to the right to increase the distance between the two boats.

"Four – three – "

The miniaturized servomechanisms produced under the Harrier brand name were seen as the ultimate in control gears by model airplane aficionados. The rudder gear now rotating slowly in a styrofoam box in the engine well of the Princess Cay was designed to turn at a controlled rate of 1.35 revolutions per second, which meant that with its specified thread count it would traverse a distance of 0.600 inches in eight seconds. The contact wires were now 0.150 inches apart and closing at a rate of 0.075 inches per second.

"Two – one – "

As Cindy Mettler, the nineteen year old daughter of Captain Don Mettler stepped off the bridge ladder and onto the stern deck, the last revolution of the precision Harrier gear brought the contact wire against the battery lead, completing the circuit and initiating a massive explosion.

*

The next morning Barnett read the article in the paper as he and Shaffer waited for their plane to Chicago.

> "The two people missing and presumed dead in the boat explosion yesterday were two senior executives who were attending the American Medical Manufacturers Association meeting at the Fountain Plaza Hotel. Mr. Randall Pellegrino from Dallas, Texas and Mr. Larry Powell, also from Dallas, were apparently killed instantly as the boat exploded and sank in 250 feet of water. Although Mr. Powell and his company had recently been verbal targets of the Animal Rights Movement for their alleged misuse of animals in research and training programs, police say at this time they have no reason to believe that the explosion was anything other than accidental.
>
> Also injured in the accident was Cindy Mettler, a second year student at Florida State University and the daughter of Don Mettler, the owner of the Princess Cay. Captain Mettler was also injured in the explosion and both he and

his daughter were picked up by a nearby boat and brought to St. Luke's Hospital where they are listed in stable condition."

"We got our guy, Jack! I told you he'd be on there. No doubt about it." Barnett reached for another cigarette.

"Listen, Lloyd, you're borderline nuts. You think this is some kind of goddamn game. I'm done working with you – you're dangerous! When we get back to Vegas I want my money and I want you to stay the hell away from me."

Barnett lit his cigarette and said, "Don't get carried aw—"

Shaffer grabbed him by the shirt and pulled him forward before he could finish his sentence. "And put out that damn cigarette, Lloyd, before I stuff it down your throat!"

CHAPTER EIGHT
The Nurse

The coverage was about as good as it could get. First page, Science Section of the Sunday *Chicago Tribune*, front page story in *The Milwaukee Journal* with a photo spread as part of the inside follow-on article, and front page placement with pictures in the local papers. **"Animal Cruelty Exposed at Northern Wisconsin U.", "Research Lab Trashed by Animal Rights Group", "Is It Science or Torture? Professor Defends Work"**.

The padded manila envelope with a Chicago postmark that arrived in Mary's Saturday mail contained the articles and a short unsigned note, "Thought you might want to see the enclosed materials. Somebody did a nice job on the photos." Actually, Mary thought, the photos were not all that good. The papers had chosen not to use the one that showed the dog with the open sores, and some of the other pictures did not convey the real impact of the squalid conditions. Mary poured herself a cup of tea and picked up the *University Daily*, which appeared to have the most detailed coverage, albeit with a somewhat sensationalized perspective.

> "The break-in over the weekend at an animal research lab in the sub-basement of Gresham Hall was obviously the work of an organized group of terrorists with objectives that extend well beyond the campus of Northern Wisconsin. The Animal Rescue Band is a worldwide organization of radical animal rights activists whose activities began in England and have only recently spread to the United States. Their complicity in the actions on this campus was made evident not only by the daring nature of the raid and theft of animals, but also by the spray painting of several messages on the wall of Dr. Kline's lab. The selection of a research lab at a small state university may be an intentional signal by the ARB (Animal Rescue Band) that no alleged animal cruelty will go unchallenged, regardless of location.
>
> The work in the laboratory was being conducted under the direction of Dr. Alex Kline, a physician and member of the Medical School faculty for the past twelve years. Dr.

Kline told our reporter yesterday that his work has been of inestimable value in the long-term analysis of skeletal muscle disease. He denied allegations that the animals in his lab had been subjected to pain and suffering, and suggested that the pictures sent to the press by the ARB may have been staged for dramatic effect.

"My laboratory has had periodic inspections by the US Department of Agriculture's Animal and Plant Health Inspection Service as well as by University officials. While it is true that some animals have died as a result of this project, we must weigh this loss against the greater good that comes from the advancement of medicine and science. The theft of five dogs along with records from past experiments will at the minimum do irreparable harm to the continuity of this research, and may eventually jeopardize the ability of the medical community at large to pursue other important research programs."

University officials have yet to comment on whether or not Dr. Kline will be given permission to reopen his laboratory in Gresham Hall. Dr. Gerald Timm, Dean of Academic Affairs for the Veterinary School, acknowledged today that the controversy surrounding Dr. Kline's work may force the School to reevaluate its policies regarding the use of experimental animals in research programs.

"My, my, my," Mary thought, "what have we set in motion? Too bad it's some backwater university instead of a major center. Imagine the coverage we could have obtained if this had been Harvard or MIT."

Mary Devlin was not given to self-recrimination, other than for the briefest moment that it took to log into her internal computer the lessons learned from prior experience. She was perceived by the surgeons at Peter Bent Brigham Hospital in Boston as distant but competent, bringing an air of authority to her position as an OR supervisor that exceeded the formal responsibility of her job. Mary Devlin had been bringing an air of authority, in some case with a focus and intensity that her co-workers found strangely discomforting, to most of her activities since she had left Birmingham in 1971. The seminal event that had wounded her psyche and shaped her personality in the years that followed was sheltered deep within by multiple layers of denial, shared only on one occasion and then locked back inside an inner compartment which even she was seldom capable of opening.

Her father, Tommy Devlin, missed his first day of work in over six years on June 23, 1950, when Mary was born. A purchasing agent for the Rover Motorworks, Tommy spent the morning of that day with Mary's mother in the hospital and then stopped at both the White Swan as well as the Queen's Head pub in the afternoon to celebrate the birth of his first child with a few pints. When Mary's brother Noel was born three years later on a Sunday, Tommy thanked his wife, only partly in jest, for the courtesy of giving birth on a day when he would not have to miss work.

The two-bedroom home at 324 Hagley Road in the Edgbaston section of Birmingham where Mary and her brother grew up in the fifties was considered to be slightly upscale for a junior purchasing agent and his family. Tommy's father had been a successful shopkeeper in Belfast before their family moved to England in 1932, when Tommy was nine years old. His Irish background, and the small inheritance he received from his father's will, were facts that Tommy never discussed beyond the boundaries of the home, and only rarely within.

"You need not tell your friends that your grandfather was Irish," Tommy had told Mary once. "He married a girl from Liverpool and they lived in Belfast until I was born, and then we moved to England. Your mother was born in Wales and you were born right here in Birmingham, so you're English. That's all anybody needs to know."

If Mary's father was reticent on the subject of his family tree, her mother helped balance the score. The pride that Susan Devlin derived from her Welsh heritage was obvious and sincere, and some of Mary's earliest childhood memories were of her mother's reminiscences of the mining country of South Wales. Susan walked across the small kitchen and poured herself another cup of tea. She was warming to her role of storyteller, the keeper of the family lore.

"I'll never forget the first time I saw your father. I'd come into Birmingham on the train to spend a week with my cousin and breathe the clean air. On the second day I was here we went to the pictures, and that's when I saw him. What a handsome lad he was, and so tall. All the girls had eyes for him, but he asked me what my name was and teased me about my Welsh accent. Wanted to know if I worked as a canary in the mines since I was so small then. What a joker your father used to be. Didn't take himself so serious as he does now. When we got married two years later it was the happiest day of my life. But when your Grandfather Devlin died and we used the inheritance for a down payment on this house, I didn't think we should be moving to this part of Edgbaston, with your father still only a clerk at Rover. It's not good to take on airs. You shouldn't try to move beyond your station, at least not too fast. Remember that, children." Years later, when her father was promoted to a manager of purchasing at Rover, Mary noted her mother's relief at the knowledge that they were now 'matching their station'. The house was in keeping with the job, and all was right with the world.

The promotion of Tommy Devlin came as no surprise to those who knew him. It was unlikely that there was a man in Birmingham more dedicated to his employer, and during Mary's high school years at St. Paul's Catholic School, her father would often discuss with her the importance of the work ethic and his pride in seeing a job done well. "When you graduate St. Paul's in two years, I'd like you to apply for employment at Rover. More and more girls are being hired now as clerks, and you could do a lot worse than to work for such a fine company. You know, Mary, here in Britain we live on an island of coal surrounded by fish. When I married your mother I promised her I would never go down in the pit, and being a Catholic is as close as I want to get to fish. This country will always need cars and we're fortunate to have one of the finest car companies right here in our own city."

In the fall of Mary's last year at St. Paul's, she took a part time job at the local chemist's shop stocking shelves. It was two weeks later, and five months before the death of her father, that Mary saw him angry for the first and only time in her life. A big man at six feet four inches and 17 stone, Tommy always surprised people with the relative softness of his voice. Men who had spoken to him only by telephone at the company were invariably taken aback when they saw him for the first time, expecting to meet a small man with wire-rimmed glasses, and instead looking up at a gentle giant extending a hand the size of a small dog. On this night her father's voice was still soft, but it conveyed an element of anger, and worse yet for Mary, an extreme sense of disappointment in her behavior.

"Mary, I stopped at the chemist's shop on the way home to see how you were doing, and you weren't there."

"I stayed late --- "

"I'm not done yet!" Mary's mother looked up from the table at this rare verbal display of emotion and nodded towards Noel to leave the room. "I spoke to Mr. Handley, and he said you'd not come in and you hadn't called. I thought you must be sick, but I see that you're healthy, so I can't understand why you wouldn't have been there!"

"Daddy, I was trying to tell you, I stayed at school to help Sister Karstens. She wanted some of us girls to tidy up the library for the meeting tomorrow. I was going to tell Mr. Handley later."

"I thought I told you about how to deal with your employer. He's provided you with a job, you're to provide him with service. It's a type of moral contract. Your education is important too, but you must tell Sister about your other commitments. I don't ever want to have this conversation with you again. Do you understand me?"

"Yes, Daddy."

It was Mary who found his body in the bathroom. She had come home at lunchtime on a Friday to get a schoolbook she had forgotten. They said later that Tommy never would have killed himself at home if he thought one of the children would find him first, but Mrs. Devlin did not return from shopping until 1:30, and by then Mary had hidden the note from her mother and called the police. Ever a neat man in his own house, Tommy slashed his wrists in the bathtub with the water running, using a newly purchased carving knife.

The police had put the story together by the day of the funeral. Some three months before, the Rover Motorworks' Birmingham Purchasing Division had declared Tommy Devlin and two other senior buyers redundant in view of consolidation of various functions with the Bristol office. Tommy had been pronounced surplus property after 19 years of service and was advised that he would be receiving six more of his bimonthly checks as severance compensation. For the past three months he had left the house at 7:30 a.m. as usual, coming home at 5:45. He had purchased a rail pass and would spend each day on a different route, never speaking to other passengers other than to comment on the new model Rover cars that he would catch sight of on the motorway from the train window. The Friday of his death would have been

69

the first day on which he would not have brought home a pay envelope.

"It all fits," the young lieutenant from the police department announced to Mary's mother. "Tragic to be sure, but it does fit. Your husband was despondent about the loss of his job after so many years, and decided to take his life. The only thing that doesn't make sense is that he didn't leave a note. You would think that a man so organized and detailed would heave a note. Still, you never know what goes through a person's mind at a time like that."

Following graduation from St. Paul's that spring, Mary was accepted into the Queen Elizabeth School of Nursing in Birmingham. Although her visits to the house on Hagley Road were infrequent, Mary did keep in touch by telephone with her mother and Noel during the three years of training. After Tommy's death, Mrs. Devlin had allowed her modest interest in roses to develop into an obsession, filling the back garden with plants and the house with small pots, color coded to denote the various mixtures of potting soil and plant hybrids. The occasional call from Mary was one of the few things that could shake Susan Devlin back into reality and out of her floral dream world.

When she was 21, Mary took and passed the exams to be a State Registered Nurse and three weeks later boarded the 9:18 morning train to London. A newly framed SRN certificate was in the side pocket of one of the two brown suitcases she carried when she arrived at Euston Station some two hours later, not the least bit nervous about the fact that the next morning she would start as a junior staff nurse on a general surgery ward of St. George Hospital near Hyde Park.

As Mary sat in her Boston apartment reading the articles about the Wisconsin raid, she thought briefly about the dramatic changes that had taken place in her life since those first days at St. George's. When had the metamorphosis really taken place? When had she gone from simple, shy nurse to strident woman to radical activist? And was there to be a next stage, and, if so, what? Her rational mind told her that the death of her father must have started her on a path of conflict with the establishment. But there must have been other steps along the way, other milestones that marked, and perhaps hastened, this change that was so evident to her, if not to others.

Mary could still remember the many new experiences she had as a young nurse at St. George's. The first patient to die in her care had been a solicitor from Dover in his mid-sixties who had presumably been well on his way to recovery from open-heart surgery. "I had just finished giving him his pills and was marking the chart," she told her mother on the phone that evening. "We were talking about the World Cup match and he suddenly collapsed. I thought he was asleep, Mum, but he was dead. I've seen dead people before but I've never actually been involved in a cardiac arrest. It didn't bother me really, although we weren't able to get him back."

She tried to keep frequent contact with her mother during those months, if not by phone then by letter or the occasional visit home. Mrs. Devlin loved to hear about her daughter's activities at St. George's. But there were some things that Mary did not share with her mother, busy tending the beloved roses some 113 miles away in Birmingham.

Mary's first lover was a young doctor from Cardiff working at St. George's on a surgical rotation. Graham Stevenson, four years older than Mary, made few promises and kept even fewer, but was gracious and caring and a pleasant exception to the shallow bravado so typical of other surgeons she encountered. Graham's uncle owned a second flat in Knightsbridge and felt it a badge of honor to share this minor secret with his nephew, reliving vicariously his own days as an intern at St. Bart's 30 years before. The visit of Graham's previously undisclosed wife to the ward one day moved Mary's relationship with him to a new phase. Although her first reactions had been of anger and distrust, she shortly renewed their lovemaking, with the now conspiratorial aspect of the affair adding an element of excitement to their ever more frequent trysts.

There were other lovers as well as occasional loves over the next few years. None were able to dramatically alter the single dimensional aspects of Mary's life, or to crack the veneer still covering what she would later acknowledge to be a smoldering cauldron of hate. None, that is, until the arrival of Jeffrey Anndover in January of 1976. 'The Winter of My Discontent,' as Mary referred to it years later, began with a hastily called meeting of the senior nurses on the orthopedic ward where Mary was then working.

"Girls, it is important that you know about a patient who will be checking in shortly," the Ward Sister began cautiously. "As you may know, Sir Malcolm Anndover has been a generous patron of St. George's during his lifetime and has specified a generous bequest in his will which we are to receive upon his death. Sir Malcolm is quite active in the Tory Party and has a reputation as a true gentleman. Unfortunately the same cannot be said for his son, who will soon be our patient. Jeffrey Anndover suffered a compound fracture of the left tibia this morning, which will require insertion of a metal pin in addition to standard orthopedic treatment. Mr. Anndover received his injuries in a rather heated scuffle with the police, who were trying to break up a demonstration by the Campaign for Nuclear Disarmament, one of a multitude of fringe organizations in which young Mr. Jeffrey is an active participant. In this case he not only suffered an injury but also was arrested and taken into custody. It was only after the intercession of Sir Malcolm that Jeffrey was released on bond and transferred for treatment here at St. George's."

At the age of 64, the Ward Sister tended to use the term "young" somewhat loosely. In this case the young Mr. Jeffrey was 31 years old. In all other aspects, Sister was remarkably accurate, and even restrained, in her description of the junior Anndover's reputation for nonconformity.

"Nurse Devlin, in view of your seniority on the ward, I'm asking that you keep an eye on young Mr. Anndover. He will not have a private nurse, so I expect that you'll pay special attention to his needs out of deference to his father. But don't stand any nonsense."

"Yes, Sister."

It began the next morning and continued sporadically for the following two days: the inquisition.

"Good morning, Mr. Anndover."

"It's Jeffrey, not Mr. Anndover. I am Jeffrey! What's your name?"

"Staff Nurse Devlin."

"No, you're not going to be Staff Nurse Devlin! What's your Christian name?"

"Mary, if you insist."

"OK, Mary, that's better. Now tell me, are you a private nurse just for me?"

"No, I'm a senior staff nurse and I have other patients to look after so please hurry up and take your tablets. I have work to do."

"Oh yes, and I suppose every patient gets a pretty nurse like you who runs in if they move just a little. I saw you out there before. Has the Ward Sister asked that I get special attention?"

"All of our patients get special attention, Mr. Anndover."

"It's not Mr. Anndover! My father is Sir, I am Jeffrey, you are Mary. Is that so hard?"

"No, Jeffrey, I suppose not."

"Now, Mary, I saw you here during the night. Are you getting special pay for an extra shift?"

"No, because it was my choice. I didn't finish my work and there were so many other things that needed doing."

"That, dear Mary, is rubbish, pure and simple. You are here to earn a decent living and have safe and pleasant working conditions. Do you understand that?"

"Yes, Karl Marx." And so it went.

Jeffrey Anndover had never, and would never, be accused of complacency in the face of controversy. His father had once quipped that Jeffrey had yet to meet a cause he didn't like, or a government agency that he did. He was an almost graduate of Queen's College Oxford, expelled for the second and last time after a demonstration supporting the service workers, just three months prior to the end of term.

Jeffrey's first actual arrest was for sabotage to vehicles used by foxhunters at the spring hunt in Oxfordshire in 1971. This was followed by a seemingly never-ending series of confrontations when participating with various peace groups or disarmament coalitions. But his foremost zeal was reserved for causes associated with animal rights.

"I should have a scrap book of all the episodes in which I have played." On this third day in the ward, Jeffrey had apparently tired of grilling Mary about her role in the workers' paradise, and was now beginning to talk about his commitment to improving the lot of society. "There were three of us who burnt that building last year at the mink farm in the Midlands. I was also at the break-in at the cosmetics company in Kent. Two hundred rabbits going blind for one more shade of lipstick, Mary. Something had to be done! Just parading with signs in front of a building does nothing. These companies will only react to one thing, and that's public pressure. We have to show how they're abusing animals in the holy name of commerce. Your medical profession is no better, you know. Some of your research labs have the worst standards of care."

"Surely you don't object to the use of mice or hamsters in medical research?"

"Mary, we have a saying, 'A rat is a pig is a dog is a boy.' Do you understand that? It's alive, and that's all that matters."

As Jeffrey's injuries healed over the next week, he spoke often about his involvement with the animal rights cause, including his efforts at providing more structure to the movement. He had been instrumental in starting a group called the Band of Mercy after becoming dissatisfied with the lack of contentiousness he had seen among BUEV supporters. The British Union for the End of Vivisection had been the beacon for animal rights efforts in Britain for years, but their distaste for militancy gave the radical left an incentive to form new groups that chose to move with less regard for the letter of the law.

Mary was surprised by her increasing interest in the subject of animal rights. She had never met anyone so committed to a cause, anyone so close to the edge of societal norms, yet persuasive in his countless arguments for change. She was not unaware that she was attracted to Jeffrey, whether because of his physical appearance, which was certainly reason enough, or because he represented a chance for her to flee the bounds of normalcy, the self-imposed bounds that moved with her from Belfast and Wales to Birmingham and London.

They became lovers shortly after he left the hospital, and within two months Mary had moved into his tiny flat near Charing Cross Station, a flat chosen with the apparent intent to dispel any suggestion that Jeffrey was the current beneficiary of a rather large trust fund. In their first year together, the Band of Mercy was broken up after one of the other leaders was imprisoned, and Jeffrey then worked with several new radical members of the movement in London to start another group which came to be called the Animal Rescue Band.

Although never as committed as Jeffrey, Mary became increasingly involved with the group's activities in the following years, participating in some of the clandestine raids on furriers and laboratories. "You must never participate in any of our public activities," Jeffrey had said. "It is essential that we protect your anonymity. The day will come when we will need a nurse in place at a particular institution, and you will be that nurse."

Notwithstanding this mutually agreed upon note of caution, they were both surprised at the relative ease with which Mary had adapted to the role of saboteur, practicing the trade craft with a degree of competency equal to that which she brought to her nursing profession. The picking of locks, techniques of radio communication, and use of animal anesthetics, were all skills she mastered quickly and passed on with increasing passion and urgency to others as their numbers grew.

"What drives you, Mary?" one of the new members she was training asked. "I don't even think you're a vegetarian. Why do you risk your career for a few beagles in Sussex?"

"It's not just the beagles or the hamsters or the rabbits, don't you see? It's the damn injustice of our system. We live in a country that today will smash the head of a chimp to test a sports helmet. Maybe next year we should make lampshades out of the dead, or leather coats from the retarded. We're a corrupt society if we turn away from cruelty at any level." The questioner glanced nervously at the other people in the room as Mary continued, her voice growing louder. "I will tell you for a fact that if we depend on the ethics of the large corporation, the large university, the testing laboratory, then we're doomed. They have no ethics! And if we're unsuccessful with the institutions, then we must deal directly with the individuals involved."

If there were any who doubted Mary's independent thinking, they had only to assess her actions while leading a late night raid on a university research lab in York during the summer of 1979. Confronted with a situation where she found four cats with severed spinal cords tethered in cages as part of an experiment on nerve regeneration, Mary quickly decided to kill the animals with an overdose of sedative.

"How could you possibly do that?" she was asked the next day in a confrontation with ARB activists. "Our mission is to save animals, not kill them!"

"There are 50 million cats and dogs on this bloody island!" Mary exploded in response. "Our mission is not to save them all! We can't possibly do that! Our mission is to stop the suffering of animals, and when we can, send the message that no program, no person, is safe if they choose to ignore the fact. It serves a greater goal for those cats to die a painless death than to let the monsters at that laboratory think they can continue unimpeded with that type of research!"

Mary's growing self-confidence was tested in yet another way several months later when she served an ultimatum on Jeffrey that it was time to move to a better flat. "You've made your statement that you weren't subverted by your father's money, and we're all duly impressed. Now I want you to cash a few of those checks from the trust. I'm tired of hot pipes and cold baths."

When it eventually came time to pack for the move, Jeffrey was intrigued by some of the memorabilia that he had found in Mary's nightstand. "And what have we here? Your SRN certificate, nicely framed and all. You are a sentimental bird, aren't you?"

"Give me that!" Mary said quickly, in a voice that surprised him.

"Not so fast, not so fast. Let's see why you're so excited about some nursing certificate."

"Jeffrey," Mary said, this time her voice more measured but still firm, "I want you to hand that to me and I want it now. Stop playing around!"

"Oh you are the cute one, Mary Devlin," Jeffrey had turned the certificate over and was sliding the backing out of the frame. "There's an envelope in here. Some long lost lover, Mary? Some hidden treasure perhaps?"

"Damn it, Jeffrey, give me that bloody thing! It's none of your business! That's a note my father wrote."

"I thought your father was dead." Jeffrey had a touch of conciliation in his voice, but he still held the envelope at arm's length away from Mary.

"Of course he's dead, you idiot! That's his suicide note! No one has seen that except me, and I haven't read it since I found the body." Mary dropped back into the chair and covered her face with her hands. There were no tears, but the anguish of painful memories now resurrected was obvious.

"I am sorry, Mary. I didn't know your father committed suicide." He handed her the envelope and waited until she had regained her composure.

"Mary," he began, "you can not always bury the past. You must learn to use it, to let it shape and mold you. If there is anger, or pain, or even love, these are forces that you can use, but only if you acknowledge their presence and build on them." Jeffrey was standing in front of the chair where Mary was sitting. His attitude had changed. No longer the playful lover, he was now once again the teacher, the master, the mentor – who could skillfully influence the direction of his student during this rare moment of vulnerability. "I want you to tell me about your father's suicide. I want you to tell me about this note. Use it as a catharsis, Mary."

"I don't want a stupid catharsis for God's sake," Mary was shouting now. "I just want peace, I just want some bloody peace and justice in this life."

"There won't be any justice, Mary, unless you and I and others like us force the process. Do you think the big companies, the big governments, are going to do the right thing because we ask it, because we sent a bunch of pickets to 10 Downing Street? We have to force it Mary, and we have to force it with disruption and violence if necessary! That's the only language they understand. When will you learn that industry doesn't give a toss about anything except money?"

"I do know that," Mary was standing again and looking out the window. "They killed my father," her voice was trailing off, "the bastards killed my father."

"I want you to tell me about it, Mary. I'll teach you how to use your anger. It's part of your destiny that you can no longer avoid. Every event in your life has a meaning, a value, but only if used. I can teach you how to use it, Mary, how to channel it, but you have to tell me."

"If I tell you Jeffrey, it will not leave this room. You're very good at manipulating people, at getting them to do your bidding, your dirty work. Sometimes I need to be manipulated, to be pushed, but I'll decide when those times are, Jeffrey, not you. Do you understand me?" Mary had regained her composure. The hubris and sense of authority which would be so evident in later years were on this day beginning to emerge. "You like to play head games, to get inside the minds of people and push the buttons. I'll push my own buttons, Jeffrey. If you help me find them you'll have accomplished enough."

And so Mary talked about her father's suicide for the first time. She described exactly how she found the body, the location of the knife, the depth of the cuts, the probably amount of blood loss and the resultant medical sequence leading to death. She sketched her father's relationship with the company to which he had devoted his life, and how they in turn had dealt with him. Finally, she described his last three months, his leaving the house each morning for a day of introspection on the train. What for most men would have been a moderate career and financial setback was for a him a complete emasculation of self, a mortal wound to his inner soul from which he could not recover. It was at this point in the telling that Mary allowed some element of self-doubt to enter the story. "If only we had sensed his pain. There must have ben some sign, some indication, no matter how small. How could we have been so blind?"

But quickly again, the crack in the emotional veneer was sealed and she continued with the depiction of the funeral and the way the family dealt with the loss, eyes straight ahead, as if reading from some moving script, unseen but by her.

"And now, Jeffrey," she said after a short pause, "I'll read his note." She opened the envelope slowly, carefully unfolded the single sheet of paper inside, and in a steady, monotone voice, read aloud her father's words.

>My dearest Susan,
>
>I'm so sorry that you must see this note, for now you know that I have failed you and the children. By my words and actions, I've tried to show the value of loyalty and trust, to my employer and to my family. I have always been so proud of my work and my ability to provide a good life for the family. But now I can no longer do that. You will soon learn that I have lost my position at Rover. If I could have found a way to work harder or better, maybe this would not have happened. I cannot face the children with this news, but most of all I cannot face you. Please forgive me and ask Mary and Noel to forgive me also. I will love you forever.
>
>   Love,
>   Tommy

"And now you know the story, Jeffrey. The company may have killed my father with their callous disregard for human capital, but I was an accomplice. I was a participant just as if I had bought the knife. I allowed my father to believe that he could not trust me, could not talk to me, and I failed to see his despair. I have been carrying a secret, Jeffrey. I have carried a secret and I've been damaged by it – and damaged people are dangerous. People like me have learned to live with our pain and we don't always have pity for those who can't do likewise. I've told you this story today, but I don't want to discuss it with you again, ever! It concerns someone you did not know at all, and someone I did not know as well as I thought."

Jeffrey was staying near the entrance to the bedroom, seemingly reluctant to move closer to Mary as she paced around the small flat. She stopped for a few seconds, as if to compose her final thoughts, and then said, "My father's death and the manner in which it came about has altered my life and has probably affected my character. I think you're right that I should use this event, that I should build on it. It might help me better understand the person I have become. You may have observed, Jeffrey, that I am no longer troubled by death. I may be afraid of life, but I'm not troubled by death."

She looked at Jeffrey again as if to be certain that he realized she was serious, and said, "Now finish packing. I want to be out of this flat and having tea in our new place by four."

CHAPTER NINE
The Board

Monday's meeting gave every indication that it would be a memorable event. Perry Robertson knew that a decision on the initial public offering could not be delayed any longer. He was also aware that an IPO could not go forward without a new president for Remote Monitoring. Although he thought he could expect three yes votes from the six members now on the board, Bob Arons' vote was less than solid, and even that might only result in a tie if the issue was forced. The key was to bring everyone along to the same decision, kicking and screaming if necessary, but at least agreeing for the record. Perry knew that if it became necessary to vote his seat on a hotly contested issue, he could end up winning the battle but losing the war.

Many early stage medical device companies face these types of tough strategic questions early in their history, and Remote Monitoring was not going to be an exception. The basic business of the company involved the development and sale of patient monitoring equipment for use in a hospital environment. The firm had gotten its start with the introduction of a line of ambulatory patient monitors that had enhanced data recording and storage capabilities, allowing for feedback of critical vital signs to a central station. Dr. Daniel Stassen, one of Remote's founders, was head of the Emergency Room trauma team at the University of Colorado Hospital when the company was started. He had worked with two industry experts, Jerry Fenton and Mike Olanski, to develop the monitors for use in emergency situations where the larger and less portable units were not available. While the initial product had some limited appeal, what had caught Robertson's interest as a potential investor was the early work that Olanski and another engineer had done on the development of the so-called "smart" patch electrodes used to monitor patients' vital signs and transmit data on a real time basis to central monitoring stations. When it became apparent that the new electrodes could serve as the basis for a number of future development efforts, the three founders set about the process of raising capital, confident that the financial world would quickly beat a path to the door of the new company.

It is indeed fortunate that entrepreneurs and their associates are, by their very nature, endowed with a sense of optimism that transcends a rational analysis of business reality. Were that not the case, none of these companies would ever get off the ground, since the formation of any new corporate enterprise is inherently risky, and even more so if the field of technical endeavor is one that is highly regulated by the federal government. While in this case optimism may be a virtue, the individuals who form new medical companies are almost invariably guilty of underestimating the amount of capital required, and overestimating the ability of the management team to bring a product to the market in a timely fashion. In this regard, the three founders of Remote Monitoring were well within the guidelines of normalcy. They were looking to obtain sizable amounts of outside investment capital and they were expecting to retain control of their company. They were also wrong.

For the first year after the company was formed, the board of directors consisted of the three founders. Jerry Fenton assumed the position of president and CEO and also functioned as the de facto head of sales. Mike Olanski was the VP of Operations in charge of product development and manufacturing. Both men were engineers by training and had been working together in technical management positions at another Denver company when they began collaborating with Dr. Stassen regarding the new concept for patient monitoring. Although an equal shareholder with Fenton, Olanski had readily agreed to take the junior of the two original executive positions when the company was formed. He was at his best when explaining the subtleties of circuit design, and had the presence of mind when conversing with a nontechnical audience to stick to a vocabulary that the layman might recognize as being part of the English language. The one disconcerting habit he did have was to avoid eye contact while speaking, writing instead in his notebook, in some form of impassioned shorthand, those points he thought to be of most significance. Dr. Stassen had assumed the title of Chairman of the Board, although in practice, he delegated all but the most perfunctory duties to Fenton, and had made it clear from the start that he did not understand the business nuances of running a company and had no desire to learn.

The first outsider to join the board was Bob Arons, an attorney in Denver with the firm of Andler, Jacobs, and Fisk. Arons would not have been considered one of the movers and shakers of the Denver legal community, but he worked for a firm that did business with a lot of new companies, and it was not uncommon for some of these start-up operations to ask their corporate attorney to take a board seat. Whether this was because of the anticipation of obtaining a new level of strategic insight in the problems of small companies, or because of a misguided expectation that the firm might get some free legal advice, was open to debate. But in either event, Arons joined the board. A modicum of strategic insight came with him, and legal fees went up.

Perhaps Arons' most significant contribution was the introduction of Perry Robertson to the company. The two men were not close friends, but they had served on a couple of United Way committees together and had shared other mutual contracts. When client companies reached the stage where they needed outside capital, it was not uncommon for Arons to make the contact with wealthy Denver investors like Robertson.

"I know you like to look at medical deals," Arons had said when he made the first call to Robertson. "I helped these guys get incorporated a couple of years ago. Two engineers and a doctor from Colorado University started the company on a shoestring. They managed to get the business up to about a million a year in revenues with fifteen employees, and now they need to raise some outside capital. I think the deal looks pretty good. I stuck some money in myself and went on the board."

The Robertson family fortune had been established by Perry's father in the early 40s with investments in several of Denver's most successful oil and gas companies. The fortune had been sustained, and eventually increased, by the timely diversification out of energy holdings and into various high tech areas when Perry took over from his father as managing partner of the family holding company in 1966. A little more than 20 years later, Perry and two associates were running a $24 million pool of venture investments under the name of Robertson Family Partnership, or RFP. As a venture capitalist, Perry invested in companies at an early stage of development, usually well before they were large enough to go public or attract capital from traditional banking sources. In theory, RFP would invest $100-300,000 in a high tech start-up, follow the company's progress for a year or two, invest another $200-$500,000 when the company needed to gear up for volume production, and then cash out their stockholdings for $3-4 million after the company went public. In theory!

"In theory, every company in which we invest must have the potential to provide us a ten times return of capital within five to seven years, or we won't make the initial investment," Perry had intoned at his guest lecture on venture capital that he delivered annually at the University of Colorado Graduate School of Business. "In practice, it never works that way. We end up completely writing off three or four out of every ten investments we make, but usually not before we have sunk in a lot more time and money. Four or five investments end in the category of the living dead, where if we're lucky, maybe one or two investments will give us back a return of eight or ten times on our money. And occasionally – only occasionally, but just enough to keep us hooked, someone in our industry will get a twenty or thirty times play."

But the successes of Robertson and RFP were not unwarranted. No one in the Denver area had better contacts, did more thorough or effective evaluation of prospective new company opportunities, or worked harder to help the small companies in which he invested succeed. And even if RFP demanded a big slice of the pie for their initial investment, in the end there was a good chance that there would at least be a pie to slice. But the man who would become the fifth director on the board was not a person to suffer in silence. Most boards of directors have one person who ends up being the dominant voice on issues of substance, and on the Remote Monitoring board it would be Robertson, not the corporate attorney.

The contrast in style between the two men was significant, the most visible illustration being their selection of attire. At the final negotiating session for the RFP investment in Remote, Perry wore a dark gray suit with a broad pinstripe, the custom tailored jacket fitting smoothly over the shoulder with a sleeve length that allowed the monogrammed French cuff on the blue patterned shirt to protrude the requisite seven-eights of an inch. A silk maroon pocket square provided a subtle touch, bringing out the background color in the Hermes tie. Arons on the other hand felt comfortable, and not at all out of place, in a light colored corduroy sport coat at least one inch too long, worn over brown pants that in all probability had never been formally introduced to the jacket prior to that morning. This outfit was complemented by a wide paisley tie, held firmly in place by a clip that could have doubled as a fishing lure in the event Arons was ever marooned near a trout stream. Despite this dichotomy in style, the two men had a high level of mutual respect. Robertson's evident self-confidence and sophistication came across in a non-threatening manner, and Arons' sartorial weakness seemed in proper balance with the personality of someone who was a journeyman attorney with other things to worry about besides the way he dressed.

One of those things that Arons and the three original directors had on their worry list was the probable addition of yet another director when the next round of capital was required. Although it had been factored into Robertson's decision process when he made his original investment, the other directors were less than thrilled to realize that the company would need at least one more round of private investment. That would mean one more venture capital group as a significant shareholder, and that in turn would mean one more outside director. This time it was Perry Robertson who made the introduction. Paul Hodson was a partner at Jefferson Summit, a California-based venture firm. In contrast to RFP, Jefferson Summit managed over $100 million of institutional money, typically from limited partners such as company pension plans or public employee retirement programs. Hodson was the senior partner responsible for investments in the healthcare area, and a friend of Perry's since they were students at Yale. The two men had been co-investors on three other transactions, and Hodson was comfortable following the lead of RFP when Robertson had done the background analysis of the company. Jefferson Summit did require a board seat when the firm made sizable investments in private deals, but it was clear from the outset that Paul would look to Perry for guidance on matters of importance.

The six-person Remote Monitoring board was now complete – three original founders, the corporate attorney, and two venture capitalists. In theory, all board seats had an equal voice, but Robertson made sure his voice was a little louder than the others. Dr. Stassen would continue to be chairman, but in matters of importance or controversy, Perry Robertson would take the lead.

*

A number of important matters had come before the board over the preceding few years, despite the fact that the company had generally been making good progress in the time since RFP had made an investment. During that four-year period, the company had gone from a revenue level of about $1 million annually to the point where it was now booking that much each month. Fenton and Olanski had found a bona fide niche in the hospital equipment market with a product that allowed for remote monitoring of patients and the concurrent storage of key medical data on a real time basis. That success had now brought on the need for the company to consider a public offering of stock, and Perry had been driving that point home with the apparently unconvinced Bob Arons before the start of the Monday board meeting.

"I don't think we have any choice," Perry said. "We need to raise fifteen to twenty million to build a new plant and expand overseas, and there's no way we can raise that much on another private round. With the market heating up for companies doing IPO's, and Remote coming off a strong year of growth in sales and earnings, this is about the best chance we'll have for awhile."

"Who are you going to suggest for the lead underwriter?" Arons asked.

"There are only two or three firms well positioned to do a medical deal this size," Perry said. "I've asked one of the partners from Brookline to be at the meeting today so we can hear their story. They may want to suggest using a Denver firm as a co-underwriter, but I think Brookline is the right group to lead."

Established in 1878, Brookline Securities was a Boston-based firm so proud of its financial heritage that it employed a full-time historian to document and memorialize its role in providing capital to American industry, fearful that any vestige of its corporate evaluation might otherwise be lost in a sea of anecdotal folklore. Despite its senior statesman status in the investment banking community, Brookline had kept pace with the rapid advancements in technology that its clients sought to finance. With a heavy emphasis on software development companies as well as those in healthcare, the firm had been able to ride the crest of successful offerings that took place in the 80s. Although the firm employed its share of bright, young attorneys and MBAs from the Ivy League schools, the core of the Brookline partner group still consisted of third and fourth generation members of some of the founding families. James

Carleton III was the senior partner responsible for the Healthcare Group of Brookline Securities and more than a little proud of his family tree.

"He does not go by Jim," Perry had told Bob Arons when they were talking about the upcoming board meeting. "He goes by James, although I wouldn't be surprised to find out that his secretary still calls him Mr. Carleton. But he's not as stuffy as he sounds, trust me. He's one of the top guys around in evaluating the market for a deal if you want to take a company public. And, having the Brookline name on the front cover of our prospectus is about as good as we're going to get."

The format for this day's meeting was to have a brief review of the current business status and then to hear from Brookline Securities about their interest in doing the offering. When Carleton got up to speak, he took off his suit jacket and placed it carefully on the walnut credenza behind the conference table. Arons could not help but observe the J.C. III monogram, sewn not only on the pocket of the light blue shirt but on each of the contrasting white French cuffs, as if to ensure that no one would miss the point that this was a custom-made garment.

"I want you to know that we think – actually we don't just think – we know, that we can take this company public. We're convinced that with your solid growth record over the past four years, we can do an IPO and raise at least twenty million in new capital for Remote." Carleton walked to the front of the conference room as if to emphasize the leadership role that he and his firm would soon be taking. "I am not aware of any other investment banking firm that has the track record of Brookline Securities for these kind of medical device deals. With our mix of institutional and retail customers, we're in a prime position to place the stock in the best hands and get the company in front of the right people when we do the road show."

Robertson had heard these presentations many times before, including at least two where Carleton was doing the pitching. The underwriters could make a convincing argument about how they would be able to move the stock if you just signed them up to do the deal. Sometimes it worked as planned. If the market got hot for IPO's, if the company's numbers kept moving in the right direction, if there were not too many other deals competing for the attention of the selling syndicate or the potential buyers, then it might work as smoothly as Carleton suggested. Sometimes it did – usually it did not.

"James," Perry said, "you'd better talk a bit about what you mean by the road show. I'm not sure everyone is familiar with that term." Carleton was still standing at the end of the conference table. He nodded almost imperceptibly at Robertson. If there was any best time to deliver the message, it was probably now.

"Well, the road show is where the underwriters, one or two people from Brookline plus maybe one or two from another firm if we use a regional company as co-underwriter – where we go around with the CEO of the company and maybe another person from top management to meet with potential investors. We do this near the end of the offering period and probably talk to fifteen or twenty groups in maybe ten different cities. Most of this will be in the US, but we might make one quick trip to Europe if we think there's enough institutional interest. We line up the schedule and help management put together the presentation, and then we hit the road. It's a pretty grueling week-and-a-half."

"And who goes from the company, would it be just Mike and me?" Jerry asked. "I don't know if we could both be gone that long at the same time."

Carleton looked over at Perry again. He could not stall much longer. "Before I get to that," he said, "let's talk a little about how we might price the deal."

Perry could not help smiling. "Carleton is so smooth," he thought to himself. "He's going to show the bait, set the hook, and then stand back and let Fenton reel himself in."

And that is essentially what Carleton did. He spent the next ten minutes going through an exercise of pricing comparable deals, the amount of capital to be raised, the number of shares outstanding, etc., etc. And then just when Fenton and Olanski appeared to be reaching their capacity for absorbing financial jargon and Dr. Stassen's eyes were beginning to glaze over, Carleton paused for affect and said, "When you take all this into consideration, we think that as long as the IPO window stays open we can price the deal in the $19 to $21 range. Call it $20 to make the math easy."

It did not need to be easy for Olanski. He had already made another entry in his notebook recording the fact that his 300,000 shares could be worth $6 million if the company went public at $20 a share.

"None of you could sell your shares on the IPO of course," Carleton continued as he watched the three co-founders trying desperately to appear unmoved by their anticipation of multi-millionaire status. "You would have to wait until at least three months after the offering, and then you could sell some stock, subject to various SEC restrictions. By that time, if we've pegged this right and the company has continued to perform, the stock could be in the mid-twenties."

Olanski was conscious of an increase in his heart rate as he tried to restrain his urge to do a detailed diagram of the pending progression of his financial future. He put his pen down and looked up at Carleton, just a moment too late to see the last exchange of glances that passed between James and Perry.

"There's one more thing we need to talk about," Carleton began again, this time with a hesitancy in his voice that was immediately sensed by the others as a precursor to a less than pleasant conversation. "My partners and I are really excited about managing this offering. We think you've got a very impressive company here and there's every reason to believe this could be one of the top IPO's this next year. But," – everyone anticipated the 'but', however none except Perry knew what would follow, "but we also believe that to maximize the possibility of a successful offering, we need someone other than Jerry in the position as chief spokesperson for the company. Someone else in the job as CEO."

Carleton had glanced over at Fenton during the prelude to this message, but was now doing his best to avoid further eye contact. "You've done a phenomenal job in bringing the company to this point in its history, but now that Remote is about to enter a whole new phase as a public entity, we, that is, my partners and I, we think it may be time to bring in a CEO that is more attuned to running a high-growth public company."

No one spoke. Olanski picked up his pen, then put it down without taking the cap off. Carleton's voice dropped another five decibels as he continued, "Of course, any change in senior management is a matter for the board to decide. We just felt that, as a probable underwriter for the company, we had an obligation to pass on this opinion." Carleton walked around the table and pulled his chair out.

"James," Perry said softly, "maybe you should give us some time to discuss this, without you here I mean. Maybe you could sit out in the lobby and we'll come get you if we have any questions."

As the door closed behind Carleton, Fenton exploded. "Just what the hell is going on here? Did all you guys know about this? Mike and I bust our ass to build this company, and now you want to dump us, or at least me! That's bullshit! What's this guy know about running a business?"

"Jerry, settle down a minute. This is something we need to talk about." Perry stood up this time, but stayed by his chair and looked directly at Fenton. "I did speak with Carleton about this before the meeting. I don't think any of the other directors did, but they can comment for themselves. I knew what he was going to say, but I thought it important for all of you to hear it from him, not from me. I think it's something we're going to have to consider if we want to take this company public."

Dr. Daniel Stassen stirred and cleared his throat. Any comment from the good doctor was so rare that the other directors looked at him as if he had just regained the power of speech. "I think you're forgetting two primary points of information," he said. Olanski had the cap off his pen, as the temptation to inscribe these soon-to-be-delivered nubs of logic proved to be irresistible. "First of all," Dr. Stassen continued, sticking one well-scrubbed finger in the air, " he did not say they wouldn't take us public with Jerry as president. He just said that to maximize the success of the offering, they would like to see somebody else in the job. And secondly," the other finger went up in what had now extended into his longest speech since joining the board, " secondly, we don't have to use these guys. There must be dozens of other firms we could work with." That said, Dr. Stassen folded his arms over his chest and shifted back to neutral.

"Well, Dan," Perry was still standing, but leaning on his chair as if to consciously convey a sense of informality, "you're right that he only talked about a new CEO as a way to maximize the deal. But I think he was easing us in one step at a time. In the conversation I had with him at breakfast, he made it clear that Brookline wouldn't do the deal if Jerry stays in place as president." He glanced over at Fenton. "Jerry, I know this sounds pretty callous right now. Hang in there for a minute, there are some things we can do to deal with a possible job change." Perry held up his hand before Fenton could respond.

"Let me cover Dan's second point about another underwriter. There definitely are other firms that can take us public, but none that have the national reputation that Brookline has. If we want to do this right and get the kind of valuation we all think the company's worth, we need to use these guys. Even if we were to try and do a deal with someone else, my guess is that we'd get the same reaction. Jerry, you've got all kinds of skills, but Carleton is right. We're going into a different phase of this company's life. Once we're public we're going to need someone who can deal with the analysts and shareholders as well as manage a fast-growth business. There are other ways you can play an important role in this company. Besides, you're going to have to spend some time learning what it's like being rich."

"Why's all this getting dumped on me today? Whatever happened to open communication?"

"Well, Jerry, I'm sorry if you think that's the case," Perry responded. "I've never tried to imply that being CEO was a lifetime job. If you remember, we talked about this topic one of the first times we met – how there might be a day when the board would have to deal with the issue of a change in senior management."

"Well, whose decision is it anyway? I'm the CEO. I don't see how this company is going to make a change if I don't agree with it."

"Bob, maybe you can respond to that," Perry started to sit down, "and while you're at it, you might comment on what you think about asking Jerry to step aside for a new CEO."

Bob Arons had been the corporate attorney since the company's inception but, next to Dr. Stassen, was the board's least vocal member. "Well, I can at least answer the first part of that," he started slowly. "As I think you know, Jerry, the shareholders elect the board of directors. There were also provisions included in the investment agreements with RFP and Jefferson which guaranteed that Perry and Paul are entitled to a seat. In any event, the six of us constitute the board of directors and we have the authority to appoint the officers of the corporation. You have a vote, Jerry, but only one out of six."

"And, Bob, what are your thoughts about making a change at this time?" Perry was not about to let Arons off the hook.

"Now that's a tougher question. As I said, the board does have responsibility in these issues, and indeed Colorado law is quite clear on this point." As Arons sailed off on a mini-lecture regarding fiduciary responsibilities of corporate boards, he removed his glasses and held them up at a 45-degree angle, peering through them as if sighting some distant navigational star. Perry was familiar with the routine. Next would come the rummaging in the briefcase for the little bottle of spray-on glass cleaner and the ritual spritzing of both sides of the lenses followed by a meticulous wiping of every spot, real and imagined, with the handkerchief stained by what was hopefully nothing more serious than some spilled coffee. All of this would be interspersed with at least three additional star sightings as Arons stalled for time to compose his off-the-cuff response. Perry had once had an economics professor at Yale who used a pipe scraping, filling, tamping, lighting, re-lighting routine to stall for time during the days when smoking in a classroom of a liberal college was not yet seen as a capital offense.

"So, where do you come down on this, Bob?" Perry was relentless.

"I don't know. Jerry deserves our support for all he's done, but this company needs capital and the shareholders deserve a chance at liquidity. If we really need another CEO to take the company public, then I think we have to ask Jerry to step aside."

Perry was nonplussed. He had never seen Arons make a tough decision before. It was all downhill after that. Hodson was polite, but unequivocal in his opinion that the company should recruit an outside CEO. Dr. Stassen, apparently emotionally exhausted after his two-point speech, acceded to the impending majority. Olanski supported his colleague but acknowledged that the IPO would benefit everyone, including Fenton. Perry suggested a co-chairman role for Jerry and pointed out the benefits to the directors of not actually voting their seats on the question but rather moving by consensus, and the deal was done. When Jerry explained it to his wife later that evening, he could not recall exactly how it all happened, but did convey the impression that it was mostly his idea.

On the topic of hiring a new CEO, Fenton had just begun to lay out his thoughts on the process when Perry interrupted. "Jerry, for this job we need the best possible candidate and we need him fast if we're going to do the IPO during the first quarter of next year. With all due respect to your contact list, we need some outside talent, and for that we need to use a search firm. The only question is which one. Paul, what are your thoughts?"

"I agree. We need to do a nationwide search. For medical device companies, the best group that I've seen is David Morkin and Associates out of Baltimore. We've used them on two searches. They're quick and they're good."

"We've used them on one here in Denver and I think you're right," Perry said. "I move that we hire the Morkin firm and that the board authorize Paul and me to work with their people to formalize a search and interview the top candidates. All in favor?"

"Aye!"

"Jerry?"

"Aye."

CHAPTER TEN
The Executive

It was in the middle of the second ring when Britta grabbed the receiver and tried to reconcile the reality of the dark bedroom with the brightness of the vivid dream in which she had been immersed only moments before. She could feel her heartbeat rapidly escalating in response to her now conscious awareness that their phone had erupted in the middle of the night. Barring the possibility of a wrong number, there was nothing good that could come from such an event.

"Hello," she answered tentatively as she extended her left arm across her body and fumbled for the switch on the bedside lamp.

"Who is it?" Tim had turned on his light and was trying to focus on his watch.

"It's for you."

"Is it Mom?" Since his father's heart attack some two months before, Tim had received a number of concerned phone calls from his mother, each one making him more apprehensive of the call that would eventually summon him to Indiana on a moment's notice.

"It's not your mother, it's someone from the plant."

"Is this Mr. Foster?" The deep bass voice was familiar to Tim, but he could not place it in context.

"This is Tim Foster. Who is this?"

"It's Darrian Colder from security. Sorry to wake you up at this time in the morning but you're the first name on the call list for this kind of emergency so I really didn't have much choice."

Tim was starting to come up to full speed as he remembered that Colder was one of the third shift security people at the plant. A shy black man in his late twenties, Darrian was dependability personified since he had gotten his life in order after less than meritorious service to the community during his teenage years.

"What time is it, Darrian?"

"It's 3:45, Mr. Foster. I'm afraid you're going to have to come in. We've got big trouble."

"What is it?"

"The dogs. Somebody stole the dogs."

"Darrian, nobody steals eight dogs from a laboratory. Something else must have happened to them."

"They're stole, trust me. You'll know when you see this place. It's been trashed. There's spray-painting all over the walls and it looks like somebody's been in the files. Are you coming in?"

Tim was already out of bed and stretching the phone cord to walk around to Britta's side. "I'll be there in twenty minutes. Call the police, and you better call the lab supervisor and ask him to come in."

"Was there a break-in?" Britta asked as Tim was pulling on his jeans and sweatshirt.

"Yes – somebody got into the animal lab and apparently took the dogs and trashed the place."

"Is that all they took?"

"Is that all? For God's sake! Don't you know what this means? If we don't find those dogs we don't get the long-term data to finish this program, and we can kiss five years' work goodbye."

"Stop shouting, you'll wake the twins. Just be thankful it wasn't your dad."

"Well, of course I'm glad it's not Dad, but you don't realize what this might mean. This could screw up not only our ability to get FDA approval on the implantable stimulator, but maybe our plans to spin out the division as well. We had big hopes for this product line. I'm not sure we can sell the idea of the Neuro group as a stand alone company if we don't have new products to introduce."

At 4:15 when Tim got to the plant, a police car was driving slowly around the parking lot, flashing a bright spotlight along the perimeter of the property. Tim rolled down his window and motioned for the patrolman to follow him around to the rear of the building where the two cars were parked near the back entrance.

"Hi, I'm Mr. Foster with Medelectro," Tim said when the two men got out of their cars. "Thanks for coming on short notice."

"I'm Dave Medlow, patrolman with the North Suburban Precinct. You guys have a break-in? You better let me go in first," Medlow said, with a note of authority and experience that belied his youthful appearance. "Somebody could still be in there."

As Tim unlocked the door he saw the patrolman take out his service revolver and simultaneously add fifteen years to his persona. "Our night security guy is in there," Tim said. "He's a tall black guy about 30 years old, so don't get carried away."

Medlow gave Foster a 'How dumb do you think I am' look, but both men realized that an intellectual insult was a lot better than taking a chance on an accidental shooting. As it turned out, Darrian Colder met them when they opened the door, and after a quick walk through the lab area it became obvious that no one else was in the building.

"I told you they trashed the place," Darrian said.

Patrolman Medlow was calling back to his office for the assistance of an investigative unit as Foster and Colder walked back into the lab to survey the damage. "Animals have rights too. Minnesota Branch of ARB." Tim was reading out loud. "Know what that means Darrian?" he asked. Without waiting for a response he said, "that means we're never going to see our beagles again."

*

The investigation of the break-in started in earnest at 10:15 that morning when Tim returned to his office after going home to change clothes. When he stopped at his secretary's desk to check for messages she said, "You've got a visitor."

"Who is it? I'm not exactly running a free schedule today."

Julie Sandowski had been Tim's secretary since he transferred to the Neuro Division four and a half years ago. A divorced mother of three who was some five years older than Foster, she kept pictures of her kids on her desk at work and a picture of Tim on her refrigerator at home. Although she had long since gotten over the giddy reaction she had had when they met for the first time, Julie was still captivated by Foster's looks and charm, as well as proud of the fact that her boss was one of the fastest rising executives in the company. "I think you'll want to see this man," she said. "He's with the FBI."

Foster's office was along the perimeter wall of the building and near the engineering labs where most of the prototype work was done by the research and engineering group that he was now heading. As one of the top four people in the division, his office was spacious but a long way from opulent. Seated at the round conference table near the window was a small, balding man dressed in a gray pinstriped suit. As Foster entered the room, the visitor stood and extended a hand.

"Hello Mr. Foster. I'm special agent Mark Sanders with the FBI. Here's my identification." With that he held out a badge mounted in a passbook size, brown leather cover that Tim stared at for a full twenty seconds despite his intentions to do otherwise.

"It's not that I doubt you're with the FBI," Tim said, "it's just that I've never seen one of those before."

"Well, I don't exactly look like most people's image of an FBI agent, so I wouldn't blame you for checking it close." Sanders had met the Bureau's minimum height requirement by something less than a quarter of an inch, and with two years to go before mandatory retirement, was at an age that seemed to accentuate the diminutive physical impression he imparted to people meeting him for the first time.

"How is it that the FBI's involved with this?" Tim asked. "I talked with the local police earlier this morning. I assumed they'd be investigating the break-in."

"They are investigating, but they've called us in for assistance. Jurisdiction is a little fuzzy at the moment, but we'll clarify that before the day is over, depending on what we find out this morning."

"I'm not sure I follow you."

Julie had brought in a pot of coffee and two cups. Sanders waited until she left the office before he continued. "At this time we have no evidence that the animals were taken across state lines, so on that count, it's a local matter. But if the Animal Rescue Band was actually involved, then this would be considered a terrorist act included within our bailiwick. Right now we're assuming that it's going to be an FBI case. I've got a technician back in your lab now working with the local police."

"Well, they sprayed 'A.R.B.' all over the wall. Doesn't that pretty much tell you who's involved?"

Sanders had his cup halfway up to his mouth but set it down to answer the question. "Not for certain. You saw where it also said 'Minnesota Branch of the A.R.B'. We don't know about any Minnesota branch, so it could be some sort of copycat group." He picked up the cup again but started talking while it was in mid-air. "I'm going to need to ask you some questions about the work that was going on in the lab." Down went the cup as Sanders pulled out a small note pad from his suit pocket. "But before you start with that, I'd like to cover some of your background. Let's start with your current position. What's your title and area of responsibility?"

"Well for the last four months I've been the VP of Product Development for the Neuro Division here at Medelectro," Tim said, as he watched the routine with the cup, wondering if Sanders would ever drink the coffee. "I have responsibility for all the research and engineering that goes into our new product activities. I've also got the clinical trial group reporting in to me at the animal lab."

"You said you've been in this job four months. What did you do before that?"

"I was the Marketing Director and before that a Group Product Manager for about two years. Both of those jobs were here in the Neuro Group and before that I was in our Cardiovascular Division working with pacemaker leads."

Tim watched Sanders lay down the pen and extend his arm towards the cup. Now the fingers were in the handle, elbow starting to bend, lips parting – almost there. Sanders glanced up and saw Tim staring at him. "Isn't that a little fast to be making so many moves?" Sanders asked as he put the cup down again.

"It is unusual to go from a Marketing Director to a VP in the research area," Foster said, "but I'm an engineer by training and I've kept current on the technical side. I think the company has wanted me to get exposure to several different management slots. At the risk of sounding immodest, I'm on somewhat of a fast track around here."

If Sanders was impressed about Foster's career progression, it was not immediately obvious. "Let's get back to the work that was going on in the lab," he said. "Why were you using animals in the research program?"

"You really can't develop a product like this without doing some work with animals," Tim said. He was starting to speak at a faster pace, as if he had made this speech before. "The basic concept is that we implant a stimulator just beneath the skin in the abdominal area and run our lead to the electrode that's been sutured on the muscle tissue that will eventually be placed around the base of the bladder. This company has forgotten more about stimulating the heart muscle than most firms will ever know, but this project is a whole new ball game."

"Why's that?"

"Well, for human implants, we'll be using the gracilis muscle that normally runs from the pubic bone alongside the inside of the thigh. But it's a fast twitching muscle that can't be contracted for a long time without fatigue."

"You're losing me," Sanders said. "Get me back to the dogs."

"That's the point." Tim took out a sheet of paper and drew a diagram showing the electrode placement. "We had to see if this muscle could be retrained over time if we did a continuous stimulation at a low frequency. Then we had to find out if there would be any negative effects. The FDA won't let you sell a device without this kind of data and the only way you can get it is with long-term animal implants. These dogs were implanted about fifteen months ago and were scheduled to be the last ones in this series."

"Okay, that's enough for now," Sanders said. He took a swallow of coffee, setting the cup back down on top of the diagram. "I want to break for lunch and check to see what the tech guys have found. Then this afternoon I'd like to go over the personnel files of all the people who worked in that lab during the past two years."

Tim looked at him and for the first time in their conversation voiced some concern. "Why do you need to do that? I trust our people."

"Well, your security guy says that whoever took the dogs had to have been in and out of the lab in the twenty-five minutes he was over at the other end of the building. The only way they could have done that and not set off an alarm is with help from somebody who knew the layout. Whoever gave them that help may not work here now, but I bet he did once."

*

Three days after the break-in, Bill Crowley was sitting at a back corner table in a small coffee shop on the red concourse at the Minneapolis-St. Paul International Airport. He had gotten a call at 7:30 that morning asking him to meet with a Susan McCoy at 4 p.m. It was now 4:25 and Crowley was on his third coffee and fourth cigarette.

Mary Devlin had been watching Crowley for the past fifteen minutes from the pay phone area forty feet away on the opposite side of the concourse. She had arrived on Northwest Flight 97 from Boston at 3:45, ticketed under the name of Susan McCoy. Mary had seen Crowley on one other occasion when he had met at O'Hare Airport with Karen Munford, an ARB activist, to convey information about the lab setup at Medelectro. Mary had been the 'tail' for her associate, checking to be sure neither Karen nor Crowley was being followed.

Even though Mary had only watched Crowley from a distance in Chicago, she did not like him then, and she did not like him now. An overweight man in his middle thirties, Crowley was wearing a Viking sweatshirt in obvious need of laundering, and a stocking cap that partially covered a thick mat of long black hair. As Mary began to walk towards the coffee shop, she watched as he stared at the waitress pouring coffee at the next table. Crowley was still staring when Mary pulled out the chair across from him and sat down. "Are you Bill Crowley? I'm Susan McCoy."

"You're English! Why the hell are you English?"

"I'm not English, I'm from New Zealand. Now, I've just flown in from San Francisco and I'm going on to New York in a few minutes. So we don't have much time, Mr. Crowley. I need to get some additional information from you."

"Well, you're the one that's late for Christ's sake, and I've got some questions for you! Why the hell weren't they blasted in the papers like your people said they'd be? One half-ass article that made it sound like we stole the Holy Grail, and no pictures! I thought we were going to nail the bastard." Crowley was leaning across the small table, gesturing with his cigarette-stained right hand. As Mary moved slightly to her left, she could see a large leather billfold in his back pocket, connected by a thin brass chain to a clip on his belt.

"Mr. Crowley, we're aware that you had a problem with a Mr. Tim Foster at the company."

"Damn right! The bastard fired me for no reason."

Mary barely slowed down, "– and we appreciate the fact that you helped us gain access to the lab."

"I want money for that! You didn't nail the bastard like you said, and now I want money!"

"The fact of the matter is, Mr. Crowley, you didn't see any pictures in the local papers because that lab was almost spotless. My associate tells me you could have eaten off the floor. We don't send pictures to the paper showing a bunch of happy dogs wagging their tails. Does that make any sense to you, Mr. Crowley?" Despite her best efforts, Mary realized that her voice had been rising. "Slow down – slow down," she said to herself, "I still need him."

"Well, it didn't used to be like that. Besides, your gal told me all animal research was bad."

"You're right, Mr. Crowley, you're right!" Mary saw her opening. "I know that you were a key part of the research group when you worked in the lab. We need to know one more thing. Our people took the dogs to a veterinarian for examination. On the x-rays he took, he can see a round metal object in the abdomen of each dog and a wire leading out from that. Can you tell us what that is and if it can be removed?"

Crowley looked at Mary for a moment and then said slowly, "What's it worth to you, honey?"

"You give me the answer and I'll tell you what it's worth. Otherwise I get back on the plane and the paper gets a picture showing you carrying dogs out to the truck!"

"You little Limey bastard. They ought to kick your ass outta this country."

"I'm not a Limey, I'm a Kiwi. Now what did he see on the x-ray?"

After a brief but losing battle with his self-esteem, Crowley said, "The round thing is a battery-powered electrical stimulator. You turn it on by putting a magnet next to it on the skin. I used to do that twice a day on each dog. The wire is a lead which goes to the electrode that they attach to the muscle."

"Can it be taken out?"

"Sure. They did that once or twice when they had battery problems."

"Thank you Mr. Crowley. Tomorrow you'll get an express envelope that will contain $500 in cash. It will also contain an 8 by 10 glossy photo of you at the lab. You won't be surprised to see that the negative will not be enclosed. Now you can leave and I will pay the check. There are two men in the terminal who will be following you out to be sure you don't have any second thoughts about our bargain."

"Bargain my ass! You are a cute little bitch!"

"Thank you, Mr. Crowley."

Mary was, of course, bluffing about the two men. Mary Devlin did not know two men in the entire state of Minnesota, let alone at the airport. As she was walking towards gate 9A on the gold concourse for her return flight to Boston, she stopped and made an 800 call to a voicemail message service, passing on the information about the dogs.

Twenty-one miles away in the northern suburbs of Minneapolis, Tim Foster was meeting with FBI agent Mark Sanders and Howard Beal, senior security officer for Medelectro's worldwide operations. Beal was an ex-St. Paul police captain who had opted for early retirement to take an industry job. Vestiges of past turf battles with the FBI were still apparent, as evidenced by the manner in which he spoke to Sanders.

"Are you absolutely sure you guys have jurisdiction?"

"Howard, I told you. We know it was an ARB raid. They've taken credit for it and the pattern matches some of the raids in Wisconsin and Ohio." Sanders continued, "Look, we need to find out if there are any other employees or ex-employees who might have had a reason to set this up. We've seen enough of the file on this guy Crowley. Who actually fired him?"

"I did," Tim said. "His supervisor had him on probation for a variety of reasons, but I was the guy who actually fired him."

"What was the cause of action?"

"He was an animal attendant who helped on some of the device activation schedules, but mainly he was supposed to keep the lab clean and be sure the dogs got a precisely measured diet and exercise regiment. He did a lousy job. That's why he was on probation. When I found out that he was falsifying the records and not giving the dogs exercise, I fired him on the spot. I could do that since he was on probation. I didn't have to jump through a bunch of hoops with the personnel department."

"Why were you so anxious to fire him?"

"I saw an animal lab get out of control once. It's not a pretty sight, and it's not going to happen here."

"Where was that?"

"California."

"When you were in college?"

Tim paused for a second and then said, "Yes – in grad school. But getting back to Crowley, I don't know if he's vindictive enough to do this. He might be. He did know the routine on the night shift so he could have set it up. We should have changed the security codes."

"Yes, you should have. I presume that's part of the procedure now if anyone leaves," Sanders said, looking directly at Beal.

"We're taking care of it, Mark. You work on getting our dogs back."

When Tim left the room for a conference call with the FDA, Sanders got up to close the door and said, "Howard, you know the routine, I have to check on Foster. Whaddya know about him?"

"They don't come any straighter. I did a background check on him when he was promoted to VP. He's squeaky clean. Good marriage, two little girls, no unusual debts – no bad habits. If the company kept a short list of people who could be CEO ten years from now, he'd be on it. Before I got here he really made a name for himself at some congressional hearing and he's been getting notches in his belt every two or three years since. I can understand why he'd fire a guy like Crowley. Foster's so damn honest and has such high standards that he couldn't put up with that shit. If I was twenty years younger, I'd be just like him."

"Sure you would, Howard. And so would I if I was six inches taller."

CHAPTER ELEVEN
The Metamorphosis

"Good morning. Morkin and Associates."

"Good morning. Is David in?"

"Yes he is. May I tell him who's calling?"

"This is Phil Martin from Southwest Venture in Dallas. We're a past client and I need to talk with David about doing another search."

"Yes, I remember your firm, Mr. Martin. I'll connect you with David."

Business had been good for Morkin and Associates over the past several years. In fact, business had been very good. Although there were several search firms that were appreciably bigger because of their willingness to take on assignments in multiple industry groups, it was generally acknowledged in the trade that Morkin got the lion's share of the searches done within the medical device and biotech segments of the healthcare field.

David had officially changed the name of the firm from David Morkin and Associates to Morkin and Associates the previous year. Although he had not told Martha the reason, they both knew it was a precursor to the day that the firm's name would be Morkin, Laudner and Associates. Martha Laudner's share in the firm had gone from 20 percent after her first year in the business to 45 percent in the six years that followed. Some of this was because of the contractual commitment in the original partnership agreement, but most of the increase was in recognition of the success achieved by the firm after Martha's computerization of the executive database and development of the search algorithms. In the previous year, Morkin and Associates had successfully completed 31 searches for 23 different clients. With an average salary of $95,000 per position filled and a placement fee of 30 percent of the first year's compensation, the firm had grossed almost $900,000 in fees. When they met with the accountants in February, David had been almost euphoric in his review of the prior year's activities.

"Martha, after netting out everything – salaries, benefits, overhead, and other expenses, our partnership profits will be around $240,000 for last year. Forty-five percent of that plus your salary of

$125,000 means you're going to be looking at a total income of $233,000. Not bad for someone who was making $18,000 not too long ago."

"We can do better, David. I can find the candidates if you can figure out how to do the interviews in half the time. We need to find you a clone."

In fact, Martha could find the candidates. Her database now included profiles on 5,400 senior technical and management personnel at over 760 companies. Each corporate file was cross-referenced several ways to show the types of products, methods of distribution, medical sub-specialty and table of organization. All of the files on individuals included various categories of information such as specific technical and management experience, education background, peer group contacts, plus a variety of demographic data. On numerous occasions over the past year or two, Martha had been able to give David a list of the top four candidates plus contact names within hours of obtaining the specs on a new search. The limiting factor on completing most assignments was the time that it took David to meet individually with each of the candidates and make his final recommendation to the client. Although time consuming, it was a task for which he seemed to be uniquely qualified. Even Martha had to admit that this was a step in the process that could never be accomplished by her ever-expanding collection of computer hardware.

"I've done it for twenty years, Martha, I should be getting good at it pretty soon," David had joked once. They had been discussing an interview where he had dug out a fatal flaw in one applicant's background that had escaped the multiple layers of Martha's screening sequence.

"Don't sell yourself short, David," Martha had said. "You've got a real touch when it comes to doing the final interviews. Plus you have a feel for the culture and personality of the client company and unless our guy fits that profile, we're not going to have a decent match. We make a good team, David."

"That we do. That we do."

Over the previous five years, Martha had been successful in extricating herself from the mundane aspects of data entry and file maintenance. At David's urging, she had hired two part-time assistants to do most of the servile work as she concentrated on software development to improve the speed and sophistication of her search routines. She was also starting to attend some of the industry meetings where she could improve her understanding of the new technical advances being made. At these meetings she had a chance to meet some of the people who were previously only bits and bites in her database of top talent. The routine of David shaking the hands and Martha shaking the disk drive began to change for the first time in 1988.

Of the many symbiotic affiliations that David and Martha had established over the previous few years, perhaps none were more rewarding than their relationships with certain of the investment banking firms that served the industry. Montgomery Securities, Hambrecht and Quist, Brookline Securities, Alex Brown, and a few others, were active in the financing of many of the rapidly growing healthcare companies and as such, were constantly involved in the evaluation of the top management talent in place at their client companies. When there was a need to fill a senior executive slot at one of these companies, and do so in a hurry, the investment firm would frequently make a referral to Morkin and then rely on David and Martha to find the type of talent that would increase the future value of the newly financed company. Most of these investment firms also sponsored conferences on an annual basis, where current and prospective client companies were showcased. It was the Alex Brown healthcare conference in May of 1990 that served as Martha's coming out event.

Based in Baltimore, Alex Brown had been holding these conferences for several years, usually at one of the major hotels near the inner harbor. Martha had received an invitation to attend the meeting from John Callard, one of the firm's investment bankers with whom she had worked in the past. "Look, Martha, you and David have done searches for several of these outfits. You really ought to come over and hear the presentations and find out more about their business. And the more you know about the companies, the easier it'll be to match up a candidate if you do another search. Plus, we've got some small private firms that we'll be presenting this year who could be future clients for you."

"New companies?"

"Yes – some of them. We always try to invite five or ten early stage operations that we think have high potential. It gives them good exposure to future stock buyers and helps lock us in to do their IPO if they go public later."

"Well maybe I should attend, especially since it's right here in the city."

"Great! It'll also give us a chance to connect. I've been talking to you on the phone for two years and I still don't know what you look like. Let's meet at the registration desk Monday morning at eight fifteen. I'll introduce you to a few people and then maybe we can hook up again at lunch and talk about what sessions you'd like to attend over the next couple of days."

In the four days prior to the meeting, Martha had some serious shopping to do. Although she had not really been a recluse the past several years, her social calendar had been limited to a few dinner engagements with David and his wife and the occasional evening out with another woman from her apartment building. Her wardrobe, never exactly cosmopolitan, was now in some serious need of upgrading if she expected to make a favorable impression at the business sessions of the conference as well as the evening social events that she knew were part of the three-day program.

So it was with a modest sense of enthusiasm that Martha went looking for new clothes, and after some halfhearted window-shopping in the Harbor Center, wandered into the Anne Klein store on the second level, where she was captured by an attractive sales woman dressed in the manner of a walking advertisement for color coordination.

"May I be of assistance to you?" Miss Color Blend asked before Martha had a chance to break eye contact.

"I'm not sure. I need a new outfit, but I don't really know if any of these would be right for me." Martha's normal self-confidence was not readily apparent in this unfamiliar environment.

"I'm sure we have something appropriate for you. What were you thinking of as your initial choice?

"Something suitable for a business conference. Maybe a two-piece outfit, black and white, size ten."

"Black and white?" Only the maturity and experience commensurate with twelve years of selling fine women's clothing enabled Miss Color to ask the question without sounding inordinately patronizing.

"Yes, black and white," Martha responded, oblivious to the subtle inference of disapproval.

After she came out of the changing room and was standing in front of the three-way mirror, Martha was joined by the sales woman who pinched the extra fabric on the skirt and said, "My dear, you're not a size ten. You should try an eight."

"Well, I don't understand that. I used to be a ten when I was at this weight before."

"How long ago was that?"

"It's been awhile. At least nine or ten years."

"And how did you lose your weight?"

"I was in an auto accident a number of years ago and as part of my rehabilitation I've spent about a zillion hours swimming and riding the exercise bike. Plus I do a lot of stretching routines."

"And you haven't bought clothes for some time?"

"No. At least, nothing of consequence."

"My dear, you should know that you didn't just lose weight. You've tightened it up and moved it around into all the right places. You've got a figure that most women your age would kill for. Don't you realize that?"

"Do you really think so?" Martha had turned sideways in front of the mirror and was pulling in the excess material around her waist.

"Absolutely! Now listen, dear – I'm sorry – what is your name?"

"Martha Laudner."

"Martha, I'm Melliss Kenworthy. You have to let me help you. I don't care if you buy a thing, but you must try on some outfits that'll show off that figure. And Martha, it can't be black and white! There's a federal law against wearing black and white if you're a size eight."

And so for the next ninety minutes, Ms. Kenworthy was a veritable whirlwind of fashion competence as she introduced Martha to the concept of coordinated outfits. Skirts that went with tops that went with slacks that went with blouses that went with sweaters. And not one of the pieces was black or white.

"With this mix and match approach, you can have dozens of combination outfits, Martha, if you pick the right color blends. With your creamy skin we're going to want to use some pale peach and peppermint greens."

"They do look nice."

"And I want to show you how to accessorize. You won't believe how we can change the look with different belts, scarves, shoes, handbags, and jewelry."

"Do you think I should change my hairstyle?" Martha had on one of the new outfits and was admiring the flattering image in the mirror while pushing her hair back with her left hand.

"Don't touch it! Soft blonde hair like that with a natural wave – that's the perfect style for you. Keep it that length with a trim once a month, but otherwise don't change it!"

There were now two other assistants helping Ms. Kenworthy locate and display the various articles and accessories that were coming together with obvious visual effect. Although Martha was aware that there was a sales process going on, she was also conscious of the fact that they were all thoroughly enjoying the results of their endeavors as they watched Martha appear even more attractive with each new look.

"Martha, this combination is absolutely stunning. If you can only buy one outfit, this has to be the one." Melliss had not brought up the topic of economics prior to this point in time, and had still not mentioned any actual prices.

"What would be the total cost if I took all of these pieces as well as the accessories?"

After a flurry of calculations and several references to the true cost of quality, Melliss managed to deliver the message – in a tone that suggested surprise as to the modest amount of money involved – that the entire ensemble could be acquired for $3,175.

"I'll take them all," Martha said without hesitation. "It's a lot of money, but I'm worth it and you're right – these outfits do look fantastic on me."

*

On Monday morning, when Martha met John Callard at the conference sign-up desk in the Hyatt Regency, any possible second thoughts about the wisdom of her purchase had been vanquished. Not only had she garnered appreciative looks from several of the businessmen arriving for the conference, but two women on the down escalator stopped their conversation and turned to watch Martha pass as she rode up to the second floor lobby.

"It's good to finally meet you, Martha," Callard said as they shook hands. "I must say you're quite a bit younger than I thought. You sound older on the phone."

"Well I'm not sure if that's a compliment on my appearance or a critique of my voice," Martha said as they walked towards the main meeting area. She had just transferred the registration materials into her black leather shoulder purse from the gray denim bag with the Alex Brown logo that she had been given at the desk. Her newly acquired sense of color coordination had been offended at the thought of seeing the gray denim in close proximity to her knit wool skirt.

After they had taken their seats near one of the TV monitors in the meeting room and were waiting for the first presentation to begin, John went through a quick review of the morning schedule.

"I've got to leave for awhile to meet with one of our big accounts, but I'd like you to join me for lunch. Let's sit at the Matrix Science table and I'll introduce you to the new president. They might be a client for you and David some day if they can figure out a way to get through the FDA labyrinth."

Martha found most of the morning to be of interest, topped by the chance to hear a presentation by a CEO that she and David had found for a Massachusetts biotech company after Martha had thought of a new way to sort through her database of PhD's. Boredom did set in at 11:30 when both scheduled presentations were by senior people from large drug firms, neither of which were potential clients. Martha used the time to read the background sheet on Matrix Science which was included in the company profile section of the conference materials. A relatively small medical diagnostics company located in the Chicago suburbs, Matrix was listed as a turn-around prospect coming back from a series of regulatory blunders.

Lunch had been set up in the main ballroom area with seating arrangements grouped by companies that were identified by placards placed on a small metal stand in the center of most of the fifty or sixty circular tables. Many of the tables were already filling up as Martha made her way across the room looking for the Matrix sign, and companies with a high level of investor interest were running out of seats fast. That was not a problem at the Matrix Science table. When Martha arrived, only one of the eight chairs was occupied. As she approached the table, the man sitting in that single chair rose and quickly extended his hand as if to insure that Martha did not slip past and escape to another table.

"Hi. I'm Joe Sheldon. Would you like to join me?"

"I'm Martha Laudner."

"I didn't mean to jump at you. If you were going over to another table, that's fine." Sheldon seemed uncomfortable standing next to Martha, glancing at his chair as if trying to decide whether to sit down again.

"No, that's fine," Martha said with a slight chuckle, "this is the table I was looking for. I read about your company this morning and thought it would be good to hear a little more about it over lunch." Now it was Martha that appeared somewhat ill at ease. Where to sit at a table for eight with seven empty chairs – next to the company president, or should she leave some space for other guests?

The decision was made for her when John Callard walked up and pulled out the chair on Sheldon's left for Martha and then took the next chair for himself. "I'm glad you two have met. Joe, this is the woman I mentioned this morning who is a partner in one of the top executive search firms. If you guys ever get yourselves back on track you'll need her to fill out your management team."

Over the next hour, Joe Sheldon chatted casually about the status of Matrix Science with a now full table of meeting participants.

"As you know, I've only been involved six months since the board made the decision to remove the previous CEO," Sheldon said in response to a rather sharply worded question about one of the current clinical trial programs. "There clearly had been some bad blood between the company and the FDA, but I think we've made good progress in establishing credibility with the agency."

Martha was impressed with this well-spoken and attractive man, and he responded to difficult questions without resorting to the temptation of dumping old ills on the backs of the now departed former management. Moreover, Martha noted that while poised when talking to others at the table, Joe seemed somewhat inarticulate when speaking directly to her. Could he actually be shy? Was she capable of having that effect on someone who otherwise seemed so poised and self-assured? She was not unaware that Joe Sheldon was a physically appealing man. With a rugged outdoor look, Joe could easily have posed for the flannel shirt ads in the LL

Bean catalog, although his vocabulary suggested something more along the lines of Scientific American. Martha was not so much surprised that she could still appreciate the attractiveness of a man as she was by the thought that this man could find her to be attractive as well. The fact that this same man picked up his water glass with a left hand that did not show any evidence of a wedding ring managed to accentuate the dynamic in which Martha attempted to analyze these rather intriguing observations.

"Well, I've got to get my slides ready," Joe said to no one in particular when lunch was over. "Are you going to catch my presentation at one thirty?" This comment was clearly directed at Martha.

"I think I can fit that into my schedule," she said, with just a touch more of a mischievous tone in her voice than she intended. "I might sit in the front row and ask tough questions about your staffing plans."

Martha did attend Sheldon's presentation at 1:30, and was once again impressed with the air of competence that he exhibited as he described the challenging but potentially rewarding area of medical science in which his firm was engaged. She could also not help but notice that of the four people who cornered him later to ask questions, three were women who seemed more interested in the speaker than the speech.

That evening, Alex Brown sponsored a cocktail party and buffet for the conference attendees at the National Aquarium on the harbor front opposite the Hyatt Hotel. Although she had not originally planned on attending, John Callard's personal invitation late in the day and the suggestion that she might have a chance to spend more time with some of the company CEOs convinced Martha that it might be an evening well spent. Later as she was looking into the thick glass windows of the main aquarium tank and trying to balance a small plate of hors d'oeuvres on top of her plastic wine glass, she sensed someone moving towards her.

"Isn't this a fabulous place?" Joe Sheldon asked. "This must be old stuff to you since you're from Baltimore, but I think it's pretty impressive."

"Well actually," Martha began while turning around slowly, "I've never been here before either, but you're right. It is impressive." She turned back towards the glass and started walking along the huge convex window. "So were you this afternoon. I enjoyed your presentation, although I'm still not sure I understand when you're going to be introducing your first product."

"There were three competitors in the audience and I was trying to be vague."

"Well, you succeeded."

As they walked past the different aquarium exhibits Martha was surprised at how comfortable she was in speaking with Joe. For his part, Joe appeared much more relaxed than he had been earlier in the day, the previous hint of shyness now being conveyed in a boyish grin which appeared as he greeted other people from the meeting. "I really wish I had brought my son along on this trip. He's just learning to scuba dive and he would have loved to see the size of these tanks and the artificial reefs."

"How many children do you have?" Martha asked, in a tone as disaffected as she could muster.

"Two – Bill is sixteen and Susan is fourteen. They live with their mother in Naperville but I see them a lot since my place is in Hinsdale just twenty miles away. We were divorced a year ago so I'm a little new at this single life." The grin appeared again although they were now by themselves. "You're not married are you? Sorry for the blunt question but it's hard to think of anyone as attractive as you not being married."

"No, I'm not. My husband died a few years ago."

"I'm sorry." They started walking towards the exit. "Do you have any children?"

"No – I don't."

Later when they walked back the four blocks along the harbor front towards the Hyatt, Martha found that the easy pattern of conversation that had marked their exchange earlier in the evening was missing, replaced by an air of nervous tension that seemed to intensify as they approached the hotel. "Why did I tell him Harry died a few years ago when it's been eight years since he was killed?" she thought. "And why didn't I mention my kids?"

As they arrived at the entrance to the main lobby, Martha said, "I'm not staying here, so I'll say goodnight and take a cab back to my apartment."

"Could I walk you there? It's a gorgeous evening." The grin returned. This time it was shyness, Martha thought.

"No – it's too far for that. I'll take a cab."

"Will you be here for the sessions tomorrow? I'd like to see you again and hear more about your business. We really didn't talk much about that."

"I'll be here tomorrow. I'm sure we'll see each other. Good night."

"Good night."

In the cab, Martha was conscious of an escalating pulse rate. For someone as structured and disciplined as she had been over the past several years, a conscious change in the pulse rate was an epiphany event. "God, I'm as giddy as a school girl," she thought. "The poor guy just wants to look at fish and talk about his kids and I'm getting clammy hands and heart palpitations." She paid the cab driver and asked him to wait until she got into her building. "Tomorrow we'll see if he's as charming as he was tonight after two glasses of wine."

The second day of the conference began with the selection of another killer outfit from the 106 combinations and permutations of jackets, slacks, skirts and accessories that Martha had spread out on her bed and dresser. An impulse to call Ms. Kenworthy at Anne Klein for a quick phone consultation was squelched when Martha conceded that no one besides herself was going to be interested in color coordination at 7:05 on a Tuesday morning. Martha did make a call to the cab company, and requested her Ukrainian woman cab driver who had been off work on Monday. The cab was waiting when she emerged from her building at eight o'clock.

"Zo, vy the color Marta? You never vor the color before."

"I just got some new clothes. It's been a long time and I needed some new outfits."

"But color, Marta, you never vor color. You met a man didn't you, Marta? You look like a new voman, you look gorgeous! Are you sleeping with him, Marta?"

"For God's sake, Neeka, I meet a lot of men! That doesn't mean I'm going to sleep with them! And just because I buy some new clothes doesn't mean I'm on the prowl for a husband."

The cab was stopped at a light on Charles Street, two blocks from the hotel. Vernika Petrosken, twice-divorced mother of three, born 1947 in Kiev, dropped her cigarette out the window and turned around slowly to look at her passenger. "Marta, don't be a chump. Ve all need love and for that ve need a man. I think you found von. Maybe you don't know, but I do. You and me, Marta, ve're not getting any younger. You're getting better looking, but you're not getting younger. Don't vaste time Marta, don't vaste time. Now here's your hotel."

It took all of twenty seconds for Joe Sheldon to see Martha when she walked through the revolving doors and into the lower lobby. He had been standing by the rail on the second atrium level and watched as she came up the escalator. As Martha walked towards the conference area he moved quickly to catch her before she went into one of the large meeting rooms.

"Good morning."

"Good morning, Joe. You're up early."

"Hey – I've been out jogging already. How about a cup of coffee? We've got fifteen minutes before the first session starts. By the way, you look gorgeous this morning." The grin was back.

They managed to spend most of that day together. She was amazed at the depth of his industry knowledge and found herself taking notes during some of his stories about the management personnel at the different companies. "Are you following me around just to get a bunch of names for your computer?" he had joked once when she had asked for the spelling of a name he had mentioned.

"I can't help it if you like to talk. I think you're just trying to impress a small town girl from Iowa."

That evening's cocktail party and buffet were scheduled to be held at the Baltimore Museum of Art. By mid-afternoon they had decided that neither was interested in another evening of balancing a plate on top of a wine glass while standing in a room filled with 300 other people.

"You live in the city. Where's a good place to eat where we could sit down?"

"What do you like?"

"Well how about seafood or crabs? Do you know any good places to get stone crabs?"

"I will by six thirty."

Steamers Restaurant on Lombart Street was starting to fill up with an eclectic crowd of early diners when Martha and Joe arrived after a hectic cab ride through the late rush hour traffic. "The best stone crabs in Baltimore," the bell captain at the Hyatt had told Martha.

College kids in jeans and sweat shirts, tourists in sweaters and slacks, and businessmen in three-piece suits all seemed intent on doing damage to as many pounds of shellfish as possible. A waitress with the longest eyelashes Martha had seen in her life walked them back to a corner table covered with clean brown wrapping paper.

"That's a nice outfit you've got on, dear," the waitress said as she handed the menu to Martha. "I suggest you put on about three bibs if you're going to have the stone crabs."

"We are going to have stone crabs," Joe said, "if you show me how to crack 'em. But maybe you can start us off with a couple of schooners of beer first. Would you like a beer, Martha?"

Martha did have the beer along with a refill as they worked their way through several piles of steamed stone crabs that the waitress — "I'm Cindy if you want more" — would dump on the center of the table every twenty minutes or so. The waitress had been right about the three bibs, but Martha wasn't about to slow down as she started on her ninth crab and third schooner. The noise level in the room had gotten higher during the last hour and Joe moved his chair closer so he could be heard without shouting. The grin was ever present now, no longer indicative of shyness, but rather of someone having a great time with pleasant company. Martha had told how she had gotten started in the search business, crying when describing the accident, laughing when talking about the cab ride that morning.

"I can't believe I'm telling you all this," she said. "Don't think you're anything special just because I wore one of my new outfits tonight. Hold still, you've got some crab on your cheek." Joe leaned towards her as Martha dabbed at his face with one of the wet towels the waitress had left on the table.

"Well, I think you're something special!" Joe was still leaning in. The knees were now touching. "I'd give you a kiss if you didn't have mustard sauce all over your chin."

"I put it there to protect myself from wild men like you." Martha ran her finger through some spots on the brown paper covering the table and then rubbed some mustard around the edges of Joe's mouth. "There — now you're safe just in case I lose control of myself in the presence of such a great orator."

"You should be so lucky." The waitress was walking past. Joe leaned back and said, "Cindy, my dear, four more stone crabs and two more schooners, and then you must promise to throw us out of here. This young lady is starting to do strange things with the mustard sauce."

It was 10:45 when they finally left and caught a cab back to the Hyatt. The mustard had stayed on his face until the check was paid. Then Martha took one of the towels and slowly wiped around Joe's mouth, finishing with a playful dab on the tip of his nose.

"Am I safe to kiss now?"

"You might be," she said, leaning forward and kissing him softly on the cheek. "I can still taste the mustard. Let me try another spot." This time the kiss was on the lips, tentative.

In the cab neither spoke for the first few minutes. They were sitting close together, holding hands and twisting each other's fingers absentmindedly. "You know, I can't remember when I've had such a fun evening," Martha said. "You were nice to listen to me blab about my life story." She pulled his hand towards her lips and kissed it tenderly. "You're a fine man, Joe Sheldon, even if you don't know how to eat stone crabs."

"Well, you're a great teacher! A little wild with the mustard, but a great teacher." Joe put his hand on Martha's chin, slowly turned her face towards his, and kissed her. "We'll need to have more lessons sometime," he said quietly. His lips gently touched hers, kissing her several times as his hand moved from her chin and traced a slow pattern along the side of her neck. "You know, I'll be leaving the hotel around ten tomorrow morning to catch my flight," Joe said, as the cab began to approach the downtown area.

"I knew you were leaving early, but I didn't know when."

"I wish I could stay until Thursday. But I really have to get back. We've got an FDA inspection going on."

"When do you think you might get to Baltimore again?"

"I don't know. I really don't come here except once a year for this meeting. I do get into Washington! I could see you then and we could go back and finish off the rest of those crabs."

"I wasn't thinking about the crabs." Martha had withdrawn her hand from his and was starting wistfully out the window into the light rain that had started a moment before. "I really enjoyed spending time with you these last couple of days, Joe. I'm pretty out of touch on these things, but I think we both would like to spend more time together," she turned back around to look at him as she finished talking.

"I know," Joe said quietly. The cab had stopped for a light and the sudden absence of street noise eradicated the invisible sound barrier that had separated them from the driver. The light changed and the cab began to move again. Joe continued, looking directly into Martha's eyes. "I've been wondering about what we're going to do when we get to the hotel. You must be aware that I'd like you to spend the night with me, but I don't really know if I should ask."

"I don't want you to ask, Joe," Martha said taking his hand again and putting it against her cheek. "I do want to stay, but I just don't know if I'm ready for all of this just yet. I'm doing a time warp back to my dating days, except I realize that things have changed and I suppose expectations have as well." She put her hand on his arm and moved closer to him. "I think I'll need a little more time, Joe. In the meanwhile, kiss me for God's sake, so I'll shut up and stop talking."

Joe pulled her towards him and kissed her passionately on the lips, pausing only to take her head in his hands, moving it slightly to the left and right to kiss her on the cheeks before once again kissing her on the lips even harder than before. Their attempt at moving into each other's arms was complicated by their awkward position in the back seat of the cab, and finally Joe slid away. "Look Martha, I understand what you're saying. I'm not the most experienced guy either since my divorce. I think we might have something special between us. I'll move at whatever speed you think is best."

Martha turned to look out the window and realized they were parked at the entrance to the Hyatt.

Joe handed the driver some bills and opened the door to get out. "I want you to take this young lady to her apartment. She's not staying here."

"Joe," Martha said, "kiss me again before you go. I will see you tomorrow, won't I?"

"That you will. I'll be the guy standing next to the escalator with the mustard bottle."

Twenty-five minutes later, Joe was just getting to his room after stopping to talk to a friend in the lobby. The phone was ringing as he opened the door.

"Hello."

"Joe? I've decided. I'd like you to come over to my place."

"Are you sure?"

"I'm sure. And, Joe – bring your toothbrush."

"I have it in the pocket of my sport coat. I took it with me to the restaurant just in case." The grin was growing dangerously close to a chuckle.

"You ass!" Martha said laughingly.

"Just kidding – just kidding. I felt we could do with a little humor."

In the half hour it took Joe to catch a cab and find her apartment, Martha's wardrobe decision anxiety level reached a new height. She went through the possibilities in her mind – ranging from no change to a robe to a Teddy. She opted for no change, except for the panty hose – they went. "I'm going to be nervous enough the way it is. The last thing I need is to be hopping around on one leg trying to get these off when I should be looking seductive."

Martha need not have worried. She was seductive. Any concerns that she had about her own capabilities melted away as Joe held and kissed her. The passion that enveloped their lovemaking was genuine and unforced, and grew in intensity as they touched each other throughout the night with ever increasing sensual pleasure. In the morning Martha was lying with her head on Joe's chest, rubbing his shoulder and arm, vigorously this time, not with the gentle teasing touch that she used before. "I'd forgotten how good it feels to be held," she said. "I don't ever want you to leave."

But they did leave, although they stayed until the last possible moment. After breakfast Joe said, "If I don't get back to the hotel and check out, I'm never going to make that flight. Do you have a car service I can call?"

Martha was reaching for the card of her favorite driver when she thought better of it and said, "Just call Yellow Cab. I don't use anybody special."

With the third new outfit on in as many days, Martha was waiting on the curb with Joe when she saw the cab approach, driven by a woman with the biggest smile this side of Kiev.

"Good morning," Vernika Petrosken said as she held open the rear door of the cab. "Vat a lovely outfit, Miss. This must be a special day. Vher can I take you and the gentleman?"

CHAPTER TWELVE
The No-Show

"Are you sure he got the other message? I called yesterday morning and he hasn't gotten back to me."

"Yes, ma'am, you've mentioned that." The hotel operator was trying to be patient but she had two other lines ringing. "The light on his phone will indicate that he has a message but it's up to him to call the switchboard. All I can tell you now is there's no answer in his room."

"Will you please leave another message for him to call his secretary, and indicate that it's important."

"Yes ma'am, I'll do that. Goodbye." She did not wait for the response. Somebody not calling his secretary back was hardly a major event. It started to become a major event the next day.

As with most big hotels, the Camelback Inn had a procedure that required the housekeeping staff to contact Security if it appeared that a guest had not been in his room for two straight nights. In most cases, the rationale was based on the concern that someone might have left early and skipped out on the bill. Occasionally it developed that the guest had been hospitalized or possibly jailed. It was not a crisis, but it was an event.

Russ Hampton had just finished talking to a guest in 317 about a lost billfold when he got beeped by the assistant manager and asked to check out 358 for a no-show. Twenty minutes later he was calling in with the report. "I doubt that it's a skip. There's clothes in the closet and a shaving kit in the bathroom. The guy checked in on Monday at four thirty and the maid said nobody used the bed on Tuesday or Wednesday night. I talked to the switchboard and they say he's got seven messages starting from Tuesday morning, so it's been a little over two days."

"You know where he's from?"

"Registration says he's from Tennessee. I saw a business card in his briefcase and it looks like he's with some medical company." Russ Hampton had been a sergeant with the Chicago Police Department until he turned fifty and took early retirement. Checking out no-shows was about as close as he got to intrigue since moving to Arizona. When he got back to his office in the basement

119

of the main building, Russ started working the phones. First, the man's secretary, who still had not heard from him. Then the local police and hospital contact list. Again, no indication that he had been picked up or hospitalized.

"We got a strange one here, Jim," he told the assistant manager. "The guy's disappeared and I'm not sure where to look. His secretary told me that he's divorced and living alone, so I don't even know what his plans were other than to attend a meeting here, and he hasn't done that since Tuesday morning. I'm trying to chase down the bellmen who were working Monday afternoon when he checked in. But the two guys I talked to so far didn't take anybody to that room. The third guy, Mike Stinson, has a couple of days off, so I can't reach him until he comes back tomorrow afternoon. I'm not sure what else I can do right now. I'm in a bit of a quandary." Although it would be eighteen months before he knew it, the origin of Russ Hampton's quandary had been spawned two weeks before, not in Phoenix, but in Las Vegas.

*

Lloyd Barnett had been playing blackjack at the Hilton since 9:30 the previous evening, and it was now 2:15 in the morning. Any hope of a profitable night had long since vanished, and getting back to even would now be considered a major victory.

The entire month had not gone well for Lloyd Barnett. A trip to San Francisco for what looked like a promising scam on a rich widow had gone sour when she had gotten suspicious of the woman who was posing as Lloyd's wife. Judie Whitely, the second half of a 'sting gone bad', was now a cocktail waitress at the Dunes Hotel after a sporadic career as a showgirl at one of Las Vegas's lesser known casinos. High cheekbones and two well-placed spheroids of silicone gel had allowed her to make a decent living until ten months ago, when the 35-year-old legs finally gave out. Barnett had met Judie at the Dunes following an all-day stretch at the tables during which time he had managed to win $3,700. He was buying drinks in the main lounge for some friends when Judie bent down to leave the check. She was dressed in a waitress outfit that left nothing to the imagination, and when Barnett put a $100 bill between those well-placed spheroids, he gained the instant attention of this long ago drum majorette from Evansville, Indiana. Two months later, Barnett and Whitely were roommates, more out of economic and lifestyle convenience than any type of romantic involvement.

"Don't get any ideas about this being permanent, Lloyd," she said while bringing up the last of her four suitcases into Barnett's second floor apartment. "I need to save up some money, and you need to clean up your act. Having a woman around your place for awhile might just do you some good."

On this day's trip to the Hilton with Lloyd, Judie Whitely was well aware that he had not cleaned up his act, and it also appeared that she was not doing him any good, at least with regard to blackjack. She was standing behind him at the table with the knuckles of her right hand pressed firmly against the small of his back. "You're four grand into your line and we're out of cash. Unless you've decided to get a job, which I seriously doubt, we're out of bucks. You blew my stash of tip money at the Golden Nugget last week and now you're damn near maxed out on your line." Judie was trying to keep her voice down without much success and the pit boss was giving her the 'tone it down' look.

Lloyd turned around and said, "I've got a bunch of money coming in a couple of days. Now get off my back."

"Where do you have money coming from?" This time she was not as loud. In her short relationship with Barnett, Judie realized there were certain facets of his life that she had yet to fully understand. This might just be one of those.

"None of your damn business where my money comes from. Maybe I got a rich uncle." The dealer had started with the new shoe, and Barnett's first hand was a blackjack. "This could be the beginning of my next lucky streak."

*

The flight from Memphis to Phoenix had been smooth for most of the way, but there was now some turbulence as the plane encountered the updrafts of warm air moving over the mountains on the east side of the city. Although Gary Lempke had been making ten or twelve flights a year for most of his adult life, he was still visibly uncomfortable as a sharp series of bumps caused a spill of coffee for the passenger sitting across the aisle. "They say it's like a boat bouncing over the waves," Lempke said, sharing his personal theory of aerodynamics with the woman now wiping up the coffee that had spilled on her tray.

"You live here in Phoenix?" she asked.

"No, I'm from Chattanooga. I'm just going to be here for three nights at the Camelback Inn. There's a medical meeting going on there and my company is trying to get some of the Docs on board with one of our new products." Gary Lempke was the penultimate sales manager, and carrying on conversations with attractive strangers was something he did with relative ease. The regional meeting of interventional cardiologists taking place in Scottsdale at the posh Camelback Inn was the sort of thing that he could do with his eyes closed, as indeed he might have done earlier in his career when his fondness for late night carousing had been at its peak. Lempke's current position with Heartflow Technologies was his third in the past seven years, and at the age of 48, he was essentially back at the same level where he had been some 14 years before, when he was with Aortek Corporation.

"I saw the handwriting on the wall when I was with those guys, and decided it wasn't the place for me," he had explained some thirty times since during various job interviews. "I could see there was some problem with the data, so I made a decision between ethics and commissions, and opted for ethics." Lempke had delivered the line so often that sometimes now even he believed the story to be true.

With the coach section of the Boeing 727 almost full, Lempke was grateful for the fact that at least he had an aisle seat. He used to fly first class when he was a hot young sales manager who was bringing in the numbers with enough consistency that he could get by with a rather liberal interpretation of his employer's travel policy. No such luck at Heartflow Technologies, where his boss was not only nine years younger than he, but also a woman who subscribed to an avant-garde theory that expense reports were to be taken seriously.

Lloyd Barnett was standing in Terminal 3 at Sky Harbor Airport when Lempke's flight from Memphis arrived, and had his camera ready when a man moved quickly to answer the page for arriving passenger Gary Lempke. "I'll know what the sucker looks like this time," Barnett said to himself.

The $10,000 had arrived in Las Vegas none too soon. Barnett really needed the money, and the sooner he completed this assignment, the quicker he would get the remaining $25,000. The instructions this time were even more cryptic than usual.

> Subject Gary Lempke will be attending meeting at Camelback Hotel in Scottsdale on Monday, March 20 to Thursday, March 23. Final action should not appear to be result of targeted event.

Barnett's interpretation of this exercise in morbid shorthand was that however Lempke died, it should not look like an assassination.

"Why the hell all the intrigue?" Barnett wondered.

Despite the cavalier attitude, Barnett did not really have any idea how he was going to complete the contract. His toughest decision was whether or not to use Judie. Rational analysis suggested that having a woman involved increased the risk of eventual disclosure. On the other hand, Barnett concluded she did not have to know exactly what the end result was going to be, and having her around could help set up some convenient cover situations.

"How'd you like to go down to Phoenix with me for a couple of days?" he finally asked her. "Should be nice there this time of year."

"What's going on in Phoenix?"

"Nothing too major. I'm going to help somebody collect a loan that's a little overdue."

"Look Lloyd, I'm not crazy about getting mixed up in your line of work." They were just finishing dinner at one of the restaurants in Caesar's Palace. "I don't know exactly what it is that you do from time to time, and I don't really want to know. Helping you out on that scam in San Francisco was about as close as I wanna get."

The waiter was bringing coffee to their table. Barnett waited until he had left and then said, "Hey, there's nothing to worry about. I'm just gonna meet a guy and remind him about the terms of his investment. All you have to do is come along and look good. Wear that wedding ring we used in San Francisco."

They were now standing in the airport watching Lempke trying to find out who left the page message. "That's my man,"

Barnett said to Judie. "Now let's get to the hotel, I want to see what kind of room they give this guy."

Although they were staying at another resort, Barnett and Judie were sitting in the lobby area of the Camelback when Lempke arrived to check in. Lloyd walked over towards the registration desk until he was close enough to hear what room number Lempke was given, and then left with Judie to drive back to their hotel.

Although Gary Lempke had no idea who Lloyd Barnett was, nor did he really care at that point in time, he was aware of Judie Whitely. When she walked out of the lobby, Lempke had watched approvingly as she made her exit. The legs no longer made it on the dance line, but they displayed well in the shorts and high heels she was wearing that afternoon.

"Are you enjoying the scenery, sir?" The bellman had also been watching Judie walk through the lobby. "My name is Mike and I have your luggage outside."

"I could watch that kind of scenery all day long and never go outside," Lempke said. This particular conference at the Camelback Inn was relatively small, with only seventy-five doctors from the Arizona-California area in attendance. Regional meetings for the Interventional Cardiology Association were always held at a top resort hotel in a warm climate, where the physicians could be assured of good weather for their afternoon golf games. "How many rooms does this place have?" Lempke asked as they walked towards one of the electric golf carts used to transport guests.

"There are over 400 casitas, Mr. Lempke. We don't call them rooms. Plus we've got two golf courses, tennis and swimming, and a spa. But the thing we've got that really makes us unique is the mountain."

"What mountain?" Lempke asked as he got into the electric cart.

"Camelback. Of course it's not really ours, but we've got the best view of it. If you look back across the pool area you'll see it now. From this angle it looks like a camel laying down. First the little hump on your left, then the big hump, then the head on the right. I've climbed it several times. It's not a technical climb. There's a path going up and some days there'll be a couple hundred people climbing. Are you interested in doing it?" They had stopped in front of a cluster of small, stuccoed dwellings. The southwestern architectural theme was evident with the smooth, rounded corners on the buildings and the soft pastel colors of the exterior walls.

"I might do that. I've been trying to get myself back in shape the last couple of months and I get awfully bored with jogging. How do I get there if I decide to climb some afternoon?"

"If you have a rental car it only takes five minutes to get there. They'll give you a map at the front desk. Just so you know, even though it's not a technical climb with ropes, it can get a bit tricky. Every year a bunch of people break an ankle or leg. Usually on the way down, and especially if it's wet. Then every other year or so, somebody gets killed when they fall off the cliff on top. There's a kind of flat spot up there and when you go up on this side it seems pretty safe. But people don't realize that it drops straight off on the other side, so once in awhile we lose a tourist."

"So when are you and your investment client going to have your little chat?" Judie asked when she and Lloyd were laying on their lounge chairs by the pool at the nearby Mountain Shadows Hotel where they were staying. The cynicism in her voice was more than a little evident. "Just how much money does this guy owe somebody?"

"Hey – you said you didn't wanna know about my business. Let's keep it that way. I'm just gonna have a little heart to heart discussion with him sometime tomorrow if I can get him alone."

"Well, whaddya want me to do now that I'm your loving wife and our two kids are staying at home with grandma?" Judie was holding out her left hand and looking in mock admiration at the one carat of false diamonds on the ring finger. Before Barnett could answer she stood up, dropped her robe, and walked slowly towards the pool, adjusting with the long index finger of each hand the bottom edges of her bikini pants, first over one well-shaped buttock and then the other, not simultaneously although both hands were free, but alternating back and forth as if to extend the amount of time that attention would be drawn to the apex of the still shapely dancer legs. Upon reaching the pool she stood on the first descending step, placing her feet into six inches of water. She completed her symbolic immersion by dipping both hands into the cool liquid, bending over slowly from the waist without unlocking either knee, thus ensuring that no single male eye within a fifty-yard radius was directed anywhere but towards her. With her bathing ritual now completed, she turned and sauntered slowly back to the lounge chair where Barnett was seated, pausing only long enough to make a minor adjustment in the alignment of her bikini top.

"Jeez – will you either cover those things up again or sit down? I'd like to be able to leave this hotel tomorrow without everybody remembering we were here. If you keep prancing around with those boobs hanging outta that suit we're gonna be the center of attention."

"Don't worry, Lloyd. Nobody's looking at you. Now tell me if you need me to do anything tomorrow or I'm gonna sign up to spend the day at the spa." Judie had picked up a brochure on the Spa at Camelback when they were in the lobby earlier in the day.

"Okay," Barnett said, after Judie sat back down on her lounge chair, "here's what I want you to do. I saw that their first meeting is at nine o'clock, so I presume Lempke might be having breakfast sometime between eight and eight thirty. We'll go over around seven thirty and sit out by the north pool area where we'll be able to see him walk from his room to the main lobby and restaurant area. After that we'll have to play it by ear, but I need to find out what he's going to be doing Tuesday and Wednesday. You may have to do one of your 'hi, big boy – can you help me' routines."

The smell of orange blossoms was in the crisp morning air the next day as they sat by an outdoor table near the north pool area of the Camelback. In a prior life, Barnett had enjoyed keeping a neatly manicured yard, trimming the hedges around his house in Cincinnati and even planting a few flowers. On this day in Phoenix he could not help but be impressed with the immaculate groundskeeping at the Camelback. Several sizes and shapes of cactus, each with a small nameplate designating the variety, were surrounded by flowerbeds, which in turns were intersected by curving sidewalks leading up to the casitas on that side of the property. From where Barnett and Judie were sitting, they had a clear view of the sidewalk which led to unit number 358. By 8:20, Barnett had gone through every section of *The Arizona Republic* morning paper and was beginning to worry that he had missed Lempke.

"He's got to come this way to go to the breakfast or meeting rooms," Lloyd said, mostly for his own self-assurance.

At 8:31 on the last day of his life, Gary Lempke closed the door to Casita Number 358 and walked down the curved sidewalk past a 120-year-old Saguaro cactus and towards the main lobby area of the Camelback Inn. As he approached the pool area, his eye was drawn to the couple getting up from the table and turning to walk towards the lobby. The woman was the same one he had seen in the hotel the day before. The legs were covered now by a pair of light gray slacks, but the rest of the figure was still easy to discern.

As Barnett got to the entrance of the Navajo Room where breakfast was being served, he glanced back and saw that Lempke was now only ten feet behind. There were four people ahead of them waiting to be seated, and the woman at the door was taking names. "Good – it's crowded," Barnett whispered softly to Judie. "Do your thing and see if he wants to join us."

There was never a doubt once Judie suggested it would be faster seating if the three of them took a table together. The loving couple introduced themselves as Bob and Nancy Erickson, and the threesome had a pleasant breakfast, for which Lempke paid. "Don't worry about it," he said as he signed a charge slip. "I'll put you down as Dr. Erickson when I send in the expense account."

"I suppose you'll be playing golf with the doctors this afternoon," Lloyd said, glancing at Judie as Lempke handed the check back to the waiter.

"No, I'm not much of a golfer anymore. I think I might climb Camelback Mountain. You two should come along. It's not a real climb. I think it's mostly a long hike going uphill. Whaddya think, Nancy? It'll be some good exercise for you."

"Well, to be honest I was thinking more along the lines of taking in the spa this afternoon. Maybe a mud bath and a massage."

"You can do that anytime, Nancy. I think we should go with Gary this afternoon." Barnett's quick eye contact with Judie made it clear that the decision was made. Forget the spa!

"You're really pissing me off you know," Judie was shouting at Lloyd when they got back to their hotel after breakfast. "I helped you meet the stiff, that's all I was gonna do. I sure as hell don't want to go hiking with the two of you."

"Look, I'm not sure he'd go if you don't. The guy's got the hots for you. Didn't you see him staring at your chest during breakfast?"

"I saw, Lloyd. I know when men are looking at me!"

"All you got to do is start the climb with us, then say you've got a bad ankle or something. I'll give you the car keys and you can come back and pick us up a couple of hours later."

If there was a time that Barnett began to seriously doubt how his day was going, it was when he saw the handrails. The three of them had started climbing Camelback at two o'clock. 'Mr. and Mrs. Erickson' had picked up Lempke at 1:45 and driven the short distance to Echo Canyon Road, where they parked the car. Twenty minutes into the hike, they reached the saddle where the trail switched back in direction. It was at this point that Judie's ankle suddenly gave out, and she started back down with assurances to return at 4:30 to pick them up.

The northern access trail on Camelback Mountain had a 1,300-foot elevation change over a distance of 1.2 miles. The climb began in earnest 150 yards after the first saddle. Metal handrails were set into the rock at a 45 degree angle, and the ancient granite on this portion of the camel's hump had been worn smooth by the thousands of hiking boots and sneakers of eager climbers pulling themselves up the steep slope, hand over hand on the metal pipe. A 200 foot gain in elevation over a distance of just 450 lateral feet could only be accomplished by one long stretch of handrail scrambling, followed by a short hike at an easier grade, and then one more steep ascent using another set of handrails.

"Come on, Bob, there's a hell of a view over here." Lempke had stopped at a junction where a side trail led on to the camel's neck.

Barnett did not respond until he got to the spot where Lempke was resting. "Gary, you've gotta slow down. You're killing me. I can't do the steep parts that fast."

"Most of the people are on their way down," Lempke said. "We're gonna have some rain pretty soon. We should've gotten an earlier start. Do you wanna turn around?"

"No!" Lloyd said just a little too quickly. "We can make it to the top before the rain hits." As he was talking, Barnett took off his small backpack and removed a plastic water bottle, carefully shielding the pack from Lempke as he zipped it shut. The other item in the pack was a handgun that he had brought with him from Las Vegas.

They started climbing again, encountering first a relatively easy section of level trail, and then, just when Barnett thought his legs might recover, they came to a steep rocky ascent of 75 yards. An upward sloping v-shaped gully with an assortment of refrigerator-size boulders strewn along its length forced them to do an almost hand over hand ascent into what was now becoming a light rain squall. A man in running shorts and no shirt, holding a water bottle in one hand and the end of leather strap in the other, came scrambling down past them at a speed which seemed to demonstrate little regard for either the well being of his ankles or for the black lab nervously tethered on the end of the six foot leash.

"We're getting there, Bob, only another fifteen or twenty minutes. Do you still want to do it? We're gonna get wet."

Barnett took a second to remember that his name was 'Bob' today. He was almost gasping for breath.

"Sure," Lloyd responded, with as much enthusiasm as he could convey. "Just take it a little easier, Gary. We're already wet. No sense rushing."

Barnett's relief when they reached the top was intense. Lempke had been there for about ten minutes when Lloyd finally struggled up the last section of the trail and collapsed against one of the rock outcroppings on the southern edge of the rounded knoll that comprised the top of the hump. He had been watching the trail behind them, and knew that no one else was coming up. However, he was shocked to see that there were six other people on the top, trying to take a group picture in the wind and rain.

"Would you mind taking our picture?" A woman had walked over towards Lloyd and was holding out a camera. Shaking his head, Barnett made it clear without speaking that he was in no condition to stand, let alone focus a camera, and pointed over towards Lempke as the photographer of choice. When the six had completed their pictures and started down, Barnett stood up and walked over towards Lempke. As he approached he took off his pack and held it in his left hand. "Hell of a view isn't it, Gary?"

Barnett had been looking over his shoulder as Lempke pointed toward the airport. The six hikers were out of view, but probably close enough to hear a shot. Lloyd was now thinking clearly enough to be concerned about the fact that they had seen him. Any investigation of a shooting might get them to volunteer with an ID. An accident should be another matter.

It was almost too easy. "Can you see the airport from here?" he asked, walking up behind Lempke.

"Over there," Lempke stepped a few feet closer to the edge and was pointing out across the valley. "It's tough to see in the rain, but it's there."

Barnett took one last look behind him, placed his right hand in the small of Lempke's back, and pushed. There was a sheer drop of 110 feet on the south side of the peak, and there was no scream, at least that Barnett could hear.

"I always thought they screamed," he thought. "Maybe only in the movies." Before he started down, Lloyd took the gun out of the pack, carefully wiped off any prints, and then threw it off the edge to his left, away from where Lempke had fallen.

It was another hour before he got back down to the parking lot where Judie was waiting in the car. "Where's your boy?" she said as Lloyd got in the car, shivering now as the effects of the wet climb and descent were starting to have an impact.

"He had a little accident. He's going to be awhile."

"You didn't do anything stupid did you, Lloyd?"

"No, he'll be fine in a few days. We'll be back in Vegas by then and I'll be getting another care package. Nothing to worry about."

It was Friday afternoon, three days later, when Mike Stinson clocked in for duty at the bell stand in the circular entryway at the Camelback Inn and was told that Russ Hampton from security was looking for him.

"What's the big deal?" Mike said. "Somebody lose a suitcase?"

"Somebody lost a guest! This guy's been missing since Tuesday morning and none of us remember taking him to his room, so Hampton figures it musta been you."

Two hours later a possible scenario was beginning to take shape. There was now sufficient concern on the part of hotel security that Hampton has advised the Scottsdale Police Department about the missing guest. Jerry Chapman, a detective on the force, had joined Russ in the coffee shop to talk about the information that was available so far.

"The bellman does remember taking this guy to his room on Monday," Russ said. Detective Chapman was taking notes, using a clipboard that seemed more suitable for the issuance of traffic tickets. "Nothing unusual about the guy as far as the bellman remembers. But he did talk about jogging and also the possibility of hiking up Camelback."

"What's the latest thing you've got that shows him in the hotel?" Chapman asked.

"Well, I went back in his room and looked at his papers and receipts on the counter," Russ said, pulling out his own notebook, this one a small spiral bound tablet. "There's an American Express stub there that shows a meal charged here in the hotel on Tuesday morning. On the back it says 'breakfast with Dr. and Mrs. Robert Erickson'. I tried to track them down but with no luck. We had a bunch of Docs in the hotel for that meeting, but no Erickson, and none were listed on the program. There are two Dr. Robert Ericksons living here in the Valley. I called both of them and they weren't at the hotel this week and they never heard of Gary Lempke."

Chapman rested the clipboard on his knee. "Any other ideas?"

"Well, I dug out one other possible lead," Hampton was enjoying his role of investigator. "I got a picture of this guy faxed to me from his office and showed it to the staff here in the restaurant. One of the waiters remembers seeing him Tuesday morning along with another couple, I guess the Ericksons."

"What'd he say about 'em?"

"Said the woman was in her mid-thirties with a great set of tits."

"What about the guy?" Chapman had the clipboard back on the table now.

"The waiter doesn't remember. I don't think he ever looked at the guy."

"That figures." The lieutenant was trying to treat the situation with some level of seriousness but without much success. "You've given me a helluva lot to go on. A new guy checks in on Monday, has breakfast on Tuesday with a woman with big tits and a husband that nobody saw, and then does a no-show for three days. Sounds simple to me."

They found Lempke on Sunday morning. Chapman had decided that the comment about climbing Camelback was a long shot but had to be checked. Two volunteers from the search and rescue squad had rappelled down the back face of the hump and discovered the body wedged behind a small ridge where it could not be seen from the base trail. It took most of the day to get the body down and to explore around the immediate area for anything out of the ordinary. It was 6:30 in the evening when the visibly fatigued Lieutenant Chapman met Hampton at the hotel. This time the clipboard stayed in the car.

"Do you think he fell off, or did something else happen?" Russ asked.

"Beats the hell outta me. We couldn't tell much by looking at him. The guy's been out there five days and it's been getting up to 80 degrees most of the week, plus there are some coyotes over on that side. Not exactly a pretty sight. It was raining late Tuesday afternoon so my guess is he probably slipped. Funny thing, though. We found a pistol about seventy feet away, all the shells in the chamber, and not much rust on it. Could've been there about the same time."

"Well, whaddya want me to do now?" Russ asked.

"I don't know," Chapman said. "I'm gonna go home and take a shower. Tomorrow I'll send one of my guys over to go through Lempke's room one more time. We really don't have much to go on. I'll wait for the coroner's report but I think this will go in the books as an accident. Keep your eyes open for the good Dr. Erickson, but otherwise, you just had the ultimate no-show."

CHAPTER THIRTEEN
The Profiler

The call to the FBI was made by Brian Davidson, Vice President of membership affairs for the American Medical Manufacturers Association, but the impetus for the call and the information on which it was based came straight from the desk of Chuck Mauer. If the gods of blue book exams had smiled on the efforts of Charles David Mauer during his European history final the previous May, he would be well into his junior year at Georgetown University instead of working for a temporary clerical agency and sitting out a semester of academic probation. With limited financial resources, and parents who made it clear that he would finish college one way or another, Chuck had opted to spend his unplanned sabbatical working in Washington rather than returning to his home in the suburbs of Arlington, Texas.

The job listing at the Washington office temps agency indicated that a position was available at AMMA for an individual to work on a project to computerize the membership records of the association. The records covered the 310 corporate members and the individuals on their staffs, most of whom were on two or three different AMMA mailing lists, depending on their areas of business specialty. With a slight Texas drawl and a well-developed reputation on campus for always knowing where the parties were, Chuck Mauer had not brought any great depth to the study of European history, but he did seem to have a flair for organization, and within three weeks of starting his job at AMMA had managed to bring some order to the chaos that had previously existed.

The first hint that something was wrong came when Mauer was updating one of the old subscription lists and found the second notice that listed reason for deletion as accidental death. Everyone at AMMA, including even temporaries such as Chuck, knew about the death of the members in the boating accident at the meeting in Florida. But these two new cases were separate incidents, one in California and one in Scottsdale, Arizona. And then in cleaning out a file of prior membership list changes, Chuck found a clipping of a story about the shooting death of John Levard in Toronto as well as a letter from a company president asking for a change in the membership listing after the company's VP of Regulatory Affairs had died in a house fire. Over the next two weeks, counting the deaths in Florida, Mauer came up with seven names of people who had been removed from one or more of the lists because of death by accident or some form of random violence.

"Brian, have you ever looked at how many of your members are dying off for strange reasons?" Chuck asked his boss after he found numbers six and seven. "I'm not sure I'd like to be on one of your lists."

Brian Davidson was a tall, wiry man in his late fifties with a predilection for wearing short sleeve white shirts in an office where most of the senior male personnel wore monogrammed French cuffs on even the muggiest of summer days. Brian had been with AMMA for six months when the two people were killed at the annual meeting, and he could remember well the shock that rippled through the organization. Now, to realize that at least five other members had died in unusual circumstances stretched the bounds of what might be a coincidence well beyond a level that could be ignored. At Brian's request, Chuck spent another week checking other old records and making phone calls to some of the companies where the file was incomplete. Two more deaths from unusual circumstances were discovered, raising Davidson's concern enough for him to get up and close the office door when he and Chuck went over the combined list.

"Nine strange deaths over a period of seven or eight years in a group of fairly healthy men with an average age of 45. Something's wrong, Brian. This ain't normal – no way!"

"You might be right, Chuck. I'm gonna brief the boss and then I'm going to have to call somebody, probably the FBI. You'll need to keep quiet about this until we know what's going on."

"The thing I can't figure out is why nobody has asked the question before. Nine guys dying of unnatural causes. It doesn't take J. Edgar to figure out something's wrong." Chuck was walking around Davidson's small office as he spoke, clearly enjoying the new role of co-equal in this evolving chronicle of intrigue and suspense.

"Nobody is gonna put two and two together on this unless they see the records like we have," Davidson said. "These people lived in different parts of the US and worked for different companies. I'm still not sure this is anything more than a coincidence, but I'll report it just in case." Brian had made the shift from 'we' to 'I'. If there was going to be any dialogue with the FBI, the AMMA side would not be presented by temporary office help on probation from Georgetown.

*

"Mr. Davidson, this is Special Agent Eric Landau. I understand you think there may have been some crime committed involving your association's members." The voice on the phone had a soft Indiana accent and the lack of enthusiasm of someone who had returned hundreds of calls in the past from well-meaning citizens who were certain that they had stumbled on some major underworld plot.

"Yes sir," Brian replied. "Actually I'm not sure there has been a crime but it does look that something strange has happened to some of our members." The recital of the string of unusual deaths from around the country was being received with a polite series of grunts by Agent Landau until Davidson got to the names of Pellegrino and Powell along with the mention of the explosion on the boat.

"I worked that case for awhile!" Davidson could almost sense Landau getting up from his chair and moving quickly over to a file cabinet. "Do you have reason to believe these other deaths are related in some way? Did these other individuals work at the same company as Mr. Powell?" Without waiting for an answer to either of these questions Landau said, "We'll arrange to have someone at your office by early afternoon today. I'm not sure just who it'll be at this time."

"How did you happen to be working on a case in Florida if you're based here in Washington?" Davidson was now curious about the sudden interest in his list.

Landau paused before responding, giving himself time to choose his words carefully. "I have some background in explosives and occasionally get called in on cases where there might be a question of cause."

Now Davidson's curiosity was really piqued. "That accident happened several years ago. Are you telling me there's still some investigation going on?"

"No, sir, I'm not telling you there is or isn't any investigation. All I'm saying is that we'll have an agent at your office this afternoon to discuss your concerns about these other deaths."

By 1 p.m., Davidson had copies of the nine membership records on the conference table in the boardroom at the AMMA office. He had also briefed Bill Samuels, the current president of the association, about Mauer's discovery and the phone call with the FBI, but Samuels was scheduled for a meeting on the Hill that afternoon and opted out of what he felt was a long shot discussion on some coincidental member deaths. Chuck Mauer was standing by and hoping to be called in, but had gotten the strong hint from Davidson to stay out of the way unless told otherwise.

If Donald Stinnett had been blessed with the genes to assure a full head of hair at the age of 46, he might have been cast as Hollywood's version of the perfect FBI agent. Tall and slender with sharply defined features, Stinnett had the physique and bearing of someone who might have been preordained for a career with the agency. His posting to the Washington District Office as a section chief four years before had not been a random personnel decision. High visibility offices tended to be staffed by the most competent and physically attractive agents that the Bureau had to offer. At least this was true in those positions that might have interactions with government agencies or other high profile organizations, including the hundreds of national trade associations that had their headquarters offices in this city of hoped-for power and influence.

The secretary in the reception area of the AMMA office on the fifth floor of the Dottler Building had been advised that someone from the FBI was scheduled to see Mr. Davidson, and she wasted no time in showing Stinnett into the boardroom at the end of the paneled hallway. On this early September day, sultry by even Washington standards, Agent Stinnett was dressed in a mid-weight worsted woolen suit with a crease in the pant leg still sharp enough to suggest that he might have had it steamed and pressed while coming up in the elevator. At his own request, Stinnett had received only a brief recap of the situation from Agent Landau, preferring to get his information and impressions direct from the source. With that in mind, he soon discovered that Davidson was not the original source of the information, and asked that Chuck Mauer be brought into the meeting. With animation and enthusiasm, along with the occasional glance at Davidson, Mauer described how he had been posting old membership and subscription list information when he stumbled on the apparent statistical anomaly that suggested something was wrong.

"And if there is something out of line here, why wouldn't you have come across it before?" Stinnett asked.

"There's a good reason for that," Davidson responded quickly, anxious to regain his role in this dialogue. "We usually get fifteen or twenty changes a month on our various subscription or membership lists. People switching jobs or retiring or any number of other reasons. What we found this time was an unusual number of deletions because of sudden death. And then when I asked Chuck to dig a little deeper and call some of the companies, he came up with a list of nine people over the past seven or eight years that appeared to have died from some type of random violence or accident, counting the two on the boat at our meeting in Florida. With all the names coming and going on our lists, we wouldn't have figured this out if we hadn't done that extra digging."

"Well, gentlemen," Stinnett said, "I'm not sure you have figured out anything beyond just a random coincidence. Still, it does seem to warrant that we take a closer look at the situation. I'll run some of the information through our national database and see if there's enough reason for concern. The death of Mr. Levard in Toronto and the drowning of the other gentleman in Mexico would not have been something we would have picked up in an initial screen, so we'll include them in any new search that we do." And with that, Agent Stinnett, having never removed his suit jacket during the 50-minute meeting in the stuffy boardroom, stood up, shook hands, and left the building with his creases still intact.

Stinnett's ability to analyze this disparate series of seemingly random events was based on another series of events, one that had done much to shape the direction and capabilities of this high-profile agency for which he worked. In July of 1908, President Teddy Roosevelt's attorney general appointed a force of Special Agents in the US Department of Justice. This new staff of 35 people was given the name Bureau of Investigation in 1909, and the rest, as they say, is history. Part of that history has been the evolution in the manner and frequency by which elements of society have managed to do violence upon themselves, and the concurrent advances in the application of technology and technique by which the FBI has attempted to impede the furtherance of such violence. Of the profusion of crimes in which the Bureau becomes involved, it is the finality of murder and the opportunity for dubious notoriety associated with multiple murderers that draws the attention and quickens the pulse of both the pursuer and the pursued. Such is the logic associated with the analysis of multiple killings, that the FBI and other investigatory agencies have developed a system for classification of these homicides by style and type. Included are such choice descriptions as: mass murderer classic and mass murderer family, not to be confused with multiple murderer spree and multiple murderer serial. Although someone such as Charles Whitman (mass murder spree), the man who barricaded himself on a tower in Austin, Texas and killed 16 people during the next 90 minutes – although such an individual can bring mayhem and tragedy upon a specific location or community, it is the serial killers, the Ted Bundys, the David Berkowitzs, the Hillside Stranglers, who intimidate entire regions of the country and require the mobilization and coordination of resources from numerous agencies in different jurisdictions. It is within this milieu of confusion and occasionally terror that the FBI now frequently rises to its finest hour. Its *raison d'être*. It has not always been so.

In the early 1970s, the Bureau opened a new academy at Quantico, Virginia, perhaps one of the last positive legacies of J. Edgar Hoover, who was at that time determined to build a first class training facility for law enforcement personnel. As some of the programs evolved, a fledgling Behavioral Sciences Unit was established, staffed by two senior instructors who spent most of their time teaching, but who occasionally analyzed violent crimes and attempted to develop a profile of the appearance and behavior of likely suspects. It was eventually determined that many of those convicted of the most hideous crimes had previously tortured, raped, or brutally murdered other victims before FBI or other agencies became aware that the seemingly unrelated criminal acts had been committed by one individual. That individual, almost always a male, might have spread his mayhem over several different states, occasionally aware, but usually oblivious to the fact that local police agencies did not communicate or share reports. Even within a single jurisdiction, similar cases were often not recognized as being part of a pattern.

Enter the FBI's National Center for the Analysis of Violent Crime, or NCAVC in the alphabet soup of acronyms that is served daily on both sides of the Potomac. NCAVC ushered in an era in which state and local agencies could discover when seemingly unrelated crimes were, in fact, possibly related. At the heart of the program was a process where reports of unusual crimes were submitted by agencies across the country, after which the computer software at NCAVC compared and matched them, looking for enough common elements to suggest some type of pattern.

While all of this was developing in Washington, Agent Jay Harris was working on securities fraud cases in Austin, Texas. Not yet one of the chosen people, Harris seemed destined to spend his FBI career in the Texas and Oklahoma districts. A divorced father of two, Harris was then living in an apartment on the outskirts of Austin, an apartment that had all the glamour of a used Chevy pick-up along with a microwave oven that bore the unmistakable signs and smells of enchilada overkill.

Jay Harris had grown up in Tulsa, Oklahoma, the son of a real estate developer and grandson of a dust bowl rancher whose one redeeming grace in an otherwise unremarkable lifetime of 67 years was the purchase of a section of land on the side of Tulsa that eventually expanded outward. After the grandfather died, Jay's father parlayed the barren acreage into a family fortune, which though small by Oklahoma standards, was sufficient to send Jay and his sister through Rice University in Houston. After graduation from college in 1975 with a degree in accounting, Harris went back to Tulsa and joined a regional CPA firm. Three years later, in one of the first recruiting efforts undertaken by the Bureau to hire candidates other than white male lawyers, he applied for a position with the FBI and was hired. After completion of training, he was assigned to the Austin field office where he spent the next two years seriously questioning his career choice, until the day he got called in to see the Special Agent in Charge, Jeffrey Whitiker.

"Harris, how long have you been with us here in Austin?"
"Twenty-six months, sir."
"And what kind of cases have you been assigned to?"

Harris's file was lying in the middle of Whitiker's otherwise empty desk. Jay had only met the man on two other occasions, but he knew enough about him to bet that the file had been read thoroughly, and certainly with regard to recent assignment activity. "Last year I spent three months assisting with the Fort Hood counterintelligence investigation," he said, "but otherwise I've been detailed to work on a variety of bank and security fraud cases."

"That's right, you're one of those new accounting types, aren't you?" Whitiker asked, glancing briefly towards the file.

"I have a degree in accounting from Rice, but as you know we're trained to deal with all types of cases." Harris was determined not to rise to the challenge about his non-lawyer status.

"Have you enjoyed your time with the Bureau?" Whitiker continued, this time looking directly at Harris.

"I'm very pleased to be part of the FBI, sir. The work I've done to date has not been overly challenging, but I know that I'll get a variety of assignments over time."

Whitiker had gotten up from his chair and was walking around his desk as if to get a closer look at Harris. "Have you ever worn a beard?"

"I grew a beard in college and didn't shave it until the morning I went in for my first interview with the Bureau. My wife had never seen me without one. She almost threw me out when I shaved." He smiled as he said that, but Whitiker apparently thought he had been serious.

"I understand why. You'd probably look better with a beard. We're going to give you a chance to grow one again." He sat back down and pulled out a large manila envelope from the top drawer of the desk. "Have you ever been to Arizona?"

Two weeks later Harris arrived in Prescott, Arizona with a well-crafted cover story and a fourteen-day start on a new beard. For the next year-and-a-half he served as an undercover agent, infiltrating the radical environmental group Earth First. With a gentle demeanor and an ersatz background as a college dropout and recovering alcoholic, Harris gradually worked his way into the group, and with a bug in his shirt recorded hundreds of hours of conversations between various members of the organization as they discussed past and present plans to disrupt construction projects around the state. During his time in Arizona, Harris was only able to get back to Austin for a few short visits, and his marriage, never exactly solid to begin with, eventually became a casualty of his service to the Bureau.

Upon completion of his undercover assignment, Harris spent another two years in the Austin field office, and then had the opportunity to return to Quantico for additional training in prisoner interrogation. After three weeks of intense but uneventful classroom preparation, he had the chance to observe an extraordinary interview with a convicted killer, an interview that set the stage for his next assignment and created the impetus for his unique specialization in the land of the weird – the profiling of mass murderers.

The guest instructor for the third week of the training program was John Dalton, who at that time in 1984 was already developing a reputation as one of the FBI's top analysts. Dalton had been with the National Center for the Analysis of Violent Crime at the Academy in Quantico for the past six years and, with the exception of the two original agents who had established the Behavioral Sciences Unit, was considered as perhaps the top prospect in the emerging but arcane art of profiling. Dalton had been impressed with Harris in class and, when he found out that Jay was originally from Oklahoma, asked him to come along to interview a convicted serial killer.

"This guy grew up in Oklahoma. I don't know if that's going to make any difference, but sometimes it helps to break the ice and get them talking." Dalton was driving one of the car pool sedans on their way to the federal prison outside of Richmond. He and Harris were scheduled to see one Gerald Bishop, an ex-barber who had confessed to killing 16 women in Arkansas, Tennessee, and Virginia.

"How many of these guys have you interviewed?" Harris asked. He had received a briefing the day before on what to wear and how to handle himself when they were in the interrogation cell, but he had not really had the chance to discuss the rationale behind the interview.

"This will make number twenty-one for me," Dalton said. "I went along with McKaskee and Grant on fourteen of their interviews and then I did six by myself."

"And all were serial killers?"

"Most of 'em. Some were just serial rapists or child molesters. Of course they would have killed eventually if they hadn't been caught. That's one of the things we're finding out. They all progress in their violence sooner or later – if you can call that progression. We're talking about some real sickos here, Harris. You sure you're up for it?"

Jay was trying not to make eye contact with Dalton as they spoke. John was the type of driver who seemed to pay more attention to his passenger than he did the road, and Harris wasn't too sure that the most dangerous part of the assignment might not be the time they spent in the car together. "I guess I'm up for it," he said. "I'm not too sure what you want me to do besides take notes and stay out of your way."

"That's about it. But I gotta warn you, this asshole is about as bad as they get. This guy not only killed these women, he would cut 'em up before they died. Sometimes called the family afterwards. The victims were getting younger when we finally caught him two years ago. I need to find out how he chose the women, what he used to cut 'em, why some were gagged but not all. Why some were raped and others weren't. A whole bunch of sick information, Harris. But when you do enough of these you start to see the patterns. Pretty soon if you're good, and maybe lucky, you can begin to predict what the killer is like when you analyze the crime. That's how Bishop got nailed. McKaskee worked out a profile on the guy after reviewing the case files and looking at the photos from eight of the early murders. Had him pegged pretty close. Knew he lived with his mother or an older sister, knew about what his age was, knew he would be a volunteer fireman or in the police auxiliary. Even guessed what type of pornographic magazines he would buy. That's how the local cops finally got him. Unfortunately he had killed three more women by then, but at least they got him."

It was about the worst three hours that Harris had spent in his career with the Bureau. Gerald Bishop was everything Dalton had said and more. The problem had not been in getting him to start talking, but rather in channeling the interview into those aspects of the crimes that could provide one more hint at how the mind of the debased and depraved functions when planning for and executing the most hideous of all crimes. Bishop at times was almost robotic in his recitation of events, staring straight ahead, seemingly oblivious to the impact of his carnage. And then just when it appeared he was beyond any semblance of emotion, he would pause, head still facing forward but the eyes now glancing to either side as he smiled slowly, knowing that he had sucked the listener into a voyeuristic cesspool – anxious to escape the sickening maelstrom yet desperately curious about the next layer of detail. During one of those pauses, Harris rose to the bait, asking a question that drew an even more aberrant grin from Bishop.

"I'm sorry about that question," he told Dalton on the way back to Quantico. "Bishop set me up, didn't he?"

"He was reeling you in and you swallowed the hook. Some of these guys get off on telling their story. This asshole's a pro. You're not the first guy he had falling off the chair."

"I didn't think I could get taken in like that."

"Most serial killers have above average intelligence and they relive their crimes over and over again in their minds. They've got all the details down. They may be sick, but they're not dumb. Not all of them like to talk like Bishop did today, but enough do that we can learn about how their screwed up minds work – figure out some of the common threads." They were almost back to Quantico now and the light was starting to fade on this late Saturday afternoon. "Come see me on Monday morning," Dalton said. "Tell me if you were able to sleep okay over the weekend and if you'd like to sit in on some other interviews with me. With the one obvious exception, you did all right today. I could use some help doing more interviews as well as correlating all the information I've been getting."

Jay Harris did not have trouble sleeping over the weekend, nor was he bothered during the next two weeks when he accompanied Dalton on three more interviews and helped document the files on several others. Harris seemed to have an almost innate ability to relate to the criminal mind when necessary, and then distance himself when it was time to analyze the sordid activity at its lowest possible level. At the end of the training period, Harris was placed on temporary duty with the Behavioral Sciences Unit, and then eventually given a permanent assignment working with Dalton to complete the interviews of 56 serial murderers that later served as the basis for the FBI's much-heralded profiling expertise. During the five years that they worked on the project, Dalton and Harris began to train others how to analyze a violent crime and develop a profile of the appearance and behavior of likely suspects. But it was Harris who took classes at George Washington University and got his master's degree in abnormal psychology. And it was Harris who emerged as the individual to whom the Bureau turned for assistance when a serial killer could not be successfully identified or profiled by others, or when a series of apparently random crimes against high level individuals threatened to draw critical attention to the FBI. It was at these times that the phone calls went out from the suits in the corner offices at the Bureau to the windowless basement domain of Jay Harris, suggesting that if Mr. Harris could kindly break free from his analysis of past mayhem and mutilation, his help would surely be appreciated on a case of current interest.

"I really don't know why I turned out to be so good at this," he told Dalton one time in a rare departure from his otherwise self-deprecating style. They were sitting in Harris's cluttered apartment, half way through a case of Lone Star beer that an agent friend of Jay's from Texas had shipped up by special courier, when the news broke within the Bureau that Harris's profile had made the ID leading to a big arrest. "You know, it used to bug the heck outta my wife how I was so detail oriented. I was the kind of guy who knew the difference between soap and detergent – between preserve and jam. I used to keep records of the gas mileage we got on our trips. Worse yet, I used to think that stuff was important. I was a real dork back then. No wonder she dumped me."

"You're still a real dork!" Dalton said as he rolled an empty beer bottle towards the growing pile in the middle of Harris's well-worn living room rug. "You're just damn lucky you found a job where you get paid for being weird."

CHAPTER FOURTEEN
The Profile

"Jay? This is Don Stinnett calling. My group is working a file here in the Washington district that has a rather strange look and I was wondering if I might stop down and talk to you about it."

It was now over two weeks since Stinnett had made his visit to the AMMA office and five days since he had come to the conclusion that something more than a random series of events was responsible for the turnover on AMMA's mailing lists. He had been reluctant to call Harris for assistance, and probably would not have done so if the case had not begun to garner some attention within the Washington office. At his Monday briefing with his boss, Stinnett had passed on the preliminary opinion that there might be a connection between the nine or ten deaths, and in doing so got an instant response from Deputy Director Bob Kaufmann.

"Jesus, Don, you think they're all related in some way?"

"I don't really know that yet," Stinnett said, surprised by the response to what up until then he had thought of as something of moderate interest. "There does appear to be the possibility of a connection, but it's a little too early to tell for sure."

"And you think it might be tied in with some radical animal rights group?" Kaufmann had swung his chair around so he could access the computer terminal behind his desk and was starting to do a call-up on the database that the FBI maintained on the plethora of radical fringe groups it followed. Most senior agents Kaufmann's age resisted using P.C.'s themselves, preferring to send their search requests to one of the legions of computer jockeys that the agency had on staff to maintain and access the complicated series of databases. Kaufmann was an exception, and always jumped at the chance to utilize his newfound expertise.

"I don't know that we've got a connection with the animal righters yet," Stinnett said, anxious to slow down the leap frogging of conclusions that Kaufmann seemed intent on pursuing. "We did think there was a connection on the boat explosion in Florida several years ago, and so far we know that at least two or three of these other deaths were senior people from companies who used animals in their research. But no group has claimed any credit on this, so we really don't know if there's a linkage."

"Listen, Don, these groups don't always take credit right away. You're on to something! Who else you got working on this?" Kaufmann was scanning a listing of animal rights groups that he had just pulled off his printer. "Here's a list of some of the fringe groups and the contact person in the Bureau who maintains the master file on each one. You're gonna have to check on what the current status is for informer reports."

"Bob, you've got to understand, I don't even know for sure that these deaths are linked, and I sure as hell don't know that there's a connection with some sort of radical animal rights group. This is going to take some more digging before I can confirm a pattern."

"Listen to me on this, Don. There is a linkage, I can smell it, and I'm sure we're going to find out it's tied into one of these whacko animal groups. I always figured that sooner or later they wouldn't be satisfied just trashing dog cages."

"I'm not so sure."

"I am! And Don, starting today this case is your number one priority. If you got other active files, get 'em offloaded to somebody else. This is a kind of case that could be a front-page article in the *Post* tomorrow if somebody at AMMA decides to talk to the press. We've got to cover our ass on this one, be sure we're pulling out all the stops. The Administration's been criticized for being too tough on the medical companies. The last thing we need is publicity that somebody's killing off industry execs while the FBI's been sitting on the case for five years. Plus I want you to get the profile boys involved. Have 'em look at the files and see if they can come up with some type of characterization that you can use to get started on this."

"I'm not sure that's necessary just yet."

"Don, you're not going to have a choice on this. I know you button-down types don't like to work with the Behavioral Science people. But Harris and Dalton have seen more serial killers than the rest of the Bureau put together. Harris in particular has a nose for seeing traits and patterns in these serial cases that some of our best investigators would miss if you laid out a map. Use him on this, and keep me informed about what's going on."

Kaufmann was right about at least one thing. The 'button-down agent types' did not rush to embrace the use of suspect profiling, particularly when it came from the Behavioral Science people who were perceived as being more comfortable reading a book on deviant behavior than they were in taking an extra hour on the pistol range. Stinnett and his counterparts held to the firm belief that cases were solved by the dogged pursuit of motive and evidence, and speculation about the personality of the suspect did little more than provide grist for the media mill and divert attention away from the basic investigatory work needed to solve the tough case. And so it was with less than complete enthusiasm that after the Monday meeting Stinnett found himself on the phone with Harris, asking for help on the case.

"I'm not sure we really have anything here that will be of interest to you," Stinnett said, "but it never hurts to have someone else take a look. I'm always open to new ideas."

"What kinda file you working?" Harris was polite but not overwhelmed with Stinnett's sudden interest in getting another point of view. He remembered that, at a case presentation he made to the local agents a few months ago, Stinnett had shown an obvious lack of interest in the role of suspect profiling. It was not likely that a religious conversion had taken place in the intervening weeks.

"We've got a situation where a Washington-based medical manufacturers association has had a bunch of its members from different parts of the country turn up dead for a whole bunch of strange reasons. My initial review tells me it's probably not just a coincidence."

"Why don't you come down after lunch and show me what you have so far? I'll need to be able to review individual case files if I'm going to do you any good."

If Jay Harris's apartment provided any subtle hints about the personal side of his life, there was no such ambiguity at his office. The manner in which he approached his daily task of trying to make sense out of the serial killer's approach to murder and mayhem was immediately obvious to even the most casual observer. Pictures of several recent homicide victims were pinned to a large cork board behind his desk with no apparent attempt whatsoever to spare the visitor from the shock of seeing autopsy photos. Taped onto the side of the file cabinet near the door was another series of photos showing close-ups of hands that had been bound tightly with various cords or ropes, in what was apparently an attempt to compare similarities in the ligatures and method of binding. On every horizontal surface in the room, including the floor on either side of the desk, were piled various folders, books, newspaper clippings, computer reports and other assorted detritus from the dozens of cases that he was apparently following as part of his daily routine. Stinnett had managed to make only one prior sojourn to the basement lair of the Behavioral Science Unit during his four years in Washington, and that trip had not included a visit to Harris's office. So it was with some sense of apprehension that he shook hands with Jay and sat down in the one visitor's chair not currently in use as a storage area. It was almost 2:30 when Stinnett arrived but Harris was obviously in the middle of lunch, with half of a vending machine sandwich resting precariously on top of a can of Dr. Pepper.

"Jay, it's good to see you again," Stinnett said with a degree of insincerity that did not seem to bother either of the two men. "I'm surprised we don't run into each other more often. You're developing quite a reputation here at the Bureau."

"Well, you field guys get a little more exposure on the outside than I do. They like to keep me and Dalton down here in the basement away from the public." Harris took a bite from his sandwich and looked around for his Dr. Pepper before realizing it was right in front of him. "If we weren't required to wear watches, I doubt seriously we'd know if it was day or night outside."

As Harris finished his sandwich, Stinnett ran his fingers slowly down the crease of his pant, knowing that Jay was consciously working the country rube angle for a little extra mileage. Although as a section chief Stinnett was technically the senior agent, both knew that Harris momentarily held the upper hand in this minor face-off of style and ego. With just enough of a final pause to remove any lingering doubts about who was helping whom, Harris cleared a small spot on his desk, pulled out a yellow note pad from a bottom drawer and said, "Let's start."

And for the next two hours, interrupted only once when Harris stopped to take a phone call from a Navy expert on knots, Stinnett went through the litany of unusual deaths that were contained in what he was now calling the AMMA File.

"I make it out to be a total of ten related deaths starting with Levard at the medical convention in Toronto in 1985 and ending with the accidental death or murder of Lempke in Scottsdale last March. The guys at AMMA had nine names. I've scratched two from that list. One was a well-documented suicide and another was a clear-cut accident. But I've added three from our database of unsolved cases. Guys who were execs with medical device companies but who apparently were not part of the AMMA group. There could be more for all I know, but it looks like there are at least ten that might be tied together some way."

"And did they all work for companies that did research on animals?"

"I don't know yet. I'm still working on that. Most of these guys change jobs every four or five years, so they might have been doing animal testing with some other company along the way. In the Florida case it looks pretty certain that there was a connection."

Harris shuffled through the pile of folders in front of him and pulled out the thick one marked Powell-Pellegrino. "Talk to me about this one," he said without looking at Stinnett, concentrating instead on the autopsy pictures that were in the back section of the file.

"Well, the Bureau did a lot of work on that case, but never made an arrest. Never proved it was a murder actually, but it sure as hell looks that way. They found traces of C-5 explosive on some of the wreckage that floated up and on one of the victims. Most of the boat sank and couldn't be recovered because of the depth and current, so they weren't able to make a case out of what they found. They were damn lucky to even recover the bodies."

"Who's this?" Harris said, pointing to one of the pictures.

"That was the captain's daughter. She was nineteen years old and was working on the boat as the mate. The press clips said she was a pretty girl but you can see by the picture that she had significant injuries."

"Where was she when the boat exploded?"

"She was just coming down from the bridge."

"So she would have been in view?"

"I suppose so. What difference does that make? If this was a murder she wasn't the intended victim. Powell was."

Harris continued with his note taking, his left hand canted at an angle to the yellow pad as he glanced up briefly at Stinnett. "Did they peg this as a timed explosion, or one that was set off remotely?"

"Well, they really couldn't say for sure. But I called the agent who did most of the work on the case and he figures it must have been set off remotely. The boat was late leaving the dock and then the explosion happened about fifteen minutes after they got out to deeper water off the shelf. It looks like somebody was watching and then set it off, probably from another boat."

"How far away?"

"Most likely within about seventy-five yards. They can't tell for sure, but the bomb guys say these are usually done with model engine controls unless they use a major electrical field change. There were some other fishing boats in the area and nobody picked up any radio interference so they figured it must have been set off by someone fairly close."

"And what do you know about Powell and Pellegrino?"

Stinnett reached across the desk to take back the file and began flipping through the pages attached to the left side of the folder by an aluminum fastener. He appeared relieved to be back on familiar ground, covering information that he had previously reviewed. "Well, Powell must have been the target. He was president of Texas Suture Company, which is a firm that makes surgical sutures. Not one of the big ones in the industry, but one that got a lot of press several years ago because they were using dogs in a training program, teaching some of their salesmen how to sew I guess. They got picketed by one of the animal rights groups. A bunch of hate mail – stuff like that."

"What about the other guy, Pellegrino?"

"I got a bio on him here in the file but there's not much out of the ordinary. Was working as a vice president of regulatory affairs for Hoffman Diagnostics when he got killed. Apparently was a friend of Powell's. They liked to go fishing together when they had the chance. Poor guy picked the wrong day to go fishing. Left a big family."

"And no claims from any of the dog lovers?"

"No, that's one thing that doesn't seem to fit. You'd think these guys would wanna take credit for some of this if they're trying to send a message. Kaufmann thinks it's just a matter of time before they do. He's scared shitless that he's gonna pick up the paper someday and see that the ARB or some other crank group has been shooting fish in our pond while we've been sitting around with our thumb up our ass."

"Give me a week on this. And leave the files."

"Jay, I'm signed out on these! I'm working on this case ten hours a day. I've gotta have these files."

"You want to see the files, come down to my office. You want me to help, you leave me the files. I can't give you a profile if I don't know every detail about how these guys died and who they were."

"You think you can develop a profile?"

"Maybe, maybe not. Check back in a week."

It was not a great seven days for Donald Stinnett. He managed to avoid going back to Harris's office by taking a trip down to Texas to visit the suture company, spending three days sorting through the records on ex-employees and looking at old threat letters. Back in Washington on Thursday, he spent the morning at the AMMA Headquarters and then went back to the FBI building where he was scheduled to do his qualification shooting with the new 10mm Smith and Wesson pistol that the Bureau was putting into service. Stinnett took pride in his weapon skills, but the Bureau's switch from revolvers to the more powerful 10mm semi-automatic had been a challenge to him in previous shooting drills, and he was not looking forward to his qualification round when he would need to get forty of his fifty shots within the scoring area. His attitude did not improve when he saw Deputy Director Kaufmann coming off one of the firing positions and walking towards him.

"You qualifying today, Stinnett?"

"I expect to. I've done all the drills."

"Piece a-cake. I shot forty-six. You shouldn't have any trouble."

Stinnett kept on walking towards the staging area but had to stop when Kaufmann grabbed his arm. "What's your progress on the AMMA File? I didn't get an update from you on Monday."

"Yeah, I know. I was checking out some leads in Texas. This is going to take some time, Bob."

"Those deaths were connected though, weren't they?"

"We're still not positive about that. I should have the answer for you in a couple weeks."

"Not good enough, Don!" Kaufmann was still holding on to Stinnett's arm. "You've gotta be moving this. I want us to be on top of this case before I get a call from some halfwit in Congress asking me why we didn't protect his favorite industry. What about the suspect profile?"

"I've got Harris working on it. I asked him to go through the files and get back to me by Friday."

"Well, be sure and tell me what he comes up with. He's the best there is on this." Kaufmann started walking back towards the locker room. "And let me know how you fired today."

Twenty minutes later, Stinnett was changing out of his shooting clothes and back into his favorite pinstripe suit. He would need to stop at the scheduling desk before he left the range. With luck he could get another qualifying slot before his next meeting with Kaufmann. Kissing up to Harris was one thing. Reporting a target score of 34 was something else.

There had not been any indication from Harris about who should schedule the next meeting. By noon on Friday, Stinnett thought he did not dare wait any longer or he would risk a phone call from Kaufmann asking for an update. The question now was whether he should just walk down to Harris's office or make a call. Stinnett opted for the call.

"Jay, this is Don Stinnett. Are you ready to go over the AMMA File with me?"

"Any time."

Stinnett was hoping for a more complete indication of interest or direction but none was forthcoming, and after a pause that seemed to extend a little too long said, "Should I come down to your office?"

"Any time you want."

"I'll be there in five minutes."

Although he would have been loath to admit it, Stinnett had actually debated what to wear on this day in anticipation of his meeting with Harris. On one hand, he wanted to look as polished and professional as possible so as to solidify his image as the senior agent on the case. However, he did not want to unduly upstage Harris at a time when he needed all the cooperation he could get from the erstwhile profiling genius. Stinnett opted for an olive green suit but left his contrasting pocket square at home. If Harris took any notice it certainly was not apparent. Instead, he sat calmly at his desk, finishing his take-out taco salad, portions of which had already made their mark on his frayed white shirt now seeing its second consecutive day of service.

"Well?"

"Well, what?" Harris responded as he threw his paper plate and plastic fork in the basket underneath his desk.

"Well, do you think there's something here? Are the deaths related?"

Harris stared back across the desk with a look of incredulity. "Of course they're related!" he said. "I assumed you knew that."

"I did know that," Stinnett said a little too quickly. "What I meant was – how do you think they're related? Were these guys killed by the same person?"

"I can't tell that from the files, and I doubt if we'll be able to reach that conclusion based on the information we have so far. But clearly these cases are related, and the deaths that look like accidents were probably murders."

"So we've got a serial murderer taking aim at a bunch of business executives?"

"I didn't say that. This is clearly not a classic serial murder case. No sexual overtones, no common mode of death, no evidence of deviant behavior." Harris had extended his arm, flipping out one finger at a time as he went through his handful of overview comments, oblivious to the irony that he no longer considered straightforward murder as a type of deviant behavior.

"So there's no pattern on this?" Stinnett sounded almost desperate, as if his one hope for assistance on this case was now gone.

"Of course there's a pattern," Harris said. "Any time you have ten deaths that are related you're going to find a pattern. What we've got here are not typical murder cases, but almost a situation of targeted assassinations. Business and research people in the medical products industry that for some reason or other have been marked for death and then killed by one or more people who clearly are pros. If I'm right on this, you really have two problems. Finding out who did the actual killing and then finding out who set it up and paid for it. And Don, you'd better hurry."

"Kaufmann? I can stall him. This information should hold him for awhile."

Again the look of incredulity from Harris. "Kaufmann's the least of your problems. You're due for another murder in three or four weeks! Didn't you at least see that? These cases started out about fifteen months apart and the time between them has gradually shortened down to about eight months. There were gaps in 1987 and 91, but my guess is you got two cases some place that nobody's tied into this series yet. That death in Scottsdale was six months ago, so you've got about a month or two to solve this before we add file number eleven."

"Geez, the people over in AMMA are gonna crap if they hear this."

"I'll have to talk to 'em, Don. Normally with serial murderers, how a crime is committed is more important than why. But in this case, why the crime was committed is more important than how. To get to the why, I have to know more about the victims and for me to know more about the victims I'll probably have to start with AMMA and go forward from there."

"And you're telling me you don't have any type of profile on the killer?"

"Oh no, I've got the start of a profile. I just don't know if it's more than one guy, and I need to figure out who his next victim is likely to be."

And then for the next hour, Harris did his information dump, detailing his observations on the ten files along with the common themes and important differences that he saw between the various cases. Stinnett took notes as fast as he could, realizing finally that if he and the Bureau were going to have any chance to break this case in the near term, it would be a result of the insights that Jay seemed to be uniquely able to generate from the sea of murky data.

"The Toronto case is another example that these were professional hits," Harris was saying. "The clean, quick kill. No witnesses, no loose ends."

"How do we know it wasn't just a robbery?"

"Mighta been, but I doubt it. There's no record of any use of the victim's credit cards. If it had been a street mugging or a hold-up gone bad, you would've had somebody using those cards."

"What else do we know?" Stinnett was starting to get religion.

"Well, we know the obvious things. The killer is a single, white male, probably thirty-five to forty-five years old. He's organized, methodical, probably has worked in some type of profession or white-collar job. He's in good physical condition, above average intelligence, decent appearance, maybe even handsome, and living in an environment where big swings in income would not be readily apparent. He has the ability to be cool and detached but can also be forceful and demanding when necessary. It's possible that he's a member of some whacko animal rights group, but I seriously doubt it. He's getting paid for this by somebody. Who that is and why they're doing it is something I can't speculate on until I find out what the common linkage is with the victims."

"Jay," Stinnett began slowly, his religious conversation somewhat in doubt again, "help me out on this. I'm sure you've got some rationale to support that profile, and I'm not trying to say you're wrong. But just in case Kaufmann asks me, which by the way is about a one hundred percent probability, give me some background on how in the hell you got to those conclusions."

Harris always heard this type of question when he discussed an initial suspect profile. There was a time when he could not understand why no one else saw the connections. But he had come to realize that not every other cop visualized things the way he did. The little nuances. Not yet patterns or even hints of patterns, but hints of hints of patterns, that when taken together with other bent twigs and subtle clues helped form the pieces which would later become the mosaic which would still later be evident to even the biggest dullard in the Bureau. And so he began again, slowly, so Stinnett could get it down.

"We know he's white because no black man could get that close to so many victims without someone taking notice. He's comfortable operating in the environment of a major resort or conference center, so he may have had a job before where he got into those types of situations. He's single, or separated, because we know from other cases that nobody's been able to sustain a normal relationship over several years when they're killing people. He's got to be above average intelligence to methodically plan this many murders, most of them with a different MO, and then pull them off without getting caught. He's obviously athletic, or at least in fairly decent shape to be able to climb Camelback in Arizona. Although somewhat of a stretch, he's probably fairly good looking in view of the woman he had along at the resort in Scottsdale. What else?"

"Something along the lines of detached but forceful."

"Yeah, this could be important. This guy must have known he'd be injuring that girl on the boat when he set off the bomb. There's no evidence that he's nuts or some type of sadist, yet he could push the button to kill his target knowing that it might take out a teenage girl. That's another reason that we can figure he's single, he obviously doesn't have any kids. But we also know he must be forceful and maybe even domineering. He had to have help on some of these kills. When there's more than one person involved in a murder, the odds of something going wrong or somebody getting caught go up exponentially. This guy has pulled it off, so he must be in absolute control at every step of the process."

"How about the age?" Stinnett was writing at full speed and trying to remember the points that Harris had outlined a few minutes before.

"Well the thirty-five to forty-five range is a pretty safe bet. This guy is a pro, and apparently able to get things done on his terms, so it's unlikely that he's younger than thirty-five. As far as a max of forty-five, that's mostly a guess based on the profiles of other killers. It's damn rare that you see a serial killer over forty-five unless he's a psycho, and there's no evidence that this guy is nuts. If anything, it's just the opposite."

"So you're confident about the profile?"

"As confident as I can be at this time. The way that I'll get more confident or else have to change, is if I see something outside the pattern when he kills again."

"You're sure he'll kill again?"

"I'm absolutely sure he will, unless whoever is giving him directions decides to stop." Harris paused until Stinnett had caught up on his note-taking and then asked, "How are your guys coming on the animal rights angle?"

"I've got two agents on that full time, plus we're shaking the tree for informers. Haven't found squat so far. There's a shit load of these groups, but my guys tell me that the only one likely to be radical enough to pursue something like this might be the ARB. Those guys also know how to milk the PR angle on everything they do, which might fit with the fact that nobody is taking credit on this so far. They may want to wait until they get to some magic number and then brag how they set this up and pulled it off without even the FBI knowing something was going on."

"Kaufmann would love that," Harris said, with just the slightest grin. "I'll tell you what I can do to help, but I'll need some assistance."

"What?"

"I need to find out more about these guys that died. I assume that you'll be going back to their families or companies to get more information, but I'll need more than just that. I need some type of industry expert to talk to. Somebody who might have a bunch of data available on execs in this industry so I can try and figure out the common linkage and maybe predict who he'll be going after next. Is there anybody at AMMA who can help on this?"

"I already asked 'em about that. They said the best place for industry data on key execs is some recruiting outfit in Baltimore."

"Got a contact there?"

"Yeah, a woman by the name of Martha Laudner."

CHAPTER FIFTEEN
The IPO

It was 7:05 Monday morning when Tim pulled into the front parking lot at Remote Monitoring Incorporated. There were signs indicating the reserve parking spots for Fenton and Olanski, but none yet with the name of Tim Foster. "Just as well," he thought. "I don't need to make Fenton any more uncomfortable than he already is." At Perry Robertson's suggestion, the Board had given Fenton the title of Co-Chairman and Executive Vice President of Research. Tim's title would be President and CEO. Although Fenton had seemingly recognized the inevitability of the change in power, whether he would continue to be cooperative in an orderly transition was another matter.

"There's really no book on how best to do this," Perry had told Tim over dinner together the previous evening. "You're going to have to take it one day at a time and see how Jerry handles the change. I suggest you make it clear who's in charge when you're alone with Jerry or in meetings with just the top people, but let him keep the perks and visible status symbols that he had before. My guess is that ninety percent of the staff will be glad to have you on board to add another dimension to the place, but they'll have loyalty to Fenton and Olanski, and you're not going to do yourself any good if you move them out of the corner offices and take their parking spots by the front door."

The front door was still locked when Tim pulled on the gray metal handle after his fifty-yard walk from the side lot. He had opted not to park in one of the visitor's spots, preferring to send a small but visible message that he was here on a permanent basis. Without a key for the door and no apparent way to attract the attention of someone on the inside, Tim retraced his steps and entered by the employee entrance on the west side of the building.

"Good morning," he said to the first person he saw in the hallway, a middle-aged woman wearing a white lab coat. "I'm Tim Foster and I wonder if you can tell me where I can find the production supervisor."

"You're going to need a visitor's badge," the woman said, with more than a small touch of annoyance in her voice, "and the front lobby doesn't open until eight."

"Well, I'm not exactly a visitor. I work here starting today. I'm the new president."

"Oh my God, you're right! I should have known that."

Tim was aware that a mailing had gone out to all employees announcing the change. Fenton had sent him a copy of the 'all employee bulletin' two weeks before which had covered the change in responsibility for Jerry along with a brief background sketch on the new president. Tim had been pleasantly surprised by the positive tone of the announcement and the inclusion of his picture under the headline 'New CEO of Remote Monitoring'.

Although Tim's first hour at the company went well, with a genuinely warm reception from the people on the production floor, it was not a harbinger of things to come. While Fenton did not publicly take steps to stymie the transaction, it was clear he was not going to roll over and salute Foster every time they met in the hall. Tim's Monday morning staff meeting a month later was a prime example of Fenton's lackluster support.

"This morning I'd like to concentrate on how we're going to get ourselves organized to work on our initial public offering," Tim began. "I expect that for the next three months this is going to occupy about seventy-five percent of my time. Brookline will do the final drafting and we'll get all kinds of legal reviews, but we have to feed them the information, including rough drafts on most of the sections. And Jerry," Tim paused and looked directly at Fenton, "you're the best guy to do the section describing the company's technology."

"If you want me to spend half my time trying to write a prospectus, there's no way we're going to make the deadline for the new data storage unit."

"Come on, Jerry," Tim countered, "you've put together a great team in the research department and I'm sure they can keep that project moving and still help with the IPO."

The prospectus did start to come together over the next several weeks as Tim had numerous conference calls and meetings with the two people from Brookline Securities that James Carleton III had assigned to the account. Obviously experienced in the process, the Brookline people used a combination of pressure, compliments, and the occasional enticement of future wealth to keep the Remote staff focused on the efforts necessary to prepare for the stock offering. But the initial excitement of having the company go public cooled quickly as the drudgery of first drafts, second drafts, and third drafts began to take its toll on everyone, including Foster.

Tim's wife and their two children were planning to live in Minneapolis until the end of the school year, and the length of Tim's work days had started to be a topic of conversation within the company, particularly since Fenton made it obvious that he now found a forty hour week more than sufficient. Although well beyond the stage of having to work hard to make a good impression, Tim knew that what he did during his first few months as CEO of Remote was going to set an expectation for much of what would follow in the years to come.

Perry Robertson was one of the first to observe that the new president had an almost innate leadership ability that was most evident in the signals that Tim transmitted countless times each day as he interacted with people at all levels of the company. Foster constantly 'walked the talk', always aware that what he did was infinitely more significant than what he said, always conscious of the importance of human interaction and the many nonverbal ways that the process of communication takes place. Who he sat with in the lunch room – how he greeted people in the hall – who he visited at their own office or work station. As with other individuals who develop into true leaders and not just effective managers, Tim trusted others, and as a result they trusted him. Over time that trust evolved into confidence and confidence into affection and eventually affection into concern about the new CEO who seemed to be working too hard for his own good.

Now several months after he had received the initial contact, it was difficult for Tim to remember his first thoughts when he had gotten the call from David Morkin. With a high profile position at Medelectro, Tim was not unaccustomed to getting phone calls from head hunters, but the call from Morkin seemed to be different, seemed to be filled with the little nuances and vibrations that sent a subliminal message that there was going to be a major change in the career path of Tim Foster, whether he really liked it or not.

"Mr. Foster, this is David Morkin at Morkin and Associates in Baltimore. I appreciate your calling back." Tim had returned

Morkin's call within twenty minutes, always a good sign according to David, who had collected his own book of key signals and body language guides during his twenty-plus years in the business of finding top prospects and convincing them to quit one known career to move halfway across the country for a chance at the brass ring on some lesser known Merry-Go-Round. "As you may know, Tim, we're one of the top executive search groups in the country and we're currently working on an assignment for a CEO position at a rapidly-growing medical device firm that plans to go public later this year."

"Where's the company located?"

Another good sign! Ask the location early in the call, Martha will be pleased. Morkin continued with the initial pitch, anxious to set the hook, knowing that the trophy fish are always cautious and rarely inclined to venture into uncharted water. "This company is in the Denver area," David said, "and one of the top technology companies in its field. At this time I prefer not to go into too much detail since this is a highly confidential search, and you can appreciate that we're going to deal very cautiously with any information on both sides. As an example, we would never disclose your name to the client without your full concurrence, and even then we'd do so only under strict conditions." – Pause – no response from Foster. Probably a good sign since he wasn't rushing to cut off the conversation. "Even though we haven't met yet, Tim, we know quite a bit about your career. We've been following your rapid career progression at Medelectro and we had a chance to hear your presentation at the recent Alex Brown meeting. Quite frankly, you have an almost ideal background for this CEO job, and given the fact that the company will be going public before long, this may just be the opportunity of a lifetime for you."

"Come on! I get a bunch of these calls!"

Tilt! Back up – slow down – stop! As soon as he had mentioned 'lifetime opportunity', Morkin knew he had made a mistake, a rare mistake, but a major blunder nevertheless. No need to hype this job. Foster is too savvy for that approach. And he's correct, he probably gets a call a week from some hotshot promising the moon.

"No – no – no, you're right about that!" David countered quickly. "What I meant was that as we've followed your career progression we've been tempted to call you on a number of occasions to discuss various VP positions or maybe CEO jobs at some mid-level firm. But we've held off until we had a client with a position we knew would justify a contact with you, a company that would meet your standards and provide you with the kind of opportunity that you're not likely to see at Medelectro for years to come." Morkin waited for a response, the recovery was in process.

"A good story," he thought, "and better yet it's true." Mostly.

"Why have you been following my career?"

The 'why are you following me' question. Recovery almost complete! David had found on several occasions that the interest on the part of the potential placement candidates in the tracking process Martha had initiated several years ago was an unintentional dividend of her system. Candidates were almost always intrigued and impressed with the amount of information that Morkin and Associates had on them. With rare exception, when David showed candidates the detail that was in their file as part of the firm's computerized database, there was a notable increase in attention and interest, almost commensurate with the stroking of ego that was taking place.

"Well, Tim, we've been following you ever since you testified at the congressional hearing at the ripe old age of 28." David was looking at the computer printout that Martha had sent over to his office earlier in the week. "We take a completely different approach than other search firms. We don't call up a hundred people hoping to get lucky and find someone with the right credentials. We track a limited number of top prospects over several years and only contact them if we're dealing with a position that appears to be an ideal fit. Quite frankly, Tim, you're one of those top prospects and we think this situation is an ideal fit."

"I'm not really looking to make a change at this time."

The perfect answer! Recovery complete! The 'I'm not really looking but let's keep talking' answer. David breathed a sigh of relief. Now he was back on friendly turf, ready to move on to the next step in completing yet one more assignment in the ever expanding business of Morkin and Associates.

"Tim, I'm going to be in Minneapolis next week and I'd like to schedule some time with you to be sure our background file is accurate, plus I want to tell you more about this position as company president. Of course I don't want to interfere with your current responsibilities so I'm looking at Tuesday evening for dinner or Wednesday morning for breakfast. Which would be better for you?"

As David anticipated, Martha was more than a little pleased when he gave her an update on the discussion with Foster. She always wanted feedback on the candidates that she dug out for David, but her curiosity about the initial response from Tim Foster extended well beyond her normal bounds of inquisitiveness.

"Just how interested is he, David? Tell me exactly what he said." They were sitting at the conference table in Morkin's office. The Remote Monitoring assignment was supposed to be the third item on the agenda for the meeting that she and David held each Monday morning with their two staff associates, but Martha was clearly anxious to find out about Foster. "This guy's an Eagle, David. If the Remote board doesn't go for him they're nuts!"

Although the spin-out of Foster's division at Medelectro had been aborted one year earlier as a result of market conditions, Tim's appearances at several road show sessions, as well as his presentation at the recent Alex Brown conference, had been duly noted in Martha's rapidly growing database.

Medelectro Exec provides update on Neuro-Division status. Division Manager Tim Foster notes significant development progress despite research setback brought about by break-in at animal facility. NY Times – May 27, 1989

"I probably shouldn't tell you this," Martha had said when she gave David her top three names for the Remote search, "but I asked Joe to talk with Foster at the Alex meeting." Dialogue with potential placement candidates prior to an actual search assignment was generally something that Martha and David avoided. The significance of Martha using Joe Sheldon as her surrogate contact was not lost on David.

"You and Joe must be getting pretty serious if you've got him doing interviews for you."

"It wasn't an interview, David, that's your job," Martha had said. "Joe just sat next to him at lunch and they talked about the new FDA regulations. And, not that it's any of your business, Mr.

Matchmaker, but Joe and I just might be getting serious if you would move our operation to Chicago. I'm not sure how much longer I can convince him to keep flying to Baltimore every other weekend."

Martha could never quite conclude a conversation in which Joe's name was mentioned without a visible sign of pleasure – a smile – a movement of the shoulders – almost a self-hug, denoting to even the most casual observer the obvious level of affection that she had for the guy. On this day she seemed to be beaming at full power, her appearance and attitude aided in no small part by one more striking addition to her newly overhauled wardrobe. Today she was wearing a beige outfit, but one that was light years away from the drab and poorly cut beige suits that she once wore with boring regularity. For this staff meeting, Martha wore a beige Armani suit with a fabric so soft that the effect was almost of a gentle fluid movement over the body. Janet Shafer, one of the two associates sitting at the table, had twice reached over to touch the sleeve of the jacket, nodding each time in silent approval of this latest testament to Martha's sartorial splendor.

"Well, in any event," David said, "I don't think the issue is going to be whether or not Foster is a good candidate. He sure looks great on paper and I doubt there'll be any surprises when I see him in Minneapolis. They key thing is probably going to be how we'll convince him to leave a fast track career path at Medelectro and head into a new situation with a couple of entrepreneurs who probably aren't too excited about bringing somebody in from the outside."

"You can do it, David. This just screams out as a perfect fit. Tell him that I'll run a magnet over my computer tapes and screw up all his entries if he turns us down."

Martha was smiling. She enjoyed pushing David just a little farther and faster than he might otherwise have moved. Never uncertain about her individual competence, Martha's belief in their combined talents had increasingly become a factor in the manner that they played off of each other's skills and abilities. The two associates watching this verbal by-play had no doubt that one way or another Tim Foster, one of Martha's Eagles, would soon be winging his way towards Denver.

*

The Eagle did go to Denver, and now in June, some four months into the job, Tim was just starting to feel comfortable, getting ahead of the power curve, getting on top of the countless details and legal matters that were required to take the company public. He even managed to take a few days off when his wife and twin girls flew out for a house-hunting trip. The family was scheduled to move during the third week of July, and Brookline's target day for the IPO was July 12.

"I think this latest draft looks pretty good, Tim," James Carleton had said during their recent phone conversation. "We'll do the SEC filing shortly and then start working on the road show presentation. We can't officially start selling until we get the go-ahead from the SEC, but I can tell you that initial interest looks strong from some of the institutions we've been talking to."

"What's your latest thinking on price?" Tim asked.

Carleton had been reluctant to be specific on the topic of offering price for the new stock issue. Always a source of tension between the underwriter and client company, setting the price of an IPO was an exercise in brinkmanship, with the investment banking firm wanting to wait until the last possible moment before making their recommendation. It was usually in the company's best interest to set a price as high as possible so as to maximize the amount of money coming in and to reduce the number of shares being sold. On the other hand, the underwriter would like to see something left on the table so that the price can continue to climb in the after market, thereby making happy campers out of all the lucky folks who bought on the initial offering and who would then stand in line to buy the next deal that the firm underwrote. In whatever manner a deal was priced, both the investment banker and the company going public wanted to do everything within their mutual power to create a situation where there is more demand for stock than supply, where there is more pressure than provision, and if necessary, where there is more sizzle than substance. It was critical that the buying public believed that the offering would be hot – that the new issue was oversubscribed.

"I think we can price this deal at the top end of the nineteen to twenty-one dollar range that we've been talking about," he postulated. "We're still set to go out with a million shares of stock, although we can expand that at the last minute if demand stays hot. We could probably push the price up over twenty-one, but I'm inclined not to, since it's really in Remote's best interest to have this pop up a few bucks after the IPO so all of your new shareholders are happy." James had temporarily mistaken what would be in his best interest with what would be best for the client, a not uncommon event in the hectic days preceding a public offering.

"Tim, my secretary said you called yesterday to ask about a preference buying list," James said, anxious to move the conversation off the pricing question. "Even though this offering will be oversubscribed, we'll put together a list of individuals that you'd like to see protected – people you want to be able to get stock on the offering. Usually we set aside some stock for employees, relatives, and other friends of the company like key customers or vendors. Is this what you're asking about?"

"Yeah, I guess so," Tim said. "I really don't know what it's called, but several of our employees have asked about buying stock and on Thursday my dad called and said he wants to buy a thousand shares."

"It's called a preferential buying list where we set aside stock for friends of the family – so to speak – so they can get shares even if the deal is oversubscribed. You'll need to send us a list with names and phone numbers and one of our people will contact them for other account information. I don't think we can circle any more than twenty-five thousand shares though, Tim, since this deal is really looking tight."

Even on a Saturday, even with the president of the company, Carleton could not break the pattern, could not ease up on the ever present hyperbole that went with the new offering game, the hyperbole that said, 'Only the chosen will play – only the fortunate will win'.

It was six weeks later that the offering was concluded, the effective date delayed some eight days because of a glitch with an amendment to the SEC filing. The three weeks preceding the IPO had been an exercise in major league frustration for Tim, as he watched the targeted offering price slip lower and lower.

"That article in *The Wall Street Journal* yesterday about Siemens introducing their new generation monitoring equipment has scared the shit out of some of our institutional buyers," Carleton had said on the first of his several bad news calls. "We may have to be looking to price at the low end of the range if we're going to keep the interest up."

"James, that article was bullshit! The equipment that Siemens is coming out with is for a whole different segment of the market. That's not gonna hurt our market share one bit." Tim had already received calls from Robertson and Hodson about the article, but neither had suggested that the news would affect the offering.

"Look, Tim, you and I know this won't affect business, but Siemens is a big company and this news has made some people nervous. Hopefully it'll blow over. We've still got two and a half weeks before the offering."

One week later it had not blown over, and to make matters worse, there was more bad news to make investors nervous. A congressional threat to take yet one more stab at tightening up Medicare expenditures had cast a pall over healthcare stocks, and the order book for Remote shares was beginning to soften – in a big way!

"Tim, I don't know what more I can tell you. We're really sailing into the wind on this one," Carleton said. "You saw the attendance at the luncheon meeting. There should have been seventy people there. We're lucky that we got forty to show up and six or seven of them were guys I called in from our local office to help fill up the room."

They were having a late dinner at a restaurant on the Upper East Side of Manhattan after a day filled with visits to the key institutional buyers plus two scheduled 'road show' presentations with brokers from several of the top Wall Street firms. Perry Robertson had flown in from Denver the day before to attend the meetings, and was now taking a close look at the wine list, hoping to find some solace in the rather extensive collection of merlots.

"When a market segment goes south like this," James continued, "it hits everybody, including the new deals. We're gonna have to price this below our original bracket if we want to get it off. Otherwise we'll have to pull the offering and wait until the market improves."

"We can't pull it!" Perry said. He had given the wine list back to the waiter and was sitting with his arms crossed, his somber mood in stark contrast to his normal ebullient attitude. "We are maxed out on our credit line at the bank and we've run up over $130,000 in legal and professional bills on this. The company needs money and I think we need to go through with the offering even at a lower price."

"How much lower?" Tim asked.

James Carleton III extended his arms to check the proper alignment of his monogrammed French cuffs, cleared his throat and made his pronouncement. "We're going to have to bite the bullet on this one. Brookline has worked this deal as hard as any we've done in the past five years." As with his attire, Carleton could never be accused of understatement. "Despite our best efforts, I think this has to be priced at fifteen dollars if we're going to get it done, and my considered opinion is that you don't dare try to go out with a million shares. We may have to cut back the size of the offering at the last minute."

As Robertson and Carleton discussed the strategy for the last week of selling effort, Tim stared out across the now empty restaurant and watched as one of the waiters went over to the Puerto Rican bus boy cleaning one of the tables. The waiter handed some money to the bus boy who put down his wet rag and counted the bills three times, mouthing the count with a deliberateness sufficient to allow Tim to follow along from across the room with his high school Spanish still proficient enough to recognize – quatro, cinco, seis. Tim knew the routine, and it brought back uncomfortable memories.

Years ago at college, one of his several jobs had been as a waiter at the Notre Dame Alumni Club. He had been a bus boy first and then spent two years as a waiter. At the end of each shift, the headwaiter would split the tip pool between himself, the various waiters, and the bus boys, on a formula agreed to by the staff, but under the watchful eye of no one but the headwaiter. Tim and his friends were convinced that they were getting shorted by the headwaiter, and Tim swore when he moved into that job during his last semester in college that he would always do a straight count. And he did a straight count, until the night the tipsy alumni from Nebraska handed him a $50 bill and told him to split it between the boys.

Now, some twenty years later, Tim still felt a twinge of guilt about having pocketed the bill for himself, using the fifty dollars to fix his car. He had needed money then, and he needed it now, or at least Remote did. Even though he had been with the company for only six months, it was sometimes difficult for him to tell where Tim Foster stopped and Remote Monitoring started. It was not going to get any easier.

When the deal was finally priced during the following week, it was not at the $15 level that Carleton had warned them about, but at $13.50. And it was not for one million shares, but for 800,000. So instead of raising $20 million for the company the offering brought in $10,800,000, and that was before the selling syndicate discounts and underwriters fees. Brookline got paid first – off the top.

"You know the worst thing about this whole deal is that my dad bought 1,000 shares from Brookline and another 2,000 through his broker in Indiana," Tim was talking to his wife as they were unpacking boxes in their house. Their move from Minnesota was now complete, but the joy of new home ownership had been tempered as they had watched the stock slide to $12 during the week after the offering as healthcare stocks continued to take a beating in the market. "I didn't know he was going to do it, but when I talked to mom yesterday she said that he took a loan against his retirement plan to buy the stock. That's all I need! I've got a bunch of employees who never owned stock before spending half their day figuring their losses, I got a company that went public but only got half the money we wanted, and a dad with a bad heart who bet his retirement plan on the hope that his son would make him rich."

"Look at the bright side," Britta said. "It's got to get better from here on out."

She was wrong! Two days later when Tim looked at the mail on his desk at the office, he saw a small white envelope hand-addressed to Tim Foster, President Remote Monitoring. The word confidential was in block letters on the lower left of the envelope. There was no return address. As Tim looked at the lettering, he felt an ominous foreboding. There was something familiar about the handwriting. He had seen it before and it was not in a pleasant setting.

"I got a letter from Maynard today," he told Britta that evening. He had originally planned not to tell her, but changed his mind as he reread the letter during the day.

"Oh my God!" she said in a voice that drew a look of concern from the twins in the next room. "How did he find you?"

"He got a copy of the prospectus on the Remote offering and saw my name listed as president holding a bunch of stock options. Even at $12 a share the options will be worth a lot some day if I stay at Remote. Maynard never much liked me when I was poor. He sure doesn't like me now that he thinks I'm rich."

"What did he say in the letter?" Britta was speaking more softly now and had closed the door leading to the TV room.

"He rambled on about how I was responsible for derailing his career at Aortek and ruining his changes for med school, and then he wrote about how his life had been screwed up ever since and how I'm the one to blame. He said he'd find a way to get even some day."

"I want to see the letter!"

"No, I don't think so," Tim said softly. Even with the subdued tone to his voice, it was obvious that he had thought about his answer for a while. "I've locked it up at the office. I wasn't even going to tell you at first, but I thought you should know in case you see anything unusual. I think he's just blowing smoke, but I'm not sure. He was nuts when I worked with him several years ago. Who knows what he's like today."

CHAPTER SIXTEEN
The Farm

Eighteen hundred miles away in Boston, Mary Devlin had seen the same prospectus. Maynard Branson had sent her a copy. No letter, no discussion, just a cryptic note – 'see page 17 – management personnel'. Branson was one of the holdovers from Mary's Animal Rescue Band days in England. One of the few people she knew who had been active in the movement in both England and the US. One of the few people she knew in the movement who gave her concerns about her own security, her own personal safety.

Although she continued to participate in a few of the ARB exploits around the Boston area, Mary had backed off from involvement in some of the more radical activities as her responsibilities at Peter Bent Brigham Hospital had grown. Now an American citizen, it had been eleven years since Mary had responded to the ad in *The London Times* and started the sequence of events that brought her eventually to the United States.

> Registered Nurses sought for employment in Boston. Assistance provided for US Immigration and Green Card. Apply in person at Medical Staffing Ltd., 416 Charing Cross Road, London.

She often thought of how different it might have been if Jeffrey was still alive. The five years they had lived together in London had, in retrospect, been one of the happiest periods of her life, although far from uneventful. In those years, Mary had been increasing her involvement in the ARB, always careful to do so without jeopardizing her position at St. George's, always cautious to maintain a patina of professionalism – no marching in the public demonstrations, no arrests, no pictures in the paper.

"You're our best kept secret, Mary," Jeffrey had said one time. "We need you working in an establishment position – allows you to do things and go places that the rest of us can't."

Mary's name never would have made it into the London papers if it had not been for the contested will and the resultant publicity in one of London's major papers.

> "*Sir Malcolm Anndover contests will that turns over £2 million estate to son's live-in girlfriend.*" Sir Malcolm states that his grief over his son's tragic death last month in an auto accident on the M4 Motorway has now been compounded by realization that the proceeds of the trust fund established for 36-year-old Jeffrey will be awarded to Ms. Mary Devlin under the terms of his son's will. Miss Devlin, 30, a nurse at St. George's Hospital, was apparently as surprised as anyone to learn of her newfound wealth. "I had no idea Jeffrey had this level of assets, nor did I know that I was named in his will. Money was not important to Jeffrey – he was a man of principle and I loved him very much."

Although the reporter had taken some journalistic liberty with the quote, the point was essentially correct. While Mary was aware that Jeffrey had some money coming from a trust, she was amazed to learn of the size of the fund, and shocked to find that she was the sole beneficiary. She was also surprised to find herself in the middle of a public flap, and the prospect of being involved in litigation over a contested will was not something that she could envision.

"I don't want to fight it," she told one of Jeffrey's ARB friends. "I came from Birmingham without money, I didn't know it was there when I lived with Jeffrey, and I don't need it now. Malcolm can have it."

"Don't be an ass, Mary," the friend had said. "Think of what that money can do, if not for you then for the movement, for the animals. If it's not needed now then put it away, or invest it. Sometime, someplace, that money will make the difference for us, for the movement. Jeffrey would have wanted you to do that. Trust me!"

In the end she compromised and settled with Sir Malcolm's solicitor. St. George's would get a donation of £1 million in the name of the Anndover family for a new pediatric wing, and she would retain the other £1 million. But the publicity surrounding the incident made it difficult for Mary to remain at St. George's, and so the opportunity to work as a nurse in Boston came at the right moment. Two weeks after her first visit to 416 Charing Cross Road, Mary was taking her nursing board exam with 120 other applicants at the Armory in Boston, and six days after that she started work at Peter Bent Brigham.

"Give me some time to settle in," Mary had told the part-time paralegal and full time ARB activist who contacted her a month later, after an introduction by Jeffrey's friend in London. "I'm not ready to get involved yet. I need to get myself established at the hospital before I go sneaking around at midnight in some dog lab."

"We really need you to help set up a training program," was the response. "We get an odd assortment of people who want to do something with us, but they all need training. We know you did some of that in England, and if you could work with the extremists over there you sure can handle the kind of people we have over here."

"Listen," Mary said, a little annoyed, "you Yanks think we had all the crazy zealots over there. Some of the oddest ducks I had at the farm were from the States." Mary did not go into any more detail on her experience with Americans in training, but the one individual who had raised the most concern was never far from her mind.

The first contact with the American had taken place the year before Jeffrey died, when she set up a meeting to talk with Maynard prior to the start of a training session. Even then, Mary thought that Maynard had enough quirks in his background to warrant some additional attention. Part of her caution was based on her inherent suspicion of the establishment, and part on Jeffrey's insistence regarding the need for subterfuge. One of their group had recently been questioned by an inspector from Scotland Yard after a tip had been phoned in by someone overhearing a conversation on the train, and Jeffrey was at his paranoid best.

"The thing you always have to realize, Mary, is that not only do we have to worry about the authorities, but the average bloke on the street will turn us in if he gets the chance." Jeffrey was on his soapbox again after the close call with Scotland Yard. "The media has the public convinced that we're a bunch of Reds trying to ruin the industrial state. Your own brother might turn you in if he knew what you were doing on weekends and holidays."

"He just might turn me in," Mary thought, "but I doubt it." In any event, on this assignment she had taken pains to ensure that no one would be aware of her schedule, and that included Maynard Branson, with whom she was scheduled to meet in one hour.

Mary had taken the Friday afternoon train from Victoria Station in London to Canterbury, and stayed overnight at the Post Hotel. On Saturday morning she arranged for one of the women from the farm to pick her up in the van and drive her to the King's Head Inn on the road to Marley. The directions that had been sent to Maynard some three weeks before indicated that he should arrive at the King's Head at 1 p.m. on Saturday, June 14th, and be prepared to spend the next seven days at a training site somewhere in the south of England. Mary arrived at the Inn at 11:30 and gave instructions to the van driver to stop back at 2:15.

The King's Head is one of those quaint English countryside inns that tourists love to look for but rarely actually find. Twelve miles outside of Canterbury on a road that leads to an area of no great importance, the King's Head had served as a local stopover for travelers dating back to 1806. With thick stucco walls, rounded window openings, and the obligatory thatched roof, the Inn boasted a total of seven sleeping rooms on the second floor, up a narrow stairway made even narrower by a collection of some 200 framed photos and assorted memorabilia collected by the current owner. Mary and Jeffrey had stayed in Room Number 3 on a cold, fall weekend a few years before. The thought of the four-poster bed and thick woolen comforter brought back some pleasant memories, but on this day, Mary was all business. Mary Devlin, ARB activist, provocateur, propagandist, trainer, recruiter, but also judge and jury with regard to this American visitor who claimed a growing interest in the radical edge of the US animal rights movement.

As Mary's experience and stature had grown within the ARB, Jeffrey had given her veto power over who got close to the group – who became privy to the organization and personnel of the British movement. Always alert for attempts at infiltration from the UK authorities, Mary was no less vigilant when it came to judging the bona-fides of the non British applicants who managed to make their way to the group for indoctrination and training. Maynard Branson had been trying for nine months to line up a visit to the farm, and had been pushing his small contact list with a level of urgency that had Mary more than a little cautious.

*

And now Mary was sitting in the dining room of the King's Head, half way through a Shepherd's pie and a glass of bitter. The tabletops in this room of the Inn were made from six foot lengths of rough-sawn cedar timber, the rounded edges of the tables and benches worn smooth by decades of arms covered by coarse sewn sleeves and jackets, and more recently by the denim fabrics popular among the modern day gentry who made their way down from London for a Sunday brunch in the country. Although most of the tables could comfortably seat six or eight people, Mary was sitting at a small side table, this one located near a huge open hearth fireplace designed and built in an era when the open hearths served multiple functions within a public building. This fireplace was so large that it contained a small niche called the preacher's cove, where folklore held that the local preacher could be hidden in the event that religious allegiances changed on short notice. Mary and Jeffrey had once squeezed into the narrow cove, drinking hot cider and warming their bones after a brisk two-hour walk in the forest which abutted the Inn's property.

On the mantle above the fireplace, barely visible after years of dirt and dust accumulation, was the inscription, "Fear knocked on the door, Faith answered, No one was there." Although she had pondered the rather enigmatic meaning before, on this day Mary thought it might be especially appropriate as she watched the door for the entrance of someone whom she knew only by one faxed photo and the description of tall and slender.

At twenty-six years of age, Maynard Branson had only been involved with the fringe edge of the animal rights movement for two years, but he had spent most of his life on the fringe of something. Growing up in the Seattle, Washington, area where his father worked as an engineer for Boeing and his mother spent much of her time lamenting the fact that her classical music training at Juliard had gone unrewarded, Maynard had a childhood that could best be described as problematic. Of all the intellectual and social pressures with which his parents burdened him at an early age, probably the most offensive was the study of the violin, reinforced by a minimum of two hours daily practice and a music camp each summer. At the end of one such camp, when Maynard was thirteen, he came home without his violin, and in what would prove to be the first of several face-offs with his parents, not only declined to talk about its disappearance but also steadfastly refused to touch a musical instrument of any description thereafter. He did manage to maintain the interest in computers that his father encouraged, and actually obtained some level of local notoriety as the school kid with software programming expertise well beyond that of most industry experts.

Always gangly and uncoordinated as a child, Maynard still had the appearance of someone who had grown too tall for his clothes. As Mary watched him enter and look around the dining room, she was immediately struck by the perception that this was a man who found very little in life about which he could be positive. Mary was careful not to make eye contact, since she wanted to observe him at a distance before introducing herself. Maynard did not know who was going to meet him, only that he was to be at the Inn no later than 1 p.m. It was now 12:40, and as Mary watched, Branson placed a backpack near the front door and walked through the dining room to an unoccupied table in the rear, ducking under one of the large wooden support beams, which although bowed slightly, had been holding up the second floor of the King's Head for over 175 years. For the next 30 minutes, Mary continued to observe as Maynard went through the motions of eating, picking rather casually through a collection of cooked carrots and potatoes while periodically reminding the waitress about the wisdom of including more vegetarian selections on the menu. When he looked at his watch for the third time, Mary thought that perhaps she had been observing long enough.

"Are you Maynard?" she asked as she sat down across from him, carefully placing a cup of tea on one of the thick paper coasters stacked near the center of the table.

"Yes, I'm Maynard Branson. I was getting a little worried that I might be at the wrong place. What's your name?" He extended a hand which Mary shook reluctantly, preferring that their meeting not draw any attention from the few people still sitting at the other tables.

"My name is Mary. It's not necessary that you know my last name, and I'd prefer that from now on you not use yours. If we take you into training you'll come to realize the importance of some basic security precautions. The limited use of names is one. You'll not be told the full name of others that you meet and they are not to be told yours."

"Whaddya mean 'if' you take me into training? Why do you think I'm over here? Gorski said it was all set up when he called me last week. He said if I was really serious about this I needed to spend some time with you Brits. Go to the farm, he said." Branson seemed to be sitting at attention, back straight, chin elevated, almost towering over Mary although both were still seated.

"I'll make the decision on who we accept into our little training program. Not one of your American friends and certainly not the name you mentioned thirty seconds after I told you not to use proper names! You are not to refer to our location again in public, and certainly not when you have a waitress twelve inches away from your nose." Mary was speaking softly but with an obvious tone of authority in her voice that was not lost on Branson. "You and I are going to have a nice quiet chat over some more tea," she continued, "then I'll let you know if we'll be spending more time together."

And then Mary began asking a series of questions, some clearly related, others not, her style still authoritarian but less admonishing than before. If someone had been listening to the dialogue without the ability to see the two participants, there would have been a presumption that Mary was reading from a list of prepared questions, so paced and methodical was her delivery. 'Do you have siblings? – Have you been arrested? – What technical skills do you have? – Why did you study physics? – Do you have pets? – Why aren't you married? – Do you know another language?' Dozens of questions. And just when Branson thought he saw a structure, a direction, Mary would switch course and probe another area of his background and thought process. But gradually there was a pattern that emerged, the nucleus around which the other atoms had been circulating – the Motivation. What was the Motivation?

Over the past several years, as Mary had gradually been developing her skills relating to the evaluation of people, she'd come to realize that her final comfort level almost always revolved around her assessment of the individual's stated motivation for involvement with the animal rights movement. Was it a hatred for all things commercial? Was there a personal experience involved? Was it the cause of the month club? There was no single best answer. Clearly every person's experiences and beliefs were different, but Mary wanted to understand the 'why'. Why were these people willing to disrupt their lives, risk arrest, and generally commit to the use of various forms of terrorism? Why were they willing to go underground, turn their backs on traditional forms of authority and then submit to new authority in some group of unknown activists? This was the gut question for Mary. Were these people, and particularly someone like Maynard Branson, prepared to follow orders within the fuzzy hierarchical structure of the ARB, or would they continue to exhibit the divergent behavior that probably brought them here in the first place. Maynard showed every sign of being a loose cannon, and Mary was already thinking that unless she could figure out a way to tie him to the deck, he should probably never see the farm.

"And so, Maynard," she said, "tell me some more about why you are here. Why do you want to join our group?" They had moved from the dining area and were now in the small pub room of the King's Head. The ceilings were even lower here and the room was almost dark, even in midday. The bartender had brought two pints of lager to their small corner booth and they were now alone. Mary had learned that the best way to get an answer to her simple 'why' question was to spend a lot of time being quiet. "Don't blink first," Jeffrey had told her once. "Keep staring 'em down. Sooner or later you might get the real answer." And so Mary stared, rubbing her finger over the top of her lager mug, looking past Maynard's left shoulder at the dartboard on the opposite wall.

"I think it's a disgrace how companies use animals in research," he began, "at least American companies. I don't know how it works over here, but some people in the States do things you wouldn't believe. I think we ought to do something about it. Put a stop to it, I mean." Mary nodded her head, looking directly at him this time. Branson was moving his upper body slowly in his chair, left to right, left to right. "I really get sick of the whole scene," he said, still rocking in his chair. "I'm not the kind who writes letters to congressmen so I decided to come over here."

Mary continued to nod her head slowly, pausing only long enough to take a swallow from her mug. She looked directly at Branson. She did not blink.

"I don't know what else I can tell you. I wanna have some influence on changing things, and you people are supposed to have the best record in getting something to happen. Action – know what I mean? Not just bullshit – carrying around a bunch of protest signs." He had stopped moving. "That's really all there is to it. That's why I'm here."

The door opened and two men in dark colored work clothes and Wellington boots came in and sat on stools by the bar. When the bar man did not come out from the kitchen right away, one of the men walked behind the counter and poured two large glasses of bitter, obviously accustomed to the casual afternoon routine. Mary watched as the men settled into a friendly discussion about cattle prices, and then she looked back at Branson. This time she blinked.

"Well, Maynard, I doubt that's all there is to it. Why don't you tell me what really got you to move? There are thousands of people in the States who don't like cruelty to animals, but they don't quit their jobs and come over to England to join the ARB. What was it that moved you, Maynard? You still haven't told me."

"I did tell you. I told you I wanted to see things changed – put a stop to this bullshit research. I saw enough of that!"

Mary leaned forward, put both hands around her mug, and stared directly into Branson's face. "You haven't told me a sodding thing!" she said, leaning another inch closer. "I don't give a toss about how you want to change the world. I need you to tell me what really moved you, what got your American ass on that plane to come over here. You've been feeding me bits and bobs about companies doing experiments with animals. Tell me about that, Maynard. Tell me what happened where you worked."

The men at the bar signaled for two more glasses of bitter. The barman was there this time, a burly-faced man who looked like he might have been bred expressly for the purpose of drawing beer in an English pub. Maynard glanced over to the bar and then looked back at Mary.

"I worked at Aortek," he said finally.

"I know that," Mary said, "I've seen the report." In fact Mary had never even heard of the company, and certainly had not seen any report. One of the many tricks that Jeffrey had taught her was to suggest that she had access to confidential information, information she could use to verify the background of an individual or the story being told. "Tell me exactly what happened at Aortek, and what you did there, Maynard. I need to confirm that you're really the person you say you are. If you can convince me of that, then maybe we'll take you out to the farm today."

And so Maynard told the story, his story about Aortek and what went on there. He talked about how he had gotten hired, what he did at the company, and eventually how he left. All the time Mary was listening intently, occasionally nodding her head as if to indicate that the story tracked with the information she had been given previously. She stopped him at one point in the telling of the story, asking him to stay at the table while she took their two glasses to the bar for a refill. There were other people in the pub now, including a woman in a dark cardigan sweater to whom Mary spoke briefly.

When Maynard finished talking, he was visibly upset. Whether from anger or some other pent up emotion, Mary was not sure. But she made the determination that his reactions were authentic, and that this was a young man driven by events that had overtaken him – by an environment that had permanently altered his viewpoint of society. He might still be a loose cannon, but she at least knew what direction he was pointed. She had the 'why'.

"Well, Maynard, that fills in some of the blanks and it squares with the report I've seen. Later this week when we're at the farm I want you to write down everything you've just told me, plus I want the names of the people in those positions you mentioned. Someday the world will know what happened there. Someday we'll get the story out in the right way, at the right time. Trust me." Mary stood up and motioned Maynard to follow her out the door.

"Are we going to the farm now?" he asked. "I have to follow you – I have a bike."

"You mean you rode out from town?"

"I rode out from London. From Gatwick Airport."

"From Gatwick? That must be eighty-five miles!"

"It's ninety-two. I like to ride a bike."

"You can't ride it, Maynard," Mary finally said. "Nobody drives themselves to the farm for the first time. Makes no difference if you've got a car or bike. Basic security. You've got to go in the back of the van." The woman that Mary had spoken to briefly in the pub had now pulled up near them in the car park, driving a dirty brown Volkswagen van. If someone had looked closely at the van, they would have observed that the side and rear windows were painted over and the registration plates were smudged with enough dirt to discourage all but the closest inspection. The inside of the van had also been modified. All of the rear seats had been removed and a wooden partition had been installed behind the front seat, blocking all forward vision from the back storage area unless a small panel was opened by the driver.

"I can put my bike in the rear of the van." Maynard walked over and was looking at the back door of the vehicle. "It'll fit in here."

Mary thought about this for a moment and then agreed. "Okay, you can put your bike in there providing that we can get the door closed. You will not be able to see out as we're driving to the farm, and when you get there you'll be searched. Clothes, backpack, bike – everything. If you want to change your mind, now's the time to do it."

"I don't."

For the next 30 minutes, they drove a series of country roads with just enough turns and double-backs to confuse anyone attempting to memorize the route while sitting in the darkened back section of the van. This was actually the farthest thing from Branson's mind, as he leaned against the wooden partition and held on to his bike so it would not rub against the two wire dog cages sliding back and forth as the van negotiated a series of hills on the road south of Canterbury. The farm that was their destination was about two miles from the small village of West Fenton. A rolling parcel of land covering 280 acres, the property had once been two farms before it came into the hands of the ARB.

A fourth generation farmer by the name of Robert Walkensford had inherited the original 160-acre farm from his father in 1953 and then purchased the adjacent 120 acres in 1967. For reasons that no one clearly remembered later, Robert sought out contact with some of England's early animal rights activists in the 60s, and then changed his land use from cattle to small grain farming. With no children or other close relatives, Robert and his wife decided to deed their property over to the use of the ARB in 1978 when they retired to a small house in Bristol. Jeffrey had arranged for a friendly London attorney to register the property in the name of a trust called Friends of the Land, and the farm had been used for a training facility and interim animal hospital ever since.

The original Walkensford Farmhouse was located at the end of a long curved lane, and had been shielded from view off the main road by a stand of aspen and poplar trees. The small house which stood on the adjacent acreage had remained in use, visible from the main road, and listed in the county records as the only home on the farm. When they had taken possession of the property, Jeffrey and some of the other group leaders decided to block off the main drive to the Walkensford house with additional tree and shrub plantings. A narrow lane, which had been cleared from behind the smaller house, was hidden behind a natural swale in the land and ran some 500 yards through the fields to the larger home. The new lane passed through an old rock wall near the small house, the narrow opening in the wall marked by paint scrapings of vehicles that had cut the corner a little too close.

The van was some five miles away from the property when Mary slid back the narrow panel in the partition and looked in at Branson. "We'll be there in another ten minutes or so. How're you doing back there?"

"My bike is getting scratched."

"There goes the neighborhood," Mary smiled a little and moved over closer to the small opening in the panel. "I want to tell you a little bit about what to expect when we get there," she said, talking loudly so she could be heard above the din of the van's engine. "There will be nine of you going through training this week. Six from the UK, two from France, and you. It's first names only for everybody, including the instructors. This is Sue, by the way," Mary said glancing over at the driver, "she's our chauffeur, cook, nurse, and general ramrod. I know I asked you a lot about your background, but don't tell anyone else who you are, and don't ask them for any information. You're going to be here for seven days, no phone, no posting of letters, no long walks. We'll eat all our meals together, work together – play together. We don't sleep together, Maynard. That and breaking security will get you thrown out."

They were turning into the driveway leading to the small house. Nigel and Elizabeth Patton had been living there for the past six years, farming the land and generally keeping an eye on things. Nigel was the uncle of one of the early ARB members, now spending a few years in a cell near Dover after a spot of arson at a meat packing plant. Both Nigel and Elizabeth had some general knowledge of what went on at the main house, but had been instructed to keep their distance and saw no reason to do otherwise. Their only tangential involvement with the activities was an understanding that they would ring up if they saw anything unusual happening on the main road. Nigel also had an old Ford tractor hooked up to a wagon, which in turn was filled with four tons of fieldstone and positioned near the gap in the wall where he could pull it into position to block any access to the lane if he were ever called upon to do so.

Mrs. Patton was standing in the yard when the van pulled through. Mary waved and grabbed onto the door handle as Sue downshifted for the rough ride on the field road. "You're the last one to arrive," Mary said, turning her head towards the panel. "Once we get there you can take your stuff to the barn where you'll get searched and then we'll start the first session on the porch at the house."

Although Robert Walkensford had not seen the property since he and his wife left several years ago, he would have been pleased to know that the large, double-gabled barn that he built in 1972 was still in excellent repair although now serving a purpose much different from that originally intended. The old milking parlor had been turned into two large sleeping rooms, austere by way of furniture and decoration, but certainly functional for their intended use. The segregated toilets and shower facilities were located in an adjacent room which had once served as the milk storage and processing area. The bedrooms and lavatories were spotless, and as each group of trainees found out on arrival, would be kept by them in that condition as one demonstration that there were certain basic levels of discipline that would be maintained during their short stay on the farm.

Several of the other outbuildings between the house and the barn had been converted over the past few years to new uses, including a large equipment shed that now served as a temporary recovery area and animal motel for the menagerie of non-human guests that were brought to the farm after liberation from various caged environs. All of the buildings, including the house, were in good condition and obviously well maintained. The first-time visitor was almost always struck by the contrast between the generally ragtag appearance of the ARB activists and the conditions maintained at the farm. The early involvement of some skilled trade unionists, and the willingness of Jeffrey to spend sponsors' money on the cause rather than the people, had started this trend towards orderliness, and some of the key players, including Mary, had pushed to see it continue.

On this day, Maynard and the others had gathered on the sprawling front porch of the old house, waiting to find out what the week would hold for them, anxious to be more involved but reluctant to make the first move. Although a few of the group were acquainted from prior association, most had never met, and with the security lecture still ringing in their ears, were now taking pains to remain distant from each other. At 5 p.m. sharp, Mary and three others came out of the house and motioned for everyone to sit down.

"I vetted some of you over the past few months so I know a little about you. My name is Mary, and you've heard the rules on names, so we won't go beyond that. For the next seven days you're going to get the best training we can provide. Nothing that we do here on the farm is illegal, but how you use it will be, and we do expect you to use it. If you haven't made that commitment then you shouldn't be here. One of the classes we'll have covers the history and philosophy of our movement. You may think you understand why we're doing this but I assure you that you have only touched the surface. Animal rights is not just a phase, it must be a mission – a passion for you. And it's not enough for you to abandon old exploitive attitudes, now you've got to roll back what others have done. You've got to help stop the atrocity that goes on every day with the treatment of animals in this country and around the world!"

Mary always tried to gear herself up for this speech when she did the introductory segment. She knew that Jeffrey was so much better at this, his passion obvious, his intensity contagious. With Mary it was something she had to work on, consciously raising her voice and making eye contact. Jeffrey was supposed to be here this week to do the overview as well as the daily lectures on ethics and principles, but he had called from London the day before saying he would be delayed. "I should be there by mid-week," he told Mary. "You can cover for me."

The other parts of the training program were less of an issue for Mary, the so-called trade craft – the tools, the techniques, the actual methods used to delay, disrupt and if necessary destroy the programs and facilities of those individuals or companies targeted for action by the ARB. For each of these topics there was an assigned instructor, either now at the farm or scheduled to arrive during the week. David Thikens, a communications engineer with British Rail, was spending a week's holiday at the farm and would be covering basic electronics, sidestepping of security systems, cutting of phone lines, use of walkie-talkies and other related devices. Ronald Atwood, a Canadian now married to an Englishwoman, brought a military background and bearing to a variety of miscellaneous subjects including the setting of fires, use of disguises, picking of locks, and other assorted tricks of the trade that he had acquired officially or unofficially over the years.

The one person on the schedule that never failed to surprise the trainees was Sue Hawthorne, the all-purpose player who was a full-time resident on the farm. A slightly overweight woman with short, curly, red hair, Sue had worked with Mary at St. George's Hospital until two years before, when a failed marriage and the overuse of medication brought about a personal crisis ending with the loss of her job and a battle with severe depression. With more than a little help from Mary, Sue had bounced back and eventually got actively involved with the ARB. Her part of the program was to discuss the concern that the movement had with infiltration, and how to spot someone trying to dig out information. She also covered the questions regarding what to do and say if you were arrested. Usually taciturn and withdrawn, Sue would become animated and verbal when she talked about dealing with the police, leaving the distinct impression that she was not basing her advice on third party information.

"One other key aspect of your training will take place on Thursday," Mary was finishing up her overview, looking around slowly to be sure she still had everyone's attention. "Dr. Ted will be coming down from London. He's a vet, and he'll be showing you how to handle animals of all shapes and sizes in stressful situations. How to do injections, use sedatives – things like that." She looked again at each face in the group, not really asking for questions but trying to determine the mood, the degree of interest. Already there was an apparent separation between Maynard and the others. While they were relaxed and communicative, he appeared withdrawn, almost distant, as if he was now embarking on a mission from which there was not likely to be a return. Mary continued, "we're going to eat at six and have our first session at seven. Not ten past, not five past, but seven, bang-on!"

It was bang-on for the rest of the week, everything on schedule as planned, until Wednesday morning during a break when Sue came running into the house looking for Mary. "He's taken off!" she yelled. "Maynard's taken off on his bike down the back lane going towards the road!"

Mary grabbed the phone in the kitchen and called the number from memory. "Nigel," Mary yelled, "I want you to move that wagon and block the gate. Hurry! There's a bike coming!"

Five minutes later, after finally getting the Ford tractor started, Nigel was standing behind the wagon looking out towards the front road for some sort of biker when Maynard rode slowly up behind him and tapping him on the shoulder. "Jesus and Mary!" Nigel shouted, turning around with a look of panic. "Don't scare me like that, lad. I was looking for someone from the front."

"Sorry about that," Maynard said, surprised himself at Nigel's reaction. "I wonder if you can move this wagon. I'd like to take a ride out on the road."

Nigel's response was cut short by the sound of a van coming at full speed down the lane, horn fully engaged. "Where the hell are you going?" Mary shouted as she jumped out from behind the wheel. "You're not allowed to leave the property during training!"

"I was just going to do a few miles while we were on break," Maynard said, almost shrinking backward from this woman standing in front of him, hands on hips, visibly upset. "I'm a biker, Mary, I've got to ride or the legs go bad. Just a couple of miles and I'll be right back."

"In the van, Maynard! You and the bike! And when we get back, your front wheel goes in my room under the bed. You can climb steps if you need a workout."

Although no awards were given at the end of the seven days, if there had been one it would have gone to Branson. Jeffrey had arrived late in the week, and even after hearing about the bike incident, was impressed, as were the others, by the knowledge and intensity exhibited by this young American.

"We have to figure a way to best utilize his skills and drive, Mary," Jeffrey had said as they were watching Maynard conduct a session on how to get false IDs. "He could be what they need in the States to really get the ARB off the ground over there."

"I don't know, Jeffrey," Mary said. "He's like a coiled spring. You don't know when it's gonna snap back and hit you in the face."

"It's energy, Mary. Pure energy. We need that. Did he give you the report?"

"Yeah – he fixed our computer and wrote a twelve-page report. It's all there, all the names, all the details."

"We'll use him, Mary. We need people like that."

"He scares me."

"I know, but we'll use him."

CHAPTER SEVENTEEN
The Queen

Jay Harris had decided to take the 8 a.m. Metroliner for the train ride from Washington's Union station into Baltimore. He could have signed out a pool car and driven the 35 miles, but he hated to battle the beltway traffic if he could avoid it, and he liked trains – even for short rides. There had been some question about whether or not he should call Martha Laudner or David Morkin to set up an appointment for the visit, but in the end it was decided to follow the 'knock on the door – flash the badge – and start asking questions' routine.

"It's not like I'll be flying across the country," Jay was on the phone with Mark Brinkman, the Baltimore agent who would assist with the local interview. "If she's tied up I'll come back in the afternoon or the next day. If I call to set something up, then we get scheduled behind six other appointments."

"Well, either way I'll pick you up at the train station tomorrow morning and we'll drive together to their office. By then I'll have a little more background on the firm. I haven't learned much so far. This is a low profile company locally, even though they apparently have a national reputation in their field. David Morkin is the founder and senior partner. This woman Laudner is the only other partner and it looks like they have two or three associates plus some clerical help. Technically they're both partners, but since Morkin is the senior one I suppose he's the boss."

"Okay. We'll talk to him first. I'll see you outside the station around 9:30 tomorrow."

Harris had been asked to move the AMMA File to top priority among the five serial cases he was following. Stinnett had finally accepted the logic that there could be another hit expected in three or four weeks, and that, plus Bob Kaufmann's concern over possible negative publicity for the Bureau, had moved the wheels of justice into high gear. Stinnett now had five agents working with him full time in the Washington office – two assigned to the investigation of various animal rights group, two coordinating the field office activities, and Agent Landau liaising with the American Medical Manufacturers Association and trying desperately to make some connection between the names. There were also fourteen field agents working the case full time, including four who were attending every 'Save the Whales' and 'Dog Lovers' protest they could find in the hopes of getting someone under cover to shore up what had been discovered to be a very weak and outdated list of informers. The other ten agents were assigned, one to each individual file, to make background checks. What was the man's job? – Were they using animals at the company as part of their testing or research program? – Had he received warnings? – Did his coworkers know any of the other names on the list?

Jay's efforts over the previous several days had been limited to polishing his preliminary suspect profile and getting it distributed to the key agents on the case. His meeting at David Morkin and Associates would be his first foray out of the basement lair – his first chance to talk with someone who might just know enough about the people in the companies and the industry to give him that extra insight – the extra footprint in the sand that he could follow to the connection and conclusion that he knew had to be there.

"David, there are two men here who want to see you." Sandy Taylor had been David Morkin's secretary for three years and usually felt comfortable handling the cold-call visitors, but she sensed there might be something different about these two dark-suited, non-smiling, uninvited guests.

"Are they selling something?" David asked.

"These guys don't look like salesmen, but in any event they wouldn't tell me what they wanted. Said they needed to speak with you about that."

When Sandy brought the two men into his office, David stood up to introduce himself but decided not to extend his hand when he saw the serious look on the faces of his two visitors. "Mr. Morkin, I'm Agent Harris and this is Agent Brinkman. We're with the Federal Bureau of Investigation and we'd like to ask you a few questions." Jay had offered his badge for inspection, but David seemed too surprised to take notice. "I wonder if you'd mind if we shut the door," Harris continued, moving over to close the office door behind a slowly departing and very curious Sandy Taylor.

As the two agents seated themselves in the chairs facing his desk, David still had not managed to utter his first word, his mind racing through a litany of real and imagined misdeeds that might have brought about this visit. "Tax returns? – Antitrust? – Inside information? That's got to be it," he thought. "I bought stock in Meridian Bio Tech after we hired the new CEO but before the public knew. They've been monitoring my account!"

"Mr. Morkin, am I correct that your firm does executive recruitment for companies in the medical device and biotech industry?" Harris asked a visibly shaken David Morkin.

"Yes, that's correct," David said, in a voice that suggested a noticeable lack of confidence.

"And as such, you have access to files and background information that goes well beyond what the general public might have available?"

David's heart rate had risen to a level that he thought could surely be heard by the two men on the other side of the desk. "I trade four hundred shares of stock and make nine hundred dollars," he thought, "and now I'm nailed. I'll have to leave the business." He stared past Harris, contemplating how he would explain the loss of a quarter million dollar annual income to his wife.

"Mr. Morkin," Jay repeated, "am I correct that your firm is concentrating your work in this area?"

"Yes, you are," David finally said, his pulse and mind still racing. Again the images flashed before him – "bring out the cuffs, I'll go quietly, you've got me."

"And is Martha Laudner working with you in this area – in the development of your database?"

A ray of hope! Martha never trades the market. For the first time David began thinking this just might be something else. Heart rate slowing – a gradual return of reason and logic to this man who only moments before was one question away from Leavenworth. He took a deep breath, looked Harris straight in the eye, and said, "Miss Laudner is very active in the development of our proprietary database, but I need to ask you what this is about. What is it that you're looking for?"

"I can give you some information about this inquiry," Harris said, "but I have to stress that it must be held in the strictest confidence. Any premature disclosure of this information could jeopardize the results of the investigation that we're conducting."

"Of course," David said, so relieved that he would have agreed to stay inside for the next year if Harris had asked.

And so, while Agent Brinkman sat passively, Harris went through a brief overview of the file. No names were mentioned, including AMMA. No more information than absolutely necessary. No suggestion that the FBI was stumped on the connection. 'A few suspicious deaths in the industry – might be connected to the use of animal research – thought we'd take a quick peek in your files to fill in a few gaps – no big deal, just need a little help with some industry background.' Harris and Brinkman had talked about the approach in the car coming from the train station. Low key for now, '– don't send 'em running for the fire alarm.'

"I wonder if you could ask Miss Laudner to join us," Harris said when he had finished with his brief overview. "We'd like to ask her how the database is structured."

"She doesn't work out of this office," David said. He could not believe how good he felt, not just a sense of relief, but almost one of exhilaration. The bullet had missed and now they were asking him for help. "Martha works out of her apartment where she has the computer set up for data entry and review. But she's not there today. As a matter of fact she'll be gone for nine days."

"Where is she? Can we reach her by phone?"

"I don't know." David was actually smiling now, his sense of relief almost at the giddy stage. "This will sound crazy, but not only do I not know where she is, but she didn't know where she was going when she left this morning. She hasn't taken a vacation in years and her boyfriend – or significant other – or whatever you'd like to call him, called up last week and said he was going to take her on a mystery vacation. Nine days – he wouldn't tell her where. They left this morning."

"What about her family? Would they know where she is?" Jay was trying not to sound anxious, trying not to look at Brinkman for assistance.

"She doesn't have a family, and no – her staff wouldn't know where she is and they can't run the database inquiries for you. Neither could I, by the way. Martha has spent twelve years setting this up, figuring out a system to do cross tabulations and sorts based on all kinds of variables. Not only do I not know how to work the system, but if I got in there and tried, she'd probably hand me my head on a platter."

This time Harris did glance over at Agent Brinkman with a 'what next' look. "Exactly when will they return to Baltimore?" Jay asked, with an air of resignation in his voice.

"She said they'd be getting back next Tuesday night and that she would be in to work first thing Wednesday morning."

"Well, Mr. Morkin," Jay had pulled out one of his cards to hand him, "if by any chance she calls you I want you to have her contact me immediately. Otherwise we'll be back first thing next Wednesday morning to meet with you and her. In the meantime, I'd like to remind you to please keep this confidential."

As Harris and Brinkman left Morkin's office, the Queen Elizabeth 2, cruise ship extraordinaire and last of the great liners to schedule regular transatlantic crossings, was gently being nudged from her moorings and pointed towards the harbor exit. The two powerful tugboats at her side looked like guppies pushing against a whale, but eventually the great ship gained momentum and moved out into the Atlantic to begin the nine day round trip cruise to the Caribbean. The QE2 made only one stop a year in Baltimore, and the crowds that had lined the inner harbor to watch her departure were just beginning to go back to their normal routine when Joe Sheldon popped the cork on a champagne bottle in suite number 8007 on the penthouse level of the Queen. "Here's to a great cruise, and a great vacation," he said as he gave Martha her glass. "We're going to have nine days by ourselves – no phones, no FDA, no computers. You deserve some time off and who better to spend it with than me."

It had been only two hours since Vernika Petrosken had dropped them off at the dock. Joe had called the cab company the evening before and arranged for Vernika to pick them up the next morning as part of the surprise. As Joe was arranging for the luggage to be taken on board ship, Vernika pulled Martha aside.

"Marta – hold out your left hand. Vat you see on that hand, Marta?"

"What are you talking about?" Martha said. "There's nothing on that hand."

"Dat's my point, Marta! There's nothing there. No ring – noting!" Joe was starting to come towards them and Vernika turned Martha around and walked with her back to the cab. "Ven you get off this big ship I vant to see a ring on dat finger. Any man who takes you on a boat like this is looking for a vife. Trust me – I know these things. I'll pick you up in nine days. I vant to see the ring then Marta. No ring and you walk back to Front Street."

Martha was smiling, thinking about that conversation as she and Joe walked down the elegant but narrow hallways on the penthouse level of the QE2 towards their room. They were in one of the suites on the top deck of the ship, $5,100 for the nine days – EACH – although Martha would never see the bill. In addition to a huge bathroom, king-size bed, and a sitting area, the suite had a sliding glass door opening out onto a verandah with views of the ocean as well as the Promenade Deck. The verandah held two chairs and a chaise longue, thus enabling the occupants of the suite to take the sun at leisure without having to mingle with the commoners queuing up for seating around the pool on the fantail. Martha was almost, but not quite, at a loss for words.

"I can't believe we're here, Joe! This has to be the surprise vacation of all surprise vacations. I've never taken a cruise and I've never been to the Caribbean – and I've never spent nine days straight with you."

"Don't forget about the nine nights. Wait till you see me in my tux. I'm irresistible. Suave – debonair – and modest. Take your pick."

"I vote for modest now, but check back this evening and I'll let you know about irresistible."

That evening did challenge the meaning of irresistible, and completely threw out any hope for modesty. After a black-tie dinner in the Queen's Grill, the top restaurant on the QE2, Martha and Joe danced for an hour in the Grand Lounge, had a nightcap at the Midships Bar, and returned to their suite for a glass of champagne and a view of the moon off the verandah. Joe had removed his jacket and was leaning over their railing watching some of the couples strolling along the Promenade Deck.

Martha had her arm around Joe, pulling him towards her as they leaned against the rail. "When's the last time you made love on a verandah," she asked as she kissed him playfully on the cheek. "I think we should sleep out here in the nude tonight – save the maids the trouble of making the bed in the morning." She now had both her arms around him, unhooking the black tuxedo cummerbund and throwing it inside the room.

"I've made love on a verandah hundreds of times," Joe said, pressing his body against Martha and kissing her softly on the neck, "although I must admit that I have not done it on the QE2 and certainly not with someone of such beauty and charm." His arms were now around her, his hands searching for the clasp on the new gown she had worn for the first time that evening.

"You're fortunate that you're with such a nautical woman, one who appreciates the sea air, one who understands that there are certain movements not caused by the waves, but rather from other more basic forces." She was now unbuttoning Joe's shirt, her hands moving slowly over his chest. "I think you may have to leave the bow tie on," she said as she pulled the shirt away. "I like my men to be formally dressed when I make love," her hands had now moved down, gently touching and teasing, knowing this was going to be an evening to remember.

"I do think that, as a gentleman, I should remind you that we are just fifteen feet above the Promenade Deck. If you should start moaning in ecstasy you might draw a crowd below us, and I will be forced to defend your honor on the high seas." He had found the clasp on her dress, and was now kissing her bare shoulders, moving his hands over her body as she pushed her hips towards him.

"I won't scream if you don't," she said.

The bed did get used that night, but it was not for several hours, and not before the deck chairs and chaise longue had been moved off the verandah and the cushions had been placed strategically along the edge near the railing. Although their lovemaking had not drawn attention from the late night strollers on the deck below, it was not for lack of passion, and Martha was still in a romantic mood when she awoke the next morning.

"Hey, sailor," she said, nudging Joe until he was awake. "I see you still have your tie on. Do you plan on going to breakfast looking like that?" Martha had thrown back the covers on the bed, smiling at the strange sight of this gorgeous man, naked except for the black bow tie around his neck. Joe was struggling to wake up, reaching to pull the covers back and trying to reconcile an overwhelming desire for more sleep with the sensual awareness of a soft body moving slowly towards him, her hands already touching, her lips kissing a bruise that he had gotten from the steel deck of the verandah just hours before.

At breakfast later, Joe was smiling at Martha, marveling at the love that he had for this woman who was now becoming an ever more important part of his life. "What are you so smug about this morning?" she said after the waiter had poured their tea and left the table.

"I'm just thinking about last night." He was still smiling, adding a teaspoon of raw brown sugar to his tea and looking at her across the table. "I wonder if anyone heard us when they were taking their late night walk."

"Well, on our way back from the Caribbean we're going to do it out on the verandah during the day. That should draw a crowd."

They did not have a daytime tryst on the verandah during the return leg of the trip. A phone call later that day, from the FBI's Center for Analysis of Violent Crime to Don Stinnett, started in motion a series of events that would eventually reach their ship when it docked in the Caribbean some 36 hours later.

"Don, this is David Chambers from Crime Studies. I hate to be the bearer of bad news, but it looks like you've got another name to add to your file."

"A new case or an old one?" Stinnett had been glued to the calendar over the past few weeks. His entire strategy had been based on a schedule where he anticipated cracking the code before the next killing, which he felt would be at least a month away.

"This is a new one. This guy died yesterday morning. You know how you asked me to watch the network for homicides or suspicious deaths where the victim's occupation was related to the medical industry? Well, the flag went up on this guy in Atlanta. The report says he was swimming in one of those backyard lap pools, where you do strokes against a current for exercise? Well, somebody musta croaked him. They thought at first he had a heart attack and drowned, but the autopsy shows he was electrocuted. Looks like the control panel shorted out. The ground fault safety circuit didn't work."

"How do we know it wasn't an accident?" Stinnett was pushing. The last thing he needed was for this whole thing to escalate in timing. This could have been nothing more than an accidental death – happens a hundred times a day.

"Doubt seriously that it was a chance event. Local cop's report says the wiring was probably tampered with. They're listing it as suspicious and may move it up to homicide when they finish their preliminary investigation."

"What do you know about the victim?" Don was now resigned to the fact that this would soon be name eleven in the AMMA File. He had opened the three-ring binder on his desk and taken out his pen to make an entry. He always used a Mont Blanc fountain pen, the fat one, despite the obvious bulge it made in his otherwise carefully tailored appearance. "Do we know where he worked, or anything about the company?"

"The guy's name was Eliot Sather. The thing that rang the buzzer on our screen is the fact that this guy's occupation is listed as VP of Marketing for VanDale Orthopedic Implants. That's all we've got so far." That was enough. As much as he hated to acknowledge another related murder, Stinnett had to act on the presumption that this was indeed going to be case number eleven in the AMMA File. Unless and until this turned out to be ruled an accidental death, Mr. Sather and VanDale Orthopedic were going to be getting a lot of attention over the next several days.

The first action Stinnett took when he hung up the phone was to cancel his appointment for the pistol range that afternoon. He would need the time to start the process rolling on this new file, and the last thing he wanted was the pressure of one more qualifying round. The next thing on his mental checklist was a call to the Agent in Charge of the Atlantic district. Bill Keller would have seen the confidential bulletins covering the AMMA File, but now he had to be advised that there was a case number eleven and it was in his own backyard. Stinnett asked Keller to assign an agent to the case immediately and to start a background review on Sather and the business of VanDale Orthopedic.

"Bill, I know you've seen a bulletin on this file. Looks like we've got a serial case on our hands and you've got number eleven in your town."

Stinnett was cautiously trying to sound calm on the phone – business as usual – send up some Chinese food and a bottle of Coors. No need to have the whole Bureau know that he was out on a limb on this case. Kaufmann had been right three weeks ago when he heard the first briefing. This was starting to get out of hand, and Donald R. Stinnett, senior agent Washington Office, twenty-two years of distinguished service and three years away from an early retirement and some serious trout fishing in Montana, that same Donald Stinnett was going to be in deep weeds unless he got on top of this sorry mess in short order.

"Do y'all have any more ideas from the profile guys?" Keller had a deep Southern accent, having managed somehow to spend all but one year of his FBI career working within a 200-mile radius of his hometown. "Which one of them is worken on it?" he drawled.

"Harris. You should have his preliminary memo in your file."

"He's the best. He saved our bacon on that Casteel case two years ago."

"Well I haven't seen any magic so far. My guess is we're gonna crack this the old fashioned way – by busting our ass, chasing down leads and working with the local cops. Still, I imagine Harris will be talking with your guy in a couple of days to get the background on Sather and his company. We still think there's a connection with the animal rights angle, although no one is taking any credit so far."

"Nothin' in the press so far from those guys?"

"Nothing – which reminds me. Be sure and keep the lid on the fact that this Sather death could be part of a serial case. Kaufmann is scared shitless that this is gonna make the front page and we'll look like a bunch of dummies. Meantime, it seems like whoever is pulling the strings on this is moving the clock a little faster."

The next call was to Harris. He would need to contact the Atlanta office to get the details on Sather and VanDale, possibly even fly down if there was a remote chance of learning something that would help develop the pattern – help make the connection they both knew had to be there.

"What do you make of the time gap? Not very long since the last one." Stinnett really did not want to ask the question, but it would surely come up later when he talked to Kaufmann, so he at least had to get Harris's opinion.

"I guess I'm not really sure just yet." Jay had made up a ten-year chart that he taped on his office wall. The blue stickers he had been using to mark the ten deaths were a lot closer together on the right side of the chart. With the new sticker that he was just putting on, the gap between numbers ten and eleven was by far the shortest. "On one hand, I'm worried we're going to see an escalation in the number of these unless we can crack the case pretty soon. "On the other hand," – Jay always seemed to use a series of stops and starts when talking on the phone. Stinnett was determined to wait him out, visualizing Harris taking a bite out of his sandwich while collecting his thoughts. " – on the other hand," Jay began again, "we could be near the end. They might be getting nervous about this leaking. They might want to finish out their list before they get ready to go public."

"Either way, we're in trouble," Stinnett said. "We've gotta move faster – push our contacts. I know you told me this morning that the woman with the industry data was traveling and wouldn't be back until Monday. We can't wait five days. You'll have to find her. I'll push on the informants and the contacts at AMMA. You chase down the woman. I'll get you more help if you need it."

And so it was that at 7:30 on the morning of Wednesday, November 3rd, Jay Harris was standing on the dock with a representative of the Cunard Shipping Line when the QE2 tied up for an eight-hour layover in St. Maarten. 15 minutes later, Jay was meeting with the ship's senior security officer, who had received a rather urgent telephone message the evening before requesting his full cooperation on an FBI inquiry of some importance.

"We realize, of course, that we have limited jurisdiction aboard your vessel in these waters," Jay said, "but our agency would be most grateful if you would assist us in speaking with one of your passengers."

Harris had been briefed by one of the Washington liaison officers on the rather delicate protocol involved with this exercise. This first port of call was in Philipsburg, on the Dutch side of the island. With an American passenger on a British ship in a Dutch port, there was plenty of opportunity for the FBI to upset one or more diplomatic covenants if Harris was not careful.

When the FBI finally found out where Joe Sheldon had taken Martha on the surprise vacation, Jay had debated calling her on the satellite phone link, but had opted again for the tried and true – 'flash the badge' routine. "I don't know if she'll fly back with me or not," he had told Stinnett, "but if I call up and ask, it's too easy for her to say no. If I'm there and ask, I double the odds that she'll end up flying back."

The QE2 security man and Harris were sitting in the Queen's Grill Lounge outside of the dining room. The penthouse deck steward had advised them that Joe and Martha had gone down to breakfast, and were then planning to disembark for a day on the island. Jay had opted to let them finish breakfast before trying to talk to Martha, anxious not to disrupt her schedule before it was absolutely necessary.

"You're not going to arrest the woman are you?" the security officer was starting to second-guess his cooperative attitude. Extending a courtesy to the FBI was one thing. Having a guest from one of the penthouse suites taken off the ship in handcuffs would be something else.

"No – of course not," Harris said, surprised that the question was being raised. "Miss Laudner has done nothing wrong. We just need her assistance to analyze some rather complicated data, and unfortunately we need that assistance right away. I'm going to be asking her to fly back to Baltimore with me."

Jay was somewhat amused by the attention his visit was receiving. At least two of the ship's senior officers had walked through the lounge in the past ten minutes, obviously alerted to the presence of an FBI agent. But perhaps the most inquisitive person on the staff was David, a short but distinguished looking man wearing a brass nameplate which affirmed his title as maître d' of the Queen's Grill. David had been instructed to advise the security chief and Jay when Martha appeared to be finishing her breakfast, and his curiosity was at bursting point when he finally walked out and told them that Martha and Joe were ready to leave.

"I wonder if you would mind telling her there's a visitor in the lounge who would like a few words with her," Harris said, trying to keep the whole process as low key as possible.

"Yes, sir," David said, "and who should I tell her is waiting?" he asked hopefully.

"The names are not important right now," Jay said, this time with a little more of an edge to his voice, "just tell her there's a gentleman who needs to speak with her."

A curious and somewhat concerned Martha Laudner and Joe Sheldon were sitting down across from Harris at a small cocktail table a few moments later. The Queen's Grill Lounge had large glass windows which looked out to the Promenade Deck and the ocean beyond. Reproductions of well-known pieces of art, prices discreetly listed in the bottom right hand corner in both dollars and pounds, added a touch of understated elegance to the room. Jay had managed to convince the security officer to give them some privacy, but had been unable to separate Joe from the meeting.

"Anything you need to ask me you can do in front of him. Otherwise, I don't know that I really want to talk with you," Martha said, with just a little more bravado than she actually felt.

Harris had agreed reluctantly, and was on his second iteration about the importance of confidentiality when Joe interrupted. "How did you know Martha was on this ship?" The fact that the FBI knew where they were when no one else did suddenly had dawned on Joe, and his logical business brain jumped straight ahead about four steps, bypassing curiosity and going straight to paranoia.

"That's a fair question, Mr. Sheldon," Jay said, stalling for time while he decided how thorough to be in his answer. He opted for completeness. "Once we ascertained your address we merely had some of our agents contact every travel agent within a fifteen mile radius of your home until we found the one that you worked with to book this cruise. Then I flew here last night so I could meet the ship this morning."

"You've gone to a lot of trouble chasing us down. I gather you think this is pretty important," Joe said. Martha sat quietly while this conversation was going on beside her. The self-assured image that she usually conveyed seemed absent this morning as she appeared to grow ever more uncomfortable with the presence of this uninvited visitor.

"Yes, this is extremely important, as I think you'll appreciate in a few moments." Harris had decided to abandon the low-key approach he had used with Morkin. The fact that he had tracked Martha down and then flown to St. Maarten to bring her back would not square with a 'gee, shucks, we were just curious' routine. Without giving actual names of the individuals or companies, Jay outlined the nature of the problem, acknowledging that the FBI had yet to make a logical connection between the victims, other than the possible linkage to one of the radical animal rights groups.

"How many have been killed so far?" Joe was on the edge of his chair, talking in hushed tones. His apparent concern for the seriousness of the situation was in start contrast to the seemingly distant attitude of Martha.

"I'm afraid I can't disclose that information at the moment," Jay said. "I can tell you that it is a significant number and we believe it will increase unless we can find the person or persons responsible. I can also tell you that we don't have much time. Every day is important and that's why we need the help of you, Miss Laudner." Jay had turned to face Martha, hoping to elicit some indication of concern, or at least apprehension. "We need you to help us go through the backgrounds of these individuals and the companies, using your database. If we can do that, then we might be able to figure out who's behind this. Maybe we can find some common thread – some way we can tie this together." Martha was still avoiding eye contact with Harris. "She's not going to make this easy," Jay thought.

"When do you want Martha to do this?" Joe was still doing all the talking.

"We'd like to start immediately. I've taken the liberty of booking two first class tickets on a flight which leaves St. Maarten at noon today. The Bureau will pay for your ticket, Miss Laudner, as well as the unused portion of your cruise fare."

"I don't want to leave this ship!" she finally spoke. "I love this cruise. I've never been on one before and I don't want to leave this one early. To tell the truth, I don't really like the idea of you poking around my database. I didn't work all these years to set it up just so the police could use it for some wild goose chase!"

"Martha, I don't think you can say that," Joe interjected. "This isn't some local cop looking for a guy who jumped bail. This is the FBI and this is serious. Those guys could be coming after me for all we know. You have to help!"

In the end it was Joe's power of persuasion that moved the mountain. Martha was more than a little reluctant to cooperate but finally agreed, provided that the Bureau would also fly Joe back and then book both of them on another cruise. Harris ended up sitting in coach on the flight to Baltimore, his first-class seat next to Martha now occupied by Joe Sheldon, to whom Jay had pledged the undying gratitude and appreciation of the FBI. Before the flight left St. Maarten, Jay had called to let Stinnett know they were on their way.

"Did you have any trouble talking her into flying back?" Stinnett asked.

"Yeah – a little more than I expected. Not only did she not want to come back, she doesn't really want to help us out with her database. We'll be back into Baltimore late this afternoon, but given her attitude I didn't want to try and start tonight. We'll get going first thing tomorrow morning."

"Let me know as soon as you see even the slightest hint of something useful. I'm heading over to Kaufmann's office right now to get him up-to-date on this. He's so worried about the case he'll probably want an hour-by-hour report."

Kaufmann was not quite looking for hourly information, but he was clearly worried, and he had news of his own for Stinnett. "Don, I had a breakfast meeting with the Director today and I decided to brief him on the case. If something leaks out on this and he doesn't know the background, he'll have my ass on a platter. We're gonna talk about it later this afternoon. I'm meeting with him again at four thirty."

"Well let me know what the party line's gonna be. I've got the AMMA guys all over my tail to release information. I can't stall much longer."

"You'll know this afternoon. I want you there with me for the meeting."

"With Nickoloff? You're shitting me!"

Walter J. Nickoloff had been Director of the FBI for only a few months, and most of the senior agents in Washington, including Kaufmann, were still trying to figure our the best way to interact with this most recent successor to the now tarnished image of J. Edgar Hoover. Appointed in the first year of the Clinton administration, Nickoloff stood in visible contrast to the legions of young Democrat attorneys and judges who had been slotted into high visibility positions at the other federal agencies. A law graduate from the University of Michigan, he had practiced only briefly before entering the service during the Korean War with an assignment in Army Intelligence. His duties in that arena lasted through 1955 and eventually served as a springboard into various positions within the CIA, some of which were still sensitive enough to necessitate closed door sessions during portions of his Senate confirmation hearings. Now in his early sixties, Nickoloff had given up a lucrative second career on Wall Street to take the helm at the FBI, his courtly manner and graying hair adding an aura of distinction to a position and institution in dire need of improved public image after several years of slippage in reputation and prestige. Stinnett had not fared well in the limited contact that he had with the two previous Directors, and was therefore more than a little surprised that he would be included in the next day's meeting with the new director.

"His idea – not mine," Kaufmann was quick to comment when he saw Stinnett's surprised look, "not that I don't think it's a good idea. Nickoloff wants you, me, and two of the hot shots from the public affairs office."

"What about Harris?"

"Not for this meeting," Kaufmann was rocking back and forth in his chair, bracing his left foot against the open desk drawer. "I must admit that I did not encourage getting Jay involved in the PR side of things. If the press gets on this, I don't want the emphasis to be on how the Bureau keeps a couple of psychology types down in the basement who get out their ouija boards if we can't catch our guy some other way. I know I pushed you to use Harris, but let's keep him under wraps if this thing goes public."

"You don't have to convince me, but somebody better talk to Harris. You can bet the reporters have his name and number filed under Serial in their Rolodex. He's going to get the first call if and when this leaks."

Kaufmann had stopped rocking but was now swiveling back and forth, his arms folded across his chest. "Maybe you should talk to him about that. Don't make it sound like a big deal, but tell him any press contact gets routed to me first with you as backup. I'm not sure we can keep him out of the limelight forever. Nickoloff likes the profile guys – thinks they add to the mystique of the Bureau. Must come from his days as a spook."

"I'll talk to Harris," Stinnett said as he started to leave. Kaufmann motioned for him to sit back down.

"Don, the main thing you need to do is get this damn case solved. If you need more resources, tell me! If you aren't getting cooperation from the regional offices, tell me! But goddamn it, let's move on this thing!" Kaufmann was biting off his words and pointing to the file on his desk for emphasis. "I'm tired of reading shit about how the Bureau had been chasing this mail bomb guy for fifteen years. My mother sent me a *New York Times* clipping about that case. Wanted to know why we hadn't caught the guy since we had a profile on him. My own mother for Christsakes!"

Kaufmann turned his chair around and was looking at the pictures lined up on the credenza behind his desk. Mixed in with several 5" x 7" family pictures were two 8" x 10" framed photos. One was a reproduction of a photograph which had appeared on the front page of *The Washington Post* showing Kaufmann making an announcement about the arrest of a suspect in the New York Trade Center bombing. The other photo was of him shaking hands with the then President George Bush in what was obviously some sort of congratulatory ceremony.

"I want to see a picture of me making the announcement on how we broke this case." He swung his chair back around to face Stinnett. "Of course you'll be in the picture, too," he said, with no trace of humor in his voice.

"Of course," Stinnett replied, equally deadpan. "I'll wear my new suit."

CHAPTER EIGHTEEN
The Reporter

"We're going to have to advise the Board, or at least the Executive Committee." Brian Davidson was sitting across the desk from Bill Samuels in a corner office at the AMMA headquarters on Louisiana Avenue in Washington. Davidson had gotten a call from one of Sather's co-workers at VanDale Orthopedics, and had then phoned Stinnett to confirm what he was now telling Samuels, that another AMMA member had died of suspicious causes. "Eliot Sather was on one of our most important committees and he was scheduled to make a report at the next annual meeting. If it's confirmed that his death wasn't from an accident or natural causes, then I think we're going to have to tell our members that something is going on. And if we're going to do that, then we really have to advise the Board first."

Bill Samuels had been president of AMMA for the past four years and was the quintessential Washington insider. A law degree from Georgetown along with Assistant Council positions on three different House subcommittees, during both a Democratic and Republican administration, had marked the start of his career and helped supply the first 100 phone numbers in the Rolodex that would serve him so well in later years when the name of the game was 'who do you know and how well'. Samuels had a well oiled propensity for organization, keeping track of things with one of those traveling leather office folders that you see advertised in airline magazines but would never consider buying yourself. Four of those yellow cards were now on the desk in front of him on this Thursday morning, one for each of the appointments he had scheduled on the hour between 8 a.m. and noon. Davidson's name did not appear on any of those cards, and such a deviation to a carefully organized day was not something that Samuels took lightly.

"I am not prepared to call a special Board meeting to make an announcement on something we are not in a position to substantiate. We have twenty-four members on our Board and if we tell them, we can just as well put it in the newsletter to all three hundred and ten, since there is no way it's going to stay confidential." Samuels had lined up the four cards in a neat row and was looking at his watch. He was seventeen minutes behind schedule for his 8 a.m. appointment. "That agent Stinnett from the FBI had asked me to keep this confidential. I'm not about to break the news on this before they do."

"Well, can we find out when they're going to say something? I'm afraid that I'll start getting calls from some of our members asking about Sather." Davidson was pushing his point, but not exactly with a high level of vigor. Although all AMMA officers theoretically served at the pleasure of the Board, Samuels always made it clear that he was the most senior, and more than capable of making life difficult for anyone on the staff who ignored the chain of command. Still, the point was valid. The AMMA staff could stonewall only so long before they would start to look stupid, and worse yet be accused of placing some of their members at risk.

"Look, Brian, I'll call the Bureau right before my nine o'clock meeting," Samuels said, tapping the second yellow card from the top. "I'll see if we can't coordinate our announcement with theirs. They should be ready to make a statement pretty soon."

At 8:55 when Samuels was placing his call to Stinnett's office, agents Harris and Brinkman were parked in front of Martha Laudner's apartment building on Front Street in Baltimore, determined to be ready to start at nine o'clock sharp on what they hoped would be a productive search for the elusive connection between the eleven deaths. Jay had spent an hour on the phone Wednesday night after his flight from St. Maarten, talking to one of the Bureau's computer jockeys about the ways that most databases are structured and the type of sort routines and co-variant query modes that might be used to get the kind of information that would be helpful to them. Jay had debated bringing along the expert, but eventually made the decision that Martha's reservations about opening her treasure trove of information to the FBI would only be accentuated if he brought along someone with another set of keys to the codes that she used to guard the Holy Grail.

"Miss Laudner, this is Agent Mark Brinkman," Jay said when they entered Martha's apartment at 9:02, "he's going to be assisting us today as we work with you to better understand the background on these individuals and their companies. Once again I want to tell you how much the Bureau appreciates your cooperation and your willingness to interrupt your cruise." Martha had seated them at her kitchen table and was pouring herself a cup of coffee as Jay was making his perfunctory 'we really are grateful' remarks. The cup that Martha was using on this morning was obviously a souvenir from the QE2, a homey touch on which Jay was about to comment until he thought better of it at the last moment.

"I wonder if we could start with the file check on Mr. Sather, the gentleman who died earlier this week in Atlanta," Harris began again. "Then perhaps we can see what sort of information you have on VanDale Orthopedics, and after that we'll duplicate the process on some other names."

And with that outline serving either as a polite request or a soft directive, Martha finally led the three of them into the inner sanctum, the war room of David Morkin and Associates. Despite Harris's general knowledge of what to expect, he still was surprised. Not only were the tape drive memory units, input stations and printers of obvious sophistication, but the room itself seemed to be worthy of something NASA might utilize, albeit on a much smaller scale. Everything from the lighting system to the counter-tops to the built-in display monitors was of the latest design, and although Martha may have started her integrated system with compromise choices on equipment, it was clear that in recent years no expense had been spared.

"I told my assistants not to come in today," Martha said as she motioned the men towards the chairs, which were slightly off to the side of the room. "Now, does your Mr. Sather have a middle name and do you know his social security number?"

Harris had both the middle name and the social security number as well as quite a bit of additional information on Sather, courtesy of a courier run from the FBI's Atlanta office the previous night. Included in the package of information were Sather's personnel file and resume, which Jay was anxious to compare with the material that Martha would generate.

"How long will it take to do the search on Sather?" Jay asked as Martha was keying in the information.

"Turn on the monitor at your station," she said with more than a little condescension in her voice, "it's on your screen now. Would you like to have it printed out?"

"Yes – please."

"How many copies?"

"Two, please."

He was just half way through reading the data on the screen when Martha handed him the two copies off the laser printer. Jay passed one to a visibly impressed Agent Brinkman and then started reading again, skipping ahead on the page, hoping to see something that would jump out as an obvious point of inquiry.

Eliot J. Sather

Aug 1985 -	VanDale Orthopedics, VP Reg Affairs
Jan 1983 – July 1985	Consultant with Sather & Co
Aug 1980 – Dec 1982	Hemograft Design Engineer
Sept 1978 – July 1980	Richardson Medical, Director of QC
Jun 1972 – Aug 1978	Howmedica, Inc., Manager Clinical Affairs

Eliot James Sather, born January 14, 1946, BS in mechanical engineering from LSU in 1968 with 3.28 GPA. Four years in Air Force as weapons officer. Left active duty in 1972 with rank of Captain and remained on active reserves through June of 1979. Primary area of expertise in materials with emphasis on non-thrombolytic coating technologies. Most recent experience related to orthopedics specialty with responsibilities in clinical affairs, quality assurance and regulatory submissions.

Search Fields: D-26, D-42. Size: 4,3. Level: 24, 23, 22. Weight: 3

March 22, 1986	Presentation at American Orthopedic Institute: "Trends in International Regulation of Medical Devices."
October 19, 1991	Presentation at AMMA meeting: "Statistical Measurement Techniques for Low Sample Size Clinical Trials."

"I'm impressed," Brinkman said. "Can you do all the inquiries that fast?"

Martha had also been reading the report on Sather, and took a moment to respond. "A single name inquiry like this is the easiest kind of question to answer. Putting information in and having it organized so you can access it in different sort routines is the tough part."

"What are those numbers near the bottom?" Jay asked. "Do those pertain just to Sather?"

"Those are part of the sort codes," Martha said. "The Search Field destination is for his area of medical specialty and job concentration. Level means just what it says, and size refers to the size of the company where he should be a good fit based on his prior experience."

"What about weight?" Harris and Brinkman asked the question at the same time.

"That's a little more subjective on my part." Martha was warming somewhat to the conversation, still uncomfortable about the intrusion into her domain, but proud to display the sophistication of her database and program. "This guy's a middleweight. If he was coded 2 or 1 he would be a lightweight. If I was doing a CEO search I wouldn't sort on any 2's or 3's. I'd be looking at the 5's – the heavyweights. I might pull up some 4's, but only if needed to fill out the list. Here, let me show you something." She motioned for them to roll their chairs over closer to her keyboard and monitor, now clearly enjoying her role as maestro of the database. "If I was doing a search for a CEO for a medium-sized ophthalmic company where we were looking for someone who had finance or marketing background and management experience at the VP level, I could tell you that I have" – she punched in six or seven entries on her keyboard, looked up at her monitor and said – "twenty-three possible fits. If I accept only candidates with a marketing background" – she hit another key – "I'd have sixteen possibilities. After that it's a simple matter for me to pull up the files and do the more subtle sorts on specific experience and education to narrow the list down to the best four or five. That, gentlemen, is why we're the top search firm in the industry today."

"How do you know Sather was only a middleweight?" Jay asked.

"Well, as I said, it's mostly subjective." Martha turned her chair around to face them and poured another cup of coffee for herself. "I look at the level of responsibility and experience the individual has, where he went to college, the kinds of outside exposure he's had. Sather has gone up in title but down somewhat in the level of companies he's worked for. You can see he had his own consulting company back in 1980 and '81, which is a polite way of saying that you're unemployed. I've got two outside citations on his record, which is low. The heavyweights might have ten or twelve and I have a few that have over twenty. Sather was a middleweight at best. He would never make my cut on a CEO search."

"Miss Laudner," Jay had been writing notes on Sather's printout, but put down his pen for a moment as he framed his next question. "As we mentioned to you yesterday morning when we spoke on the ship, there's a possibility that one of the radical animal rights groups might be involved with Sather's death and the deaths of some of the other individuals whose cases we're reviewing. Can you pull any information from your database that would help us address that question?"

"You saw all I have on Sather. There's nothing there about him doing research using animals. It would be rare to see that on a file unless it was part of the individual's specific job description. That doesn't mean he might not have been involved with that kind of research, it just means it's not picked up in his file."

"What about if we looked at what you have with VanDale Orthopedics?" Brinkman asked. He had been an almost unseen and unheard bystander up to this point. Jay had brought him along primarily to insure cooperation from the Baltimore Regional Office, but Brinkman was now getting into the details of the case, intrigued by the paper chase on which they had embarked.

Martha ran a company profile on VanDale and then later on Heartflow Technologies, the company for whom Gary Lempke worked, the man who was victim number ten courtesy of a fast descent off Camelback Mountain. Both company profiles showed the general medical nature of the business and the organizational charts, including the positions that he had held over the past ten years and the fact that Martha had his weight quoted as a 2, notwithstanding his extensive industry experience. Despite a fully ingrained sense of optimism that he would find some shared theme to link the two victims, Harris could find no similarity in the records for Sather and Lempke. No common education, job, or company where they had been employed together. No hint that there was any unusual involvement with research on four-legged patients, and it got no better as the morning wore on and they tried to access the files on the other nine victims. In each case they were greeted with the short and cryptic notation on the monitor that the file was deleted.

"I do that if I know the individual's retired or deceased," Martha said. "I guess that on Sather and Lempke we had not seen that news. On the others, my assistants must have seen some notice and dumped the file. We've got a lot of memory here but it's not endless. We like to do some housekeeping once in awhile or the response times get a little slow."

"Miss Laudner," Jay began, hoping that she would finally lighten up and say, 'call me Martha,' "Miss Laudner, this might be a good time to take a break for lunch. You've been most helpful this morning but I think we'll go back to our office for a while and check on some of our other information. Then we'll come back around two or two-thirty if we have additional questions."

"What other information do we need to look at?" Brinkman asked when they left the building.

"I really don't know," Jay said. "I was just stalling for time. Her setup is pretty sophisticated but it doesn't help us much if we can't get into those other nine records or find some type of linkage. I want to call Stinnett from your office and see if we've gotten any more information from Atlanta on Sather."

*

"I'm sorry, but Agent Stinnett isn't available to take your call at the moment." Janelle Davis had been Stinnett's secretary for three years and had been with the Bureau since 1987, when she had moved to Washington from Des Moines, Iowa, in what was still an unsuccessful quest to add some level of excitement and glamour to her otherwise uninspiring clerical career.

"This is Jay Harris, and I know that Don is going to want to talk with me. Any idea where I can find him?"

"He's with Deputy Director Kaufmann right now, and I don't really think I can interrupt him. They've got a little bit of a crisis going on. They're meeting with someone from the Public Affairs Office." This anticipated but dreaded event had occurred twenty minutes before, at 12:15, the call from the press – although Denise Altman from the Bureau's Public Affairs Office was not yet ready to concede that Michael Montgomery was emblematic of the press.

"He's a junior reporter for God's sake," she was telling Stinnett and Kaufmann. "He's fishing. Probably heard some rumor and now thinks he's going to be the next Woodward and Bernstein. Hampton is the reporter at the *Post* who does ninety-five percent of the coverage on the Bureau. Montgomery's a rookie. I checked him out with a friend. He was an intern last summer and now he's on general assignment. He's a young black kid. Probably part of an affirmative action program."

"I tell you, this guy knows something!" Stinnett was standing behind a chair across from Kaufmann's desk. Still worked up about the call, he had asked Denise to join them on short notice, hoping to get some help on the call or at least lay off the blame if the story broke prematurely. "He's not just fishing! He asked about the Sather case and whether or not it had anything to do with the deaths of other industry executives."

"Did he know any of the other names?" Denise asked.

"He didn't mention any and I sure didn't offer. But it sounded like he knew there were others."

"That proves my point." Denise Altman had been in the Public Affairs Office at the Bureau for twelve years, having previously worked in a similar capacity at the Department of Treasury. She was usually quick to venture an opinion on matters of how to handle a touchy situation with the press, and in more cases than not she turned out to be correct. In this situation she exuded a level of confidence in her judgment almost equal to the level Stinnett lacked in his. "If this kid knew something more he'd have names on the other cases. He doesn't have anything – trust me!"

"I think Denise is right," Kaufmann said slowly. He was leaning back in his chair, wanting desperately to put his feet up on his desk but aware that would look just a little too pompous. He settled for resting his elbows on the padded arms of the chair, pressing his fingertips together and occasionally touching his chin to the apex of his digital triangle. "I think we can hold the line on this for awhile longer," he said. "What did you tell him, Don?"

"I gave him the party line. I said we were cooperating with local authorities in the investigation of Sather's death and we were not aware at this time of other cases which tied specifically to the Atlanta situation. I said we're always working on other investigations around the country, but we're not at liberty to discuss details on cases that are in process."

"And did he accept that?" With his chin touching the fingertips again, Kaufmann was rocking slowly in the chair, concentrating on looking knowledgeable.

"I didn't give him a choice! I told him that was the situation and if there was a change we'd be in contact. If he calls back I want you to talk to him, Denise. But keep him away from Harris. I don't think he can lie with a straight face."

"I'll talk to him, Don, you can relax. We're in control of this story. You won't believe the good press we're going to get when we break this case. I've got the fax numbers ready to roll and background memos drafted. We'll do the first announcement at around three thirty on the day you make your arrest, and we'll be the lead item on all four network evening news broadcasts. You guys are gonna be famous."

"At least for fifteen minutes," Kaufmann said. "Warhol was right about that."

*

Michael Montgomery had not yet had his fifteen minutes of fame, and was not likely to get it if he stayed on the same general assignment beat that he now had at the *Post*, working third tier stories of marginal interest to even local readers. Eighteen months into his job and so far down the assignment list that he could almost get better stories as a stringer, Michael kept himself motivated by the consciously generated mental image of the day when he would pick up the paper and see his byline on a story of national interest. As a teenager growing up in Selma, Alabama, he had been fascinated by the power of the written word, newspapers, magazines, books – and the process that transformed independent and sometimes divergent thoughts and sentences into stories which could captivate the reader and move him to an opinion or conclusion.

Michael had his first experience of breaking in a story of importance as a fledgling writer on the student newspaper at Howard University, researching and documenting a series of articles about academic oversight that resulted in a change of policy by the University. His internship the next summer at *The Washington Post* gave him his first exposure to the workings of a large daily newspaper, as well as a shot at a full time position upon graduation. Denise had been right about Montgomery being an affirmative action hire, but to underestimate Michael Montgomery was clearly an error. Although lacking in polish, experience, connections and even physical stature, the 5'6", twenty-four year old reporter had the quality most required for eventual success in a difficult profession: singleness of purpose. Michael Montgomery was driven! His quest for his own National Affairs byline was such that he would record CNN news during the day on the VCR in his apartment and then write lead paragraphs at night, working on style as well as substance, striving to put together a sequence of 100 words in such a way that no editor could do anything but marvel at the turn of a phrase and the skillful use of the hook. A hook intriguing enough to pull the reader into the text that followed but sufficiently subtle so as not to insult the intelligence of the *Post* subscribers, who read on average at the 12th grade comprehension level, some three grades higher than their counterparts out in the hustings.

Not yet blessed with contacts in the city and unlikely to cultivate any of substance while doing stories on bus line fare increases, Michael assiduously worked the bars and restaurants where the legions of government secretaries went to meet the legions of young and single clerks and appointees and hangers-on who went to meet the secretaries who went to meet the legions of junior staff attorneys who usually went home alone, ready for the next night's game of 'meet your mate'.

"Every one of them has a story," Michael told a friend of his at the *Post*. "They may not know it yet, but each one has access to some information that will one day be the germ of a story that I will dig out, nurture, and then present in such a compelling fashion that no editor in his right mind will be able to keep it off the front page!"

And so each evening when Michael worked the circuit, he was Mr. Glad-hand, Mr. Hello – How are you? – What agency do you work for? – That must be fascinating – Can I call you sometime if I need to confirm some background for the story? – What's your number? It would all get written down in the little spiral notebook. And when Michael got back to his apartment that night, and after he had drafted his paragraphs, the data from the little book would go into the Macintosh, cross-referenced by government agency – department – and section if possible. Names and phone numbers, ready to call on the day he got the lead that would get him the start of the story, the story that would take him off general assignment forever.

It was not a government employee who dropped the first hint, the first raised eyebrow with the 'if you only knew what I know' look. It was a college student from Texas, drinking at a bar in the Georgetown section of Washington on 35th Street near the University. Smitty's was the type of place that had cigarette burns on the tabletops and popcorn on the floor. With a two-for-one cocktail hour and a rather liberal policy of checking IDs, Smitty's appealed more to the young secretaries and nearby Georgetown students than to the GS twelves and thirteens that you would see at the Willard Hotel.

Chuck Mauer, now back in college on a full time basis with a renewed sense of academic conviction but a lingering affection for the party life, was not about to turn down a free beer from the short black guy at the table now that Happy Hour was over. Mauer had been regaling the two secretaries from Agriculture about his expertise with computers and how he had almost single-handedly straightened out one of the biggest trade associations in Washington.

"You should have seen how screwed up this place was," he said. "I was only temping, but I hadda fix up their whole damn membership record system. If I hadn't done that they still wouldn't know about those guys getting killed."

The twenty-year-old secretary from Ag who typed field agent report on corn yields all day long had never seen anyone quite as cute as this Georgetown senior before, one who only moments earlier had mentioned the possibility of a fraternity party on Saturday night. "Chuckee," she drawled with just the right mixture of adoration and curiosity, "we never heard about a bunch of business men getting killed."

"Secret – secret – secret," Chuck said, leaning over towards her and waving his index finger back and forth in front of her face. "I'm sworn to secrecy. Cross my heart and hope to die. The FBI's involved now."

"Hey, Chuck," Michael was consciously controlling his voice, slowly reaching for his pen but not yet taking out his notebook. "What do you think the FBI's going to do?"

"I don't know. They cut me out of the loop pretty quick. Some guy named Stinit or Stinett or something like that came in and it was all hush-hush. I've got to go."

Michael got up from the table. "I have to go, too," he said as they started to walk out. "You know, Chuck, my company might

215

be able to use someone like you to do some consulting on their computer setup. You gotta number where I can reach you?"

Forty-five minutes later, Mauer's name and number were going into the Macintosh. On this night the paragraphs did not get written. This night Michael Montgomery came into his apartment, took off his elevator shoes, turned on his computer, entered Mauer's number, and then began looking through his listing of FBI names and phone numbers. Somewhere there was a secretary who said she worked for a guy named Stinnett, and although she did not know it yet, she was going to help a Mr. Michael Montgomery get his first byline.

CHAPTER NINETEEN
The Connection

"Agent Harris? This is Janelle Davis. I'm glad I tracked you down. Don's back in his office and he needs to talk to you! Hold on a minute."

Harris had just finished a lunch which, even with his notable tolerance for marginal food, had been a long way from acceptable. "How in the hell can you eat Mexican food this bad?" he had been complaining when Brinkman's pager went off, starting the process that now had him using the phone in the manager's small office at the restaurant, talking with an obviously excited Agent Stinnett.

"We may have something, Jay. I'll need you to check it out with your woman who has that computer setup. Have you learned anything from her so far?"

"Not a heck of a lot. We've only gotten into two victim's records. Looks like she pulled the others off when they died."

"Did Lempke ever work for a company called Hemograft? I just got a call from Keller in Atlanta. He told us Mrs. Sather said that a friend of her husband's had also been killed several years ago. A guy named Barry Decker. Recognize that name?"

"He's number five!"

"Bingo, Charley!" Stinnett's excitement was almost contagious. "The late Mr. Decker turned up dead in a hit and run accident in 1986. One that looked strange enough that he made our happy little list of eleven. Decker and Sather used to work together at Hemograft. What does your ouija board make of that little piece of news?" If gloating over the phone could be converted to a digital signal, Stinnett would have needed an extra line. He was on his way! He was going to nail this case and he was going to do it soon!

"Well, it is interesting," Harris was not yet ready for gloating. "There could be a connection and it's something worth checking out. I have to tell you though that Lempke didn't work for Hemograft. I remember that name from Sather's file, and I know that when we compared their two records there wasn't any match on companies."

"Shit!" Stinnett's attitude quotient was taking a rapid slide down towards the humble marker on the gloat scale. "Maybe he

217

shouldn't have been on the list to begin with. Maybe that was an accident after all."

"Sorry, Don, I think he should have been on the list. Remember there was a gun found not too far from the body? The killer had a backup plan – plus Lempke was a fairly good athlete. Guys like that don't fall off small mountains by themselves. He was pushed."

"Well – check out the others for a connection on Hemograft. It's still a possibility. We tried calling the company, but they've been out of business for a while. We're trying to track down their history through some other sources, but Laudner may be our best bet for information."

"I'll check 'em out, Don." Harris was almost consoling in his response, "and I'll check Lempke again. Maybe we missed something."

"Call me back this afternoon when you're done. Either way, whether you've found anything or not. Call me at home if I've left the office."

"I will, Don. Don't worry. We'll find the connection if it's there some place." Harris was trying to end the conversation. The restaurant manager, a gentleman with a poorly trimmed mustache along with an attitude problem, had been standing outside the door to the office, trying his best to look like he was doing the US Government a very large favor.

"And, Jay," Stinnett would not quit, "there's a reporter trying to fish for information on this. Remember the sequence. Kaufmann first, me second, and the Public Affairs group third."

"I don't even read the papers. I'm sure as hell not gonna talk to 'em."

"I'm just reminding you. Let me know if you get a call."

"Relax, Don. We're the good guys."

When they returned to Martha's apartment at two o'clock, David Morkin was at the kitchen table. Martha did not appear to be overly excited to have him there, and even less thrilled when he offered Harris and Brinkman a cup of coffee.

"I don't have a chance to get into Martha's war room all that often," David said. "I figured as long as you guys were going to be here, I'd come over and watch. I might be able to help a little depending on what you need to find out. Martha would like us to believe that these tape drives of hers have all the data that's worth knowing, but I've been around a few years, and once in awhile I can beat the computer." Morkin still seemed to convey the sense of elation that he had exhibited after the first visit when he realized he was not the point of inquiry. For him this had now taken on the sense of adventure. Serious to be sure, but still exciting.

"Well, we appreciate that, Mr. Morkin." Jay had turned down the invitation for coffee, anxious to move things along. "We'd like to remind you that this whole inquiry must be held in strictest confidence. We may ask a few questions this afternoon that could be sensitive as far as some individual companies are concerned. It's absolutely critical that nothing gets communicated on this subject except by us."

Jay opened his notebook and placed it on the table. "Miss Laudner," he began, "I wonder if you could tell us a little more about how your company records are structured. What information do you or your assistants post to the files, and then how do you access that data? What kind of inquiries can be made?" The four of them were still sitting around the kitchen table. Harris was reluctant to move into the computer room, preferring to remain in neutral territory as long as possible.

"Well, the company files are basically a data dump off of the executive names," Martha began. "When we load an individual's name along with his position and dates of employment, either from one of our sources or an old resume, we key in the different companies he's worked for and the dates. The program code is written to automatically duplicate the individual data and dump it into the company files where he's worked."

"And how do you play it back?" Brinkman asked a little too quickly, generating a brief glance from Harris.

"Maybe another way to phrase the question, Miss Laudner," Harris asked this time, "is if you wanted to see the names of people who worked for a particular company over a period of time – would you have that data?"

"We'd have that, but only for the senior positions. In a medium sized company that might mean the top ten or fifteen names. For a company like J&J we probably have over two hundred names."

"And what if that company was no longer in existence? Would you still have that data?"

"That depends. If it got bought out then I might merge that file into the successor company. If it just died a slow death we may still have the data on tape."

"One other question," Jay said. This was the big one, but he was trying not to signal its importance just yet. "This morning you said that if someone retired, or you found out he died, that you would delete his file. Is that correct?"

"Yes."

"And a little while ago you said that when you set up a new individual's file that it automatically updates the company records."

"That's right."

"Now when you delete an individual's file, does that pull him off the company file or does that file remain intact?"

"I know that one!" David responded, obviously pleased to be back in the loop. "Those names stay in the company file. I talked Martha into that so we could see how a company's organization chart evolves over the years in case we get them as a client. I must admit we haven't used it much. Martha always wants to delete stuff, but memory's so damn cheap now that I keep talking her out of it."

"You may have done us all a big favor, Mr. Morkin," Jay said. "I wonder if we could try out the system again on another company – Hemograph."

"Hemograft?"

"Yes, that's right. I'd like to see who you show worked there as senior management when the company was in business."

They moved into the computer room without any additional conversation. Morkin had dropped his giddy look, apparently sensing that the search was getting serious. Harris and Brinkman knew they were close to a critical point. Would there be a match on names besides Sather and Decker? Only Martha seemed relaxed, but that also changed when she sat down at one of the workstations and turned on the monitor.

"Spell the name for me."

"H-e-m-o-g-r-a-f-t," Harris said slowly.

"One word or two?"

"One."

Martha typed in the letters and then touched the return key and watched as the monitor lit up, showing what was obviously a canned format with entries after certain of the categories.

"It must have been a small company. I've only got seven names on the listing."

"Can we see the names please?" Jay said softly.

"The last name went back on in 1984, but it came from an old resume," Martha said.

"Can we see the names?"

Martha moved the cursor onto the second data field and touched the return key again. Harris and Brinkman almost hit heads as they leaned in for a closer look. Jay had his notebook under his arm but it was not needed. He knew the eleven names on the list by heart, and of the seven names now on the monitor, six were on the list. Sather, Decker, and four others. "I wonder if you could print that out for me," Jay said softly, conscious that his heart rate had escalated, hoping that his voice would not betray his attempt to underplay what was clearly the biggest break in the case so far.

"Does that tell you anything?" David asked, aware that both Harris and Brinkman had stopped talking.

Jay had taken a seat at one of the other workstations. He was debating whether he should leave the room to call Stinnett, but opted to hold off for a while. "It may be helpful to us," he said, without looking at David. He was staring at the one name on the printout that had not appeared on this list. "Miss Laudner, I wonder if you could check for an individual file on a Mr. Robert Haberman. The company file lists him as CEO of Hemograft."

It took less than 30 seconds to get the response that Harris expected. "There's no file on Haberman," Martha said. "Since he was in the company file, I must have had him on the system at one time. But that's an old company file so he's probably retired."

"Or dead maybe. Is that possible?" David was back in the hunt again.

"That's possible," Jay said.

They sat in silence for a few minutes as Harris paged through his notebook debating what to do next. David walked back out in the kitchen for a refill on his coffee, offering again to get Harris and Brinkman a cup. Martha sat passively at her keyboard, exuding an air of indifference, in sharp contrast to the unspoken but obviously heightened tension exhibited by the other three participants. Finally Harris spoke, his soft Oklahoma accent once again in evidence as he chose his words carefully, like someone stepping slowly into a small boat that was close to the water line. "This morning when you ran the individual file on Gary Lempke, it showed a number of different companies that he worked for." Jay was holding the printout in his hand. As a number two lightweight by Martha's rating system, Gary Lempke had moved a lot during the past fifteen years.

Gary W. Lempke

Feb 19, 1990	Heartflow Tech, Regional Sales Manager
Oct 1987 – Jan 1990	Gelmar Laboratories, Sales Manager
Feb 1986 – Sept 1987	Medtel Systems, National Sales Manager
Oct 1983 – Dec 1985	Cellmed Optics, Dir. Sales and Marketing
Jan 1982 – Sept 1983	Vicor Medical, Regional Sales Manager
Mar 1978 – Dec 1981	Aortek, Sales Manager
Jun 1975 – Feb 1978	Inwood Labs, Salesman
Jul 1972 – May 1975	Boston Dynamics, Salesman

Gary William Lempke, born February 16, 1945. BS in History from the U. of Michigan in 1968. Sales experience in multiple specialty areas. Mid level sales management experience.

> Search Fields S-4, S-5   Size 3, 2
> Level 15, 14   Weight 2

"Miss Laudner, I wonder if you could please run the company files on each of these firms where Mr. Lempke worked. You did Heartflow Technologies this morning, where he was working when he died. If you could do the other seven names now I'd really appreciate it."

"Do you want to see them on the screen or just get printouts?" she asked.

"Why don't you just give me the printouts. You don't have to call 'em up on the monitor." Harris was not sure what he would find, if anything, but if there was something of value he did not particularly want Martha and David to know what it was.

Martha typed in the seven company names and then handed Jay the sheets as they came off the printer. On the fifth sheet he took slightly longer to scan the names, but then as before, he turned that page over and picked up the next one, staring at the words, but not concentrating, his mind racing with the explosive information that he had just seen on the previous company profile. There were five names listed for that company and four were on the AMMA File list. Now all of the eleven names except Powell were accounted for and shown as having worked for either Hemograft or Aortek. Plus there was another name, Robert Haberman, on the Hemograft list, who would probably end up being listed as victim number twelve, and yet one more name on the Aortek organization chart, Jin Daieje, whose name Jay was now writing down as a potential number thirteen.

"We'll need to check all this information out later," Jay said as he slipped the company profiles over to Brinkman with a 'don't say anything' look. "We have just a few more questions for you today. I wonder, Miss Laudner, if you could please check your database for a file on a Mr. Jin Daieje. I believe one of these company records said he was a PhD if that makes any difference."

Harris had written out the spelling of the name, and as Martha entered the information he closed his notebook and looked briefly at his watch, thinking momentarily about how quickly he could get back to Washington for what he knew would be a series of crisis meetings on this major breakthrough. The news that they might be up to thirteen names was going to send Stinnett and Kaufmann into orbit.

"Here's a printout on Daieje," Martha said, bringing Harris back to reality.

"You have a file?" he asked, the surprise in his voice evident despite himself.

"It may be out of date, but I've got a file. It shows he got his PhD at Stanford and then worked at Aortek from 1983 to 1988. Then he went to a company in San Jose called Barkley Avionics. That's the last I have on him. Barkley looks like a non-medical company so we may not have picked him up on other subsequent moves."

"But he's still in your system?"

"Yes."

Jay was standing now, reaching for the printout on Daieje that Martha had run off without being asked. Was Daieje a suspect or a possible next victim? Either way it was imperative that they run a check on him immediately. If he was not number thirteen yet, he could be shortly. As Harris was staring at the data on the sheet, trying to think whether Daieje's Korean background might have anything to do with the case, Brinkman handed him a note. 'Current status of two companies? Need to know.'

"Miss Laudner," Jay began again, still waiting for the 'call me Martha' that was apparently not going to be forthcoming, "we'll have to check out all of these companies of course, but I wonder if you could tell me what you know about two of them, Hemograft and Aortek? The printouts indicated that they were out of business, plus I saw that both of the companies listed their product area as vascular grafts, but what other information might you have on 'em?"

This time Martha looked at her watch, sending a visible and none too subtle message that she was beginning to run a little thin on patience. "That's really all I have. The only way we know that they're out of business is that I have my assistants go through the files once a year and call each company to get the latest financial report. If the number's disconnected and we can't find any forwarding information, then we show that company as being out of business. We've got more important things to do than chase down the reasons they close the door."

As Martha was talking, David picked up a phone and dialed a number. "I told you I could beat the computer once in awhile," he said. "I've got a good contact at the business reference desk at the Baltimore Library who digs out corporate history stuff for me once in awhile. He – hold on a second – John, this is David Morkin. I wonder if you could check out two companies for me and tell me what's happened to them. The first one is Aortek." David turned the received sideways so he could give Harris the response. " – Filed bankruptcy 1986. Okay, how about Hemograft?" Once more Morkin spelled out the name and then waited, drumming his fingernails on the counter-top. "Name change? To what?" Again the fingernails. Now he looked over to Harris, smiling as he repeated the information he was receiving. "Name change in 1984 to Aortek. So they're really the same company? Okay, thanks a lot John." David looked back towards Harris as he hung up the phone, unaware if what he said had any major significance.

"Guess those two companies were actually the same one. But I'll tell you something else that's more interesting," he looked over towards Martha, "wait till you hear this, Martha. I told you I can beat your computer sometimes. My friend at the library reminded me that Aortek was the company that had all those problems with their implants several years ago. Now I remember where I heard that name before. One of our recent CEO hires used to work for 'em, but he's not listed on the company profile."

For the first time that afternoon Martha was showing interest – extreme interest – "Who was that, David?" she asked.

"You see," David was looking at Harris and Brinkman again, proud of his little discovery and anxious to share the tricks of his non-computer world. "Martha and her assistants set up their files off an individual's resume, or what that person might list as his relevant experience when he applies for a job someplace. But I've learned over the years that a lot of people have gaps on their resume where they had a job that didn't work out very well, or maybe when they were unemployed for awhile."

"Who was it, David?" Martha asked again.

"Hold on, Martha, I'm getting to it," David said. He was standing now, looking like he was getting ready to deliver a lecture at a small business seminar on how to conduct employment interviews. "You see, almost everybody leaves something off their resume, and usually they adjust the dates on either side of that to close the gap. Most of the time there's a good reason, but I always like to try to find out what it was just in case they're covering something up. This guy had worked for Aortek and apparently wasn't very proud of it – wanted it kept off his resume."

"David, are you going to tell me who it was or do I throw a stapler at you?" Martha was trying to portray a friendly interest, but something about her look told Harris that she was serious.

"It was one of your Eagles, Martha. Your hotshot Eagle that we sent out to Denver – Tim Foster. He worked at Aortek right after he got done with grad school in California. I don't remember what he did, but I remember he didn't like it much."

They were in Brinkman's car now on their way back to Washington. There was a Metroliner leaving in 30 minutes, but Harris had made a quick decision and figured out they could beat the train provided they made it into the city before the rush hour traffic. He had placed a call to Stinnett on Brinkman's car phone, talking in cryptic word groupings, anxious to convey the importance of their findings but cautious about breaking security on a mobile phone that half the scanners in Maryland could monitor.

"We found the connection, Don, and we're on our way back."

"The name I mentioned this noon?" Stinnett was about as excited as his button-down image would allow. "Kaufmann said that Nickoloff wants an update this afternoon. Can I tell him we've got the connection and we're getting closer to a suspect?"

"I think you better hold off until I get there, Don. The connection is more than the one name you gave me. Plus, the list is probably longer than we thought."

"Shit! How much longer?"

"At least one name and maybe two. And we've got another name that we're gonna have to warn, although I suppose we have to consider the possibility that he could be a suspect."

"Then I can say that was might have a suspect?"

"I wouldn't. This name might be a future target. We really don't know. We're going to need some field help right away, Don, in Denver and in San Jose, plus the company name you mentioned this noon used to do business out of Dallas. We're going to need a lot of help there and probably in a hurry."

"When will you be here?"

"We're coming up to Highway 95 now. We should be at the office in twenty minutes."

Harris's next call was to his secretary, who relayed a message that Jay did not want to hear. "He's called twice, Mr. Harris. He said he needs to talk to you."

"What's his name?" Jay was holding the phone in his left hand, his right hand extended out towards the dashboard to guard against sudden stops. Brinkman was driving the car, moving rapidly through the afternoon traffic. They had opted not to put the light on the roof unless they hit heavy congestion.

Jay's secretary was a floater from the office pool. Harris and Dalton had never been successful in keeping a full time secretary for long, the basement office location and gruesome details of their case files serving as dual incentives for the clerical help to transfer out at the earliest opportunity. This secretary was all of four days on the job, and more than a little uncertain about how to deal with a situation where her boss was getting called by the press.

"He said he's a reporter with *The Washington Post*. His name is Michael Montgomery. He asked if you were the Jay Harris that does the profiles on serial murderers."

"What did you tell him?"

"I said I didn't know. I said you were the only Jay Harris at the Bureau, but I really don't know what you do." The phone connection was breaking up slightly. "What should I tell him if he calls back?"

"Tell him to call Deputy Director Kaufmann first, and if he's tied up to talk to Stinnett. If that doesn't work, have him call Denise Altman in Public Affairs. In any event, tell him I won't be able to call him back."

*

Michael Montgomery had been a busy young reporter the past few days since his conversation at Smitty's Bar in Georgetown. A quick wire service file check had picked up the item on the death of the Atlanta businessman during the past week. Michael had also logged on to the paper's computer link with Newsfile, the database used by a consortium of major daily newspapers and wire services to track stories of national interest. With this service it was possible to retrieve old articles off a mainframe somewhere underground in Colorado, articles that could be reviewed line by line on the 14" monitor that was part of Michael's word processing unit, provided he could figure out which key words to use.

The *Post* had a crackerjack research librarian on staff, a woman who could pull the most obscure reference out of the voluminous Newsfile database or one of the many others to which the paper subscribed. Unfortunately, she also had the bad habit of asking for the assignment code so the computer billing could get allocated to the correct department. With Newsfile, Michael had an account under his own name and running budget where he could generate billings of up to $50 a month without attracting attention. Once the billing went over $50, the system would deny him access until he had an additional authorization code or budget number that he would have to get from his editor, necessitating a conversation Michael did not want to have until he was ready to lay out the whole story line.

On his first do-it-yourself try, Michael typed in a request for a listing of articles on 'FBI investigations' and got a rapid and none-too-pleasing response that there were some 312 citations listed under that key word designation and it would cost $36.80 in computer time to get the summary reports. After trying 'FBI murder investigations' with 127 citations, Michael finally settled for 'FBI serial murder investigations' with 21 citations and a budget charge that would still leave him some room for future digging.

Although the names of FBI agents McKaskee and Grant were mentioned in many of the early articles dating back to the mid 90s, it was Dalton and Jay Harris who were referenced in several of the later articles.

> Georgia law enforcement officials today announced the arrest of Juan Casteel in Atlanta and have charged him with the murder of eleven prostitutes over the past four years. Local authorities say the break in the case was directly related to the information that the FBI had compiled regarding the probable characteristics of the individual responsible for the strangulation deaths of the women. Agents Jay Harris and John Dalton of the FBI's Washington office had been assisting the Atlanta Police Department throughout the investigation of the serial killings.

Three other references to Harris in articles published over the previous two years was all that Montgomery needed to zero in on his first contact at the Bureau. The phone call that afternoon, and the fuzzy conversation with Harris's secretary, had not provided any confirmation that there was a major story waiting to be had, but Michael was not dissuaded. There were other calls to make.

"Chuck? Hi, I'm glad I caught you in this afternoon. This is Michael Montgomery. Remember – we met over at Smitty's a few nights ago."

Michael's names and phone numbers were going to pay off! All those inane conversations, all those patronizing comments from the hangers-on to the Washington social circle who spoke of liberal attitudes and then looked with disdain at the young black reporter who did not yet have a reputation or position that brought him in contact with a name that could be dropped. How ironic that his first big lead would come not from one of the self anointed coterie, but rather from an unassuming college student who, like Montgomery, had so far found little reason to be impressed with the level of intellect of the individuals with whom he had interacted in this city of pomp and pomposity.

"I guess I remember. Are you the black guy?" Mauer asked, not in a pejorative sense, but rather as a casual way of helping to catalog the names and faces of the people that he had met.

"I'm the black guy," Michael said, smiling to himself. "I'm the short black guy who was talking to you the other night about some of the computer work that you did over at AMMA. Remember?"

"Yeah, I guess so."

"Well, I wanted to call today and get the name of your boss for a quick reference, since we might have a project over here where we can use you on a part-time basis."

"I could have gotten a little carried away the other night. I'm not exactly a computer whiz. I just helped straighten out their membership records that were all screwed up."

"That's probably what we'd need over here. Who would be the best person to contact at AMMA if I wanted to understand the process a little better?"

"The only guy over there that really knew what I was doing was Brian Davidson. I'm not sure if he'd give me a recommendation. I was only there as a temp."

"You have his number?"

*

"Mr. Davidson? This is Michael Montgomery at *The Washington Post*. I'm working on a story about the number of AMMA members that have been killed recently, and I just need to confirm some information for background purposes."

Michael was sitting at his word processor, his head tilted to the left so he could hold the phone against his shoulder. He was typing rapidly with both hands. Nothing that was readable – just striking the keys with enough force so the sound could be heard by Davidson, who would take away the mental image of a story going out on the wire as they spoke. "First of all," Michael continued, "the Mr. Sather who was killed this week in Atlanta was one of your members, wasn't he?"

The pause was critical. Michael was praying for a pause, praying for a tentative response that would be the first clue, the first confirmation that there might be something to Mauer's comments. As each second went by, Michael's heartbeat rose. Finally Davidson broke the silence. "The firm where Mr. Sather worked belonged to AMMA. That's correct."

"And counting Mr. Sather, how many of your members have been killed over the past few years?" Michael was pounding the keys again, the high tech clicking clearly audible to a shaken Brian Davidson wearing his trademark short sleeve white shirt as he stood next to his desk in the AMMA offices some ten blocks away.

Again the pause, this time longer, this time more important as a confirmation that there was something going on. "I can't really comment on that," Davidson responded slowly.

"I understand," Michael said. "We're just looking for background to confirm another source. Would you say the number is between five and ten? Between ten and fifteen?" This time Michael sensed that the delay in Davidson's response was because he was actually debating which answer to give, not whether he should respond. Michael thought for a moment that Brian might actually give a number, but finally the response came back with another version of 'no comment', again with an affectation in the voice that did nothing to dissuade the young reporter that he was charging down the right track.

The next call was back to Harris's office, one more try at locating the profile expert who would have to know about this if the FBI was really involved as Mauer had indicated. "I'm sorry, but Agent Harris has not returned. He did call in and said he wouldn't be able to talk to you."

"He said that?"

"Yes, he did," Harris's secretary responded with just a little more sense of self-importance than was justified. "He said that if you called back you'd have to talk to Agent Kaufmann or Stinnett or Miss Altman in Public Affairs."

Stinnett! The bell went off in Michael's memory bank. That was the name of the guy for whom one of Michael's secretary contacts worked. That was the name of the guy whose secretary might just remember Michael and might just provide the information that would tip the scale and remove all doubt. The fact that Harris had set up a triage system for his call was almost evidence enough, but the secretary's name would be an unexpected blessing.

"I'm sure you're right that I should call one of those other individuals. I've dealt with Agent Stinnett before. Remind me, what's his secretary's name again?"

Five minutes later Michael Montgomery was staring at the morning edition of that day's *Post*. There was a two-paragraph story on page 26 that he had written concerning the new rules that would go into effect for the taxis serving National Airport. But Michael was looking at the front page articles, the ones that carried the bylines of reporters who got their calls returned, reporters who created the stories that turned into series with follow on articles and sidebars and unlimited research budgets. Michael Montgomery was going to be one of those reporters. He had his lead! Janelle Davis had confirmed it a few minutes before.

"Hi Janelle, this is Michael Montgomery. Remember I told you I might call you sometime? We're doing a story about the deaths of the AMMA members. You know the case that Agent Stinnett is working on? The AMMA people indicate that their number of members killed is around eight or nine. Does that sound right to you?"

"Did they tell you that?"

"Well they didn't give me the actual number, but it sounded like it was around that level."

"I don't think I'm supposed to be talking to you about this, Michael."

"It's only for background. I just need to confirm our other source."

"You won't use my name?"

"No of course not. I'll probably be talking to Jay Harris later, but I wanted to get a quick confirmation on the number."

"Well, the last I heard it's more than ten. I think it's eleven."

"That makes more sense. I thought their number was too low. Thanks for your help."

Michael Jay Montgomery, twenty-four year old rookie reporter from Selma, Alabama, got up slowly from his chair, carefully adjusted his tie, and then shoved his fist in the air and let out a yell that could be heard by the lead reporters two floors above. He was on his way!

CHAPTER TWENTY
The Deadline

It was ten minutes to five when Harris and Brinkman walked down the corridor towards Stinnett's office. They could see him standing out by his secretary's desk, looking like someone waiting for the mail. "We're set up in conference room 2B," Stinnett said as the two men approached. "I've got our four DC agents ready and most of the field guys standing by for phone calls if needed. Kaufmann is going to be joining us in a couple of minutes and Denise Altman from Public Affairs is on her way over. Nickoloff might stop in also." Stinnett was unconsciously brushing off the lapels to his suit coat as he spoke, his excitement about the breaking events almost orgasmic, but not yet sufficient to overpower his instinctive need to be well groomed.

"I told you I don't think we've got a suspect yet," Harris said. "I don't know what we're going to tell the Director."

"Outta our hands, Jay." Stinnett had stopped the brushing but was now checking his cuffs. "Kaufmann told him we may have a break in the case. This thing is starting to take on a life of its own. You better be ready to make a report on what you've found."

"I'd really like some time to get this organized." Jay was holding a page of names and dates that he had written out during the short drive back from Baltimore.

"We don't have the time," Stinnett said. "Have my secretary run off an overhead transparency for the meeting and then type it up later. And, Janelle," he turned to his secretary, "I'd like you to plan on staying late tonight. We may need to have some faxes sent out and I don't want to use pool help on this case."

Conference room 2B was on the same floor as Stinnett and Kaufmann's offices, but in a section of the building rarely seen by most agents and only once before by Harris. With seats for twelve people around an oval table plus an additional four chairs on each of the two sidewalls, the room was normally used only for senior staff briefings or meetings with liaison officers from other federal agencies. Passive sound baffling and active electronic generation of spurious signal noise ensured that room 2B was the most secure area in the building other than the Director's office. "A bit of an overkill," thought Harris, but Kaufmann was never one for underplaying a situation if there was an opportunity for drama.

When they entered the room the four other Washington agents assigned to the case were already there, standing near the table, apparently uncertain of the seating protocol in a room that had one picture of President Clinton and two of J. Edgar Hoover. Stinnett motioned for everyone to sit down in chairs near the head of the table, then moved quickly to the small podium at the front of the room.

"Before we get started I want to mention again that we will be joined shortly by Deputy Director Kaufmann. It is also possible that Director Nickoloff may stop in for part of the briefing. He'll sit down in the end chair if he joins us. For those of you who haven't interfaced directly with him before, you should know that he likes short, straight answers to his questions although your best bet is to defer to Kaufmann or me." All of this seasoned advice was coming from a man whose only meaningful conversation with the Director had taken place just 24 hours before. "Now," Stinnett paused for effect, "since I don't know just when they'll be coming in I want to get started, and Jay, I'd like you to tell us what you found out in Baltimore."

As Jay got up and started moving to the podium, Kaufmann entered the room along with the Director. "Gentlemen," he said as he approached the table, "this is Director Nickoloff. We're both on a tight schedule so please continue with the briefing." Robert Kaufmann had been with the FBI for 28 years, during which time he had seen four Directors come and go. As a deputy director for the past five years, he was accustomed to cutting a rather broad swath when it came time to take command on a mission or an important investigation. Having the Director sit in on the briefing would help foster the image that he wished to convey, the image that Deputy Director Robert Kaufmann was in command – on top of the details – leading the troops out of the landing craft and onto the beach. Unfortunately the Director had not visualized the same image, or if he did, he at least wanted to tag along for the landing.

"Hold on a minute, Bob." Nickoloff had taken off his suit coat and was hanging it over the back of his chair, exposing a rather ample girth which did not seem to be of the least concern to him. "I haven't met all of these men." And with that he went around the table shaking hands and introducing himself, asking each man about his assignment and his experience within the Bureau. When he came to Harris he mentioned that he had reviewed the report that Jay had prepared. "It seems to me you might have profiled the wrong person," Nickoloff said, not in a remanding way, but rather with a congenial tone of 'let's talk about this for awhile'.

"What do you mean by that, sir?" Jay asked.

Nickoloff had moved around the table and was motioning for everyone to sit down. Kaufmann seemed reluctant to take his seat, aware now that the briefing was taking on a new leader. "What I mean," the Director continued, "is that while it's obviously important to figure out who's pulling the trigger, it seems to me that the most critical issue is to figure out who's behind all of this – what's the motive for these killings? Questions like that."

"You're absolutely right, sir." It was Stinnett this time. "We've made some dramatic progress on that point within just the past six hours. We found the linkage, and it should give us the break we need to nail down the motive and then the group behind all of this."

"You still think it's some group?" Nickoloff directed this question at Kaufmann, apparently aware that the deputy director felt in need of rejoining the fray.

"Yes we do!" Kaufmann said, a little more loudly than he intended. "I felt from the beginning that one of these radical animal rights groups is behind all of this, and I think we're going to be able to confirm that before long. We've beefed up our undercover work with some of these groups and I think it's just a matter of time before we have some hard evidence."

"What do you think about that, Harris?" Nickoloff said. "Do you think the guy you profiled would take directions from the animal righters?"

Harris had just been handed an overhead transparency from Janelle Davis and was glancing at it briefly before answering the question. "I'm not so sure any more that the person behind this is tied into the animal rights movement. There may be that connection, but we can't prove it on what we've found so far. We should be able to give you an answer on that in a few days once we check out this company." He held up the transparency and glanced towards Stinnett, looking for some indication that it would be okay to move to the podium. Nickoloff made the hesitation unnecessary.

"Tell us what you've got," he said, this time his attitude a little less congenial, aware that the concern over the pecking order in the room was rapidly starting to get in the way of conveying information. "There's an overhead projector on the cart, and the blue button on the podium will drop the screen. Let's see what you found out today."

For the next 20 minutes Jay described the process that he and Brinkman had gone through with Martha Laudner, using as his main talking point the listing of names and dates that he had prepared on the way back from Baltimore.

Case #	Date of Death	Name	Where Killed	Time at Company
1	May 13, 1985	John Levard	Toronto	3/77-6/80
2	Jul 16, 1986	Frank Ryan	LA	2/74-11/75
3	Sept 8, 1987	Randy Pellegrino	Florida	2/76-2/77
4	Sept 8, 1987	Larry Powell	Florida	Never There
5	Nov 12, 1988	Barry Decker	Boston	10/80-12/82
6	Oct 16, 1990	Richard Wendt	DC	8/83-12/85
7	Sept 2, 1991	Mirek Santarel	St. Paul	2/81-6/84
8	Aug 29, 1992	Howard Keppner	Portland	4/83-6/86
9	June 11, 1994	Spencer Mahler	Cleveland	10/76-4/78
10	Mar 21, 1995	Gary Lempke	Scottsdale	3/78-12/81
11	Oct 13, 1995	Eliot Sather	Atlanta	8/80-12/82

As he recapped the data that was available on the eleven deaths, there were several questions asked, initially by Stinnett and Kaufmann, but then just by Nickoloff as it became obvious that his interest in the case had gone from passive to active in a major way.

"What about those other two guys, Haberman and Daieje? What's their status?"

"We'll be having the field check on that as soon as we break from this meeting," Jay said. "My guess is that they're no longer alive. I won't be too surprised if they don't end up filling in some of the blank spots on our time line. If they are alive they're in danger, or possibly suspects."

"And what about the name of the guy Morkin came up with? Foster?"

"Same response for Foster," Jay said. "We need to have our Denver office make an immediate contact. I'm sure he's okay since Morkin interviewed him just a few months ago. But we'll need to warn him, although once again we have to consider that he could be a suspect."

"And what about Powell?" Heads turned again towards the Director. "Why was he killed if he didn't work for either company?"

"He wasn't the target." Jay was getting more comfortable at the podium, his initial unease about stepping on Stinnett or Kaufmann's toes had now subsided as it appeared obvious that the Director was more interested in getting the case solved than he was in worrying about interoffice politics. "We'd always assumed that Powell was the target and Pellegrino was the unlucky tag-along since Powell's company had the run-ins with the animal rights groups. But now it looks just the reverse. Pellegrino was the target because he had worked at Hemograft. Powell was the guy who was in the wrong spot at the wrong time."

Nickoloff had gotten up from his chair and was walking towards the front of the room to take a closer look at the information projected on the screen. "Tell me about the first guy that got killed – Levard. When did he work at the company?"

Jay took the laser pointer from the podium and directed the light onto the section of the screen that showed Levard's dates of employment, choosing not to tell the director that the information he was looking for was right in front of him.

May 13, 1985   John Levard   Toronto   3/77-6/80

"And the company filed bankruptcy in 1986, less than a year after this guy was killed?"

"That's right," Jay said, not quite sure where the Director was heading.

"What I don't understand," Nickoloff said, still staring at the names and dates on the screen, "is why it's taken over ten years for someone to make the connection on this. Why didn't the people who worked there, or their families, figure out something pretty bad was going on?"

"I guess we're as surprised about that as anybody," Jay said after awhile. "But if you look at the sequence of when these men were killed, you can see a pattern, which the more I think about it must have been intentional. The first five who were killed never worked there at the same time, and they were all killed in different parts of the country. It's unlikely either those men or their families would have known each other. It's only with some of the later files where there was an overlap on employment dates, but even with those cases the hit took place in different locations. These guys had taken new jobs, moved around the country, and probably lost contact with each other. They'd have no way of knowing what happened unless they kept in touch some way, which was apparently the case with Sather and Decker since Sather's wife knew that Decker had been killed."

"What about some of the people who worked there for several years? They should have known that something was happening to their ex-employees." Stinnett was back in the discussion, asking another question. "What about Haberman? It looks like he was there the whole time. He must have known something was happening if he had any contact at all with the people who left."

"I think Haberman's got to be our top suspect," Kaufmann said.

"I think Haberman's dead." Jay was surprised to hear the conviction in his own voice, not knowing why he felt quite so confident in that opinion. "We'll know within twenty-four hours, but I bet he's dead. He'll be number twelve on our list."

"Okay, let's get the assignments nailed down. We've got to get the field moving on this."

Don Stinnett was back in business, getting the troops organized and orchestrating a multi-state exercise that before the night was over would have 24 agents deployed in three different cities: Dallas to check out Haberman along with whatever trail was left on Hemograft and Aortek; San Jose to follow up on Jin Daieje; and Denver to warn Tim Foster and find out what he might remember about Aortek and the people who worked there.

During the hour of phone calls to the regional offices, Kaufmann and Nickoloff left the meeting to put in an appearance at a retirement ceremony for one of the associate directors. Stinnett had asked his secretary to have some food brought in, and the agents, along with Denise Altman who had now joined the session, were finishing their sandwiches and potato salad when the Director and Kaufmann returned.

"Any more news?" Nickoloff asked.

"Not yet." Stinnett was now without his suit coat, a rare event but a luxury he occasionally allowed himself when a working session stretched into the evening hours. "We've got the field up and running with this latest information. We might have some feedback yet this evening, but if not, we'll definitely know a lot more by noon tomorrow." As he was talking, his secretary brought in a message which Stinnett glanced at briefly.

"You want me to wait?" Janelle asked.

"Yes," Stinnett responded, motioning towards one of the chairs along the wall. "I may need to respond to this." He passed the message over to Kaufmann. "We have our first information back on Daieje," he announced to the group. "A records check indicates that he was indicted by the State of California for insurance fraud in 1986. No information yet on what happened to the indictment. We need to find out, but at least we know he was alive then."

"And in some kind of trouble," Kaufmann interjected. "He could have been working with Haberman! Maybe that's the fit!"

The Director had gone over to the side of the room to say hello to Denise Altman. Although she was buried about ten levels down in the organization, Nickoloff had worked with her on several occasions over the past few months as part of his campaign to rebuild the Bureau's rather tainted image that he had inherited from his two predecessors.

"I'll be very surprised if we see any connection between these two men, although it's possible." Harris had managed to find one extra container of potato salad which had been consuming his attention for the past few minutes, but he was now back in the discussion. "The thing we have to remember is that while these two guys and Foster might be suspects, they may also be targets. We're going to have to walk both sides of the street with 'em until we know a little more."

"What about the other targets?" Nickoloff was heading back towards the conference table when the thought hit him. "What makes you think there aren't five more names on somebody's hit list? Just because some woman in Baltimore only had twelve names in her computer for this company doesn't mean there might not be more!" The Director was standing by his chair now, but with no apparent intention of sitting down. His demeanor had changed to one of all business, challenging a shaky premise before it became the basis for a faulty strategy.

"Well there may be more, sir," Stinnett responded. "That's one of the things we'll have to find out as we dig into the background of the company and talk to these three men."

"That may take too long, or you may not get the whole story. What about using the press on this? Get the news out so that anybody else who worked for this outfit can be forewarned." As Nickoloff looked around the room waiting for a response, Denise got up from her chair and moved over to the conference table, taking a seat next to Brinkman.

"Maybe I can respond to that," she said, when it became obvious that no one else was going to answer. "We made a decision earlier not to inform the media until we had the case solved. I'm sure that decision can be revisited, but I think there's some good reasons why we should hold tight on this for awhile."

"Well I'd sure like to hear 'em. Seems to me that's a pretty risky strategy unless we know for sure who's a target and who's a suspect." Nickoloff had been looking at Stinnett when he spoke, but once again it was Altman who responded.

"The thing we have to remember is that it's only been a few hours since we found out this connection with Aortek. Before that, if we'd gone public, we wouldn't have known who to warn. Plus, I think the Bureau might have had a tough time explaining why we couldn't tie all the deaths together some way. You've seen how the press treats us with our mail bomber case."

"But now we have tied these together. Why not go public now?"

"Well, sir," Denise paused, knowing she was now moving onto shaky ground, "it would appear that we may be within days of breaking this. That could give us an almost unparalleled opportunity for a controlled news event. We can announce the culmination of an extensive investigation and at the same time disclose the arrest of our suspect. With a case of this magnitude, I can almost guarantee that it will be front page news. It's the best opportunity that we've had for favorable PR in an awfully long time."

"And what if we don't solve the case that fast? Who else are we going to be putting at risk?"

"I think we can limit that, sir," Stinnett said. "We should know in two or three days at the most about the organizational structure and other people who worked for Aortek. We can contact each one individually, even assign protection if necessary. And by not going public, I think we have a much greater chance of cracking the case. We won't tip our hand to whoever's behind this."

Nickoloff was no longer standing, but it was evident by his posture and tone of voice that he was still very much concerned about the issue, aware that this was a decision that should be made at his level – a decision that could blow up in his face if events did not occur as expected. "What do you think, Harris? How much time do we have before the next hit?"

"Well, sir, we all know that the time span has narrowed with these later deaths." Jay was tempted to use his laser pointer once again to highlight the dates, but realized that might be dwelling on the obvious. "But even considering that, we should have at least a month before we're at risk. You can maybe come up with an argument that if we went public now we'd actually increase the risk since the person behind this might want to finish the list quickly before the targets go underground. On the other hand—" Stinnett actually cringed when Jay started the sentence, knowing that what followed would only confuse the issue, "—on the other hand," Jay repeated, "the very fact that the FBI's scurrying around the country asking a bunch of questions might tip somebody off that we're on the trail, and that could push 'em to move faster."

Kaufmann had remained silent throughout the discussion regarding the press. As the original architect of the 'don't talk to the paper' rule, he had the most to gain if it worked, and the most to lose if it did not. Unless – unless the decision to hold tight was basically ascribed to Denise. His 28 years' experience as a survivor in an organization that greatly rewarded success and severely punished failure was about to pay dividends once again.

"So, Denise," he said, "is it your recommendation that we hold off informing the media for awhile, based on your review of the pros and cons?"

"Well, yes," she said, a little surprised that she seemed to be the focal point of the decision process. "There may be some risk as Jay pointed out, but the opportunity for favorable PR is just phenomenal if we hold off to break the story until we arrest our suspect."

"I think we have to follow Denise's recommendation, Walt." Kaufmann was the only one in the group who used the Director's first name, and he did so in a manner that suggested a degree of camaraderie greater than what actually existed. Kaufmann never used the first name in private conversations and Nickoloff was too nice of a guy to call him on it in public.

There was an awkward silence for a few moments following the "Walt" comment. No one else wanted to go on record with a formal recommendation until it was clear which way the Director was leaning. Jay got up and turned off the overhead projector, realizing they were at the end of the briefing. Finally Nickoloff stood up and walked around the table to the podium, surprising the rest of the group with this delayed specter of formality.

"I want to thank everyone for your work on this case," he said. "I think you're right about the impact this would have on the image of the Bureau if we solve it quickly. But we are at huge risk if we don't solve it and someone else dies. Today is Thursday. I want to be briefed on your progress at least every other day. We'll hold off going to the press for now, but if we don't have an arrest in ten days and if we have any doubt about who else we need to warn as possible victims, then we'll go public the next morning with whatever information we have at that time."

"If I may, sir?" Stinnett actually held his hand up, but quickly pulled it down after realizing how juvenile it looked. "I'd like to stress how important it is in the meantime that we not let anything leak. There's a guy from the *Post* who's snooping around on this. The worst thing that could happen is that we put a hold on our release and then the news breaks anyway. That could make it look like we've been covering something up."

"He tried to reach me today, Don," Harris said. "Some guy named Montgomery. I had my secretary tell him to call you or Bob."

"Well, he hasn't called me yet, but all of us have to be careful on this. Absolutely no contact and let Denise or me know if Montgomery calls you." As he paused for effect and looked around the room, he failed to notice that Janelle Davis had turned a rather unique shade of eggshell white, her breathing now at an elevated rate and her mind racing with contingency plans to be brought into play if the young Mr. Montgomery ever disclosed his source of information within the department. She was expecting that any moment Stinnett would go around the room asking if someone else had talked to Montgomery, and she was aware that if that happened she might actually become physically ill. It was only when she heard the voice of Deputy Director Kaufmann that she began to think there might be a chance to finish out the evening with her secret intact.

"I know it's important to keep this under wraps," he intoned, "but I've got contacts over at the *Post* and I can always put the pressure on 'em to squelch the story. I'm not worried about taking on the press if we have to."

Director Nickoloff was still standing at the podium. He leaned forward slightly, one hand on each of the burnished walnut side panels. In his office some 50 feet away were several pictures of him with his children and grandchildren, all portraying the image of a warm and gentle man basking in the love of his family. But at this moment Walter J. Nickoloff was not the kindly grandfather. Walter Nickoloff was the seventh director of the Federal Bureau of Investigation and he had heard enough posturing for one day.

"You all know that I'm new with the Bureau," he said slowly but firmly, "but I've had more than a little experience with the shaping of public opinion and the subtleties of dealing with the fourth estate. My rule on this type of issue is to never do battle with an entity that doesn't have a cardiovascular system. I'd like you all to remember that. Now you've got ten days! After that we talk to the media."

CHAPTER TWENTY-ONE
Day One

Friday, November 5, 7:45 a.m. – Washington, DC

It had been a busy night for some of the agents in the field, and the reports were starting to come back into Headquarters where Stinnett had set up a command center in a separate conference area with secure telephone linkage to the district offices. The agent in charge of the Denver office, Craig Knowlton, had personally made contact with Tim Foster at 10:45 Thursday night, and procedures had been established to provide protection at Foster's home as well as at Remote Monitoring. Knowlton and another senior agent would begin questioning Foster on Saturday morning to ascertain his knowledge about other Aortek personnel, as well as to make a preliminary determination about whether or not Foster should be considered as a possible suspect.

Activities in Dallas overnight had been somewhat more hectic, with numerous agents deployed in the attempt to unravel the Aortek corporate history, and other agents assigned to determine the status of Robert Haberman. The latter task had been the quicker of the two to accomplish. By midnight the Dallas office had not only determined that Mr. Haberman was indeed going to be listed as victim number twelve, but they had also located his ex-secretary, who apparently had some knowledge of the events that had transpired at Aortek. The call from Field Agent Frank Callahan of the Dallas office had been transferred to the conference phone in the command center when he called in at 8:10 Friday morning.

"Okay, you've got Special Agent Harris listening in and this is Section Chief Stinnett. Tell us what you have so far."

"This is all pretty early, but I thought you'd want to know as soon as we had something. Haberman's dead. Been dead since November of 89. The records list the cause of death as suicide by jumping from the twelfth floor of a luxury apartment building. We haven't had a chance to talk to the local cops who did the investigation, but the file indicates there was some reason to doubt if it was suicide. We'll be following up on that the next couple of days."

"Anything yet on the company?"

"I'm not working that end, and the agents who're assigned haven't completed their initial report. I can only cover so much." Callahan had intended on taking his son dove hunting near San Marcos over the weekend and was less than thrilled to be pulling extra duty to help the Washington office haul its fat out of the fire. "I do have a witness who worked at the company. A Mrs. Dorothy Latrobe."

"That's great!" Jay said. Now along with Tim Foster they had at least two names of people who had worked at the company, both of whom could hopefully shed some light on its history. "How'd you find her so fast?"

"Looked her up in the phone book and gave her a call." Callahan was yawning as he held the phone to his ear, the excitement at his end of the case nowhere near a level sufficient to keep his adrenaline pumping. "Her name was listed in the record of Haberman's suicide. I gave her a call and confirmed that she used to be his secretary."

"Did you bring her in?" Stinnett asked.

"Are you kidding? She's seventy-four years old. I got her out of bed when I called at eleven o'clock. I sure wasn't going to haul her downtown last night. I've arranged to pick her up this morning and we can set up a conference call with you guys at nine thirty your time."

The San Jose efforts had so far yielded few if any positive results. Other than the original indictment record on Jin Daieje, the local office was still chasing dead ends when Harris and Stinnett met Kaufmann in the command center.

"We've made contact with Foster in Denver and we've also found out that Haberman is dead," Stinnett said, "but nothing so far on the third guy."

Kaufmann had arrived at the building early, determined to be involved in the action during what he expected to be the last few days before an arrest. "Well, Jay, you were right about Haberman," he acknowledged, punching Harris lightly on the shoulder as part of his 'one of the boys' routine. "Now we need to double our efforts to track down Daieje. I've got a feeling about him. Are you checking with the Korean authorities – finding out about his background?"

"We're working it Bob," Stinnett said. "These things all take time. We're pushing our people as fast as we can."

"We've only got ten days. You may have to push 'em a little harder."

Over at the *Post*, Michael Montgomery thought he might have pushed just a little too hard. The funeral for Eliot Sather had been held in Atlanta on Thursday afternoon, and now on Friday morning, Michael was talking by phone with a rather upset young man who was apparently one of the Sather children.

"I really don't think my mother will want to speak with you. We've already been hassled by the local reporters and I don't understand why we should be talking with someone from *The Washington Post*."

"Perhaps I can explain that." Michael was sitting at his desk, but this time not touching the keyboard, recognizing that a more restrained approach would be in order. "We're aware that the FBI is involved with the investigation into your father's death, and the *Post* is in the process of conducting its own investigation into a series of deaths that have taken place recently among executives in the medical industry." Michael was listening to himself talk, almost as if he was across the room observing. "I'm getting pretty good at this," he thought. "This is how the pros do it. Spin the dial and ask questions. Everyone has a story sometime."

"How many deaths?"

"Well, Steven, I can tell you that there have been eleven people killed in what we think may be related incidents. That's why I wanted to speak with your mother. I wanted to ask if she was aware of anyone else who may have been killed?"

"She's not going to want to talk to you. I can tell you what she told the police. One of my dad's friends was killed six or seven years ago by a hit and run driver. That's the only name my mother knows about."

"Can you tell me, Steven, was that in Atlanta also?" Michael was consciously trying to be as courteous as possible, recognizing that he might be getting closer to another significant lead, but that he might also be only one wrong question away from losing a phone call.

"No, it was in Boston. But they worked together when we lived in Dallas several years ago."

"What company was your father working for then?" – "one more question," Michael thought – "one more!"

"I think it was called Hemograft."

"And just one more question, Steven, what was the name of your father's friend?"

"Barry Decker."

*

"Janelle? Hi, this is Michael Montgomery."

"I can't talk to you, Michael! Don't call me at the office!"

"Do you want me to call you at home?" Michael had debated waiting until Friday night to call Janelle Davis, but opted to call her as soon as he finished his conversation with Steven Sather. He was on a roll. Good reporters push their stories, they don't wait for the leads to walk into the front lobby of the newspaper!

"Don't call me at home either!" Janelle had turned her face towards the padded wall of the secretarial station, speaking firmly into the phone but trying not to draw any attention from the other people in the area. "I can't talk to you any more, Michael! I shouldn't have talked to you yesterday. Don't ever tell anyone that I spoke with you!"

"I just need to ask you one question Janelle. Is Barry Decker one of the eleven names on that AMMA list?"

"I can't talk Michael! I won't answer any more questions. I'm not gonna lose my job just to do you a favor!"

"Did they tell you not to help me on my story?"

"Michael, you don't have a story, don't you understand? They'll be having a press conference on this. Give it a rest!"

It was like a blow to the stomach. Michael actually felt as if he had been kicked. How in the hell could they hold a press conference on his story? He had dug it out and was bringing it along as fast as he could. It was his story! His story!

"I've got to hang up, Michael."

He was actually surprised she was still on the line, not certain how long she had been holding. "When's this press conference gonna be?" he asked finally.

"I don't know. I think in ten days. Probably a week from Monday. I've got to go, Michael."

He stared at his keyboard for a full two minutes after she hung up, his emotions ranging somewhere between anger and pain. Although Michael knew he was inexperienced when it came to digging out stories, he was extremely confident about one thing. This was the kind of opportunity that he might not see again for five years – maybe never. He had the lead on a major national story that involved a possible cover-up by a federal agency. It was his story!

And so Michael Montgomery reached in the bottom drawer of his desk, took out a large yellow pad and turned it sideways. Using a ruler, he divided the first sheet into ten equal sections. At the top of each section he listed the day of the week, starting with Friday and ending with the next Sunday, the day his story would run. Then he began to fill in action items for each of the ten days. It was possible he could do it. It was possible!

Friday, November 5, 9:28 a.m. – Washington, DC

Kaufmann was getting anxious. He was aware that the conference call was scheduled to start at 9:30, and if punctuality was a virtue, the deputy director could qualify for sainthood, so strong was his obsession with being on time. When he was promoted to his current job, one of his most treasured gifts had been a watch with two faces to accommodate the time zone shift that he encountered during his frequent trips to Chicago, thus reducing the remote possibility that he might err by a few minutes when he moved the hands forward or backward an hour.

For this meeting, Kaufmann had arrived at his customary three minutes before target time, although he had to ask his secretary where the room was located. Deputy directors did not usually sit in on conference calls from the field, but Kaufmann was aware that with Nickoloff's involvement, the case had taken on a new tone. The room that Stinnett had reserved as the command center for this investigation was a major step down from the ornateness of Conference 2B where they had met the previous evening, but it did have certain advantages, the most visible of which was a 30-cup coffee pot. Harris had apparently brought his personal cup with him, a mug that looked like it was washed only on special occasions, and then with very little vigor.

"Will we be starting at nine thirty?" Kaufmann was sitting down, but looking like he might be more comfortable standing, at least until he was sure of getting started on schedule.

"They're going to be originating the call in Dallas. I'm sure it'll be coming through any minute."

Harris was aware of Kaufmann's obsession with timeliness, almost feeling sorry for him as he might for a person having an inordinate fear of cars or some other common facet of daily living. Jay was in an unusually indulgent mood on this morning, particularly given the late night session and lack of sleep. This was the part of his job that he really enjoyed, getting information that should help tie together the files that he had been living with for the past several weeks. In most serial cases he spent the majority of his time working with individual data points, like studying isolated cities on a map without the benefit of being able to see the roads or sequence of stops. Once he could access the road signs and the mileage markers, the destination and estimated time of arrival could be determined. This morning Mrs. Latrobe was going to help Jay read the road signs. He hoped!

In Texas, Agent Callahan had spent the previous 20 minutes sitting in his office with a very talkative Mrs. Dorothy Latrobe. A tiny woman who could have served as a poster lady for an osteoporosis campaign. Callahan had picked her up at her apartment, and during most of the drive time had been forced to listen to a recitation about how all the people in Dallas drove too fast. This from a woman who may well have been incapable of seeing over her own steering wheel.

Now in the office, Callahan was trying to set the stage for the conference call. "What we're going to be doing, Mrs. Latrobe, is speaking with some of our agents in Washington. They'd like to ask you some questions about Aortek, where you worked for several years. We're going to use this speaker phone on my desk so they can hear both of us and we can hear all of them."

"Is this one of those TV phones where they can see us?"

"No, ma'am. It's just a speaker phone."

"My son wanted to get me one of those phones so I could see the grandchildren in Michigan."

"That would be nice."

"I'm not so sure I like the idea of people seeing how I look all the time."

Callahan thought briefly about mentioning the on and off switch but chose to cut short the discussion on modern communication technology in the interest of staying on schedule.

"Agent Stinnett? This is Frank Callahan in Dallas. I've got Mrs. Dorothy Latrobe here with me."

The call had come in at 9:32, barely within the grace period for Kaufmann's score card on punctuality. Stinnett made the introduction at the Washington end, which included himself, Kaufmann, Harris, and Eric Landau. Callahan started by telling them that he had given Mrs. Latrobe some general information about their area of inquiry. He had confirmed that she had been Robert Haberman's secretary for nine years, until the company went out of business, and that she might remember some of the other people who worked there but she 'hadn't thought much about it' over the past several years.

"Mrs. Latrobe, this is Agent Harris." They had agreed that Jay would ask most of the questions to cut down on the confusion for someone trying to sort through the voices coming out of a speaker 800 miles away. "I wonder if you would tell us about the people you remember working with at the company."

"Well as I told this gentleman here," she said, nodding towards Callahan, whose name she could no longer recall, "I don't remember many besides Mr. Haberman. One of my best friends was Irene Nieland who worked in accounting. Then there was Elizabeth Maloney who was a secretary in the marketing department. Goodness, it's been almost ten years. I haven't kept in contact with any of those people."

"I understand, Mrs. Latrobe, but what about some of the executives, some of the men who worked there?"

"There was someone named Barry. He worked in the production department."

"Barry Decker?"

"Yes I guess so. I don't remember his last name. Most of the men didn't stay too long. Mr. Haberman ran a tight ship and some of the people didn't meet muster. That's what he used to say. He'd been in the Navy during the war. He liked to use nautical terms." Kaufmann had pushed a note towards Harris and was pointing to the speaker phone they were using in the Command Center, obviously wanting a question asked of Mrs. Latrobe.

"Did you know a man by the name of Jin Daieje? He might have been called Dr. Daieje. I believe he was there when you were at the company."

"Was he the Korean?" Mrs. Latrobe was leaning towards Callahan's desk, bending her frail body in the direction of the speaker and almost shouting, as if to ensure that she could be heard by the people in the echo box on the other end of the line.

"Yes, he was Korean," Jay said, looking towards a now excited Bob Kaufmann. "What can you tell me about him?"

"I didn't like him very much. That's not nice to say I suppose, but he used to argue with Mr. Haberman a lot. Then one day he got fired. I don't know what happened to him after that."

"And what did they argue about Mrs. Latrobe? Do you remember that?"

"I'm not sure. Something about the research program. He didn't think that the company was doing the right kind of test with the dogs and Mr. Haberman disagreed, so he fired him."

Harris spent another 20 minutes with Mrs. Latrobe, patiently going through the names of the victims who worked there when she was at the company. Mrs. Latrobe thought she recognized certain of the names, but could come up with no others on her own. She was able to confirm that the company used animals in some of the research projects, but could not recall any details of the programs other than the fact that Daieje apparently was unhappy about the results.

"A lot of the men complained too much, but I stayed on." She paused for a moment, looking as if she needed to justify her statement. "I was loyal," she said, "he was my boss. I was loyal."

"Mrs. Latrobe," Jay asked, still on the hunt for more names, "who do you think took the records of the company when it shut down? Employment records, things like that? Would Mr. Haberman have taken those?"

"Oh goodness, no! Everything burnt in the fire. That's when the company filed for bankruptcy, right after the fire. There was financial trouble before but I guess the fire was the last straw."

"Was that when Mr. Haberman committed suicide?" Jay was looking for his list of names and dates.

"It was three years later when Mr. Haberman died." The chill in the voice was suddenly obvious, the kindly grandmother was not leaning towards the phone any longer. "I was never certain that it was suicide."

"What do you think might have happened?" Now the four men in Washington were leaning towards the conference phone, anxious to hear the response. Earlier that morning Stinnett had received a copy of the Dallas police file. There had been no note or witness, but in the absence of other evidence the police had ruled it as a suicide.

"I'm not sure what happened," Mrs. Latrobe said, "he might have slipped or maybe something else. Some people thought he might have killed himself because of the deaths. But I never thought they were his fault. I told him that too. I was loyal. I never got a dollar of pension money because of the bankruptcy, but I'd still work for Mr. Haberman if he was alive."

Afterwards, Harris complimented himself and the others on how well they had handled themselves with the open phone line. There had been the immediate impulse to shout 'What deaths?' How could she have known about the eleven deaths, and who would have been blaming Haberman for it in 1989? When Jay finally asked, in a calm voice, for a better understanding as to which deaths Mrs. Latrobe was referring, he got the answer that none of them had expected, and the answer which was now starting them on a new slant in their investigation.

"The patient deaths," Dorothy Latrobe said, "the patients who died after having the graft implanted. I thought that's why you were digging out this old information on the company."

*

For the next hour there was a flurry of activity in the Command Center as this new piece of information was added to the dynamic of the investigation. Calls went out to initiate computer searches of additional databases in an attempt to ascertain the number and specific causes of patient deaths associated with products produced by Hemograft or Aortek. Two additional agents were assigned to contact the FDA to review old files on medical device regulatory filings and facility inspections. Mrs. Latrobe had been unable to recall the number of patient deaths, only that there were some, and that they resulted in major legal and financial problems for the company.

"Maybe that's why Daieje got fired. Maybe he was blowing the whistle on the company – got fired – and then later on started taking his revenge." Kaufmann was obsessed with the Korean connection, and became even more so when the call came in from the San Jose office with an update on their findings. One of Daieje's ex-coworkers at Barkley Avionics had told the local FBI that the scientist talked incessantly about his negative experience at Hemograft. He also said that Daieje apparently lived frugally, but had access to a lot of capital from his family, who were part of some successful industrial group in Korea.

"We've got to push this," Kaufmann said. "We've got to push! This guy must be back in Korea. He's been pulling the strings from there. Who's doing the liaison with the Korean National Crime bureau?"

"Hancock's been working on it since yesterday," Stinnett said. "We really didn't do ourselves any favors last year the way we handled the investigation on Korean sales of attack rifles in the US. The KNC guys thought we ran a little roughshod on that and they're not exactly busting their ass to help us on this."

"Screw 'em! I'll have Walt talk to the ambassador if necessary!" Kaufmann was looking at his watch, concerned about how he was going to push his point on Daieje and still be three minutes early for his next meeting.

"Bob, let's hold on that for a while and try to keep this in normal channels," Stinnett said. "If we don't have any more information in the next twenty-four hours, then we'll bring out the big guns."

"That guy's going to drive me nuts!" Stinnett said when Kaufmann left the room. "We oughta send him to Korea."

"Don, I want to fly out to Denver this afternoon," Jay said, changing the subject. His interest in Daieje as a suspect had never been high, and it was obvious he thought other elements of the investigation might be more important. "I want to talk to Foster direct and get a better understanding of how that company worked. Plus I want to know more about these patient deaths. We may have something from the FDA search today, but I want to find out what

Foster knows. I'm going to ask the Denver field office to hold off their meeting with him until I get there."

"You know, Jay," Stinnett said, "what we really need from you is another profile on the person who might be behind all of this." Later that night when he thought about it again, Stinnett would be surprised that he was the one asking for a profile, but at the moment it seemed to make sense. "Nickoloff was right to push you on that. You did a profile on the trigger man, but then you tell us somebody else is pulling the strings. We need a profile on the second person or Kaufmann is going to have us all on the next plane to Seoul."

"I know," Jay said. He was getting himself another cup of coffee, the fifth one that morning. Landau had been keeping count and wondering when the caffeine would take hold. Jay was starting to pace. It was apparently beginning to have an impact, proving that even cast iron digestive systems are not immune to the basic laws of metabolism. "I've been thinking about that since we talked with Mrs. Latrobe. I've got some ideas and I'll work on a draft during the flight out to Denver." He had stopped walking but was now standing near the table, rhythmically tapping his hands on the top of one of the chairs. "Don, who's our in-house medical expert? I need to talk to somebody about implantable grafts," Jay said, "the kind that Aortek made. I need to find out how they were manufactured, what kind of patients used them, and how they failed. I want to get up to speed before I talk to Foster." The caffeine was definitely working.

The FBI had standby consulting agreements with two medical schools in the Washington area, under which the Bureau could access faculty members and specialists when it was necessary to learn more about a specific medical or anatomical question that might come up in the course of an investigation. There were also three MDs on the staff at Quantico whose primary duties involved reviewing case files and investigations where there might be some question regarding cause of death or the accuracy and completeness of an autopsy report. Stinnett knew that one of them, Dr. Jordan Browning, was an ex-vascular surgeon and probably had the best background for this line of inquiry. After medical school, Browning had spent 20 years as an Air Force Flight Surgeon and at retirement could never quite reconcile the thought of going into civilian medicine with its attendant requirements for malpractice insurance and claim forms. The FBI position allowed him to double-dip in the federal well and still keep his certification, thereby allowing him to attend the odd medical convention and impress his colleagues with discussions on bizarre causes of death.

Friday, November 5, 11:25 a.m. – Washington, DC

By the time Dr. Browning arrived at the Command Center, Harris had received a message from the agents reviewing files at the FDA. There was apparently a great deal of information available on Aortek, much of it negative, and it would take an additional three or four hours to sort through the material and copy the items of importance. In the meantime, the agents had sent over a copy of a product brochure on the company's aortic aneurysm graft. Jay handed the copy to Browning who seemed intent on taking his time to review the two-page document.

"You're not really giving me much to go on, you know," Browning finally said. "If I had the specifics on their clinical data I could be a lot more helpful."

"We'll have that for you eventually." Harris was tempted to get up for another cup of coffee but didn't want to lose eye contact with the doctor. "We'll have more in a day or two," Jay started again, "but right now we need a quick overview so we can ask some intelligent questions."

"I do remember reading something in the literature several years ago about a series of deaths caused by graft failures. I'm not sure if it was this company. We didn't do a lot of aortic aneurysm repairs in the Air Force – patient base was too young. They probably do a lot in VA hospitals. You might wanna check there for some history."

This time it was Harris worrying about punctuality. He was booked on the 2:35 United flight from Dulles Airport into Denver. "We've got to move, Jordan. I'm going to have to ask you for the shorter version."

He never did get the shorter version, but somewhere between the doctor's desire for scientific accuracy and Harris's need to catch a flight, they got enough of an overview to provide Jay with the background he would need when he spoke to Foster. With periodic trips to the board to illustrate an anatomical point, Dr.

Browning delivered his lecture on Aneurysm 101 and Implantable Grafts 102.

"The first things you need to know," he began, "is that an aneurysm is basically a ballooning out of a vessel. An aortic aneurysm is where you get this ballooning, or dilation, in the aorta, which is the biggest blood vessel coming out of the heart. Normally in an adult male the aorta is about an inch in diameter, but sometimes you get an aneurysm the size of a grapefruit. If that thing ruptures you can start painting X's on the eyelids because this guy isn't going to be around for surgery tomorrow morning."

Browning paused for effect, hoping to elicit a chuckle over his lighthearted description of death. His casual attitude towards medical issues and attempts at being 'one of the boys' had not yet found an audience among the agents at Quantico, despite the fact that earthy humor was very much in evidence at the Bureau, much to the consternation of officials dealing with a number of sexual harassment suits.

"How common is this problem?" Stinnett asked.

"You probably see it in two or three percent of the population," Browning said. "It's more common in men than women, more common in older people than younger. A sixty year old guy who smokes a lot and has high blood pressure is a prime candidate, but it can happen to anybody."

"So what about the grafts? Where do they come into the picture?" Harris was back to the coffee pot again. His secretary had brought in some boxed lunches which nobody except Jay had touched.

Browning moved up to the white board at the front of the room to draw a rough sketch showing the main branches of the cardiovascular system. "You can get an aneurysm just about any place in the vascular tree, but with aortic aneurysms, about ninety percent occur in the abdominal area. From what I saw in that copy of their product literature, that's the kind of graft the company was producing. One that could be used to repair abdominal aortic aneurysms, AAAs in the trade. If they burst you're probably dead like I said before, but if they can be diagnosed ahead of time you can do a surgical repair where you cut out the damaged section of the aorta and replace it with a synthetic graft. It's tough surgery!"

"You ever do one?" Jay asked.

"I've done 'em in the peripheral arteries, but not in the aorta. That's big league surgery. Usually those are done at major centers where they see a lot of cases and have a surgical team that's well trained to handle any problem."

"What kinda things can go wrong? If some of these patients died, what do you think might have been the problem?"

Harris was looking at Browning, trying to remember which was the good eye. The doctor's eyes did not line up exactly square, one always pointing five degrees off center, and Jay could never remember which eye was dominant. He had asked Browning about it one time at an agency party when both men had consumed enough wine to lower the barriers of acceptable conversation. He thought the doctor had said the left eye was the one to look at, but Jay was still uncertain, and often wondered how Browning could have done precision vascular surgery if he was focusing in on two different suture lines.

"I don't know what went wrong. I told you before that once I see the clinical data and FDA reports, then I can be a lot more helpful. Having said that, there are some obvious possibilities." As Browning walked back towards the board for yet one more diagram, Stinnett looked at Harris and nodded his head, recognizing the need to wrap up the meeting.

"Jay's gonna have to leave in a few minutes to make his flight, Jordan," Stinnett said.

"Hey – you guys are asking the questions," Browning responded with an edge to his voice, "I'll give you the short version." He put down the felt tip marker and held up three fingers. "Three likely causes of failure. One – damage to the red blood cells because of interaction with the prosthetic material of the graft. That's really a long-term problem that would be slow to develop. Two – rupture of the graft itself, which probably means instant death. And three – failure of the anastomosis. That's the juncture between the graft and the natural vessel. You've got two anastomoses to make on a triple A implant. If one of them fails, you better check your malpractice insurance. You've got a dead patient. That fast enough for you, Donald?"

On the three and one half hour flight to Denver, Harris began drafting a second profile, the one that Nickoloff was looking for and the one that Jay knew might be key to a quick resolution of the investigation. This was a new experience for him, trying to ferret out the motives and characteristics of an entity that had systematically directed the murders of at least twelve executives, murders which were carried off in such a way so that the common thread between the cases had not been detected despite the sophistication of the FBI's criminal statistics and data analysis software.

The information they had received that morning on patient deaths had introduced a new dynamic into the equation, the possibility that the second profile could be driven by revenge. Once Stinnett had the FDA information on Aortek product failures, the team might be able to put together a list of people who would have some reason to seek reprisal. But that would take time, and they would still need some way to screen the names – some way to lock in on those individuals who might have the warped personality and characteristics which would drive them to plan and finance a series of execution style murders over the span of a decade. They needed a second profile!

Friday, November 5, 4:25 p.m. – Denver

By the time the United flight landed at Stapleton Airport, Harris had finished the draft and rewritten it so it would be legible when he faxed it to Washington. He was met at the gate by Alex Meyers, the Denver agent assigned to the case. Meyers had managed to find a secure phone line at the airport so they could fax the draft to Washington before they left for the downtown office. Stinnett read it as it came off the printer in Washington, surprised as always by Harris's ability to write with a style that belied his folksy demeanor.

Second Profile

> The person responsible for these serial murders is a methodical, well organized individual, who is driven by a passion or cause that is sufficiently intense to sustain itself over a period of some ten years. The timing of the crimes suggests a pattern of planning carried out with great attention to detail so as to minimize the possibility that targeted victims would be aware of other deaths. The geographical dispersion of the murders and the fact that several occurred in cities where the victim was visiting, also

indicates an attempt (largely successful), to reduce the appearance of linkage which authorities might otherwise have perceived.

The great care taken to minimize detection, the absence of any attempt to seek credit for the crimes, and the fact that these murders were carried out over such an extended period, all combine to suggest that the individual responsible is not likely to be at the fringe edge of society or actively involved with some radical organization where the risk of a security lapse could increase the chance of detection and subsequent apprehension. Although it is possible that the entity behind these homicides is not an individual but rather a group or an organization having some common motive or cause, I find it highly unlikely that this is the case. It is almost impossible to conclude that a group could retain a common objective over this period of time and successfully coordinate the planning of eleven separate crimes. We must therefore assume that it is one single individual responsible for the formulation of the plan to systematically kill these executives. This person would in all probability have been between the age of 40 and 50 at the time of the first murder. Although it is plausible that our subject is a woman, the brutal nature of the crimes and the ability to interact with the actual killer or killers suggests that the subject is male.

The relationship of this individual to Aortek is as yet unclear. In all probability this person was never employed at the company but may have been affected directly or indirectly by events which took place there. These events could have involved the use of animals in research, but more likely were tied to the failed graft implants which subsequently led to patient deaths.

With regard to personal characteristics, this individual is very likely to be an intelligent, well organized, detail oriented person who is now between the age of 50 and 60. We can expect that the subject is either single or in a marriage that is not close and is without children in the home. We can also expect that the individual is employed in a professional position with sufficient monetary resources available to finance an extended series of hired executions. This person is very much in control of his emotions and will appear outwardly normal to other individuals with whom he interacts. Accordingly, he will be very difficult to identify unless he can be tracked via contact with the actual killer or unless a more definitive motive can be established after closer examination of the events which took place at Aortek.

Given the obvious level of planning that was undertaken by this individual, it is possible that the killer may not even be aware of the identity of the person directing the crimes. Therefore, apprehension of the killer may not result in the identification of this second profiled person, and may also not preclude additional murders taking place. Although there is not yet evidence to suggest that any of the twelve murders were carried out by the second individual, the subject may now be so driven by the goal of finishing the list that he could personally kill the final victim or victims. Said another way, the identification and arrest of this person will put an end to the killings, whereas the apprehension of the hit man may not.

"Did you get the fax?" Jay asked when he reached Stinnett by phone. It was almost seven o'clock in Washington, and even though this was a top priority case, Stinnett was hoping to get out of the office early on this evening and make it home for his daughter's birthday party. "I got the fax," he said. "I copied in Kaufmann but haven't sent one to Nickoloff yet, even though he's looking for the second profile. You haven't given us much to go on, Jay. I don't know if you told us much more than we already knew."

"You want the guy's name and phone number?" Harris had been down this path before. Despite all the caveats, some people still expected enough detail in a preliminary profile that they could go out and make an arrest. "It's an initial profile," Jay said, "not a list of suspects. I should be able to improve on it after I talk to Foster and after we learn more about some of the patients who died."

"You're really sure it's a man that's behind this?"

"No, I'm not sure! I think so but I can't be positive." Harris got up and shut the door to the office he was using at the Denver Headquarters. "I can tell you we have a compulsive person who is absolutely driven to complete a mission. Those characteristics are usually reflective of the male criminal mind, but could be a female. I am sure it's a single individual and not some group thing. If this guy's in some radical animals rights organization then he's operating on his own. The group wouldn't even know that something was going on. You getting any help from our undercover agents by the way?"

"Nothing yet," Stinnett said. "Now that we know about Haberman and Aortek, we're pushing that angle for information. I hope to have something soon."

There was a knock on the door to the office and Meyers' secretary brought in a sandwich and a cup of coffee. It was only five o'clock in Colorado but Jay's stomach was still on East Coast time and not to be denied. He took a swallow of coffee and then continued with his phone conversation. "I'm gonna be meeting with Foster in the morning. He's coming to this office, and Meyers and I plus maybe Knowlton will be talking with him about Aortek. In addition to finding out about the patient deaths, I hope to get some more names of people who worked there. You need to push the Dallas office to help on that. Nickoloff might have been right about the list. There could be more names than we think."

"We're trying to find those two women that Mrs. Latrobe mentioned – see if they can remember other names." As a section chief with prime responsibility for directing the investigation on the case, Stinnett was always a little less than enthusiastic about getting unsolicited advice. Still, he knew that Harris had a good feel for key elements of a serial crime, and God forbid that Kaufmann or Nickoloff ever thought that Jay was being kept out of the loop. "We also talked to the State Employment Bureau – looking for old workers' compensation or social security records on Aortek and Hemograft."

"Good idea." Jay was starting on his sandwich, keeping his response short between bites.

"I thought so too. Unfortunately they only keep records for seven years and these guys have been out of business for longer than that, so no help there."

"Did you see where Haberman fit on the schedule?" Jay asked, switching subjects.

"Whaddya mean?"

"Haberman was killed in 1989. That was one of the gaps that we had on the list of twelve murders. I forgot about it until I was going over it again on the plane. The other gap is in 1993. I'm sure we're going to find another name and he'll have been killed in '93. Part of the profile. Our subject likes to stick to a schedule."

"What time do you talk to Foster tomorrow?" Stinnett was anxious to get home.

"I think we're scheduled to get started at eight or eight thirty. They tried to get it lined up for tonight, but Foster's got some family thing and wouldn't change it."

"Call me as soon as you're done."

"You gonna be in the office? Tomorrow's Saturday."

"I'll be in. Tomorrow we'll be down to nine days before Nickoloff's press conference. I want to break this case before then. Altman is right. If we can announce an arrest when we go public, it'll be the best PR we've had in a hell of a long time."

"Don't hold your breath on an arrest. We've got a ways to go."

"I think we'll do it. Things are starting to come together. But what do you think about Foster? Is he at risk? If this guy gets hit on our watch then Kaufmann and Nickoloff are going to have both our heads."

"I'll give you a better answer tomorrow after we've talked to him. Right now I don't think he's got anything to worry about. I think he was too low in the organization. Actually I'm beginning to think that we may be at the end of the list. I wouldn't tell that to Kaufmann yet but the Atlanta case could have been the last one."

Friday, November 5, 9:45 p.m. – Los Angeles

In California, Enrique Moreno was just starting his shift as a pressman at *The LA Times* printing plant on Hillman Avenue. The personal section for the first Saturday of the month always seemed to be a big one, and this week's was no exception. It would be another twelve hours before Lloyd Barnett picked up a copy of the paper in Las Vegas, but in Los Angeles, Enrique had already seen the ad as he scanned the tear sheet from the section, looking for print alignment and ink density. Married for almost thirty-eight years, he smiled as he read the ad at the top of the right hand column.

Happy 40th Anniversary Uncle Ed and Aunt Sheri
From David, Susan and Bill

CHAPTER TWENTY-TWO
Day Two

Saturday, November 6, 9:05 a.m. – Denver

Tim Foster was not his usual picture of self-confidence as he shook hands with Jay Harris in the lobby of the FBI office in downtown Denver. Since the phone call from Agent Knowlton, Tim had been reviewing in his mind the events that had been going on at Hemograft when he was employed there – events that he had consciously tried to forget over the years since he had left the company. Despite attempts to distance himself from that experience, he was aware that the company had changed its name to Aortek, and he also knew that it had since gone out of business. The information that Knowlton had passed on about a number of executives being killed over the past several years had still not registered completely, as he tried to put the breaking events into perspective and understand how all of this was going to affect him.

When he had gotten the phone call Thursday night, he had neglected to tell Agent Knowlton about the letter he had received from Branson. Several times on Friday he thought about calling the FBI to advise them about the letter, but opted to wait until the Saturday meeting when he could show them a copy. Now he was sitting at a table with three agents, but instead of feeling secure, he was suddenly even more concerned as he sensed the air of tension that seemed to permeate this small, windowless, conference room.

"Mr. Foster, we'd like to record this conversation if you don't mind," Agent Meyers pointed to the microphone in the center of the table. He was handling the preliminary details as agreed, but Harris would bear the prime responsibility for the questions on Aortek and the other people who worked there.

"Before we start I've got a question," Tim said, ignoring the comment about the microphone. "I've got to know if I'm in danger or if my family's in danger. I thought about this yesterday, and how do I know if this guy might not be looking for me next?"

"Mr. Foster," Jay said, as calmly as he could, "that's what we want to find out also. But we really need to spend some time going over several other questions before we can answer that."

"But I really need to know! I need to make a decision if I should tell my wife and maybe have her leave for awhile with the girls."

Harris saw that he would have to deal with this immediate issue before Tim would be able to relax enough to talk about the other areas of interest. "Let me ask you a couple of quick questions and maybe I can answer that," he told Foster. "How long did you work at the company?"

"Just a year and a half. Most of that time I was still in grad school so I was working part-time. After I got my Masters I worked full-time for the last six months."

"And what was your position?"

"I was a design engineer. I helped on some of the work with the grafts and the animal implants."

"And were you a manager or an executive at that time?"

"No way! I was just out of grad school."

"Well, Mr. Foster, we're still early into the investigation of Aortek and we'll have to take certain precautions in any event until the case is solved, but based on what we know about the other men who were killed, I think we can safely say that you are not a target."

It was less than an hour later when Lloyd Barnett picked up the Saturday edition of *The LA Times* and saw the ad. He had developed an almost uncanny ability to guess when there was going to be a message for him in the personal section, anticipating correctly this time that there would be a shorter interval between the new job and his last assignment. It could not have happened at a better time – for him. Maxed out on his credit line at the Hilton, Barnett had been spending more time at the downtown casinos, playing the low stake tables and trying desperately to get another winning streak started. There had been other dry spells in Barnett's gambling history, but this one seemed to have unusual staying power. Judie had loaned him $2,000 and was now threatening to move out if he did not come up with the cash. This was more than an idle threat, since she had been paying the rent for the past three months. Even his one good Visa card, the previously sacrosanct symbol of normalcy and his lifeline in case he needed to disappear in a hurry, even that was at risk because of late payments.

As he read the ad for the second time, he thought how he would use the money when he finished the job. Priority one should be the Visa bill, but after that he might consider some high stakes blackjack at the Luxor hotel before he paid back Judie and the Hilton. In any event, he needed to respond with his own ad in Monday's edition of the paper, and then think about whether or not he would use Jack Shaffer again. With luck he could have the first payment in four or five days. One more annuity check. Still working the list!

Saturday, November 6, 12:15 p.m. – Washington, DC

Michael Montgomery was sitting at the kitchen counter in his small apartment in a mixed income section of Washington. He was now on the fourth draft of the ten-day schedule that he had first tried to sketch out the previous morning when he found out about the FBI plan for a press conference. Day one was over and he had little to show for his efforts. A call to the business reference desk at the Dallas public library had been moderately successful. Michael had learned that Hemograft had a name change to Aortek in 1984, and that there was a subsequent bankruptcy filing in 1986. No other data was available at the library other than the fact that the company had produced implantable vascular grafts and the president's name, listed in the bankruptcy filing, was Robert Haberman. A dialogue with a career civil service employee at the FDA topped off Michael's first afternoon of frustration.

"Some material may be available on the company and its products," Michael was told, but a Freedom of Information request would have to be submitted and only then would available records be copied, at a rate of 50 cents per page. Expected turnaround time could be one to two weeks depending on the need to screen the records for information which might be considered of proprietary value to the company.

"How can anything be of any proprietary value to the company if they're bankrupt?" Michael asked.

"The regulations specify that a company can indicate what they think is proprietary, and then we can't copy that under FOI, unless there's some type of court order or administrative ruling."

The clerk behind the window at the FDA's Silver Springs office was a tall black man with a neatly trimmed beard and a pair of half glasses balanced precariously on the bridge of his nose. As he tilted his head back to peer downward at Michael, he was successful in conveying the impression that he was unimpressed by the brandishing of press credentials that the reporter had offered in a hoped-for display of authority.

"How do I know if there's any proprietary information in the record?" Michael asked.

"You file an FOI request."

"And how long will that take?"

"It depends on how much proprietary information's in the file."

Michael's luck improved with his call to Boston. He had managed to locate Barry Decker's widow, who confirmed that her husband had once worked at Hemograft in Dallas with Eliot Sather. Mrs. Decker was intrigued to hear about the possibility of some connection between the death of her husband and others in the industry. "We always thought there was something suspicious about the way Barry died," she told Michael during their phone conversation. "I've got some of his old files here, and if you want to look at them you're sure welcome."

And so Michael made an appointment to meet with Mrs. Decker on Sunday afternoon at her home in Boston, an item that he was now entering onto day three of his schedule. His problem was not with day three, nor with days eight and nine when he would be in final draft and rewrite stage. His story would have to run in the following Sunday's edition, day ten of the schedule, and one day before the FBI press conference. The blank spots on his yellow legal pad for days four through seven were his problem, and would remain so unless he got some assistance with his research. He was going to have to talk with Karl Bonnert, his editor, and convince him of the merits of the story, a story that Michael did not yet have and a story that was clearly outside his area of responsibility at the paper. "I have to have the lead paragraph," Michael thought, "I have to have the first hundred words and they've got to set the hook so deep that Bonnert would be nuts to take me off the story."

As he thought through the strategy for a Monday meeting with Bonnert, Michael realized that he would also have to involve Larry Hampton, the reporter at the *Post* who traditionally covered stories involving the FBI. No editor would turn over a top story to a rookie reporter without touching base with the writer who normally covers that beat – no matter how good the first 100 words were. And so Michael took one more clean sheet from his yellow pad and filled in his action items for the next two days.

<u>Day 3 – Sunday</u>

1. Meet with Mrs. Decker in Boston
2. Draft first 100 words
3. Call Hampton at home

<u>Day 4 – Monday</u>

1. Sell editor on story
2. Work on remaining research

Taking the shuttle flight to Boston on Sunday would have to be at his own expense, but the front page story would carry his byline. He could afford to fly to Boston for a byline.

Saturday, November 6, 1:20 p.m. – Washington, DC

It had been an hour since Harris had called. He had been surprised when Stinnett was unavailable to take the call and even more surprised to have to wait this long for a call back.

"Sorry about the delay," Stinnett said when he did call. "I've been on the phone to our liaison contact at the embassy in Seoul. Kaufmann was in the office this morning and thought we were moving a little too slow on the Daieje angle. He had me on the horn with Korea for so long I could almost smell the cabbage."

"Did you learn anything?"

"Who you kidding? It's six o'clock tomorrow morning over there. I got our embassy guy outta bed and about the last thing he's gonna do is call up his KNC contact at that time of day. They do know that Daieje came back to Korea in 1987, but that's it so far. We should have more news before long."

"He's not our man, Don."

"Tell it to Kaufmann. I'm not the guy you gotta convince. What did you get outta Foster this morning?"

Stinnett was aware that there had been some information obtained from Foster that morning which had resulted in the questioning of a possible suspect in Seattle. Harris proceeded to discuss the details, reviewing the letter that Foster had received from Maynard Branson and the subsequent trace that had ended up with two Seattle agents flashing a badge in front of Branson when he showed up for work.

"You sure he's not involved?" Stinnett asked.

"I don't think so. This guy was in prison from 1987 to 1993. We're checking him out but I think he's a fruitcake. He doesn't fit the profile." As soon as Harris mentioned the profile he knew it would trigger a response from Stinnett. When there was no immediate reaction, he asked, "Are you still alive, Don?"

"I'm here! I'm looking for my copy of your second profile. I thought you said the suspect was driven and committed. He could've been directing all of this from a cell someplace, you know."

"Not likely. I'll fax you a copy of the letter that Branson sent Foster. The guy's a flake. We need to watch him, but he's not gonna be our prime suspect no matter how much we'd like the case to fall into our lap."

"Why's this guy so pissed at Foster?"

"Claims Foster got him demoted. Branson wanted to steal the dogs outta the research lab and Foster turned him in. Apparently they both thought it was bad research and terrible conditions in the lab, but Foster wanted to clean it up and Branson wanted to play God. Branson lost. But forget about him for a while. I spent some time asking Foster about the patient deaths. We really need to move on this, Don. If you can shake loose some more help, this is where you need to use it!"

Tim Foster had not been eager to discuss the patient deaths. In fairness, most of them occurred well after he had left the company, but it was obvious that he felt a residual guilt for his past involvement with the product. Tim had apparently kept some level of contact with the company for a few months after he left, and knew that there were several legal cases pending at that time.

"I can only guess that there must have been several more in the early eighties," he had told Harris. "The company produced over four hundred of the Series C grafts and we found out later that they could have a five percent failure rate after a few years."

"What caused them to fail?" Harris asked.

"They started coming apart at the point where the graft was attached to the suture ring. They tested okay on the bench, but that was without any sterilization. Before they were implanted in patients they were gas sterilized at the hospitals. That apparently affected the integrity of the bond and caused some to fail. That's where the dogs came in."

"Help me out here, Mr. Foster," Harris had said. "I don't follow the connection."

"After the company realized that the grafts might be failing because of the gas sterilization, they had to scramble to find an alternate design. So then they started accelerating their animal implant testing. The problem with long-term implants is that they might not fail for years in a normal test setting, and Haberman couldn't wait that long. He decided to speed up the tests by putting high stress at the critical juncture of the graft. Heavy exercise of the test animals, elevated blood pressure – things like that. What he should have done was to take the product off the market for a couple of years while the company got long-term data, but he wouldn't do it."

"Is that when you left?" Jay asked. He was aware that Foster was reliving a painful experience, a part of his life that he not only had kept off his resume, but a part that he also had tried to block from his memory. Harris was giving him a way out, suggesting that Tim chose to leave the company when he realized that appropriate standards were not being met.

"I left after the blow-up with Branson over the dog lab. I should have talked to the FDA or the surgeons or somebody. I was too inexperienced at that time to realize just how bad the situation was."

"Did any of the other engineers or managers discuss this outside the company?" Harris sensed that he might be closing in on a key element, but Foster was not able to add much to the story.

"I don't know," Tim said. "I think Daieje tried to get Haberman to change the process. Most of the senior guys did try to make some changes at one time or another, but eventually most of them copped out and left. Everyone was scared of going against Haberman and screwing up their resume. It was easier just to leave."

"Who do you think might want to have those men killed, Mr. Foster? Who do you think would know where they all went, and then still have the motivation to want to see them dead after all these years?"

"I don't know. I really don't know." Tim was emotionally exhausted. Between the concern over his own safety and the rehashing of the Hemograft experience, he had about reached his limit for one day. "The only name I could come up with now is this guy Branson, but I don't think he's capable of killing people. He apparently still has it in for me, but I don't think he ever cared what happened to the patients – only to the dogs. If you're looking for a motive, then I think you better look at the patients, or the families of the patients."

"Thanks for your help," Jay said, realizing that he had pushed Foster enough for one session. "You've had a lot to swallow the last couple of days. I still don't think you're in danger, but I believe it'd be prudent if we arrange for some protection until we've finished our investigation."

"Just so you know, I'll be doing some traveling next week. My VP of sales and marketing has resigned and I'll be taking a trip to interview some replacement candidates."

"Okay, but keep us informed about your schedule."

"So have you got the protection started?" Stinnett asked when Jay had finished the recap of his meeting with Foster.

"The Denver office is working it out with the local cops. We're okay on that. I'm gonna be flying back to Washington this evening. The place we need to be spending more effort is on the patient deaths. Crank it up, Don! I think Foster was right. That's where we're gonna find the fit, the second profile."

Saturday, November 6, 5:10 p.m. – Boston

"How did you get my number?"

"I still have contacts in the Animal Rescue Band. I knew your address when I sent you the prospectus on Foster's new company. You got that didn't you?"

"I got it, Maynard. But my phone number isn't listed. Who gave it to you?"

"Relax, Mary. That's not important. I wanna know what you're gonna do about Foster, now that you know where he is and what he's doing. When are you gonna do something?"

"Why should I be doing something, Maynard? What possible reason would I have to be concerned about him? I'm not that active in the movement anymore, and even if I was I wouldn't be chasing off to Colorado at the drop of a hat just because you send me some advert on a company."

"Mary, that wasn't some advertisement. Didn't you read the part I marked? That new CEO is Tim Foster! He was at Aortek. He was one of the people I wrote about in that report I did for you. Plus he used to be at Medelectro. Ran the dog lab there. I know you were involved with that one, Mary. Don't give me this crap about not being active."

Just about the last thing Mary Devlin needed on this Saturday was a call from Maynard Branson. Now a head nurse in the pediatric unit at Brigham and Women's Hospital in Boston, Mary had spent the last week trying to manage an understaffed unit with a patient census that was technically two people over the limit. Now the intrusion of this man's agenda into her otherwise carefully orchestrated life would at best be disruptive and at worst put Mary at risk for disclosure of the relationships and activities that she still maintained, despite her protestations to the contrary.

It had been a long time since Mary had seen Maynard during that week of training at the farm. In her first few years in America, Mary had heard the occasional story about him from some of her contacts in the ARB. As Jeffrey had anticipated, Maynard had become very involved with animal rights activities, although his attitudes and behavior, radical by even ARB standards, had precluded him from moving into any sort of leadership role. Mary knew that while most people in the movement were capable of maintaining a reasonable balance in their lives, along with some level of prospective for the importance of the issue versus other events, Maynard always seemed to represent the extreme fringe, that small minority for whom animal rights was the sole focus of their existence. And now, someone from this extreme fringe had her unlisted phone number and was on a mission – his mission!

"What did you ever do with that report, Mary? You and Jeffrey were awful anxious to get it. Did you send it to somebody – make copies of it?"

"Maynard, I barely remember that report and I sure don't know where it is now. Times have changed! Jeffrey's dead, and I've moved on to other things." Mary clearly wanted to end the conversation, but was reluctant to respond in a manner which might sound overly negative, knowing that Maynard would find other ways to push his agenda, ways which could be even more threatening to her security and peace of mind.

"The FBI came to see me this morning, Mary. I'm minding my business working in a bike shop here in Seattle, and two FBI types come storming in like they owned the place. Flashed their badges and scared the shit outta everybody in the shop, including me. Then they gave me one of those invitations that you can't refuse about coming downtown to answer a few questions."

Now Mary did not want Branson to hang up. He was talking to the FBI and he knew her address and phone number – not a good combination. "Why did they want to talk to you, Maynard?" she asked as calmly as she could.

"I made a small tactical error a few months ago. I sent Foster a nasty gram. He showed it to the FBI and they tracked me down in about five minutes and were awful anxious to talk to me – and I bet you know why, don't you Mary? You've been a naughty girl, Mary. You've been doing things that they didn't teach back at the farm."

"Maynard – what did you tell them? You didn't talk about the farm, did you?" Mary wanted to scream. She wanted to drag his smiling face through the phone line and pound his head on the table. How could he jeopardize her security – her position?

"I didn't talk about the farm, Mary. Actually they weren't very interested in the animal rights thing. Only about my time at Aortek. There's been some bad things happening to some of the people I wrote about in that report, but I bet you know about that, don't you, Mary? They went through all the names with me," he said, his voice now somewhat tentative, unsure of whether or not to believe Mary's disclaimer of knowledge. "They asked about Haberman and Daieje plus most of the other managers and engineers. Wanted to know about what I've been doing the past ten years. Wanted to know if I talked to anybody else about the company. Any families of patients who died. Things like that."

"Why do you think they're asking about this now?"

"They wouldn't say, but I think some of those guys have been killed. Somebody's been taking them out, and now the FBI's on the trail. That's the way they were talking. 'Who might have a reason to want to kill those men?' Questions like that."

"Do they think you're involved?"

"Not anymore. I was in jail for six of the years they were asking about. Small matter of getting caught in a stolen truck with explosives after we did in a research lab in Portland. I shoulda been on my bike."

"So who do they suspect is behind all of this since you had the good fortune to be in jail most of the time?" Mary asked.

"Well, I didn't tell them about the report I gave you, Mary, if that's what you're concerned about. At least, I haven't told 'em so far." There was a pause for effect. The inflection in the voice had changed, and the mercurial personality that Mary had once described as a loose cannon was starting to roll across the deck one more time. "I really don't know what you did with that report, Mary, and I'm not sure I want to know right now. But I do think that if you passed it on to somebody, you might also want to pass on the news about Foster, and if you do that then I think I might be able to forget about the farm. I'm sure the FBI would love to find out about all the things you've been doing over here in the States, but my memory can be very spotty sometimes. Know what I mean?"

Again the pause. Mary remembered the 'don't blink first' advice that Jeffrey had given her years before. This time it was Maynard who was doing the long-distance equivalent, waiting for Mary to respond, knowing that she was thinking through her options, choosing her words carefully.

She briefly thought about denying knowledge of everything and threatening Branson with some form of retribution if he brought her name up with the authorities. Instead, responding calmly in measured tones, she was once again the head nurse who was now the valued employee of a respected institution, volunteer at a Boston women's shelter, US citizen, registered voter, and a payroll deduction contributor to the local United Way.

"Maynard, I want you to listen very carefully." As she spoke she was conscious of her own speech pattern, hopeful that the modest favoritism most Americans extended to women with English accents would work in her favor. "I have no idea what happened to any of those people at your old company. I do remember you writing a report, but I have no idea what happened to it. As I told you before, I'm in a different phase of my life now. What I did in England and for a short time in this country is behind me. But it would be difficult for me if my old life was ever brought to light. If you have any feelings for the cause that we once shared, then you'll respect my need for privacy and keep my name and my history out of this current investigation. You will do that, won't you, Maynard?" And then, without waiting for a response, Mary slowly depressed the receiver button on her telephone, ending the conversation with a small but obvious symbol of defiance, hoping to recapture some vestige of the authority that she once had in her past relationship with Maynard.

If her action was indicative of someone in complete control of her emotions, then that message had not yet reached her autonomic nervous system, which was at that moment sending a panic alarm throughout her body, increasing respiration and heart rate as part of a response which evolution had intended as a reaction to predatory attacks. Maynard Branson was Mary's equivalent of a twentieth century predator, one whose actions could shatter the lifestyle and image that she had so carefully developed over the past ten years. The report that Maynard had drafted at the farm was in the bottom right hand drawer of her desk. Mary knew exactly where it was. She had put it in that drawer after she had made the one copy that she mailed in 1985. She had read the report several times since then, returning it always to the same location. On this day she would destroy the report, but not before she read it one more time, troubled as before at the hate that Branson had emoted when he transcribed his version of the events that took place at the company.

> My name is Maynard Branson and this is my report about the events that transpired at an American company that was originally called Hemograft and subsequently called Aortek. This report will document the callous disregard that corporate management had for their employees as well as for the patients served by the company. This report will also detail the malicious treatment of the dogs that were used as part of the company's so-called research program, a program which caused the suffering and death of dozens of animals with no discernible benefit other than the enrichment of the company owners.
>
> I was hired at Hemograft in July of 1975 by Frank Ryan, who was an engineer with the company. My first job was to help him set up test fixtures where the woven fabric used in the implants was attached to a suture ring and then gradually pulled apart to measure the breaking strength of the bond between the two different materials. This was the

first of many tests that were done improperly and which no doubt contributed to the deaths of certain human patients as well as the suffering of many non-human subjects.

The original company was founded in 1974 by Robert Haberman, who had previously worked as a scientist for another firm that made implantable grafts used in small vessel repair. Haberman started Hemograft to make large diameter grafts which could be used to fix aortic aneurysms. In 1974, the FDA did not have any formal authority over medical device companies and Haberman thought that he could get these products to the market quickly and then take the company public. Without any outside monitoring, companies like Hemograft could determine their own standards and testing procedures for the products they made. If they could convince doctors and hospitals that these products were safe then they could start selling. That's exactly what happened with this company, despite my best efforts to stop it.

Mary skimmed the next several pages of the report, which included references to each of the company managers and key technical personnel. Maynard had taken pains to comment on the purported deficiencies of each of these men, and the contributions that they made to what he perceived to be a horrendous example of research and product development. It was clear that he had never seen himself as a part of the organization despite his several years with the company. His report, although written in the first person, sometimes read as if he had been observing from afar, monitoring the activities of all the people at the company, including Maynard Branson.

When the news had spread through the company that a patient died after one of the grafts had failed, Maynard wrote of the event as if he were reporting on a ball game. He did remark on the efforts within the company to ascribe blame for the failure on the surgeon involved, but again, the commentary was restrained and dispassionate. It was only after several patient deaths and the ensuing degeneration in the animal research protocol that Maynard changed from being a recorder of events to an analyst – to a critic. As he described the accelerated testing of a new graft design on the dogs in his lab, his writing became terse, opinionated, filled with invectives against those individuals who were involved, even if only peripherally. His recall of specific animals, identified by cage number, appeared to be total, as he described each experiment and subsequent autopsy result with a furor and intensity that was conspicuously absent when he wrote of the failure in humans. But he saved his most caustic review for the description of events involving Tim Foster.

> After all my attempts to change the system via the normal process had fallen on deaf ears, I realized that the only way this program could be stopped would be to release the animals and arrange for their transport to some safe location where they would be properly cared for. Because I would need help to do this, I shared my plan with Tim Foster, a young engineer working on one of the design projects. Foster had previously complained about the manner in which the dogs were treated and I felt confident that he would work with me. Unfortunately, Foster turned out to be the most sinister of them all, for he knew exactly what was happening to the animals, he knew of their suffering in the name of false science, and yet he failed to act. Not only did he fail to act, but he blocked my actions by disclosing my plan to Haberman. Of all the vile activities that took place at this company, Foster's actions have to rank as the most heinous. Over the next several years, dozens of other animals suffered and died because of the actions of Tim Foster – and this company, which could have been forced out of business, continued to produce inferior products and implant them in patients.

There were three more pages to the report, but Mary had read enough. The phone call had reminded her of the concern that she had about Maynard when she met with him before driving out to the farm. The 'why' question! What was his motivation? She had been wrong before! Maynard's 'why' had little to do with animal welfare, and more to do with a vendetta. Oblivious to the paradox, Maynard Branson was taking pleasure in the deaths of the human researchers, now that the non-human subjects were no longer at risk. The ultimate form of retaliatory action!

Saturday, November 6, 6:40 p.m. – Hinsdale, Illinois

"Dad? Hi, it's Martha. I haven't talked to you for a while. How are you doing?"

Martha Laudner's call to Iowa was made, not from her apartment in Baltimore, but rather from a house in Illinois. After the aborted QE2 trip, Joe had invited her to spend the weekend with him at his home in Hinsdale. Although Joe normally traveled to Baltimore for their frequent weekend visits, Martha had been at his home on two previous occasions. Both were times when he had his children with him for the weekend. But on this weekend the children were with their mother, and Joe had spent the past day doing something that he had originally planned to accomplish when they were on the cruise: proposing.

"Dad, I thought you might want to hear some news. I'm going to be getting married."

"That's wonderful. You must be very excited." Mr. Baumgardner had been standing near the extension phone in the kitchen of his house in Davenport, Iowa, when the call came from Martha. He was in the middle of fixing a meal for himself and Mrs. Baumgardner, and he was trying desperately to sound excited for Martha's benefit and at the same time put the potatoes on the stove.

"You remember me talking about Joe Sheldon, don't you Dad?"

"Yes, I believe so. He lives somewhere near Chicago, doesn't he?"

"That's right. He's the president of a medical company. I met him at one of the industry meetings. We've been seeing a lot of each other over the past several months, and now we've decided to get married. Joe was married once before but he's been divorced for a while."

"Does he have children?"

Now Mr. Baumgardner was sitting down at the small table in the corner of his kitchen next to the double frame window. It had been a beautiful fall day in Iowa, but Marcus Baumgardner was not looking outside at the autumn colors. He was looking through the open doorway and into the living room where a large family photo was hanging over the couch. The photograph was a professional portrait shot of Martha and the two children. It had been a Christmas gift from the children to their grandfather, and it was the last picture that he had of them. There had not been a single day since the accident that he had not looked at the photo, sometimes actually touching it as he walked past, as if that degree of contact could bring back some association with the two young lives that had been lost in such a tragic fashion.

"Joe has two kids," Martha said, not realizing the intensity of her father's curiosity. "A boy and a girl. Real nice kids. They live with their mother most of the time, but Joe has them on weekends and vacations. They're a few years younger than Thomas and Jennifer would be now."

"Will they be your children after you're married?" Marcus was standing now, the phone cord stretched as he moved towards the doorway to be closer to the picture. He was staring at the images of the children, wondering what they might look like if they were still alive. "Will you be their mother?" he asked finally.

"No, Dad, they have a mother, she's just divorced from Joe." Martha was still missing the hurt in her father's voice, her ebullient mood overshadowing the sensitivity that she usually brought to these conversations. "We'd like you to come to the wedding," she continued. "I'm afraid it's a rather short notice but we were wondering if you could come to Baltimore this next weekend."

"I don't think your mother would be up to it," Marcus said. He was now at the stove again, back in real time, looking at his watch and turning on the burner. "If I come it would probably be by myself. Your mother isn't much on flying."

"I didn't think she'd come, but Joe and I would like you to be there. We'll send you a ticket and all the details. You'll need to arrive sometime next Friday. The wedding will be Saturday afternoon in Baltimore. We're not sure where we'll be living, but we just didn't want to wait any longer."

"I understand, Martha. I'm happy for you. I really am."

"Dad, you do understand about Joe's kids, don't you? They're not going to be my children, and unfortunately they aren't going to be your grandchildren. As much as we miss them we can't turn back the clock. You know that don't you, Dad?"

"Of course – of course," Marcus said, this time with a stronger voice. "I understand and I'm glad you're getting married again. I'll see you next Friday."

"We'll pick you up at the airport. I love you, Dad."

"I love you, Martha. Be an eagle."

The potatoes were starting to boil as Marcus hung up the phone and walked into the living room. Staring at the photo over the couch, he kissed the tip of the index finger on his right hand, and then gently traced the outline of each of the children's faces before turning and walking slowly back into the kitchen. He would go to Baltimore. Maybe Joe would bring the children.

CHAPTER TWENTY-THREE
Day Three

Sunday, November 7, 10:30 a.m. – Denver

"Mom, there's another police car coming down the street. Why've they been driving around our neighborhood so much this weekend?" The Foster family had just left their house and were on the way to early service at St. James Methodist Church. Kerry was always the most inquisitive and verbal of the twins, intrigued by every event of daily life in contrast to her sister, who was at that moment reading the Sunday comics in the back seat of the car. Now eleven years old, the twins had made a reasonably painless transition into a new school after their move from Minnesota.

"I think that somebody had a bike stolen out of their garage last week, so the police are watching the area a little more closely. That's why we asked you and Kelly to let us know if you see any strange cars or people around." Britta Foster had been looking straight ahead when she answered her daughter's question, but now she glanced briefly at Tim as he turned on the car radio. They had agreed on a cover story the previous evening, knowing that sooner or later the twins would become aware of a change in the pattern of activity around their house.

On a Saturday evening, with the twins at a friend's house for the night, Tim and Britta had been briefed by an FBI agent regarding the security procedures that were going to be put in place. The one-hour session with Keith Sanford of the FBI's Denver office left them both a great deal more concerned about their vulnerability than they had been before.

"What we'll be initiating, starting tonight, is something we call a medium-level security watch," Sanford began, in a voice that seemed more suited to a group lecture than it did for a brief discussion at the kitchen table where they were sitting. "Our office coordinates this with the local police department. They'll be doing periodic drive-bys in the neighborhood, and they've also been advised about the need for a possible quick response if you call for assistance. We won't be doing a twenty-four-hour watch. That's only done in extreme cases and really doesn't seem warranted in

279

your situation. Over the next couple of days the local police will visit with each of your neighbors and ask them to report anything unusual. Then on Monday I'll be going out to your company and talking to some of your people, asking them to be on the lookout for anything out of the ordinary."

"Do you have to tell them what's going on?" Tim asked. "I don't want to blow this all out of proportion."

"Your neighbors can be told that there's been some burglaries in the area. We can use that line with them, but at your company I'll probably have to disclose the reason for increased security. While we think the chances are remote, there is a possible threat to your life, and we need to act accordingly." Sanford had gone through this drill many times before. A tall man in his early 50s, his attitude as he continued down his laundry list of precautions appeared to convey the message that "if you get shot it'll mess up my day something terrible". Tim almost thought he should be taking notes as the agent rattled off a rapid-fire list of things to do and not do. "Alter the route you take to work; change the times that you normally do things; keep your car locked and don't park in any out of the way locations; keep your drapes drawn; get better locks on your doors; get a mobile phone and take it with you in the car but bring it into the house when you are home," et cetera, et cetera.

On this Sunday morning before the girls came back from their friend's house, Britta still had the same look of incredulity, based in part on a firmly entrenched belief that something of this magnitude could not possibly be happening to her family.

"It just can't be that somebody would want to kill you for what went on at Hemograft years ago," she said to Tim. "You tried to change things there! You weren't responsible for any of those grafts failing. You tried to point out the problems and nobody would listen to you. This can't be happening! It's not fair – it's not fair!" And now she was crying. The possibility, however remote, that Tim could be a target, was in itself almost unthinkable. But the fact that he was not at fault was an even crueler blow, as if fairness was a component that should receive significant emphasis in a death threat situation.

And now as they were driving to church, Tim made a point to hum along with the song on the radio. He was the very picture of hope and confidence, but he was also glancing in the rearview mirror yet one more time as he turned a block early. He would park on the other side of St. James this morning. It would do the girls good to get some exercise.

Sunday, November 7, 11:45 a.m. – Washington, DC

This time they were going to be meeting in Nickoloff's office. It would be just the three of them: Harris, Stinnett, and Nickoloff. Harris had gotten the call from Don Stinnett 40 minutes before.

Jay, can you come in to the office for a few hours? Nickoloff wants a briefing. He'll be out of the city for the next couple of days and doesn't want to wait until he gets back on Tuesday. It'll just be you and me. Denise might be joining us later if we can reach her in time."

"Where's Kaufmann?"

"He's in New York on some kind of problem. He asked us to wait until tonight, but Nickoloff's flying out this afternoon so we need to do it before then."

"I don't have a lot more to talk about besides what I told you on the phone yesterday."

"All we can do is tell him where we are on the case. He's going to want to know what you found out with Foster. My guess is that he'll also have some questions on your second profile. Kaufmann gave him a copy of what you wrote."

It was the 'second profile' comment that had Jay thinking as he drove to the FBI headquarters. He had hoped to take another look at his draft on the flight back from Denver the previous evening but had opted for a nap instead. As confident as he was with his original analysis of the person behind the serial murders, he was also aware that he had little backup for his set of postulates other than his experience with a number of serial murder cases and a well-developed sense of the criminal mind. Whether this would be sufficient for Director Nickoloff was still an open question.

"Thanks for coming in on a Sunday morning," he said when Harris and Stinnett got to his office. "I have to fly out to San Francisco on short notice and this is really the only time I've got to do this." The Director had apparently stopped at his office on the way back from a Sunday church service. He had taken off his suit coat but still had on his tie along with a matching pair of suspenders. The combined set had the markings of a Father's Day present which

281

had made it into the selection pool for weekend wear even if it did not meet the standard for Monday through Friday office attire.

"How much time would you like to take, sir?" Stinnett was all business. He had given up his Redskins ticket for that day's game, but knew that it was a great tradeoff. Giving the Director a private briefing on a Sunday would result in bragging rights for months to come! "I've brought along the reports from the agents who have been reviewing each of the twelve murders. We've also got updates from the undercover work with the animal rights groups, plus more FDA information on the company and its products. We can go into as much detail as you'd like, but it really depends on your available time."

"My wife dropped me off and she's coming back to pick me up at one o'clock. That gives us a little over an hour. Maybe you can start with what you've found out about the company, and then I'd like to hear your progress on narrowing down the list of suspects." As he was talking, the Director took out a spiral bound notebook from a drawer on his side of the conference table. Stinnett and Harris watched with some apprehension as Nickoloff entered their names and titles along with the date and time, thereby sending a less than subtle indication that he was serious about the briefing.

"Well, I'll start with the field agent reports." Stinnett had twelve files stacked neatly on the floor next to his chair, but was referring now to a typed set of notes that he had on the table in front of him. "As you know, we've assigned one agent to each of the cases, and over the past several days we've gone back and had each of them contact the respective family once again now that we know that each victim worked for the same company at one point in time. We're getting some general information about the problems that went on there, but not a lot of really useful data. It's been somewhat amazing that the families didn't really know a lot about the company, whether it was called Aortek or Hemograft. This guy Haberman apparently ruled with somewhat of an iron fist. A couple of the wives knew that some patients had died because of failures in the grafts, but nobody had any names."

"Did any of the wives know about this Korean scientist?" Nickoloff asked.

"Two of them did," Stinnett said, without looking at his notes. "I had each of the agents ask specifically about Daieje. Two of the wives recognized the name and knew he had been fired from the company. Neither one had any idea of where he might be now. While I'm on that subject I might as well tell you what we've found out about him, which unfortunately isn't much." This time Stinnett did refer to his notes, and then spent the next five minutes going through a recap of the trail the agency had followed on Daieje; from Texas to California to Korea. "I'm afraid that we still haven't been successful in locating him in Korea," Stinnett concluded, "although we should have something on that within the next 24 hours."

"You getting decent cooperation from the KNC?" Nickoloff asked.

"It's improving. They made their point and now I think we're back on the front burner."

"What do you think about that guy?" the Director asked Harris. Do you think he fits your second profile? I read it yesterday and I've got a couple of questions about it, but do you think this Korean guy could be behind all of this?"

Harris had been comfortably watching the briefing develop over the past several minutes as Stinnett had been doing the talking. Although Nickoloff had been taking meticulous notes, there had been a generally relaxed atmosphere to the meeting so far, the weekend temperament obviously having taken the edge off what might otherwise have been a very tense session. But now it was Jay's time to come through with some salient comments, and he was more than a little nervous.

"I can give you my answer on Daieje," he began, "I really don't think that he's a factor in this case, and he doesn't fit the profile if that's your question."

"That's part of the question. I guess I'd like you to tell me more about your profile. I'm generally familiar with the process, but I don't have an understanding of how much weight to give something like that in the overall investigation. What's the risk that your profile gets everyone pointing off in one direction and then we find out too late that our guy isn't really a guy but some organization or group of people with their own agenda. I'm not suggesting you aren't good at what you do, but what's the risk in this? Seems to me it could be pretty high if we put too much emphasis on a profile."

Now Harris had a reason to be nervous. Although Nickoloff had asked the question in a non-threatening tone, he had put his finger on the very thing that always made Jay sweat during the later stages of a serial case.

"Well, sir," Jay began, "there is always the possibility that a group of individuals or some other type of organization could be responsible for these murders. I'd be willing to give that more consideration if these deaths had taken place over a period of two or three years. But I think the extended period of time that we're talking about here makes this a totally different situation." Harris was beginning to regain his confidence as he spoke, remembering the rationale that he had for this particular profile. "The fact that there've been at least twelve deaths over ten plus years tells us an awful lot about the character of this individual. As I mentioned in my draft, when we find this guy I'm sure he'll be somebody who's above average in intelligence and probably working in a professional job, or maybe as a general manager in a small company where he's accustomed to giving direction."

"Could he have a military background?" Stinnett asked.

"It's possible. I hadn't really thought of that, but my guess is that he isn't military because they move around too much, which would have made it difficult for him to stay in touch with whoever he hired to do the actual killing. One thing I didn't mention in the first draft is that it's very unlikely this individual will have any sort of prior criminal record. Again, the patience and systematic attention to detail that we've seen in this case is just not characteristic of a person driven by normal criminal motives. When we find this guy I can almost assure you his neighbors will be shocked. He's not likely to have close friends, but the people who do know him will have a difficult time believing he was behind something like this."

"So you're telling me that you think this profile is accurate?" Nickoloff was looking directly at Jay.

"Well, of course, we can never be absolutely sure – there's always some element of doubt – this isn't an exact science." Jay's usual display of self-confidence was beginning to fade again.

"Look, Harris," the Director put down his pen and closed the notebook, "help me out on this. I'm not going to hang you by your toes if you turn out to be wrong. I know this is not a science. What I'm trying to understand is the general likelihood that your profile is reasonably accurate, and then what I *really* don't know is what the hell we do with it! We can't put out an APB describing our suspect as a non-criminal type who's a manager in a small company. That sure isn't going to do us any good."

"The best use of a profile is to help narrow down the list of suspects." Now Jay was back on ground that was a little more comfortable. This was part of a lecture that he had delivered several times before, and he could see the light at the end of the tunnel. "It's rare that a profile can be specific enough to actually lead you to the guilty party, although that has happened on occasion. What's far more common is that its use is restricted to pointing you in the right direction so you can concentrate on a particular category of suspects. And in that regard, I think this profile leads us away from the animal rights nuts and the disgruntled former employees like Daieje – and maybe leads us towards another type of individual, perhaps someone who wanted to retaliate for the death of a family member."

"Okay, I can buy that." This time, Nickoloff was smiling. He liked the down-home attitude and demeanor of Harris, and was pleased to see that Jay could hold his own with some difficult questions. "Let's move on to another topic," the Director said. "What have you found out so far about the patient deaths? How many were there and do we know the names yet? If you're right on this profile, then it seems to me that the failures of the grafts should be our main area of investigation."

"It's one of our main areas investigation right now," Stinnett said, "but I'm sorry to say that we aren't making progress as fast as I'd like. We've really been stymied by the fact that there are no records left for this company. Then the very fact that almost all of the senior people have been killed takes away the other main source of information that we would have otherwise. Foster was some help, but he wasn't really there long enough or in a senior level position at the time to know the details of what might have happened." Stinnett was referring to another set of notes, spreading out the pages in front of him as if to emphasize the amount of work that was being done on this part of the case. "We have two agents over at the FDA going through every file that might be relevant. They've found several references to problems with the company's products, but so far no patient names. These failures happened before it was a requirement that device companies send in reports of complications or deaths. We've also done a detailed literature search trying to find reports in the medical publications describing these problems. On the only one we've found so far, the doc who wrote it has since died. Of natural causes," he added quickly when Jay looked at him. "We're trying to get ahold of his old patient records to go through, but so far haven't found anything."

"There have to be some other ways to chase this information down," Nickoloff said. "What about trying to get some help form one of the medical groups? They might keep records on these things."

"We're working on that idea already. Dr. Browning obtained a listing of the surgeons in the US who might have been doing these kinds of graft implants in the seventies and early eighties. We've got a group of agents trying to locate and contact them to see if they can remember the names of any patients who died. Unfortunately, there are over six hundred docs on the list and a lot of them have retired or moved, so it's a long process. Then when we do locate one, even if he's still in active practice, he usually isn't too anxious to dig out names of patients who died. Surgeons don't like to talk about their failures. Partly pride and partly malpractice concerns. Nobody likes the lawyers these days. Everybody's scared about getting sued."

"Have you worked that angle?" Nickoloff started to ask, but then stopped. "Wait a minute, it looks like Denise is here. Come on in, Denise," he said. "We'll get to you in just a bit. I've just had an idea on one of our other questions."

"Do you want me to wait outside until you're ready?" Denise Altman was noticeably out of breath, having run down the hall to gain a few seconds, worried that she would not arrive in time to be a part of the meeting. "I was at a brunch with my mother when I got the page. It took me awhile to get here."

"That's fine, Denise, don't worry about it," Nickoloff said with a casual wave of his hand. "We'll get to the media questions in a minute. I've got another idea I want to pursue and I'd like you to hear it. We may need some press on this if we can't get the information we want any other way. Let me go back to where I was a minute ago," he said. "Have you thought of looking for the legal cases in this area? Think about it!"

He was grinning now, looking back and forth between Harris and Stinnett, obviously proud of his insight and aware that they had not yet seen the connection. "What do you think probably happened when one of those grafts failed and the patient died? Somebody filed a lawsuit! Right? Even ten or fifteen years ago people sued on these kinds of cases. Not as much as today, but they still sued. That can be your trail! Any product liability or malpractice attorney worth his salt can get you a listing of cases that would have been filed. The legal records will have the plaintiff's name along with the attorney who filed the suit. You'll be able to get the names of other family members from the court record or from the attorney. And I'll tell you one other thing." He stood up to make his last point, fighting hard to contain his excitement over what he now was sure had to be a correct sequence of logic. For the first time since assuming the senior position at the FBI, Director Walter J. Nickoloff was going to be making a direct contribution to the solving of a case. He knew it, and now Harris knew it, as a look of recognition came across Jay's face.

"You're right!" Jay said, without waiting to hear the Director complete the description of his one other thing. "We concentrate on the cases where the plaintiff lost. That's where we find the guy who works up enough hostility to carry him for the next ten years. Damn it! I should have thought of that!"

Stinnett still had somewhat of a quizzical look on his face, but it was clear that Nickoloff and Harris were on the same wavelength. "It definitely fits with the profile scenario," Jay said. "Someone dies because of a graft implant, the family files a lawsuit looking for compensation and justice. They lose the suit for some reason, and then somebody decides to be the judge and jury himself. Even if it takes ten years they'll get even. It definitely fits. We'll work on this angle right away. I think you've come up with the one approach where we can find some names, even if all the other files are lost."

"I think we're on to something," Nickoloff said. He seemed about ready to expand on his new thesis when a phone rang. It was a different sort of ring, one clearly pitched at a different tonal level so as not to be confused with calls that might come in on the two other phones on his desk. "That must be Ann calling me on the car phone," Nickoloff said, taking on the chagrined appearance that most men get when their wives call them at the office and others are present. "She must be waiting for me outside."

"Yes?" he said as he picked up the phone, looking at his watch and doing his best to appear in charge of the conversation. "I know, I know. We can still stop there on the way to the airport." Again, the glance at the watch to be certain there had not been a change during the last five seconds. "I'll be out in just a few minutes. Ten at the most." Again the pause, but this time with a glance to the conference table and a roll of the eyes upward. "I know. I'll be there as soon as I can."

"We're just about done, sir," Stinnett said, anxious to give the Director a face-saving out. "We've got plenty of things to work on."

"Yes, I've got to get moving," Nickoloff said, "but just a couple more questions. Denise, what's the status with the media? Does it look like we've got any leaks or any chance of this breaking before we call the press conference?"

Denise Altman had arrived at the briefing dressed in a manner that could best be described as 'smart casual', the sort of outfit that a career woman might wear for a Sunday brunch with her mother at one of Washington's better hotels, which was indeed where Ms. Altman had planned on being at about this time. With navy trousers, and a red sweater and cardigan cashmere twin set, accentuated perfectly by a double strand of pearls, Denise looked like she might be the sort of woman who had a BMW in the city and a wealthy husband in the suburbs. In fact she was single, a point that Harris had never reflected upon until this day, when he realized for the first time just how attractive this woman was.

"I think we'll be able to keep this under wraps until the press conference," Denise said. "There haven't been any more calls the last two days from this Montgomery reporter at the *Post*. Nobody else has been asking any questions about the case, so I think the paper is our only concern. On Friday afternoon I called the *Post* to speak to Hampton, the guy who has the FBI beat there. I was going to give him some material on our EEO hiring plans. His secretary told me he left early because he was heading off for a hiking trip in Nepal. They sure aren't working on any deadline story if their main guy is out of the country."

"What about a press conference," Nickoloff asked. "What are your plans for that?"

"My department is getting it ready to go. We'll have all the standard notices ready plus special contacts arranged for some of the health industry groups. We can be ready within an hour after you've made the arrests, but it's usually best to time it so you hit the evening network news. I'm even more convinced than I was before that this will be the biggest story we've had in a long time. This will show the FBI at our best. Serial murder, difficult and complex investigation spread over half the country, and everything carried out in secrecy until the case is solved."

"I do want to remind everyone that the case isn't solved yet," Nickoloff said. "I'm still going with the ten-day limit. If we don't have an arrest by then, we go public with the story anyway. We can't take a chance that the story leaks or we end up putting other people at risk. What's the story on Foster, by the way? Are we giving him some protection?"

"Yes, sir," Stinnett said. "We've got him under a medium-level security watch with the Denver office and the local police. No indication so far that he's at risk."

"Well, remember the ground rules. If there's any chance that we're putting people at risk by keeping this under wraps, then we go public. Otherwise you've got seven more days and we go public in any event, although right now I'm a lot more optimistic that we'll have an arrest by then and give Denise the big story she wants. It'll make you guys look pretty good, Don."

"Thank you, sir. It's been a team effort." Stinnett was tempted to expand on his modesty speech but was cut short by the off-key ringing of the Director's private line.

"I've got to run," Nickoloff said. "Let me know as soon as anything breaks. Otherwise I'd like another briefing on Tuesday when I get back."

Sunday, November 7, 3:05 p.m. – Boston

"Mrs. Decker? I'm Michael Montgomery from *The Washington Post*."

Despite the phone conversation the previous day, Mrs. Decker had one of those 'who are you and why are you here' looks on her face when she opened the front door and looked at Michael. In the seven years since her husband's death, Cindy Decker had raised three children, completed work on her master's degree, and had twice been promoted at her job with the insurance company. But she was still uncomfortable being in the house by herself, and despite her well-intentioned social consciousness, she was doubly uncomfortable being there by herself when the person at the door was a young black man that she did not know.

"We spoke on the phone yesterday." Michael could sense her apprehension. He had seen it many times before. Middle-aged white women clutching their purses, moving to the other side of the street if they saw a black man walking towards them. "You told me I should be here Sunday at three o'clock," he said.

This time it clicked. Mrs. Decker pushed the door forward to release the chain lock. "I'm sorry," she said in a voice that made it clear that she really was sorry as well as more than a little embarrassed. "I guess I was expecting someone a little older."

Despite the rocky start, the two hours they spent together that afternoon proved to be a gold mine for Michael. Although Mrs. Decker had not followed events at the company after her husband left, she did have an old Christmas card mailing list that included the names of several of the people who worked at Hemograft during the two years her husband was there.

"I really didn't know those people except for the Sathers. Hemograft wasn't the kind of company where people socialized after working hours."

"What about Mr. Haberman? Did you know him?"

"I met him once or twice. He was always rather distant with the wives. Not the sort of man you would get to know very well, despite the fact that he had been president of the company from the time it started."

"Do you think he still lives at this address?" Michael was copying down the names and addresses off the list.

"He committed suicide several years ago. We found out from Mr. Sather. Eliot used to keep closer contact with the company." Mrs. Decker was on her third cigarette, apologizing each time she lit one for what she described as her only weakness in life. "Is it really true that Eliot's death wasn't an accident? I just can't believe that anyone would want to kill him. He was such a sweet man."

"But you said yesterday that you always thought there was something strange about your husband's death." Michael was trying not to act like a reporter, trying not to push the questions, hoping instead that this pleasant woman would open up and talk about what she thought might have happened.

On the flight back to Washington that evening, Michael reviewed his notes as a prelude to beginning the draft of his first one hundred words. Mrs. Decker had indeed opened up as her comfort level with the young black reporter increased. She spoke about the strained relationships at the company, the controversy over the use of animals in the research lab, and then the trauma associated with the patient deaths – knowing the product you worked on had failed in a patient and had been the cause of his death. She knew there had been lawsuits, but did not know any of the names or how the cases were resolved. And she was still uncertain about her husband's death. What had been a tragic and unsolved hit and run accident seven years before now seemed to be a candidate for intrigue, linked perhaps to at least one other death and conceivably tied in to a serial murder case. Mrs. Decker's mood had gone from cautious to grim during the last thirty minutes of their conversation, as she contemplated the fact that someone might have consciously planned the death of her husband.

But Michael Montgomery was far from somber. Michael Montgomery was on the giddy side of ambivalent, trying not to feel elated at the expense of other people's tragedies. He now knew where he would need to direct his research over the next few days. But for the next few hours what he needed to work on was the first draft of his 100 word lead paragraph. Day three was almost over but he was making progress. He was back on schedule.

Sunday, November 7, 5:00 p.m. – Washington, DC

Although there were now some 23 agents assigned to the case, Harris still operated on the perception that it was his to solve. In his rational mind he knew this was not correct. It was not his case, nor was it Kaufmann's or Nickoloff's. It was Stinnett's case based on the formal assignment process used within the Bureau. Kaufmann would probably use some revisionist latitude to take credit if everything went down smoothly, but it was really Stinnett's case. Jay had gone through these head games before in other serial cases. As it began to appear that a suspect could be identified, he would get increasingly involved with the case, chasing down details and following up on long shot leads that occasionally resulted in his stepping on the toes of other agents – agents who took a somewhat more traditional view of assigned areas of responsibility.

On this Sunday afternoon he was sitting in his office, touching up the draft of his second profile to take into account the legal angle that Nickoloff had surfaced earlier in the day. The more he had thought about the failed lawsuit theory, the more he was convinced that the Director had hit upon a unique idea. If the records on old court cases were as available as Nickoloff suggested, it might be possible for them to be narrowing down a list of suspects within the next one or two days. Even for someone as experienced as Harris, it was easy to slip into the realm of wishful thinking, a quick ID on a suspect who matched the profile. The time it was Stinnett's phone call that brought Jay back to reality.

"You won your bet."

"On what? I don't remember making a bet."

"On Daieje," Stinnett said. "He's dead."

"How didya find out?"

"We got the fax in from the KNC just a few minutes ago. A whole bunch of bad English about why it took 'em so long to track him down, but the long and short of it is that Daieje's dead. Been dead for quite a while. You wanna guess when he died?"

Jay started flipping through the papers on his desk, looking for the listing that showed the dates of death. There had been one gap on the original list that had been filled when they found out about Haberman, and another gap that was still open. Harris knew where Daieje's name would go. He always fought a little with his emotions at times like this, feeling good about his ability to analyze a case and predict patterns of behavior, but also wondering if it might not be just a little strange that his single area of expertise revolved around the subject of multiple deaths. "Daieje was probably killed sometime in 1993," Jay said after he found the list.

"June sixteenth, 1993, to be exact," Stinnett said. "Your guy sure liked to stick to schedule. The good news is that I don't think there are any other gaps on the list, so thirteen should be it."

"What do the Koreans know about how Daieje was killed? Any suspects?"

"Not much to go on. They closed their case without an arrest. Closest thing they had to a lead was a note in the file that he had been seen talking to an American in a hotel bar on the day before his body was found. No description that was worth anything. We all look alike to those guys."

Sunday, November 7, 8:40 p.m. – Washington, DC

Procrastination and avoidance had reared their ugly heads the moment Michael landed at National airport after his flight back from Boston. He knew that if he was going to be talking to his editor in the morning, then he would have to talk to Bill Hampton tonight. Michael had done a file check on Hampton, pulling every story that he had written on the FBI during the four years he had been with the paper. Although most of the 20 plus articles in the file were on topics of minor importance, there were at least five stories that even Michael had to admit were worthy of the front page byline Hampton had managed to secure. None however could be compared to Michael's story, the one that he might have to share with Hampton unless he could convince the senior reporter to cut him some slack with regard to territorial rights. Sooner or later Michael would have to ask, and he had delayed just about as long as he could.

"Hello, Mrs. Hampton, this is Michael Montgomery. I work with Bill at the *Post*. I wonder if I could speak with him for a few minutes."

"Didn't you know? Bill left yesterday for one of his annual hikes. He's going to Nepal this year. Talked your travel editor into doing a story on the trip so he could get some expense money. Is this important? He might be calling when he gets there."

"No, that's all right. This can wait."

It had to be a sign, Michael thought. This was going to be his story and his alone. He would beat the deadline for the press conference, and now he had clear sailing at the *Post*. A small matter of convincing Bonnert that he should be on the story, and just a few details about getting a ton of research done in the next few days, but it was going to be his story. He had the 100 word lead paragraph. He would polish it one more time tonight and then lay it on Bonnert in the morning. It would be his story!

CHAPTER TWENTY-FOUR
Day Four

Monday, November 8, 8:50 a.m. – Washington, DC

Michael had been at work since 7:30, making several changes to his lead paragraph during the past hour before finally hitting his self-imposed limit of 100 words. Dr. Harold J. Brown had been the journalism professor at Howard University who had drilled the hundred-word target into Michael. A slender man in his mid-sixties with a predilection for wearing bow ties, Brown would start off each new group of students with the same directive.

"I want to see discipline in your writing, the parsimonious use of words and phrases. Any damn fool can write a synopsis in two hundred words. I want to see a paragraph that gives me the essence of the story but then pulls me into the rest of the article like a boot into quicksand, and I want to see it in one hundred words."

Hundred Word Harry, his students used to call him behind his back, Michael included. News writing assignments for his class stipulated that the exact number of words in the lead paragraph be written at the bottom left corner of the first page. In the initial three weeks of the semester you were allowed a five-word leeway, then three, and then none. Stories always circulated in the journalism school about the student in some previous year who was set to graduate with honors and then got marked down because he tried to slip an extra two words past Hundred Word Harry.

In the week before graduation, Dr. Brown had invited Michael and three other seniors to dinner at his home near the Howard campus. "I want you to know how proud I am of each of you," he said as they were finishing their evening together, "and I'm sure you must know by now that it's not the hundred word limit that's important, it's the discipline. Words are like precious jewels to me. They're not to be squandered just to please some editor who's trying to fill up so many column inches between ads."

Michael had tried to maintain that spirit of discipline in his early assignments at the paper but found it increasingly difficult to do so when writing about residential zoning changes and bus fare increases. He was also aware that the journalistic style at the *Post* tended to lean towards single sentence first paragraphs of 20 to 25 words, followed by a second paragraph only slightly longer. "Too short is no good either," Professor Brown would have said. "You have to hook the reader, you have to give him some reason to move into the body of the story."

Michael had his hook! Michael had his 100 word lead paragraph that would give the reader a glimpse of what was to come and then pull him in like that boot in the swamp. This was a story that cried out for a great lead paragraph, one that would meet the exacting standards of Dr. Brown. Michael had planned on how he would call Hundred Word Harry on this next Sunday morning. Dr. Brown would have already seen the article, would have seen Michael's byline, and would have read the first paragraph. Michael would not need to tell Dr. Brown the number of words in that paragraph. He would know.

On this morning the only reader Michael need to hook was Karl Bonnert, and Karl was late. "He's at a breakfast meeting over at the Press Club and then he's scheduled for a 9:15 interview with a job applicant. I'm not so sure he'll have time for you this morning, Michael."

Karl Bonnert was the managing editor of the *Post* and a man with more than a small degree of influence at the paper. This was an apparent fact that he would not unduly call to your attention, but his secretary certainly would. Margaret Laker had been with *The Washington Post* company for 23 years and had intimidated more than one rookie reporter during that time. She was also a woman given to the pursuit of various social causes, the most recent of which was the plight of the African elephant. Capable of quoting herd sizes in at least five National Parks, she had once publicly berated the senior copy editor when she discovered that the poor guy had a small piece of carved ivory on his bookshelf. Today it was Michael she was staring down.

"You should have called me for an appointment," she said. "He's really very busy and I have to keep him on schedule."

"I know that, Margaret." Michael was not going to lose his chance at this story because of a secretary, no matter how intimidating she was. "I would have called but this just came up over the weekend and it can't wait. It'll only take a minute."

As Ms. Laker was regrouping for her next defense of the daily calendar, Karl Bonnert came around the corner and Michael moved quickly towards him before Margaret had a chance to intervene. "Karl, I've got something hot and I need to see you for just a few minutes."

"Okay, Michael, come on in but I'm running tight. Margaret, when's my next appointment?"

"It's at nine fifteen, Karl. You really don't have much time."

As Bonnert closed the door to his office he motioned Michael towards a chair. "You still working on that zoning story? I got a call from a city councilman the other day who thought you had your facts screwed up on the economic impact. Wanted us to print a retraction."

"Yes, I know," Michael said. "He called me too. But that's not why I'm here. I've got something more important. What if I told you that I uncovered a story about a major serial murder case where some top business execs are being killed? And it's a case where the FBI won't release any information. They may even be consciously trying to keep it quiet – keep it under wraps."

"What if you told me that, Montgomery?" Bonnert had turned around and was hanging up his coat. If he was at all intrigued by Michael's comments, it was not immediately obvious. "If you told me that, Montgomery, then I would probably tell you to go see Hampton. If your lead checks out he may want you to help on the story. Might be good experience for you."

"I called Hampton last night. He's on his way to Nepal or somewhere. Won't be back for a couple of weeks."

"Then, Michael, I'd tell you to wait until he gets back. He does the FBI stuff. You're on zoning the last time I checked."

"This can't wait, Karl. They're gonna go public with this a week from today at a press conference. Right now we're the only ones working on this, and it's big, Karl! A serial murder case of medical execs and we're the guys with the story." Michael had thought about this part of his pitch, consciously using "we" instead of "I", hoping to move Bonnert towards the conclusion that this was in the best interest of the paper and not just for the benefit of Michael Jay Montgomery. "I've got half the work done on pulling together the facts and verifying the information. I can finish the story this week in time for the Sunday edition – but I need help on research."

"Well, settle down, settle down." Bonnert was grinning, enjoying the enthusiasm of the young reporter, remembering his own early days at the paper when exuberance and ambition could overcome low pay and boring assignments. "Tell me what you have so far. What makes you think you've got in inside track on serial murder case that the FBI's covering up?"

"Well, let me tell you how I first got on to the story and then I'll lay out the facts I have." And so Michael took him through the chain of events; the first lead that he had gotten from Chuck Mauer, the call to Brian Davidson at AMMA, and eventually the contacts with Steven Sather and Mrs. Decker. Bonnert began taking notes about halfway through the sequence and started asking questions when Michael got to the brush off from Stinnett's secretary.

"But she did say there was going to be a press conference soon?"

"That's right. She said it was schedule for this next Monday. But she didn't want to talk to me, she was scared of losing her job. Somebody really must have put the pressure on to keep things quiet."

"And she's the same one who told you before there were eleven deaths?"

"Yes, but I'm sure she wouldn't confirm that now and I don't know who else to talk to over there. I've got two of the names and I think I can come up with most of the other names if I can get some research help. The AMMA people may have the names but they seem afraid to talk. They know something's going on, but I can't get them to go on record."

"Did you talk to Samuels?"

"No, I talked to a guy over there by the name of Davidson, plus Chuck Mauer who worked there on a temporary basis. I guess I don't know who Samuels is."

This would have been the perfect time for an editor to come down on Michael, pointing out with more than a little emphasis that if the reporter did not know that Samuels was the head of AMMA, then he had not really done his homework. Bonnert knew Samuels, had met him on a number of social occasions, and had quoted him as an industry expert on some of the major pieces that the paper had done recently on the national healthcare debate. But Bonnert also knew that young reporters do not have the social and business connections that managing editors have. Right now his contacts were young secretaries and young government agency attorneys and college students at bars in Georgetown. But someday they would be

297

executive secretaries and chief counsels for congressional committees and presidents of trade associations, and someday Michael would be calling them first. Right now it was Bonnert who would make the call.

"I know Bill Samuels. I'll give him a call. Let's see what he has to say about your serial murder case." And with a visibly nervous Michael Montgomery watching, Bonnert got Samuels on the phone, and after the requisite small talk about Clinton and the Redskins, asked him the question of the hour.

"Say, Bill, we're working on a story about this series of murders of industry executives. A lot of them are your members I guess – employed in the medical device business. Our sources over at the FBI tell us there have been eleven deaths so far. We're just trying to confirm that number – see if it squares with your information."

"You're doing a story on this?"

"We're working on one. I don't know when it'll run." Bonnert motioned for Michael to pick up the extension phone and listen in on the conversation. "You know, I'm a little surprised that your group or the FBI hasn't made some announcement on this. Seems to me this is a pretty significant sequence of events."

"Are they talking to you? The FBI, I mean." Samuel's legal training was beginning to surface. Give a little – ask a little, but no questions where you don't already know the answer, or think you know. "Are they starting to talk to the media on this?"

"Well, they're about ready to schedule a press conference. I imagine that you'll be getting a notice in a few days."

Michael had scribbled a note as he was listening and now was holding it up. "Names of victims??"

Bonnert took about a microsecond to pick up on the cue. "Bill," he asked, "do you have the names handy of the men who were killed? I know the FBI will cover that at the press conference, but we're just trying to get some of our background work done ahead of time."

The 'give a little – ask a little' pendulum was now swinging too far towards the 'give' side for Samuel's comfort level. On this question he decided to tighten up on the outward flow of information. "I don't think I can really disclose that, Karl. You'll have to wait for the press conference. If the FBI decides to release those names, then there's not much we can do about it."

"I suppose you're right. But you know, much of this is public information already." Bonnert was still pushing.

"I don't think so." The legal training was coming back again as Samuels moved the little yellow cards around in his mind, but this time the structured logic and ordered patterns of thinking carried him one step too far. "The only names that have been made public are the two men who were killed in that boat explosion in Florida back in 1987. Otherwise the names haven't been released and I think we have to keep it that way."

When the conversation was over Michael looked at Bonnert, almost expecting a handshake or some form of congratulations. Samuels had come about as close as he could to confirming that there had been a series of murders, and the lead on the two deaths in Florida would mean that Michael could have at least four of the eleven names by the end of the day.

"It's a start – it's a start," Bonnert said when he saw how Michael was looking at him. "It does look like you may be on to something, but you've got a ton of work to do if you think we can run a story on this by next Sunday."

Before Michael had a chance to respond they were joined by Margaret Laker, who made it clear that the schedule she had so carefully arranged for the day was in danger of major slippage. "You're almost ten minutes late for your 9:15 interview Karl, and then we have you set to meet with Senator Kennedy's press secretary at ten o'clock. That was arranged over a month ago, you know."

Bonnert held up his hands in mock surrender, now in danger of losing one more battle in the never-ending war with his secretary over schedules. "Relax, Margaret. We'll make the ten o'clock. The applicant can wait a little longer."

"He came all the way from California."

"I've seen his stuff, Margaret, he can wait. Right now I want you to call Kathie McDonnell and ask her to come to my office. Tell her to drop what she's doing. We're going to need some help from her and it's going to have to be on a priority basis."

As Ms. Laker beat a somewhat ruffled retreat, Bonnert turned his attention back to Michael. "You've got a load of research to do in the next few days, not to mention a lot of contacts that you're going to have to make in order to confirm what little bit of information you actually have so far. Kathie should be able to dig out the information on the boat explosion in Florida pretty quick from one of her databases, but that'll still leave you seven more names to find, not to mention a motive. Have you thought much about the kind of information you'll need to chase down?"

"I've got a list right here that I worked on over the weekend." Michael was holding up a typed sheet that he had prepared, hoping that Bonnert would ask the question. "I think that we can get a lot of this from press clips around the country if I can get some time from Kathie and her help on the computer. The rest of the stuff I'll have to get by riding the phone and maybe visiting some of the families of victims. I know that at least two of the eleven worked at the same company. The firm's gone out of business, but there should still be some background information available."

When Kathie McDonnell arrived they went through Michael's list, with Bonnert adding several items that he thought might be important. Kathie was a research librarian of the new school, very much at home on a computer keyboard, but visibly uncomfortable during those rare occasions when she had to physically set foot inside an actual library. She had the capability and reputation of almost always coming back with more information than you asked for, not necessarily in volume, but certainly in scope and parallel areas of interest. Those reporters who knew how to ask intelligent questions and work effectively with Kathie ended up writing articles that were not only well founded on fact, but also accompanied by sidebars that were frequently of equal interest to the main story.

"How soon do you need this?" she asked, when they seemed to be running out of items to add to the list. In her three years at the paper she had never been given a deadline that was in any way reasonable, and this assignment was not likely to be different.

"I think that if Michael is going to have any chance at finishing a story before the FBI press conference blows our lead, then we have to start getting stuff back from you this afternoon. I'm sure there will be follow-up research that we'll need later, but unless we get a running start today, we won't have time to confirm our primary sources."

"Why am I not surprised?" Kathie said.

*

After McDonnell had left, Bonnert did one of those lean-back-and-stare-at-the-ceiling routines that editors do when they think it is time to ponder some mystery of the universe, or of a story. After just enough of a pause to build up Michael's already high anxiety level, Bonnert asked his question. "I wonder why the FBI is keeping a lid on this? You'd expect that if there were a series of murders of business execs going on around the country, then the FBI would want to make it known, either to warn other possible victims or to help identify the killer. I don't see their logic in this."

"I've thought a lot about that," Michael said. Bonnert had not really asked for his opinion, but Michael felt it appropriate to respond. "Samuels said the two guys in Florida were killed in 1987, so this has been going on for at least eight years, maybe more. We don't know how long the FBI has been on the case. That'll be interesting to find out. But maybe now they think they know who's responsible and they don't want to tip their hand. Or maybe they know who the potential victims are and can give them protection, so they don't have to tell the public and scare the crap out of every other guy in the medical products business. If we can figure out any linkage between the victims, then we might be able to understand why the FBI isn't talking yet."

Bonnert was staring at the ceiling again. "Go on," he said. "I'm still listening."

"That's really all I have. I wonder if maybe you should call one of your contacts at the Bureau and see if you can get any background on this."

"I think not." This time Bonnert looked at Michael. The pondering time was over. "If I were to call, it would tip them off that we're closing in on a story. They haven't announced this press conference, and they probably won't until just a few hours before they're ready to go. If they think we might steal their thunder with an exclusive story, they could move up the release time, and then we're in the same boat with everyone else in town. It's better that we know a little rather than everyone knowing a lot."

Michael was starting to get concerned about the time. He had been in Bonnert's office for 25 minutes and still had not discussed the lead paragraph. If there was going to be a time, then this was it.

"You know, Karl," Michael said slowly, "I realize that I've got to get a lot more information put together before this is a real story, but I've written the lead already, just to kind of help me set the tone as I put the rest of the piece together. I'd appreciate if you'd take a look at it for me." And with that, he handed over the paragraph that he had written and watched as the editor took all of 15 seconds to read the words that had taken Michael some six hours of writing and rewriting to forge into a sequence of rhythmic prose. A sequence that might just possibly have been acceptable to Dr. Harold J. Brown.

> At first it was an isolated crime, a hit and run in Boston, a murder in Atlanta. But now this paper has discovered that there have been eleven mysterious deaths of business executives from different parts of the country. Deaths separated by geography and time, yet linked by some common and still unknown motive. Adding to the intrigue is the fact that throughout the duration of their investigation, the FBI has chosen not to make any information public, thereby putting other potential victims at risk, in what is certainly one of the most baffling serial murder cases of recent times.

"A little long, don't you think?" Bonnert finally asked after what Michael thought was an unduly protracted period of reflection. "We typically use a little shorter lead here at the *Post*."

"It's only four sentences," Michael said. He had promised himself that he would not be defensive if Karl suggested any changes, but right now he was having trouble remembering just how open to criticism he had planned to be.

"You could break it into two paragraphs. It would cover the same information but show a little more movement. Might make it somewhat more readable."

"I'd really like to keep it one paragraph. I think it'll draw the reader into the article. Give him the basics of the story but make him want to read more."

"We'll see," Bonnert said, handing the sheet of paper back to Michael. "In any event, you've got a lot more work to do before we even know if there's going to be a lead paragraph." He was opening the door now, nodding to Margaret, the keeper of all things timely. "Tell me one more thing, Montgomery. Is Hampton really in Nepal?"

"That's what his wife said. I didn't check his desk this morning."

"You didn't buy his ticket for him, did you?"

"I don't even know where Nepal is. The farthest I've been away from home is Boston, and that was yesterday. And I did buy that ticket!"

Monday, November 8, 10:45 a.m. – Baltimore

The Monday morning staff meeting at Morkin and Associates had just finished. Business had continued to be good for the partnership, despite a general slowdown within most segments of the healthcare industry. With the firm's reputation well established, many of the new assignments were now coming from clients for whom work had been done before – a vice president of regulatory affairs in a company where David and Martha had already filled two other positions, a director of new business development in a company where they had just filled the CEO slot. This was the kind of business that most search firms would kill for, but rarely got. It also was the kind of business that was inordinately profitable, since little incremental expense was required to understand the subtleties of the client company, and Martha's database could frequently turn out a top-four prospect list within a few hours of initiating the search.

On this Monday morning, David sensed that there was something else that Martha wanted to discuss besides her database. During the years they had worked together, they had established a rather unique blend of friendship. David had often thought that had he not been married, his relationship with Martha might have developed into more than a friendship, more than just a successful business partnership. At least he liked to think that might have been the case, and perhaps it would have been, had Martha not met Joe Sheldon. But she had, and that was the topic on her mind this morning.

"David," she said, in a rather formal tone of voice, "you need to know that this past weekend Joe and I made a decision that we're going to get married. We've been talking about it for some time, and finally decided that if we're going to do it someday, that it might as well be now."

"Well, it's about time. Congratulations." David's mind was already clicking forward to the possible implications of this announcement, but he was trying desperately to appear positive in his response. "Have you set a date?"

"It's going to be this Saturday, here in Baltimore, and we'd like you and your wife to be at the ceremony. I know this all sounds like pretty short notice, but the more we thought about it, the more we came to the conclusion that it doesn't make any sense to wait." Martha knew the question that David would now be framing in his mind, and she also knew that he would have a tough time bringing that question forward while trying to maintain his 'I'm so happy for you' face.

"You're probably wondering what my plans are for continuing work on the database," she said, in a generous effort to take him off the hook.

"That's not really important right now." They both knew he was lying, but he had managed to say the words with enough sincerity that Martha was touched. She got up and walked around to David's side of the table and gave him a kiss on the forehead.

"That's very sweet of you, David. That was a nice thing to say. But it is important, and I want you to know I realize that. I have a tremendous amount of pride in what we've accomplished over the last several years. There's no way I'm going to let that slide, not to mention the income we generate each month. I'm sure I can set this whole process up to do most of it from Illinois. Meantime, I'll be staying on top of all our current searches, so you don't have to worry about something getting lost in the shuffle."

"You know that I've got some interviews set up this coming weekend for that VP job at Remote?"

"I know. I'll have the reference list for you by Wednesday. Foster will like these guys. Any one of them would fit well with his style of management." Martha was getting ready to leave but she had one more item for David. "Did the FBI ever call you back with any additional questions after all that activity last week?"

"No, they haven't, and I'm really curious about what's going on. I'll let you know if they contact me."

"Do that, David. I'd like to know what happens."

Monday, November 8, 10:15 a.m. – Las Vegas

It was 10:15 on a Monday morning in Las Vegas, an hour of the day that Lloyd Barnett saw only on rare occasion, and then it was usually on the way home. This Monday morning was different. On this morning he felt compelled to get up and check the early edition of *The LA Times* to be sure his ad was there. There was no longer room for error in the timing of Barnett's personal financial projections. At this particular point in his life, the possible loss of his line of credit at the Hilton, his cozy living arrangement with Judie, and even the cancellation of his much beloved Visa card – even these potentially disastrous events paled in comparison to his foremost concern. Lloyd Barnett had lost $5,000 of Marty Pastorie's money over the weekend, and that equated to exactly $2,500 a kneecap if Mr. Pastorie chose to debate the point, as was his wont.

In the several years that he had been pursuing his checkered career path in the unique business environment of Las Vegas, Barnett had studiously avoided a lucrative but risky type of money-generating exercise that some of his associates gently referred to as the 'hard con'. One version of this exercise involved the exchange of cash as part of a money laundering scheme, where if you were fast of hand and speech, and had enough front money to lay on the table, you had a decent chance of making several thousand dollars in the space of an hour. With his financial picture bordering on desperate, Lloyd had decided to work this scam on some out of town lowlifes. Unfortunately, his first exchange went out the door in the wrong briefcase, and the front money advanced by the humorless Marty Pastorie was now on its way to Miami. Hence the Monday morning concern about the timing of this next assignment.

Barnett had calculated that if he got the usual $10,000 first payment on Wednesday or Thursday, and if he could somehow avoid contact with Pastorie for the next three days, then it just might be possible that he could make it through the week. The Hilton, Judie, and probably the Visa bill might have to wait until the assignment was completed and the big money arrived. Lloyd knew he would need some cash to cover expenses on the job, and there was that high stakes room at the Luxor hotel and casino. He did have priorities!

305

CHAPTER TWENTY-FIVE
Day Five

Tuesday, November 9, 9:20 a.m. – Washington, DC

Of all the things that the FBI does well, and there are many, the rapid accumulation of data from a variety of scattered sources must certainly rank as one of their strongest suits. If the huge computer files within the Bureau are not capable of belching up the requisite information on a moment's notice, there is always the mother lode of data held under the purview of the Justice Department. And should even this commodious reservoir of knowledge prove insufficient, legions of government and civilian agencies stand ready to burn the midnight oil in the search for material requested by even the most junior of FBI agents. On this particular search, it was not a junior agent who had initiated the process, but rather a section chief, and even more to the point, a section chief who was not shy about mentioning Director Nickoloff's name in the listing of people who were anxiously awaiting the results of the query.

"You do know that the Director has taken a personal interest in this case, don't you?" Don Stinnett would ask during the course of almost all of his calls.

At one time on Monday afternoon there had been as many as sixteen agents and staff personnel tracking down information on lawsuits that had been filed over the previous ten years, suits which either directly or tangentially involved the type of graft that was produced by Aortek. Despite the massive effort and the access the Bureau had to court records, it had not been an easy undertaking. Now on Tuesday morning, Stinnett was meeting with Deputy Director Kaufmann and Agent Harris to review the progress that had been made over the past 24 hours.

"When's Nickoloff due back?" Stinnett wanted to get his main question answered before they went any farther. "He had asked for another briefing today but I'd like to delay that until late this afternoon if possible. We still don't have a tight list of lawsuits."

"I think he'll be back in the office right after lunch," Kaufmann said. "I talked to him early this morning before he left

California. He does want an update this afternoon, but he didn't tell me what his schedule was."

The three men were meeting in Kaufmann's office, sitting at a small round table that rarely was used for its intended purpose. Kaufmann normally liked to stay behind his desk, having visitors face him across a broad expanse of mahogany, maintaining a degree of distance and authority that he felt appropriate for his position. Sitting at a small conference table and shuffling files back and forth was a little too collegial for his normal style, but Stinnett and Harris were already parked at the table when Kaufmann arrived, leaving him little choice in the matter.

"Well, let me tell you what we have so far," Stinnett said, "then we can talk about how we want to brief the Director." Stinnett was chewing gum as he spoke, a rare breach of etiquette for the button down section chief. Five weeks into a self-imposed no smoking program, he was about one stick of Spearmint away from getting out the carton of filter Kools that he kept locked up in the bottom drawer of his file cabinet.

"I gotta tell you first of all that this is probably gonna take longer than I thought," he began. "We busted our ass yesterday chasing down every legal resource we could put our hands on, trying to come up with a short list of people who sued because of a graft that was made by Hemograft or Aortek. The problem is that lawsuits don't get nicely labeled like that. Some legal pleadings identify a product, some don't. Some list a company as the primary defendant and some might just list the doctor or the hospital. Take a look at this."

Harris stood up to get a closer view as Stinnett spread out several sheets of paper on the table. Each page had ten to twelve court cases listed, each reference showing name of plaintiff, jurisdiction of the court, and finally the outcome of the case. Jay could see that some of the cases went back to 1975, while some were as current as 1994.

"We really don't need anything that's more recent than 1985," he said. "If this theory holds true that a lawsuit went against our guy and pushed him off the deep end, then it would have happened sometime before May of 1985, since that's when the first murder took place."

"That's not my problem," Stinnett said. "It'll be easy to sort out the dates. The tough part is to find out what kind of product was involved with some of the older cases. I've got four agents calling the judges and lawyers who were listed in the court records, trying to see if they remember the details of the case, or if not, then seeing if we can get access to a trial transcript. We'll be able to chase all this stuff down eventually, it's just taking more time than I thought. If Nickoloff is still pushing for the ten-day limit, we may be in trouble."

"He's still pushing, trust me. When I talked to him on the phone this morning he was the one that brought it up. Reminded me that this was day five and we'd need to schedule the press conference for Monday if we don't have an arrest by this weekend."

Kaufmann was beginning to have some mixed feelings on the subject of the press conference. Although he had hoped to announce an arrest concurrent with the culmination of a long and complex investigation, the thought of coordinating a number of press conferences was not without some appeal. Legions of reporters shouting questions, pressing for more information, and at the center of the storm would be Deputy Director Robert Kaufmann, on top of the details, cool under pressure. A man clearly in charge of things and competent to lead an ongoing investigation that now was undoubtedly going to take more time, more meetings with the press, and more on-camera interviews to keep the worried public informed. Not an altogether bad sequence of events.

"Right now the only lawsuit we've identified that definitely involves a graft from Aortek, along with a suit where the company won in court, was a case that went to trial in Lincoln, Nebraska in 1982." Stinnett handed one of the records to Kaufmann and then continued, pausing only long enough to stick one more piece of gum in his mouth. "It looks like there may be some others that involved the company, but we need to see the court records to be sure. We should have most of them checked out by tomorrow."

"What about this Lincoln case?" Kaufmann asked. He had been reading the brief recap of the trial that was part of the court record. "Looks like this suit involved the death of a 64-year-old man after the failure of a graft. The children sued the doctor and the company alleging negligence but lost the case for some reason."

"As of right now that's our top lead. Actually it's our only lead. We've got three agents on the way to talk to the different people involved with the trial. We're also checking out the background of the family members, looking for anything out of the ordinary."

"I haven't seen the record yet," Jay said, "but I doubt if this is going to get us anywhere. We need to find a court case where the person who died was younger. Unless there was really something unusual going on in Kansas it would be pretty tough to carry that much hate over the death of a 64-year-old man, even if he was your father."

"Has anybody talked with the trial lawyers group?" Kaufmann asked. "They might have some old records on these kinds of cases."

"Who are they?" Jay asked.

"Oh yeah!" Stinnett said, with a touch of levity in his voice that had been noticeably lacking the previous few days. "I keep forgetting that we have a non-lawyer in our midst. Did you know that, Bob? Harris is an accountant and amateur shrink. Never went to law school like he was supposed to. Think it's too late to give him a legal education?"

The Trial Lawyers Association of America, as Stinnett explained to Harris in agonizing detail, is the primary industry self-help group for attorneys who made their living by suing companies, governments, organizations, or any other part of the establishment that might be a visible target. The trial lawyers do this on a contingency fee basis for plaintiffs who have reason to believe that they have been harmed in some way or another. The national association serves as a platform for a variety of lobbying activities and continuing education programs, and provides a forum for the member attorneys to share information in tactics for use in the litigation frontal attacks that they wage daily in America's courtrooms against some segment of industry or government. Attacks that might happen to be justified on the basis of fact, or perhaps merely lucrative because of particular trends in public opinion and run-away jury verdicts.

"You wouldn't believe what it looks like if you went to some of their meetings." Stinnett was smiling again, enjoying his role as the purveyor of inside information on the tradecraft practiced by some of his legal brethren. "There'll be rooms set up where the lawyers filing certain types of lawsuits get together to share information. One room for the guys doing asbestos cases, one room for the guys going after breast implants, one room for air bag injuries. But these affinity groups change over time depending on what's hot – where the big verdicts and quick settlements might be. This year it might be age discrimination and shopping mall safety. Back in 1985 maybe it was graft implants."

"What have you found out?" Kaufmann asked.

"We haven't found squat so far. We're still working on it. They were never too anxious to keep good records on the different groups. Apparently thought they might be skating a little too close to the anti-trust regs. There probably was some type of plaintiff's lawyer group for the graft cases back in the mid eighties, but we haven't been able to find anybody yet who will admit to being part of it."

"What kind of organization do the defense attorneys belong to?" Jay asked. "They must have something similar."

"They really don't." Stinnett stopped chewing gum for a moment as he thought about the question. "Most of the defense guys are getting paid by an insurance company to defend the manufacturer."

"What kind of insurance company?" Jay asked. "Who insures for this type of liability? There can't be too many companies who do that."

"Jeez, you might have something," Stinnett said, once again with the chewing back at full speed. "It would be product liability insurance! You're right, there can't be too many of those companies, and if we can find out who insured Aortek they should have the records of the cases that went to court, and they sure as hell would remember the suits they won."

In what passed for something resembling a compliment, Kaufmann thanked Jay for his contributions to the meeting and then suggested that both Harris and Stinnett get their butts out of his office and back on the litigation trial. "Since this was more or less the Director's idea about finding someone who lost a suit on a graft implant, I strongly suggest you have more for him this afternoon than what we have so far. I'll set up a briefing at four. That should give you time to chase down this insurance carrier angle. And, Don–"

"Yeah."

"Ditch the gum this afternoon."

Tuesday, November 9, 12:30 p.m. – Washington, DC

It was what people who are employed in an office setting like to refer to as a working lunch. This oxymoronic description for a uniquely American custom covered a forced feeding of bad sandwiches and warm Cokes consumed while pushing projects against a deadline. This was what Kathie McDonnell had to do in order to have any chance whatsoever of meeting the unrealistic schedules that were imposed upon her by the writers and editors at the *Post*. This was the pressure-packed environment that required her to juggle priorities, make rapid decisions, and find new ways to dig out information that other people couldn't find – and she loved every minute of it! And on those rare assignments when she was working with a reporter who had an appreciation for her talent and the intellect to use it effectively, she loved it even more.

On Monday morning after the meeting with Karl Bonnert, Kathie and Michael had met to discuss the list of research questions that Michael had prepared. Their first order of priority was to determine the appropriate division of labor – namely, who could chase down the required information the fastest and then who would follow up for additional background information. In most cases, the first part of the job went to Kathie on the computer and the second part to Michael on the phone. The information relating to the two men killed in the boat explosion in Florida was the quickest hit. Kathie guessed that she could dig out the reference in fifteen minutes. It took twelve. A search on the computer base of back issues for *The Miami Herald*, using the key word locators of 'boat explosion' and 'medical' and 'executive' all appearing within the same paragraph, turned up the article along with the names of Randy Pellegrino and Larry Powell. Michael's part of the search took a little longer and required a lot more human interaction.

There had been ten names and addresses of business contacts on the Christmas card mailing list that Mrs. Decker had given Michael on his trip to Boston. His first task was to contact those men, or their families, along with the families of Pellegrino and Powell.

"I've got to find out if any more of those names might have been on the FBI's list of eleven, or if their families know of any other deaths of friends or associates. I'm not exactly looking forward to calling up some woman and asking if her husband's still alive."

"We could do a search of death records for the main population centers but it would take too long. You're better off making the call and hoping they don't hang up on you."

"How am I going to get the numbers?"

"I've got a CD-ROM database of all the major telephone directories in the country. I'll have to cross reference that against the actual telephone listings for these men at the addresses they were living at back in 1980. There won't be a pure match. Some of these names are pretty common, so my guess is I'll probably end up with eighty or ninety phone numbers and you'll have to keep calling until you find the right Powell family or whomever you're looking for."

She was not far off. There were 109 telephone numbers on the list that Kathie gave Michael on Monday afternoon, and he had been calling ever since. At first he debated trying to get help from some of the interns or clerical staff at the paper, but after his first few calls he realized this was going to be a task that would take a special brand of chutzpah. The 'do you know – did you know – are you related to – I'm sorry I woke you up' brand of chutzpah. He had been on the phone until 10:45 Monday night and had started again at 7:30 on this Tuesday morning. Now five hours later, clearly elated despite some les than desirable phone conversations, he was sitting down across from Kathie McDonnell at a cluttered table in one of the second floor conference room at the *Post* building.

"You won't believe what I have," he said. And before Kathie could start asking questions, he moved her Coke over to the side of the table and spread out his notes. "The first ten or fifteen calls were complete busts," he said. "The wrong people – the wrong numbers – nobody knew any of the names on the Christmas card list or the men who were killed in Florida. Then I got ahold of a Mrs. Mirek Santarel who lives in St. Paul. Her husband was killed in 1991. Unsolved murder, and he used to work at the same company in Texas where Sather and Decker worked. She also knew that another man who used to work at the company had been killed, a sales manager named Lempke. He apparently died in some suspicious accident out in Arizona several months ago. And get this," he paused for effect, "she's been contacted by the FBI!"

Michael had brought a plastic-wrapped cafeteria sandwich with him to the meeting. If he had any intention of eating lunch it was not readily apparent as he moved the sandwich to make room for one more list. "I've finished most of the other calls now, and I'm up to six names counting this Lempke guy. That leaves five more if there really were eleven on the FBI list. Mrs. Santarel also said that the company president had committed suicide, so we need to check that out. It could be there are more than eleven names now."

"I'll check *The Arizona Republic* database to see if I can find any article that mentions Lempke." Kathie had been patiently listening to Michael's discussion regarding his phone contacts. She had found several other items of interest and was anxious to pass on the information. "Let me tell you about some of the other things I found," she finally said. "I've had a very productive morning. I think you're going to be a happy camper when you see what I have." And he was!

McDonnell had pulled over ten articles from various Dallas publications, references which would prove invaluable to Michael as background and contacts on the main article he was writing as well as for the sidebars and follow-on articles he expected to writer later. Kathie had not only dug up material from the major Dallas newspapers, but she had also searched a number of obscure sources to pull out information from various Texas business and legal publications. As a result, she had a wealth of background material on Hemograft and Aortek as well as information on their product problems and the senior people who had been working to solve them.

"One of the articles I found covers the suicide of Haberman, the president of the company, and gives the name of his secretary. And yes, I have a current phone number for her, thank you kindly."

Michael was sorting through the material that Kathie had spread out on the table, his mind racing forward, thinking about how he would tackle the job of pulling the various items together into a coherent sequence that would tie in with the primary story of a serial murder case. "What about their product area? Do you have any more information on that?"

"I thought you would never ask, my friend." As she dumped out the contents of one more manila file folder onto the table, Kathie could not help but smile at the reaction of the young reporter. "I've got every thing you wanted to know – and more – about aortic aneurysms, implantable grafts, animals testing,

313

complications, etcetera, etcetera. This company had a lot of problems! They had problems with their implants and with the FDA. Then later they filed for bankruptcy and their building burnt down. But I've got one other thing for you, Michael. This could be important."

"Well?" He had his notebook, wondering what else this one-woman Library of Congress has to offer.

"I got to thinking about what happened if their products failed in a patient, so I did a search where I was looking for medical lawsuits that mentioned the company. I doubt this is a complete list, but I found one case in Lincoln, Nebraska where the company was sued. They won that lawsuit but the court record should have some interesting information on the people who testified. I called a service out there and they'll be running off copies and sending them out express this afternoon. We'll have 'em tomorrow morning."

"This is fantastic stuff, Kathie. You're amazing!"

"You're right! I am!"

Tuesday, November 9, 4:05 p.m. – Washington, DC

The briefing had taken all of five minutes. Kaufmann was just getting warmed up to cover some other elements of the case when the Director cut him short.

"Have you found out the name of the insurance company?" Nickoloff asked.

"Yes, sir, we have," Stinnett said. "We've talked to the company already and found out that they defended Aortek ten different times when the suit went all the way through trial."

"Well?" It was starting to get obvious that the Director was not in a chatty mood this afternoon.

"In seven of those cases Aortek lost, and in three they won." This time Stinnett was going to answer the next question before it was asked. "Those cases were in Lincoln, Nebraska, Cincinnati, Ohio, and Jesup, Georgia. We've got people chasing down the court records as we speak."

"Let me know what you find out. You've got five days left." The meeting was over. Nickoloff had made his point.

Tuesday, November 9, 5:30 p.m. – Boston

For a person accustomed to taking things in stride, the past few days had been anything but typical for Mary Devlin. The phone call she had received on Saturday had caused her to spend much of the weekend thinking about some of the problems she might have in front of her if the vitriolic Maynard Branson was still out there stirring the pot. She had brought along his troublesome chronicle of past events when she went to work on Monday, unwilling to throw it in the trash at her apartment. There was a shredding machine in one of the patient record vaults at the hospital, and Maynard's report was now thoroughly sliced and diced and mixed with the confetti of two hundred lab test results. Later during the day on Monday, Mary had spoken to the one friend at work who she could trust to keep things in confidence. Virginia Carston, an ex-nun who had worn out her welcome in the convent several years ago after a number of arrests for social causes, was now working as a patient advocate at the hospital and was the only person there who knew about Mary's history with the ARB.

"I'm not aware of anyone asking about your background," she told Mary, "but you have to remember that if the FBI came marching in here it's not too likely that I'd be the first person they'd come to for a recap on staff loyalty. Still, I think that sooner or later I might hear something, and so far I haven't."

With that modest bit of good news in hand, the toughest thing that Mary had left to do on Monday was to arrange to have dinner during the week with an old friend – an old lover, to be exact. The object of attention was Joel Packard, a surgeon now practicing at Massachusetts General Hospital. When Mary first arrived in Boston and started work at Peter Bent Brigham, Joel was the handsome young American doctor on staff who befriended the nurse from England and helped her feel welcome in the new city. It was never all that innocent, of course. Although new to the country, Mary knew a wolf when she saw one, but enjoyed Joel's company and found herself at ease with the surgeon who was even then developing a national reputation within his area of specialty. Their relationship lasted almost two years, until Joel finally succumbed to the call of the suburbs and a marriage with the daughter of one of Boston's finest families in a wedding that made the society pages of the Sunday paper. Mary had not seen Joel for over three years, and he was more than a little curious when she called and asked him out to dinner.

"It's good to see you again," Joel said when he joined Mary at a back corner table in a small Italian restaurant near her apartment. "I remember some pretty romantic evenings we spent in here over pasta and a bottle of Chianti. You look just as great now as you did then, even if I've gotten a little older. I'm really pleased that you called." Mary knew that even with the wedding ring on the hand that was now holding hers, the good doctor was still capable of playing the romantic lead, and she was a little concerned that he might have misjudged the intent of her invitation.

"It's great to see you again too, Joel, and I appreciate you making time for dinner on short notice. I think I should tell you up front why I needed to talk to you."

If he was disappointed about the lack of sentimentality that Mary conveyed, he managed to disguise it well, and for the next half hour as she cautiously spoke of her recent contact with Maynard, Joel worked his way through two glasses of wine without one more suggestive comment. The more that Mary talked, the more it became obvious that she was really concerned about the weekend phone call, and Joel realized that sooner or later she was going to ask him about the report.

In 1984 when he had been a young vascular surgeon on the staff at Peter Bent Brigham, Joel had co-authored an article in one of the specialty medical journals on the subject of graft implants for aortic aneurysms. After the publication appeared he had been asked to serve as an expert witness in a lawsuit where an individual had died after failure of an aneurysm repair, and Mary had given him a copy of Maynard's report to read, thinking that it might be of some value in understanding how the products were made. When Mary first had asked Maynard to write a detailed report about his time at Aortek, her goal was to better understand how a company could have abused animals so badly in the development of new medical implants. She never would have anticipated what Maynard was implying—that his report had started the FBI on a paper trail that could eventually lead back to her.

"Joel, you remember that I gave you a copy of the report that Maynard wrote?" Mary was leaning across the small table and speaking quietly. She had ordered a small dinner salad but had not yet touched it, concentrating instead on the conversation which, up until this point in time, had been primarily one-sided.

"I remember."

"What did you do with it after you read it? Do you still have it?"

"I don't have it, Mary, and I don't really know what finally happened to it." The restaurant had gotten crowded since they had arrived, and the guests at the other tables near them were in various stages of animated conversation as the dinner hour progressed. Despite the noise level, Joel was now speaking softly, aware that this was a matter which had suddenly turned serious. "You remember I told you there was some plaintiff's organization that was in attendance at the trial? I loaned the report to one of the men to read. He was supposed to send it back to me but I never got it. I'm sorry, Mary. There's no way I could have known it would turn out to be this important."

"Who was the man you gave it to?" Mary was staring into Joel's face, uncertain if she really wanted to hear the answer.

"That's the problem, Mary. I never knew his name. He was just one of the men at the trial each day. Seemed like a nice guy – said he'd send the report back to me in a few days. He never did." Now for the first time Joel was looking at his watch, sending the message that perhaps he had helped enough for one day. "I doubt the guy ever did anything with the report. That was a long time ago."

"Some people never forget, Joel! You'd be surprised how long they can keep their anger – their hate. I was there once."

CHAPTER TWENTY-SIX
Day Six

Wednesday, November 10, 10:15 a.m. – Baltimore

With only three days to go before the wedding, Martha was still the picture of normalcy. Business as usual. Two phone calls from David Morkin and a review of a new stack of resumes with one of her assistants, but essentially, business as usual. It would be different on Thursday when she would be arranging some of the last minute details at the Regency Park Hotel.

On this morning the main task still remaining was to complete the reference list on the four candidates for the vice president of sales position at Remote Monitoring. One of the four had been in the running for a position at another client company and David had met with him at that time. The other three prospects had been interviewed the previous week by David who subsequently arranged for Tim Foster to see all four as part of the final selection process.

"I'm pretty sure I can predict which one will get the offer," David had told Martha the day before when they were having lunch together, "but I think it's important for Foster to interview them all so he gets a feel for the kind of candidates we can deliver. I expect to be filling two or three more positions for Remote over the next year. On those we should be able to show Foster just the final one or two applicants, but for that to work he has to get comfortable with our judgment."

"What about the reference list?" Martha had asked. "Isn't it a little early to be getting that ready?"

"It is early, but I want him to see our system, plus he wants to be able to move fast after these interviews. He'd like to be in a position to make an offer next week. That's why he's doing the interviews this Saturday. I've got all four people lined up to come into Baltimore, and Foster will be flying in Friday night. He can see them on Saturday morning and I can meet with him in the afternoon to help make the final decision and structure the offer."

"You're not forgetting about one other little item that we have scheduled for this Saturday, are you?" They were having lunch at one of their favorite Chinese restaurants, a block from David's office. Martha had ordered a bottle of wine and made it a point to tell the waiter that she would be picking up the check. There would not be a lot of lunches together after she moved to Illinois, and she wanted to be sure this one would be special.

"It seems to me that I do remember something else going on this Saturday," David said with an exaggerated look on his face, "but I can't seem to recall what it is. I wonder if it's important."

"You turkey!" Martha said. "You'd better be there on time. The wedding is at eleven and the reception will start at noon. I don't do this every week you know."

"I know – I know. Relax, I'll be there on time. I won't need to meet with Foster until after your buffet lunch. Actually he'll be staying at the same hotel. I reserved a suite for him so he can do the interviews right there. It'll save everyone some time and make it convenient for me." David had been helping himself to some rice as he was talking and had not seen Martha's reaction.

"Maybe you should invite him to your reception. He's one of your eagles, isn't he?"

"We'll be set up for twenty people, David, not twenty-one," she said coldly. "Foster is a client, but that doesn't mean we need to invite him to my wedding reception."

"Hey – I was just kidding. It's your reception. You can invite anybody you want. The guy's an eagle though, don't you think? He's going to turn that company around out in Colorado. I just bought some more of their stock last week."

"I don't know, David." Martha was looking for the waiter, anxious now to get the check. "I'm not sure I believe in eagles anymore. Hawks maybe, but I'm not sure about eagles."

She still was not sure about eagles on Wednesday morning as she finished the reference list and got ready to fax it over to David's office. Martha realized that as the day of the wedding approached she had been thinking more and more about the possibility of actually leaving the search business – selling her partnership interest back to David and then doing something different in Illinois. "It's not as much fun without eagles," she thought. "It's really not much fun at all."

Wednesday, November 10, 11:10 a.m. – Washington, DC

One of the agents assigned by Don Stinnett to chase details on the lawsuits had made the contact on Tuesday that eventually resulted in finding the company that had insured Aortek. The call to MedTech Mutual had uncovered the fact that the Virginia-based carrier had initially written the liability insurance coverage for Hemograft as well as for Aortek in later years after the name was changed. That same call had also turned up the information regarding the names and dates of lawsuits on the graft implants in the early 1980s, including the three cases where the plaintiff lost. The MedTech underwriter who had been responsible for the Aortek file, Jason White, was now retired and living in Silver Springs, Maryland, but at this moment, Mr. White and some of his old files were in the back seat of an FBI executive car. He was being driven to FBI headquarters for an 11:30 meeting with Section Chief Stinnett and Special Agent Harris, and he was wondering for all he was worth about what possible information he could have that would warrant this type of attention.

The insurance business by its very nature is involved with different degrees of risk. In most types of coverage the risk is reasonably well understood, and the possibility of loss in any given period can be determined with some level of certainty. Actuarial tables can be used to estimate life expectancies. Prior history and good statistical analysis can be used to predict the numbers of houses that will catch on fire or cars that will be involved in accidents. Some risks are higher than others and the premiums are set accordingly. There will also be the occasional underwriting surprise when two hurricanes hit in one year, but for most lines of coverage the companies will at least know what their losses are at the end of the day or the close of the year. Not so with product liability, and especially liability coverage for medical devices.

"It was the tail that killed us!" Jason White explained when he met with Stinnett and Harris. "It was that goddamned tail!"

Jason D. White was not the sort of individual who looked like he had spent 37 years in the employ of an insurance company. With a flat stomach and a full head of hair, the 63-year-old Mr. White looked more like a football coach than a retired underwriter. Stinnett had given him a general overview of the investigation when their meeting had started, and had then asked White to spend a few minutes explaining the vagaries of the product liability business.

"It damn near killed our company," White said again. "That's about the long and short of it. We wrote ten or twelve different kinds of coverage, and product liability was only about five percent of our premium business, but it damn near killed the company!"

"Maybe you can help us understand how that kind of coverage works," Harris said. "In particular how it was structured during the period 1980 to 85." Jay was still marveling at the stroke of luck they had in finding the actual person at the insurance company who worked on the Aortek account. It was obvious that Mr. White remembered the problems with the graft implants. If anything, he was still upset about the whole situation some ten years later.

"The problem we had back in the early eighties was that we wrote coverage on the basis of the claims the company had in that particular year. We'd charge a premium that was maybe two or three percent of the company's sales, and then at the end of the year if there weren't any claims we'd pat ourselves on the back and think we were pretty damn smart. What happened was that the claims didn't show up in the first year, or maybe even in the second or third. When the grafts started failing in the fourth year we realized that we had a hell of a liability on our hands. But then, even if we double or tripled the premium, or for that matter if we canceled the policy, we were still stuck with defending the claims which turned up for the early implants. They were still covered under terms of the policy! Damn near killed the company!" White paused for a moment to look around the conference room where they were sitting. "You guys mind if I smoke?" he asked.

The overview of the liability insurance business continued for another five minutes as Jason White enjoyed his cigarette and Don Stinnett took deep breaths. With only an occasional review of files that he had brought along, White confirmed that his company had defended Aortek in ten cases, losing seven and winning three.

"I wonder what you can tell us about those cases. We're particularly interested in the people who were involved. Not the technical points of law or things like that, but anything you can remember about the people. Relatives or anyone else who might have been upset when the verdict went against them."

It was three cigarettes later, one for each case, when White finished his review of the lawsuits. He had been right about his past involvement with the litigation. Although he occasionally reviewed the files for certain names and dates, it was obvious that he still remembered most of the other details, including the attitude of some of the participants.

"You never really know what a jury is going to do," he said when he was reviewing the lawsuit that had been filed in Lincoln, Nebraska. "During that trial the plaintiff brought in a doctor from Boston to testify about graft implants. This guy had one of those 'I'm from the East Coast' attitudes and I think it really turned off the Midwest and small town folks who were in the jury. That was the first suit we won."

"What about the family? Were they upset about the verdict?" Stinnett had been eyeing the package of Winstons that were on the table next to White's elbow. The gum might not hold him today.

"The family didn't really seem like they were too surprised. As I recall they probably wouldn't have even brought the suit if they hadn't been pushed a little by one of the local attorneys. It was kind of the same way with the Georgia suit. If you're looking for someone who was really upset when they lost the case, it would have to be the one in Cincinnati. That guy was a piece of work!"

Later they spent a few minutes getting some of the details on the suit in Georgia, but White's comments about the Cincinnati case had clearly gotten the attention of Harris and Stinnett. That trial had lasted for six days and the jury had deliberated for another two before they brought in the verdict. The woman who died had been in her early 30s, which meant that she had been a rather unusual candidate for the surgical implantation of an arterial graft.

"Our attorney really played up that angle," White said. "He tried to make the point to the jury that maybe this woman shouldn't have had the operation at all. For some reason the woman's husband had decided not to sue the doctor or the hospital, so we threw a lot of bricks their way and tried to muddy up the water about whether or not she died because of a graft failure or maybe just bad practice of medicine. It was a gutsy call on our part from a defense strategy point of view. I remember sitting in on some of the discussions the day before our attorney made his closing argument. It could have backfired, but the plaintiff was asking for half a million dollars so we thought we didn't have much to lose."

"And you won?" Harris knew the answer but was looking for more background.

"The plaintiff lost. That might be a better way to put it. He gambled on a big emotional verdict and we pushed the preponderance of evidence argument. I don't think the jury liked either side but they ended up ruling for us. The husband pretty much blew up when they read the verdict. Yelled at the jury and stormed out of the courtroom."

"Tell me about him," Jay said. "What he did for a living, how he dressed, who he spoke to during breaks in the trial. Anything you can remember. When he testified, what did he say about his wife? What were his emotions? It's all important. Even the small points."

These slices of human data were the raw materials from which Harris's profiles were built. They were his emotional nutrients and he loved every little morsel, every tiny grain of information that would have been a throwaway bit of trivia for someone else. And he wanted even more. Jason White might have left a piece of his stomach in those courtrooms back in Nebraska and Georgia and Ohio, but he brought back a lot of information, and his recall was close to perfect. White remembered all the details about the man in Cincinnati, remembered what he looked like and how he reacted to the testimony of defense witnesses, remembered that he had once been a successful real estate broker before his wife died. And he remembered being surprised to find there would not be an appeal of the case because the husband had left town shortly after the lawsuit.

"I'm sure you have all the names and addresses in your file," Jay said finally.

"It's all there. It's been several years since the trial so the address won't be any good, but I'm sure you can track the guy down if you want. His name was Barnett. Lloyd Barnett."

Wednesday, November 10, 1:30 p.m. – Las Vegas

In a city where the word 'excessive' was not part of the official vocabulary, the two casinos that had recently opened for business were setting a new standard for opulence and luxury that would be difficult to equal in years to come, even in this recognized capital of self-indulgence. The Luxor and the Bellagio were grandiose in architecture and scale, flaunting a level of extravagance that seemed almost vulgar against the desert background of sand and cactus. Pretentious, brazen, perhaps even garish in certain aspects of design, but not excessive. Never excessive. Not in Las Vegas.

The ex-real estate broker from Ohio had found the Luxor to be of particular interest. His fascination with the new hotel and casino complex was not based on its huge entertainment area or unique pyramid shape that drew the conventioneers and tourists and blue-haired ladies who took pictures of each other as they rode the elevators up the slanted exterior of the building. Instead, the attraction that brought Lloyd Barnett to the Luxor was in the main casino area and on the other side of the velvet rope that separated the high stakes blackjack players from the lesser gamblers. On this afternoon, at almost the same time as Don Stinnett was initiating an FBI records search to locate the man who moved from Cincinnati, Barnett would walk past that velvet rope and enter the exclusive domain of the truly high stakes player. Lloyd Barnett had just picked up an envelope containing $10,000, and he had a new system.

The procedure was the same as before, even if the response was faster. This time it was the president of a Denver area firm that was targeted. His picture was included along with the address and phone number for the company, but that was the extent of the information supplied. There were no suggestions for other locations – no medical conventions, no out of town sales meetings. Barnett would have to go to Denver, and if he wanted to solve his financial problems, he would have to go soon.

He had gone over the instructions one more time while eating lunch at the coffee shop in the Luxor. The target was a man named Tim Foster, CEO of Remote Monitoring in Colorado. "Pretty sparse on the details this time," Barnett thought. "Not much in the package, except of course, the envelope containing the ten grand." Lloyd had counted the money as he waited for his sandwich. He would have to make some choices shortly on the spending priority for the stack of hundred dollar bills that was currently stuffed in his pocket. It did not turn out to be a lengthy decision process. He had other things to do, including making a few phone calls.

"Judie, has anybody been looking for me so far this afternoon?" This was more than a casual question. Barnett knew that if he had been getting any visitors, it was a good bet they were not dropping by for a cup of tea.

"Where are you, Lloyd? I'm not covering for you any longer!" Judie Whitely had never really been a ray of sunshine even under the best of circumstances, and on this day her attitude had been going from bad to worse at an accelerating rate. "Your close personal friend Marty has been over here once already and said he's coming back again. He's driving me nuts, Lloyd. You have to get him some money!"

"I've got the money and I'll pay him back today. Tell Marty to take a hike. We're back in the bucks."

"You owe me $2,500, Lloyd. If you've got money, I want it! You've been giving me a line of crap for two weeks about paying me back. I need that money, Lloyd!" She paused for a moment as she thought about the odds of Barnett rushing over to the apartment to give her a pile of cash. "Where are you, Lloyd?" she asked. "I'll come over there."

"I'm at the Hilton," he said, without missing a beat, "but I'm gonna have to head out of town later this afternoon. I'll stop by the apartment on the way to the airport and drop off your money."

Barnett was capable of lying with such little forethought that occasionally he accidentally mixed in some fact with the fiction. He would need to arrange a flight to Denver, and besides, after he won big at the tables with his new system, he would need to assume a low profile for a day or two. The Luxor might have relaxed some of their rules during the grand opening phase, but no casino would let him win big money for a long stretch without suggesting that he move along and share his business with another spot in town.

Barnett approached his pending excursion to the high stakes table with a degree of optimism that was surprisingly well-insulated from the reality of past experiences. Despite a history of losses that would have broken the spirit of most men, Lloyd was able to look himself in the mirror on any given day and unequivocally state that he was capable of winning $100,000 at the tables. His ebullient attitude on this particular day was clearly influenced by the half-inch-thick stack of hundreds that he momentarily possessed, along with a recently acquired card counting technique that had been taught to him by one of his mathematically inclined but socially maladjusted acquaintances.

'Card counting' is a catch-all phrase that covers a variety of blackjack playing strategies, all of which are based on the premise that, as each new deal begins, the house has a slight advantage, and will retain that advantage so long as the deck stays balanced. However, if the hands are dealt out in a pattern that results in a disproportionately large number of high cards remaining, the advantage can shift to the player. An accomplished counter who detects this kind of temporary imbalance will significantly increase his bets when the deck is 'fat' and decrease his bets when the deck is 'thin', and thereafter will go on to lead a life filled with wealth, happiness, and the company of attractive companions. So goes the theory, at least.

To test this theory, one only has to look around at the number of casinos that go broke because too many gamblers are walking out with huge winnings night after night. It does not happen, and one of the reasons it does not happen is that long ago the casinos began using multiple deck card racks, or shoes. When the house is dealing from a six or eight deck shoe, it is almost impossible to keep track of the cards. And for the one out of a thousand players who can count cards in a six-deck shoe, there is another technique that the house employs to discourage the practice – they ask you to stop playing. Politely at first, and then with an escort to the front door and a picture in the book for the guys watching the security cameras. All of this was known to Barnett, but his friend with the math skills, Mike Beardsley, suggested that a window of opportunity might just be available for a few weeks after the two new casinos opened.

"They'll want to attract the high stakes crowd away from the other places in town, so they'll set up a couple tables with a two-deck shoe, and they won't push you out the door right away if you start winning too much. I can't play since I'm in their book already. They've got pictures of all the known card counters in town. Most of the Las Vegas casinos share that kind of information. Besides," he said, "I don't have the kind of cash you need to work the system. If you're gonna do it right, you need to be playing with at least $5,000. Do you have that much?"

"I can get it. You teach me to count cards and I'll give you half of what I win," Barnett said, with a straight face.

"You should be able to win two or three thousand in a couple of hours if you bet at the levels I taught you," Beardsley said, "but you can double that if you do a separate count on the fives. The five card is good for the dealer since he has to take a hit on sixteen. If the shoe is short of fives and you have a fat count, then you've got the best of both worlds."

Lloyd was now waiting patiently for the best of those two worlds to materialize. He had walked past the velvet rope some 45 minutes before, and while Judie was looking for him at the Hilton casino, and a legion of FBI agents were scanning criminal records trying to find some trace of the man who had left Cincinnati on short notice some ten years before, Lloyd Barnett was sitting at one of the high stakes tables at the Luxor, trying to add and subtract points and look cool at the same time. It had taken the pit boss all of five minutes to realize there was a counter at the table.

"I've seen him play when I used to work at the Nugget," he told the floor captain. "He's a loser, but he wasn't counting back then. Right now he's up a thousand – down a thousand. Nothing to worry about so far."

"Let me know if it changes."

It did not change much over the next hour, except for the range. Up two thousand, down two thousand – up three, down three – and so forth. Barnett was starting to get comfortable with his counting, now able to do it without being as obvious. Up until this point, he had not had a really fat count, but with the current shoe it was beginning to look like he might have his best chance to capitalize on his new found skill. Down $4,200 at the moment, Lloyd knew that the remaining 25 cards in the shoe were mostly 9s, 10s, and face cards. He also knew that seven of the eight 5 cards had been played. This was the time to do it, to make the bet that would get him back on the plus side. He pushed out ten purple chips, $5,000. It was the most he had ever bet on one hand in his life.

This time the pit boss and the captain watched as the cards were dealt. If Barnett won, his picture might go in the book. Maybe this guy was turning into a decent counter.

Lloyd was dealt a Jack and a Queen and the dealer got a 6 as his up card. This was the way it was supposed to work. With a majority of high cards left in the shoe, the dealer was an odds on favorite to break. There was only one card he could get that would beat Lloyd, and there was only one 5 left in the shoe.

Later when Barnett was back on the other side of the velvet rope, he actually experienced a rare moment of self-doubt. Maybe he never would be a winner at blackjack. When the dealer hit on 16 and got the last 5 card, Lloyd realized that once again, he had managed to put himself back into the big assemblage of losers that start out each story with 'if only'. He was once again part of that big walking pool of streak gamblers, system users, hunch players, and other assorted suckers for whom the casinos would gladly pay expenses to fly to Las Vegas if thousands and thousands of them did not already come so willingly on their own. Lloyd now had $800 to his name, along with a growing number of people who wanted to discuss his near term plans. Lloyd Barnett was in a world of hurt, and it was about to get worse.

Wednesday, November 10, 5:21 p.m. – Washington, DC

"We think we know where he is, and I'm going to fly out there. I was wondering if you wanted to come along." Stinnett was still off the cigarettes, but it had been touch and go the past few hours. Now with the apparent success on the computer search, the tension was lessening. He might just make it until the end of the week.

"How didya find him?" Harris was back in his own office, having decided it would be a good idea to give Stinnett a little breathing room.

"We did a records check on state licenses for real estate agents. Barnett turned up with a license in Nevada and a Las Vegas address. The license was renewed nine months ago so we think there's a good chance that he's still there."

"What's your plan if you locate him? You can't arrest him based on what we have so far."

"I know. We don't have enough probable cause for an arrest and I doubt we even have enough for a search warrant. We've got the local agents checking with the Las Vegas police to see if there's some other reason for a warrant. Otherwise we'll put on a tail and then maybe try to bring him in for questioning. That's why I'm going out. I want to be there if he's brought in. We don't dare screw this up."

"I'll stay here for now. I'm still not sure just where this guy fits. Remember that we're looking for two people. It looks to me like Barnett might be closest to the second profile, but depending on what you find out when you talk to him, he may be a closer fit on the first."

"I think its only one guy, Jay, and I think we're about six hours from having him in a set of cuffs."

CHAPTER TWENTY-SEVEN
Day Seven

Thursday, November 11, 7:10 a.m. – Denver

The remodeling project had been underway for the past four days and the large dumpster that had been left near the back entrance was nearly full with the remnants of old plasterboard and insulation that had been removed from the building. It was difficult to see the car that had pulled in behind the dumpster unless you drove through the employee parking lot and continued back towards the loading dock area. At this time of day there were no deliveries being made, and in the dim light of early morning the man sitting in the car had not been seen by any of the people hurrying into the side door of the plant.

It had now been almost two years since Tim Foster had been named president of Remote Monitoring Incorporated, and some 15 months since the public offering that had been such a traumatic event for the company. After watching the stock slip some 30 percent from its initial price in the first few months after the offering, Tim and the other shareholder employees were more than a little pleased to see that a new trading high had been reached earlier in the week. Foster's secretary, Alice Lindstrom, was one of the people at the company who checked the security prices in the paper first thing each morning to see how the stock had closed on the previous day. With her 50-share position and a newfound interest in the stock market, she had been pleased to get the phone call late Wednesday afternoon from the securities analyst who was planning to write a report on the company.

"My firm is going to initiate coverage on Remote's stock," the man with the deep voice said, "and as part of our research process I'll want to meet with company management, starting with the president. Since I'm going to be in the Denver area tomorrow, I wonder if you can tell me what Mr. Foster's schedule will be first thing in the morning."

The man in the car was thinking of that conversation now as he lit another cigarette. He never ceased to be amazed at the amount of information that people would give out to a complete stranger over the phone if you had a plausible story and asked your questions in the right sequence. Mrs. Lindstrom was only too pleased to inform the caller about how early Foster got to the office and what his schedule would be on Thursday.

"If he's not traveling you can almost set your watch by when he gets to work," she said. Mrs. Lindstrom knew that there had been two reports published on the company during the last month by local brokerage houses. Another positive report by a national firm could only boost the stock more. "The production shift starts at seven a.m. and the office people an hour later. Mr. Foster likes to spend some time with the manufacturing group each morning so he comes in around 7:15."

Now at 7:20, the man with the cigarette was wondering just how accurate the helpful secretary was with regard to her ETA for Foster. What Mrs. Lindstrom had forgotten was that on this Thursday morning, Tim would be taking the twins to school for an early conference with their French teacher. He was planning to stop briefly at the office to pick up some documents for a meeting in the city later that morning, but would then go directly to the school for the 7:30 conference with the girls and their teacher.

It had now been several days since Tim and Britta had met with the FBI agent to discuss the possible dangers that might exist in view of the past Aortek relationship. The borderline paranoid that Tim had felt the first few days after the meeting was beginning to wane as logic and reason started to outweigh what he now believed had been an irrational concern. They did change the locks and buy the portable phone, but the daily patterns were otherwise back to normal and Tim no longer spent much time looking in the rearview mirror of his red Audi. Today with the girls in the car he had taken his normal route to the office, anxious to get there quickly and hesitant to do anything out of the ordinary that might scare the twins. He was one block away from the entrance to the parking lot when he was spotted.

The car next to the dumpster had moved forward several feet so the driver could get a better view of the entrance to the lot. The man behind the wheel was looking through a small set of binoculars at the red car that was turning into the parking area, checking to see if Foster was being followed. He could see that it was Foster driving, and as the car approached the building he could also see that there were two girls sitting in the back seat. There was a special parking spot designated for Foster. The man had made a point to note the location when he had first scouted the area.

And now as Foster was pulling into that spot, the other driver started his engine and moved his car forward another few feet. Tim saw the movement out of the corner of his eye and realized that something did not compute. There was not supposed to be a car in that section of the lot, and certainly not one where the engine was running and the driver was getting out. Tim had to move, and he had to do it fast as he could, now seeing that the man was holding something in his right hand.

"Daddy, what's wrong?" Kerry could sense that something very bad was happening. She could see the panic on her father's face as he threw the car into reverse and pulled out of the parking spot.

"Get down, girls! Get down!"

Tim could see that the other man was pushing a button on whatever it was he held in his hand. The complacency that Tim had displayed earlier was now turning to anger as he realized how he had put the twins in danger. He should never have taken them with him in the car! He should have been more careful! He should have done a lot of things!

And then as he heard the noise, and in the half second it took his brain to catalogue the source, he looked once again towards the other car and watched as the man standing next to it put a telephone to his ear, the telephone on which the call had been placed to the portable phone which was lying on the passenger seat of the red Audi and ringing for the second time.

It took several minutes for the heart rate to return to normal, and another few minutes to assure the girls that this was all part of a normal process, something that he did once in awhile with the FBI. But when Tim had managed to answer the phone on the third ring, he was a long way from believing this was all a normal procedure.

"Mr. Foster?" the deep voice again. "This is Agent Keith Sanford. I hope I didn't scare you and the girls."

Tim did not answer. At that moment he was still breathing too rapidly for normal speech. The girls were now looking around trying to understand what had just taken place.

"You're not really following the procedure that we agreed on, Mr. Foster." Sanford was only 75 feet away. He could have walked over to Tim's car and spoken to him directly, but he chose to stay on the phone. "We would like for you to call us when you leave your house in the morning, give us a chance to follow you or check out the area where you're going. There could easily have been someone else parked behind the dumpster."

"I get your point." Tim could not yet reconcile his emotions, not sure if he should be mad at Sanford or relieved that the situation was over and the girls were not in danger. "I'll call in from now on."

"And, Mr. Foster," the agent was now only 40 feet away but apparently intent on keeping this a phone conversation, "you'll have to do a better job of telling your staff how to handle inquiries about your schedule. When I was talking with your secretary yesterday afternoon she would have given me your shoe size if I had asked. She was just a little too helpful."

"I'll talk to her again. I may have underplayed the situation just a little when I spoke with her on Monday."

"Hopefully this won't go on much longer." Sanford had stopped walking and was standing about 15 feet from the Audi. It was now obvious that he did not want the twins to hear what he was telling their father. "I spoke with our Washington office yesterday. They think they're getting close to an arrest. As soon as that happens we can pull back on this protection route. In the meantime you and your family could be in significant danger."

"I understand."

"Have a nice day, Mr. Foster."

Thursday, November 11, 10:15 a.m. – Washington, DC

The meeting was originally scheduled for nine o'clock, but had since been changed twice. Margaret had made the first call to Michael on Wednesday afternoon and had then called again on this morning to make the second change.

"Something else has come up that's very important, but I can't tell you what it is." As private secretary for the managing editor, Margaret was never shy about letting people know when she had access to confidential information.

"I don't need to know, Margaret." Michael had enough to do without guessing what real or imagined trail of intrigue the self-possessed Ms. Laker was now pursuing. "Just tell me if Karl still

333

wants to review where we are on the story, and do we still have forty-five minutes? I need that much time. We've got a lot to go over with him."

"I do have the meeting on the calendar for forty-five minutes, Michael. You'll have to be done right on time though, since I have Mr. Bonnert scheduled for another appointment at eleven."

Story meetings with one of the editors at the *Post* were not all that uncommon, but 45-minute conferences with the managing editor were unusual, particularly if they were being scheduled at his request. Bonnert had left a message on Wednesday requesting that Michael Montgomery and Kathie McDonnell meet with him on Thursday morning to discuss progress on the serial murder story. Michael had seen it as a good sign, an indication that there was, at least, continuing interest in the story and perhaps even outright enthusiasm. Now after hearing Bonnert's opening salvo, the outright enthusiasm aspect seemed to be in serious doubt.

"I'm not so sure we should be pushing this story," Bonnert said when he came rushing into his office at 10:20. Michael and Kathie were already waiting in the office, going over some of their notes and talking about the questions they needed to cover. "We've got to be careful that we don't get out ahead of ourselves on this one," Karl said, in a managing editor tone of voice that he used only on rare occasions.

It took a moment for the response. Michael actually just stared at Bonnert for a few seconds, wondering if he might have misunderstood what was being said. Finally it was Kathie McDonnell who spoke, the librarian who was now immersed in details of the story to a degree that she was taking on a sense of ownership.

"I don't understand, Karl. Wait till you see what we have! Michael has background on at least seven of the men who've been killed and we may have two more after we check a few things later today. Plus, I've got reams of material on the company that these men worked for and on the product problems they had there."

"Karl, this is going to be a major story!" Michael had recovered and was now ready to do battle. "There is no doubt this is going to be front page news when it breaks. The only question is whether or not it will be in every other paper or whether we'll have an exclusive, or at least a major head start. I don't see why we should be slowing down just when we're making such great progress!"

"Take it easy. I didn't say we wouldn't do the story. I just want to be sure we're not too far out ahead of the facts – screwing up some ongoing investigation."

This was the type of discussion and decision process that justified the rather generous salary that *The Washington Post* was now paying Karl Bonnert. Managing editors in hundreds of papers around the country made countless decisions each day on coverage assignments, story emphasis, and a variety of other details that went into the process of getting out newspapers that would do justice to their mastheads. "All the News That's Fit to Print," as *The New York Times* proclaimed each morning. But besides the normal trade craft that goes with putting together an informative and readable daily publication, there are perhaps one or two situations that come up each week where the editor needs to exercise significant judgment over and above the normal call of duty. Bonnert obviously thought this was one of those situations.

"I should tell you that I got a call yesterday from Bill Samuels over at AMMA." Bonnert's body language seemed to suggest that he was not overly comfortable with this part of the conversation. "I know that Samuels has an ax to grind on this, but he's worried that if a story comes out too early it'll screw up the FBI's investigation – maybe put some more of the industry people at risk. I think he may be right."

"He's worried about covering his ass!" Michael had started slowly but was now working up a head of steam. "They didn't tell their members what was going on over there and now Samuels is trying to buy some time. He's worried about his people reading about it in our paper instead of their newsletter."

"I'm not worried about the AMMA connection. We do one story on them every ten years. It's the FBI relationship that concerns me." Bonnert was leaning back in his chair again, his fingers pressed together as if he was practicing some form of stress relief. "If they are at the sensitive part of an investigation, then we may have some obligation not to screw that up. Hampton's been working hard to build up his contacts over there at the Bureau. I'd hate to blow it all away on one article. We're gonna have to call them – verify our facts and give them a chance to ask for a hold on the story if they really think it's warranted."

Now Michael was starting to get his breathing back to normal. Calling the FBI before the story ran was a reasonable request. There was always the possibility the Bureau would hoist the 'not in the public interest' flag, but even that would mean that the *Post* and its aggressive young reporter would be in a position of some influence when the story did run. There was the matter of timing, however. When should the call be made, and by whom?

"I don't think we should call before late Friday afternoon," Michael said, willing to accede on the issue of making contact, but hoping to retain some influence on the timing. "They could arrange for a press conference on Saturday, but I doubt they would do that since it wouldn't have a lot of network interest. So, even if we call them on Friday we should still have a good chance for an exclusive in the Sunday edition, providing they don't start pulling rank on what's in the public interest."

Bonnert was starting to smile again, the serious tone that he had displayed earlier in the meeting no longer evident as he listened to the young reporter present the same argument on timing that he himself had made earlier in the morning when talking with the publisher. "And tell me, Michael, just who do you think should make the call to the Bureau on Friday afternoon, the one where we tell them we're running a front page story in two days about how they've screwed up the investigation on a long-term serial murder case of national interest?"

"I think that's your decision, Karl. You're the managing editor, I'm just the hard working reporter." Michael was trying not to smile now. He had caught the reference concerning the front page placement, but did not want to appear overconfident. "Why don't we go over what we have so far and then you can decide the best way to handle the contact with the FBI."

For the next 20 minutes, until Margaret came into the office at 10:56 to deliver another of her schedule manifestos, Michael and Kathie gave Bonnert an information dump on all the material they had acquired over the past few days, and they did so with a level of intensity and energy that was calculated to remove any lingering doubt that Karl might have had about their commitment to the story. It was all there – background on the seven victims identified to date, details on the company they had worked for and the products that were produced, a chronology of the work the FBI had done on other serial murder cases, even an overview of the medical device business in the United States and the numbers of companies involved. Not only was it all there, but Michael also made it clear that it was there with confirmations and second sources.

"Kathie even found a reference article that covered the suicide of the company's president. I talked with the woman who had been his secretary up until the time the company filed for the bankruptcy. She's been interviewed by the FBI! So have the family members of most of the other people involved, and most of the interviews were done in the past ten days or so, not back when the men were killed."

"Tell him about the doctor you spoke to." Kathie was pointing to one of the files that Michael was holding.

"I talked to a doctor that testified in one of the lawsuits that the company had. This guy is an expert on grafts. I was going to use him as a source for background on implants, but he ended up asking me about the number of executives that have been killed. That suit went to court over ten years ago but this guy is aware that something is going on now. It's all coming together. I'll have a first draft tomorrow and be ready with the final by deadline on Saturday."

It was 11 a.m. Michael had one question left. "Who makes the call to the FBI, Karl?"

Bonnert had his answer ready. It was obvious that he had been thinking about the call during the time Michael and Kathie were presenting their background information. "We want to be sure they take us seriously on this," he said. "They need to understand that we have a story that's ready to go and we're just giving them a courtesy call to check a few facts." He was standing now, getting ready to leave for the next appointment. "I'll make the call," Karl said. "It's your story, but I'll make the call."

Thursday, November 11, 3:40 p.m. – Las Vegas

He had been in Las Vegas for 18 hours and was starting to remember why he did not like the city. As an FBI section chief based in Washington, Don Stinnett was generally provided some modicum of respect and attention on those occasions when he found it necessary to interface with various city and state police officials. Not so with the men in blue from Las Vegas. This was a city where the public servants had long since grown accustomed to the visiting hoards of out of town investigators who would come riding in on their aluminum horses expecting to be greeted by local traffic cops who would no doubt be grateful for the assistance of these oracles from the east. As a result, the LVPD had not one, but four liaison officers on its staff, each one a thick-skinned veteran who had seen his share of hotshot investigators come and go.

Sergeant Gary Prescott had drawn the straw on this most recent FBI contact, and had spent the better part of the day reminding Stinnett that they were in Nevada, not the District of Columbia. At the moment, the part of Nevada they were in happened to be Prescott's small office, a drab and cheerless room that seemed to be almost intentionally devoid of any personal identification with the primary occupant. In addition to Stinnett, there were two agents from the FBI divisional office, both of whom were visibly uncomfortable as they watched the interplay between the Washington visitor and his local handler.

"Let's review this one more time," Prescott said. "You call me yesterday afternoon about four o'clock my time, tell me you want everything we have on a Lloyd Barnett, and that you may want him brought in for questioning. You don't have a warrant for his arrest or probable cause for a search. You don't have a picture or much else in the way of help on an ID, and now you're pissed at our troops because we haven't tracked this guy down for you. Is that about right?"

"No, Sergeant, that's not what I'm saying. The assistance that we've received so far from the Las Vegas police has been excellent." Stinnett was doing his best to be cordial despite an almost overwhelming desire to pull rank. "It's just that this guy is a prime suspect in a serial murder case that involves thirteen people and could involve more if we don't bring it to a conclusion. One way or another we have to talk to Barnett, and I'm just wondering if we can't find a way to get some additional resources allocated from your department."

"Why don't you tell me just where you think we should be looking and I can tell you the odds of getting more cops assigned to beat the bushes. For all we know the guy is in LA or New York. He's got a lot of reasons to be out of town."

The sergeant's enthusiasm for helping the FBI did not appear to be growing. When Stinnett arrived in Las Vegas on

Wednesday evening, Prescott had given him the initial briefing covering the information that had been pulled together from various sources within the local police department. The picture that emerged on Barnett was that of a full-time hustler and part-time gambler. Although there was no arrest record under the name of Lloyd Barnett, he had drawn the periodic attention of some of the officers in the bunco unit as someone who was on the fringe of the law with a variety of schemes to part the tourist from his cash, but who had not yet stepped across the line that would get him arrested.

"We've probably got hundreds of guys like him in the city," Prescott had said. "They come in from out of town expecting to win some money at the tables. Maybe they look for a job, maybe they don't. Pretty soon they've got an apartment and an expensive habit of one form or another, so they start hustling. Eventually they push it too far and get in trouble with us or someone else. So far it looks like your guy is either lucky or smart. Doesn't really seem to me like he's got the kind of background to be going around the country killing people."

"We have other reasons to consider him as a suspect besides what he's done here in Las Vegas," Stinnett had said. "The main help we need from your department is to locate him for questioning. We'll be responsible for making the case." And now on Thursday afternoon, after a grand total of three hours of sleep in the last day and a half, one of the FBI's finest was again doing verbal battle with the fully rested Sergeant Prescott.

"What do you make of this guy that Barnett's girlfriend told us about?" Stinnett asked.

"Marty Pastorie? He's another of our local hustlers. A couple steps up from your guy. We think he's doing some money laundering but we haven't been able to make anything stick so far. If he's looking for Barnett like the girlfriend said, then it's probably because Barnett owes him some money. My guess is that your guy is on the run from Marty. Probably doesn't even know you're looking for him."

"Where would he stay if he was out of money and on the run?" Stinnett was determined to ask some intelligent questions, if only for the benefit of the other agents in the room.

"Who in the hell knows?" Prescott was tempted to laugh but thought better of it as he saw the look on Stinnett's face. "This is a big city. He could be staying any place if he's still in town. I suppose we could check to see if he has a line at any of the hotel casinos."

It took a few minutes for the Vegas tutorial on how lines of credit work and the freebies gamblers can get if they are comped at one of the hotels. This was new stuff for Stinnett, whose idea of a big bet was $10 on the Redskins. The thought of a free room at a hotel as a side benefit for heavy losers would never have occurred to him. It did occur to Lloyd Barnett on Wednesday after he left the Luxor.

*

Barnett had been in a fog when he walked out of the casino, as if the loss on his last hand had triggered the onset of a catatonic stupor. For a while he had even contemplated the possibility that he might never gamble again, that maybe this was time for a life change. But today he was back to reality. He knew that he would gamble again and had even been thinking about a way to improve on the counting technique. He also knew that on this day he needed to stay out of sight in Las Vegas, and better yet to stay out of sight in Las Vegas by spending the next few days in Denver. He had a job in Denver and a solution to his money problems. At least, some of his problems.

With only $800 and change in his pocket, Barnett knew he was running out of options. The room at the Hilton was free, as were the meals and drinks he had ordered through room service, but the disadvantage was that he had to register in his own name. Sooner or later Judie could track him down and Marty Pastorie might not be far behind. It would be better to fly to Denver and spend the next night there.

For the next two hours, Barnett worked out the details. This was where he had a real skill, a talent that he had already used on 13 other occasions. He would need a gun, and since he had no contacts in Denver where he could buy an unregistered gun, he would have to buy it in Las Vegas. And since he would have to take it with him on the plane, he would need to check luggage, and for that he needed a small suitcase. The gun and suitcase were purchased via a phone call to a fellow hustler acquaintance who agreed to bring them both to the hotel for $250 cash. The few things he needed to hold him over in Denver and to stuff the suitcase could be ordered from the hotel gift shop. Details, but the sort of details that Barnett did well, and actually enjoyed. He still needed to buy his ticket for the flight to Denver, but he could do that at the travel agency in the shopping area off the main lobby. He always liked to pay cash for tickets to be sure there would be once less record in somebody's file, but cash was now at a premium so this trip would have to be charged.

As Barnett left his room to check out of the hotel, Sergeant Prescott was on his way to the Hilton with Stinnett and the other two FBI agents. One of Prescott's contacts had dug up the information that Barnett had a line of credit at the Hilton, and a call to hotel security confirmed that Lloyd had checked in the previous evening.

"We'll go up to his room when we get there," Prescott said as he pulled his car into one of the designated police parking spots near the front door of the Hilton. "I'll get the room number from the VIP desk where they handle the comp rooms. Those guys should know Barnett since he has a line here. You and I will do the door," he was looking now at Stinnett, "and your two partners can handle backup in the hallway." The sergeant was starting to get serious. He may have had doubts about how someone with Barnett's background could be a serial killer, but he knew that you don't grow old on the police force by walking into hotel rooms with your hands in your pockets.

Sara Jeffrey had just finished with a phone call when Lloyd walked into the travel agency located in the shopping atrium at the hotel. This office of Sunride Travel served mostly walk-in clients, many of whom found it necessary to change their return travel arrangements when their plans for a five-day gambling trip turned into a two-day disaster. Sara was always amazed at the number of people who would bet their last dollar and then come in to charge a ticket to Cleveland or Houston or wherever home might be. In several cases, the credit limits on their cards had been reached, or exceeded, and she would get a message on the computer asking her to cut up the card. Although there was a $25 reward for doing so, it was not a task she relished, given the temperament of most people who were already down on their luck. She had actually seen people cry when she pulled their card, but when she brought out her scissors to cut Lloyd Barnett's Visa in half, he opened up a suitcase and took out a gun.

It was almost ten o'clock in Washington when Stinnett reached Harris at his apartment. There had already been an official report of the action that had gone through normal FBI channels. Stinnett had also spoken to Kaufmann, giving him the details of the shooting, knowing that the deputy director would want to call Nickoloff. The call to Harris was mostly a courtesy gesture in recognition of Jay's involvement with the profile work.

"We found Barnett, Jay. When we went to the hotel where he was staying they told us he had checked out and was on his way to a travel agency in the lobby area. We caught up with him there and now he's dead. You wouldn't believe what happened. A goddamned gun battle! We walked in and he started shooting at us. We returned fire and Barnett was killed. I've been in the Bureau over twenty years and this is the first time I've been shot at." Stinnett still had the adrenaline pumping some three hours after the event. He was also smoking. The first thing he did after he could leave the scene was to buy a pack of cigarettes.

"Why did he start shooting? Had you talked to him at all?" Jay's first reaction to this news was one of extreme disappointment, not necessarily over the death of Barnett, but over the loss of a prime information source.

"He didn't say anything. He was in this travel agency and they had just pulled his credit card. He was arguing with this woman when we walked in and started to identify ourselves. Then he started shooting. We think he may have mistaken us for someone else. And wait until you hear this, Jay," Stinnett was lighting another cigarette. "Barnett had a picture of Foster in his pocket, along with his name and address. The woman in the travel agency said he was trying to buy a ticket to Denver. We got him just in time. We'll need to make a match on the other cases, but I'm sure this is the guy that did all thirteen."

"Did you say they were pulling his credit card?"

"Yeah. I guess that's why he was so pissed at the woman in the office."

"I'd like to see his charge activity over the past several years."

"I'll get you a copy. We've already put in a request. Thought it would help tie him in with the other cases."

"Don, I'm not sure this is the only guy that's involved. I'd like to hear more about what you found out about him when you get back tomorrow. I'm still working on the theory that we have two profiles. I doubt that this guy fits both. By the way, Don, who fired the shot that killed Barnett?"

"I did. At least I'm pretty sure it was me. I never shot anyone before. But it was him or me. I didn't have much time to think about it."

Over the next several days an FBI forensic team would go over every inch of the Sunride Travel office. Any time an agent fires a weapon in the line of duty, there is a report to be filed, and when the action involves a death or injury, that report is prepared in exhaustive detail. In this particular case, it was confirmed that "Mr. Lloyd Barnett fired his weapon three times, resulting in three bullets lodging in the wall near the entrance to the office. Section Chief Don Stinnett fired his 10 mm Smith & Wesson revolver four times. Three rounds entered the wall behind Mr. Barnett and one round shattered the computer monitor at Miss Jeffrey's desk. Agent Ronald Hanson fired one round which punctured the left atrium of Mr. Barnett's heart resulting in his immediate death."

CHAPTER TWENTY-EIGHT
Day Eight

Friday, November 12, 8:40 a.m. – Washington, DC

The meeting had been arranged on short notice but Deputy Director Kaufmann had managed to get the large conference room near Nickoloff's office. They were expecting a small crowd, possibly including the Director who was scheduled to arrive in the building sometime after nine o'clock. There was almost an air of celebration in the room as the different players began arriving. Stinnett had taken a late flight from Las Vegas to Los Angeles in time to catch the red-eye back into Washington. Somewhere along the line he had managed to find a clean shirt and a shave, and despite getting only a few hours of sleep, was more than holding his own in the early morning banter.

"And there wasn't any warning that this guy was going to start firing at you?" Kaufmann asked. Three other agents who had been working on the case were in the room along with Kaufmann, Stinnett, Harris, and Dr. Browning, all of whom were standing next to one of the side tables drinking coffee. Denise Altman was expected to arrive in a few minutes, at which time they would start the formal briefing.

"It happened to fast you wouldn't have believed it," Stinnett said. "The woman at the hotel's VIP counter told us that when Barnett checked out he asked her where the travel agency was. When we walked in there we saw this guy yelling at the clerk. He had a gun laying on the counter, like he was trying to impress her, and when the Vegas police sergeant calls out Barnett's name he picks up the gun and starts shooting at us. Never said a word – just started shooting!"

"And you returned fire?" Kaufmann was rocking back and forth on his toes, obviously enjoying the conversation as they replayed the previous day's action.

"I didn't have a choice! This guy was going nuts. He was trying to kill us."

"And you were the one who shot him?"

344

"I guess so. We don't know for sure yet, but it must have been me. Hanson only got off one shot."

"You know, this is what we get paid for," Kaufmann said, looking at the junior agents as if delivering an orientation lecture. "The public thinks we sit around reading ransom notes and going through fingerprint files all day long. They don't understand that we put our ass on the line every time we go out on one of these field assignments. That's why we qualify on the range each year. That's why we're using the Smith and Wesson." He looked back at Stinnett. "We're damn proud of you, Don. Damn proud!"

They had been joined by Denise Altman during Kaufmann's soliloquy, and after another round of felicitous remarks and instant replays, they started the briefing. Kaufmann was at his ingratiating best, laying on the praise once again, complimenting everyone on the role they had played in bringing the case to a conclusion.

"All of us made a contribution. Don was on the firing line – literally, but all of us played a part, including the Director. He was the one who helped us focus in on the individuals who lost their lawsuits. And Denise –"

Kaufmann was never really comfortable when speaking to women professionals, unsure of how to give direction without slipping into a condescending speech pattern. "How in the hell am I supposed to communicate?" he had asked one of the other old time agents. "If I talk to them like they're one of the boys, then I catch a ration of crap for that. But if I get overly polite or deferential, I get accused of talking down to 'em. There's no way I win on this." Some of the women in the Bureau made a conscious effort to help the deputy director out of his dilemma when he was speaking to them. Denise Altman was not part of that group.

"Denise," he started again, "we'll be talking about the public relations angle a little later, but I want to remind you now to position this story so that the senior people at headquarters get their share of credit. We can't give out all the details, of course, but I'm sure you can find a way to get the point across that this case was solved with the very active involvement of our top executives."

"I'm sure we can find a way to do that, sir," she said, "if you really think that's the primary message we want to get out to the public."

"We'll talk more about the press conference when Walt gets here," Kaufmann said, choosing not to ask for a clarification of

Altman's guarded response. "Right now I'd like Don to do a wrap up on the case and tell us what we've learned since the action yesterday afternoon in Las Vegas."

Stinnett had just started talking when Nickoloff entered the room and walked over towards the side table. For a moment Stinnett thought the Director was crossing the room to shake his hand until he realized that Nickoloff was just getting himself a cup of coffee.

"Go ahead, Don. Don't let me interrupt you."

"I was just starting to say that after we were able to leave the scene of the shooting, we went back to Barnett's apartment. Since we'd found the information about Foster on Barnett's body, we had probable cause for a search and could also question the girlfriend as a possible accessory. We didn't find a hell of a lot, I'm sorry to say, although they were still going over some of his things when I left."

"What about the girlfriend? What else did she say about Barnett?" This was the first time that Harris had joined in on the conversation, and by the tone of his voice it appeared that he was not yet ready to send out for party hats and streamers.

"She pretty much confirmed what the local cops had told us about Barnett. He played blackjack every time he had money and hustled when he didn't. He was a small time con artist, but obviously successful enough to finance trips when he killed those men. The girlfriend was along when he went to Phoenix." Stinnett was shuffling through a number of file folders as he was speaking, wishing that he was a little better organized in front of the Director. "We've got the travel dates on that trip so we can tie him into Lempke's death, but we're still not sure how he tracked the other people who used to work at Aortek. The picture he had of Foster came out of a prospectus, so he might have been watching the financial news or maybe he had a contact who used to work there."

"Don, just what type of tie-in do you have on the other deaths?" Nickoloff asked. "It does seem you found the man responsible, but before we start patting ourselves on the back I'd like to have a better understanding of why we think this guy killed all thirteen of the men on the list – and did it by himself."

"Well, the first thing we have is motive, and we have you to thank for that." Stinnett paused for a moment, as if expecting to hear a 'thank you' from the Director. "Barnett's wife was implanted with one of the Aortek grafts and, as you know, after she died there was a lawsuit that Barnett lost. We think that's what set him off."

"Tell him about the passport information," Kaufmann said before Stinnett had a chance to continue.

"We just got this information back in the last hour. Barnett traveled to South Korea in 1993. The dates tie in exactly with the time that Daieje got killed. The other thing we did last night was to send a name and photo on Barnett to the police in the cities where the other murders took place, asking if there was a match with someone fitting that description being in the area at the time of the crime. So far we've heard on two cases where they think they have a fit. We should have more responses back this afternoon."

Stinnett went on to talk about the other ways the FBI and local authorities were working together to verify that Barnett was the man responsible for the various deaths. Airline travel logs were being screened and Barnett's Visa card record had been subpoenaed to see if any charge slips would place him at a particular location at a given time. To his credit, Stinnett had initiated a wide variety of checks and inquiries which were expected to establish beyond a reasonable doubt that Lloyd Barnett was indeed responsible for the deaths of 13 men and would have killed one more if he had not been stopped the day before.

"He's our man, I don't think there's any doubt about it," Stinnett said. "We haven't made the positive match on each one of the 13 cases yet. Actually we may not be able to do that on all of them since he covered his tracks pretty well, but he's our guy. We called off the protection on Foster last night. Didn't tell him how close he came to being a target. Just said that he was no longer in danger. It's been some kind of week. I'm looking forward to taking a few days off."

"I want to go back and cover the question of the two profiles," Nickoloff said, seemingly oblivious to the interjection by Kaufmann. "Weren't we taking action on the basis that there were two people involved, one who was the hit man and another who was behind the scenes?" He had directed his question in the general direction of Harris, but once again it was the deputy director who responded.

"You're right, we were going with that theory initially," Kaufmann said. "We thought that it was one person responsible for the actual deaths and another behind the scene who had the motive.

347

Now we know that it was just one person. Barnett was doing the killing and he obviously had the motive. The profile work helped, but it was only one person, not two."

"What do you think about that, Jay?" This time Nickoloff looked directly at Harris and used his name, removing any doubt that he wanted an answer from the Bureau's leading expert on the use of profiles in serial murder cases. Jay had been doing his best to remain on the sidelines as the dialog had progressed over the past 20 minutes. He knew that sooner or later he would have to go on record with his reservations about Barnett acting alone, but he was not overly anxious to be the first one spitting into the wind. Now he had run out of stall time.

"Well, sir, I still think we are looking for two different people. Apparently Barnett was the triggerman, but that still leaves one other person. This guy fits the first profile like a glove, but he doesn't fit the second. Given what we've found out about him so far I don't see any way that he could have sustained a ten-year serial crime series on his own. Somebody else was involved. There's one other person out there who fits the second profile, and it isn't Barnett."

"Jay, that's just bullshit!" Kaufmann was going out of his way to play a dominant role at the meeting. Whether this was out of conviction or just to impress Nickoloff was unclear, but he seemed unusually willing to express a strong opinion, in sharp contract to his normal practice of covering both sides of the street. "Do you actually think that somebody else wanted to see these guys dead, and then went out and hired a hit man, who coincidentally had a wife that died after one of these grafts failed? What do you think the odds are of that?"

"I'm not sure what to make of that connection," Jay said. "Obviously that wasn't a coincidence. Barnett must have come into contact with the other individual somewhere along the line. Maybe at the trial. But whatever the connection, I'm sure there's still another person out there who fits the second profile, and if that's true then our man Mr. Foster is still in danger."

"Are you planning to hold a press conference this afternoon, Bob?" Nickoloff asked.

"We sure are! I don't see any reason not to schedule one for today since we definitely don't want to do it over the weekend.

We'll lose half of the impact if we try to do it on Saturday or Sunday, and it could be old news by next Monday."

This was a decision that might have been made by Stinnett or Kaufmann if it had not been for the fact that the Director was in the room and had been so directly involved in the case. It soon became clear that Nickoloff saw this issue as more than just a question of when to hold a press conference.

"I think it will be okay for you to go ahead and schedule the press conference for this afternoon, but I must tell you that I'm not all that comfortable that we're really at the end of the trail on this case. Jay has made some good points that we may still have another player out there somewhere. On the other hand, you make a good argument for not waiting too long before we inform the public or else we run the risk that this story gets out ahead of us." Nickoloff could see that Denise Altman was patiently waiting to say something.

"Before we ask Denise for her thoughts on all of this," he said, "I just want to make two other points. If anything else turns up today that casts more doubt on the premise that Barnett was acting alone, then we hold on to the press conference. And secondly, I don't want the focus of any story to be on two or three senior people here at headquarters. My name should not be mentioned, other than for some quote about how proud I am of the way the bureau can handle a complicated investigation that was spread out all over the country. You agree with that, Denise?"

"I do indeed." Despite her best efforts, she could not help smiling as she responded to the Director. "I've already started working up a position statement and series of quotes for you to approve. And just so everyone else understands," she said with a note of authority in her voice, "to make the network news this evening, the latest we can hold a press conference will be at three thirty, and to do that I'll need to send out the announcement over the wire at two o'clock. We don't have much time left, gentlemen."

Friday, November 12, 10:15 a.m. – Washington, DC

"When's the latest they could announce a press conference and still pull it off today?" They were sitting in Bonnert's office at the *Post* and Michael was doing his best to maintain the attitude that his story

349

was going to continue sailing forward without a hitch. Kathie McDonnell was not at this meeting, working instead on one more background search to build the reference base on previous serial murder cases.

The last 24 hours had been a hectic time for Michael Montgomery as he continued to race to identify and contact the friends and families of the people who had worked at Aortek. Although the research on the story could have gone on for days, at this point in time, 36 hours before deadline, Michael and Kathie had accumulated enough material to support and substantiate the first major article. Now it was a matter of filling in the details, drafting and redrafting the main body of the article, working on sidebar stories, and of course, doing everything possible to ensure that the managing editor of the *Post* did not lose the courage of his convictions at the last moment. Hence the meeting with Karl Bonnert and a review of their intention to contact the FBI later in the day.

The agreed-upon plan involved getting in touch with the public relations office of the FBI to inform them that the *Post* was going to run an article on Sunday covering the serial murder of the medical company executives. Bonnert would call one of his contacts at the Bureau, probably Denise Altman, to inform her about the forthcoming article. Hopefully this would encourage some last minute cooperation on the part of the FBI to confirm facts and lend the patina of authenticity to the story. The implied *quid pro quo* was that the FBI would have a chance to put their slant on the facts and the *Post* would have a few hours of exclusivity before the rest of the media world got copies of a 20-page press release.

The key to this bit of mutual back scratching was the timing. Neither the FBI nor other government agencies would consciously hold off the rest of the media just to help the *Post* with a story. But – if it was too late to call a press conference – if the paper already had the story going to press – if it appeared to be a generally favorable article, then it only made sense for the Denise Altmans of the world to make the best of a sticky situation.

"I'm sorry to tell you, Montgomery," Karl said, "that in this day and age of the fifteen-second sound bite, press conference times are set on the basis of network news schedules rather than on how long it takes our ink to dry." Bonnert had enjoyed his interaction with the rookie reporter over the past few days and was now occasionally taking on the role of a friendly tutor, educating his young charge in the subtleties of the news business. "They wouldn't schedule a press conference to start after three thirty if they wanted to make the evening news, and they'd need to make the calls and send out the notice on the news wire an hour and a half before that. That means that I shouldn't make my phone call before two o'clock, and preferably fifteen to twenty minutes later just to be on the safe side. I don't want to wait much longer or it'll be too late to get any decent information out of them today. I guarantee you we'll hear some assholes snap shut over there when we tell 'em what we're working on. It's going to take them some time to decide on their response."

"So you'll make the call around two fifteen?"

"That's what I said, Michael. I'll worry about the call and you concentrate on polishing up the draft. How's that lead paragraph coming, by the way? You shortened it up yet?"

"I really want to stick with the style I showed you before. I think it's the right compromise between setting the hook and providing some substance."

"How long is it?"

"Four sentences – one hundred words."

"Exactly?"

"Exactly!"

Friday, November 12, 11:30 a.m. – Baltimore

The flight arrived ten minutes behind schedule, but Martha was just getting to the gate when her father got off the plane. "Hi, Dad," she said, "I'm sorry I'm late."

"That's okay. I just got in. I didn't have to wait."

"I know, but I wanted to get here in time for Joe to come in with me. We got caught in traffic so he's waiting outside in the car. He's looking forward to meeting you."

"Did he bring his children along?"

"No, they'll be flying in late this afternoon from Chicago. Their mother didn't want to take them out of school today, but they'll be with us at dinner tonight and at the wedding tomorrow."

Marcus Baumgardner seemed to have aged a great deal since the last time that Martha had seen him. He had traveled to

Baltimore periodically over the past several years, but it had been almost ten months since his previous visit, and Martha was struck by the change in his appearance. Always a spry and energetic man before, he now seemed to be lacking in energy, almost lethargic, as he sat in the back of Joe's rental car during the half hour drive into the city.

"Have you been feeling all right, Dad?" Martha asked. "You seem a little tired."

"I'm okay. I had to get up pretty early to catch the flight into Chicago."

"Well, tomorrow's my big day so I hope you'll be feeling all right. You can get a good night's sleep tonight. You're going to be staying at the Regency Park Hotel. That's where the wedding and reception will be, so you won't have to do a lot of chasing around. You can relax and enjoy yourself."

Twenty minutes later when they were beginning to enter the downtown area, Joe made another attempt at small talk as they stopped for a traffic light. Although this was the first time that the two men had met, Mr. Baumgardner seemed to have little concern about making the situation easy for Joe. Martha had made an effort to engage her father in conversation, but that too seemed to be of limited interest to him. Finally he cleared his throat and asked the question that apparently had been on his mind for some time.

"Why did you decide to get married tomorrow?" he asked.

"Well, Dad, as I mentioned before, we've been talking about it for a while and this date works well for both of us. We can take some time off next week before it gets busy again."

"But why on November thirteenth? You know what that day is, don't you?"

"I know, Dad. Tomorrow would have been Jennifer's birthday. I don't forget the dates."

"She would have been twenty-one tomorrow. Thomas would be almost eighteen. It doesn't seem appropriate to be having a wedding on her birthday."

Now Martha was getting concerned. This was the first time that she had seen her father in this mood so long after the accident. She glanced over at Joe, hoping to get some help in the conversation.

"As Martha said, we just picked tomorrow's date since it worked so well for our schedules. I didn't realize that it was going to be on your granddaughter's birthday."

"Well, it is."

"You'll have a chance to meet my two kids tonight." Joe was still trying to help, looking back at Martha, wondering if he was doing the right thing. "I'm sure you'll enjoy talking to them."

"They're not my grandchildren."

"Well, no, sir, I guess that's right. But you'll have a chance to see them from time to time after we're married."

"But after you're married, they still won't be my grandchildren. Will they?"

"No, sir, they won't."

Friday, November 12, 12:15 p.m. – Washington, DC

"I've got the copies of Barnett's Visa bills. They just came in on the fax twenty minutes ago and we've been going through the charges. He's our guy!"

Don Stinnett had brought the new file down to Harris's office without calling ahead, knowing that the reclusive agent was not likely to be out having a big lunch. Stinnett had the new suit on. Sometime during the busy morning he had found time to slip home for a change of clothes. Nickoloff might want to go low key on the personal credit, and that was fine for an agency director who had plenty of other chances to see his name in lights. But for a section chief, this was a golden opportunity to get some well-deserved exposure near the end of a distinguished career, and there was no way that somebody wouldn't want a picture of the agent who shot the serial murderer.

"In ten of the cases we have a charge record that puts him in the city where the killing took place," Stinnett said. "Sometimes he charged an airline ticket and other times he must have paid cash. But if it wasn't a charge for the airline, then he charged something else like a car or hotel."

"Can I see the file, Don?" Harris cleared a spot in the middle of his desk. He had two other serial crimes under active review, and his office once again was filled with the type of pictures that tended to keep the secretaries at bay.

"It's really solid, Jay. I don't know what else you need to look at."

"I want to see the outstanding balances, how big the bills would get before he paid them off. And I want to see when they were paid."

It only took Harris five minutes to find the pattern that he expected. As Stinnett watched intently from the other side of the desk, Jay went through the several pages of records, circling the amounts and dates of payments. Then he took out his listing of the 13 cases and compared the dates. Finally he looked back at Stinnett, who was not smiling. Harris was.

"It's right here," Jay said, "like growth rings on a tree after a wet spring. Barnett would run up the outstanding balance on the card to his maximum credit limit and then the bill would be paid off within a week or ten days after one of the murders. This guy was getting big money and it was coming in on schedule – coming in from the person who fits the second profile. Your case isn't over yet, Don."

"Oh, crap!" Stinnett was standing now, looking over the list of payments that Jay had given him. "Kaufmann is going to flip when he hears this. He put himself out on a limb this morning in front of the Director and now I'm the guy that gets to cut it off. Is there any way this could be a coincidence?"

"Not likely, but there is one other thing we can check, just to be sure. If this guy had a line of credit at the Hilton, my guess is he'd have been paying that off on a similar schedule. If you put the two together there's no way Kaufmann can say that we don't have a second person out there."

"I'll check it out. Listen –" Stinnett was getting ready to leave but obviously felt he should say something more to Harris after his latest contribution. "I appreciate your insights on this stuff. I don't really like the result, but I guess we're better off finding it out now rather than later. We'll be meeting in the conference room again at one forty-five for a quick session, which was going to be to give the go-ahead on the press conference. I may have to pull the plug on that now. I'd appreciate if you'd attend."

"I'll be there," Jay said, as he started going through his pictures again. "By the way, Don, that's a good looking suit. I should get one like that."

Friday, November 12, 1:05 p.m. – Denver

Although it was supposed to be confidential, the news that Foster was no longer in danger had spread through the company in record time earlier in the day. Agent Sanford had driven out to the Remote Monitoring offices at 8:30 to advise Tim that the individual responsible for the murders of the other men was no longer a threat. After Sanford left, Tim called the company officers to pass on the news, requesting that they continue to downplay the entire episode.

"I don't think that I was ever really in danger," he told them. "But in any event, they apparently got the guy who was behind all of this, so we're back to business as usual." The business as usual on this day involved Tim leaving the building at noon to catch his flight to Baltimore. The call that came in for him shortly after one o'clock went to Alice Lindstrom, who was still working on her defensive phone techniques despite the news that her boss was no longer in danger.

"I'm Mr. Foster's secretary," she said to the voice on the phone. "He will not be available today, but if you'd like to leave a message I can pass it on if he calls in."

"It's really quite important that I talk to him. I wonder if you can tell me where he'll be this afternoon and perhaps I can reach him there."

"No, I'm sorry, but I can't give out that information." Alice was rather proud of herself as she stood her ground against this assertive caller. This was a new version of Alice Lindstrom, polite but firm, capable of holding information in confidence – but still helpful. Perhaps too helpful. "Mr. Foster is out of town on a recruiting trip and really can't be reached."

"Yes, I know that." Maynard Branson was also polite but firm. He had gotten information from secretaries a lot tougher than Alice. "I was one of the applicants who was supposed to meet with him, and I need to change the schedule."

"You were meeting him in Baltimore?"

"Yes. My name is Mike Duffy. I might not be on the list that you have since the recruiter just got ahold of me this morning. I need to know where Mr. Foster is staying in Baltimore so I can get him a message."

"I'm surprised that Mr. Morkin didn't tell you that. He set up the interviews to take place at the same hotel where Mr. Foster is

355

staying." Alice was still hesitant, still trying to balance the need for caution with her inherent desire to be friendly.

"Well Mr. Morkin did call, but my wife lost the information. She's pretty embarrassed about it so that's why I'm calling back."

The balance shifted to the friendly side. By the time Maynard hung up the phone he had the name, address, and phone number of the Regency Park Hotel. He also had Foster's flight schedule, and now he was dialing the phone again. It was time to give Mary Devlin a call.

Friday, November 12, 1:55 p.m. – Washington, DC

They were back in the conference room again. This time it was just Kaufmann, Stinnett, Harris, and Denise Altman. Denise had spent the past several minutes reviewing the procedures for the press conference after first reminding everyone that she had not yet been given the green light to go ahead. Stinnett was waiting for an appropriate break in the conversation to tell her there could be a problem with the carefully orchestrated schedule that she had been pursuing. He had told Kaufmann about the information on Barnett's Visa payments, although he had downplayed the importance, choosing to wait for the credit line information from the Hilton to use as they key determining factor. That information was expected any moment, but it was going to be a close call on timing.

"Denise, we're going to have to wait a few minutes before we can make a final decision," Stinnett said. "I'm waiting for a fax from one of our agents in Las Vegas. We do have a possibility that Barnett wasn't acting alone on this and if so, it might make sense to hold off on the press conference until we identify and arrest the other person."

"I thought you folks were back to the one man theory," she said. "We can't change our story line in the middle of a press conference."

Denise had just shifted from cruise control and back into third gear. She prided herself on the network and reputation that she had developed over the past several years within the Washington press corps. The task of rebuilding the image of the FBI was something that she took very seriously, and she knew in her gut that the proper handling of this story could go a long way in that rebuilding process.

"I don't really think it's all that important if it's one person or two," Kaufmann said, in a misguided attempt at revisionist analysis. "We can always indicate that there was one main person involved and that we're continuing our investigation in case there were others."

"No, Bob! We can't do that." This time it was Denise using the first name, something she rarely did at Kaufmann's level, but something that seemed appropriate under the circumstances. "We only get so many times up to the plate with a major story. We can't look stupid when we get there! It's important that we come across as a competent investigatory body, acting with surgical precision on a difficult case of national importance. I'd rather hold off a few days before we make our release if there's any doubt on this second person theory. How soon will we know for sure?"

"I should get the information from Las Vegas any minute now," Stinnett said. "But let me ask you, Denise. If we hold off on our release for a few days, how confident can we be that the story doesn't get out from another source?"

"I can't guarantee that something else won't get out. The longer we wait, the greater the risk, but right now it looks pretty good for a few days at least. I haven't had any contact directly on this, and it's been several days since that guy from the *Post* was asking questions."

It was 25 minutes later when she received the phone call from Karl Bonnert. The meeting in the conference room had lasted until 2:15 when Stinnett's fax finally arrived, confirming what Harris had predicted – Barnett's credit line at the Hilton was paid down shortly after the date of each murder. Even Kaufmann had to admit that the evidence pointing to the involvement of a second person seemed overwhelming, and the plan for the afternoon press conference was quietly dropped. Don Stinnett had been dispatched to brief the Director on the new development, and Denise had just returned to her office when the call came in from Bonnert.

"Hello, Karl. This is a pleasant surprise. What can I do for you today?" It had been several months since Denise had seen Bonnert at one of the various trade functions where their paths could be expected to cross. Although she did not know him well, she was certain that this was not going to be a social call, and her accelerating heart rate was telling her that it might just be about the serial case. She did not have to wait long to find out.

"Denise, I just thought I should tell you that we're going to be running a story on Sunday about the serial murder case you folks are working on, the one involving the deaths of the medical company executives." After a calculated pause that Denise chose not to fill, Karl continued, glancing down briefly at the notes he had made before placing the call. "We've been working on this article for some time, as you may know. We've spoken to most of the families that are involved, and frankly they're wondering why there hasn't been something in the press already."

"Karl, you know that we're really quite restricted about what we can say if there's an ongoing investigation." Denise was choosing her words very carefully, not wanting to paint herself into a corner from which it would be difficult to escape.

"I know that, Denise. I was just wondering if you would like to comment on when this might be brought to a conclusion."

"Is this just for background, Karl?"

"I don't think I can say that. We basically have our story put together. What we'd like is a comment for the record from the FBI concerning just where you are when it comes to solving this case."

This was a tough one for Denise. If she said nothing was going on, she would severely damage her credibility when the full story became available. On the other hand, if she allowed the *Post* to go forward with an incomplete or inaccurate story, then the very argument that she had used against Kaufmann would come into play, and once again the FBI would look like an organization that was incapable of bringing a difficult case to a final conclusion. It was time to make the pitch that she knew Bonnert would be expecting.

"Karl, what I can tell you, off the record, is that there's an investigation going on, and we're at an extremely sensitive stage in that process. There's been some major progress made within the past few days, but one key element is still missing. If you were to go forward with your story right now, it could put our entire investigation in jeopardy."

"She's good," Karl thought. "Doesn't ask me point blank to hold the story, but makes it clear that's what she'd like to have happen." He looked back at his notes again.

"I have a suggestion to make, Denise." Karl had used this approach on one other occasion with a major story coming out of the defense department. It did not work then, but he was hoping for better results this time around. "We know that Agents Stinnett and Harris are actively involved in this case. We presume that Harris has developed the profile that you're using in your search. We'll set up a meeting with the two of them for six thirty tomorrow evening, at which time we'll let them read the draft of our story. If they can convince us that we'll be publishing something that will jeopardize your investigation or put people in danger, then we'll either make a change or hold on the story."

"I'll need to get approval for that kind of a meeting."

"I understand that. And Denise," now it was Karl's turn for the pitch, "I think this is an extremely generous offer on the part of the *Post*. I'd be very disappointed if someone else got ahead of us on the story."

"You know that I can't promise exclusivity."

"I know that, Denise, but you'll have to admit this is a very generous offer."

"It's fair, Karl, provided that I'm at the meeting."

CHAPTER TWENTY-NINE
Day Nine

Saturday, November 13, 8:15 a.m. – Silver Springs, Maryland

In contrast to most of her friends of a similar age, Delores White was still able to sleep late in the morning, particularly on a Saturday when none of her favorite news programs were on television. The fact that she was now plodding around her kitchen, fixing her husband bacon and eggs, did not bode well for her weekend humor.

"I can't believe that you're going to get dressed and drive into the city on a Saturday. What's so important that they can't talk to you over the phone?"

"Delores, I'm a retired insurance man, sixty-three years old, and the most exciting thing I do each week is read the Sunday travel section. All of a sudden I get a call from the FBI asking for my help on solving a murder case. What do you think I'm going to do? This is exciting stuff!"

"But you did all this on Wednesday. What else do they need?"

"I don't really know." Jason White was getting ready to leave and was tempted to ask his wife to fix a thermos of coffee for the drive, but thought better of it. "All I can tell you is that this Agent Harris that I talked to before called me again yesterday. Apparently they had some kind of hitch in their investigation and now he wants to talk more about the other court trials I attended. When I mentioned that I had a videotape of the one in Georgia, he asked if I'd bring it in for him to look at."

The very fact that there was a tape at all was somewhat of a serendipitous event. When Harris had called on Friday afternoon, he had asked Mr. White to once again review the two other trials where the plaintiff had lost the suit. If the second profile theory was going to hold water, then the type of person who had the hostility and passion for revenge could well have been associated with one of the losing court cases. With Barnett removed from contention for the honors, that left the cases in Nebraska and Georgia for consideration.

"I'm not sure what more I can tell you about those two cases," Jason White had said on the phone. "From what I remember, the families that brought suit were solid citizen types, no more emotional than what you'd expect given the fact that someone had died, allegedly because the product failed."

"How was it that you and your client were able to win those two suits?" Jay was grasping at straws, hoping that there might have been an unusual event in one of these cases that could keep this theory alive. Otherwise it was back to the drawing board for another approach.

"Well, I told you about the case in Nebraska when I was at the Bureau on Wednesday. That was the trial where the plaintiff brought in this doctor from Boston."

"What about the trial in Georgia?"

"That was a strange situation. I'd never seen a trial quite like that. The man that died was a truck driver, and what made the case so unusual was that he actually died in a traffic accident. The family claimed his graft failed and that caused his death, or at least made him pass out and lose control of the truck. Although the autopsy results did show a graft failure, our attorney was able to raise some element of doubt about the actual cause of death and whether the failure had happened before the crash or after."

"Was the family upset with the verdict?" Jay was still hoping for something.

"Well, they didn't seem to be any more upset than you'd expect," White said. "Actually, you can see their reaction if you'd like. There was a local station that televised part of the trial. I testified in this one since there was an issue about the amount of coverage, so later on our attorney sent me a copy of the tape."

With little else to pursue in the way of possibilities, Harris asked Mr. White if he would bring the tape in to FBI headquarters. Now, as the retired insurance man got ready to leave and head off for his moment of glory and intrigue, his wife made one more attempt to bring him down to earth.

"Why can't you just send them the tape, Jason?"

"I don't know, Delores. They seemed to think it was important enough for me to show it to 'em on a Saturday morning. I'll ask Mr. Hoover about it if I see him."

Saturday, November 13, 8:40 a.m. – Boston

If she had left her apartment two minutes earlier, she would have missed the call. As it was, she let it ring several times, debating whether to answer and run the risk of another conversation with Maynard Branson. He had phoned three times in the past week, including once at the hospital where he managed to convince the floor supervisor to get Mary out of a staff meeting so she could speak with the doctor calling from the Mayo Clinic. In each contact, Maynard had escalated the level of dialogue, strongly suggesting that he would expose Mary's background if she did not take some action against Tim Foster.

"Hello," she said tentatively, as she picked up the phone.

"Mary? Hi, this is Joel Packard calling. I'm sorry to bother you so early on a Saturday, but I really need to talk to you." Mary was as surprised to be getting a call from Joel as she was relieved to be not getting one from Maynard. With the exception of their dinner together earlier in the week, she had had almost no contact with Dr. Packard since their relationship ended several years before.

"I must admit that I'm a little surprised to hear from you, Joel," she said. "What's got you so worked up this morning?"

"You know that court case where I testified several years ago? We were talking about it at a dinner the other evening. Well, guess what?" he said, not waiting for a response. "I got a call on Wednesday from a reporter at *The Washington Post* asking me about that trial and wanting to know more about graft implants. Then I check my service last night and find out that he's called me back again! What's going on, Mary?" Packard's decibel level was going up with each question. "Who did you talk to about that report?" Now he was almost screaming into the phone. It was not his smartest move.

"Don't you yell at me!" she shouted back at him. "You're the one who gave out the copy of the damn report. You think you have problems just because some reporter's calling? How would you like it if I gave your number out to the guy who wrote the report, so he could call you once a day in the operating room?" Now Mary was working up her own head of steam, using Joel as a surrogate to vent the anger that had built up after the calls from Branson. "This guy is going nuts, Joel, wanting me to do something about the last man he wrote about in his report ten years ago. All you've got to worry about is some reporter who calls and leaves polite messages!"

If the good doctor could have thought of a way to gracefully hang up he would have done so, as he now recognized that his problem was relatively benign in comparison to the situation with which Mary was dealing. An apology seemed in order.

"I'm sorry, Mary. I didn't realize this had gotten so serious. Why don't you call the authorities and report this guy? It sounds like he's making some kind of threats. I think you should report him."

There was a noticeable pause as she decided how to respond to the obvious question. Mary had successfully isolated Joel from her prior involvement with the Animal Rescue Band, and she had no desire to open the door on that segment of her life at this point in time.

"I can't really go into the details right now, Joel, but it just wouldn't work for me to ask for outside help on this. Branson has some old information from when I used to live in England that he's threatened to use against me. If I have to call the police some time then I will, but right now I want to see if I can work this out on my own." She was trying to sound confident.

"So what are you going to do? I don't see how you can solve this by yourself."

"I'm going to see Tim Foster. He was the last one that Branson wrote about in that report. I was just leaving when you called."

"Is he here in Boston?"

"No. He's staying at the Regency Park Hotel in Baltimore. I'm going to fly down there today to talk to him, warn him about Branson. That's how I found out where he is. Maynard called me last night and told me."

"What if he shows up at the same place? Aren't you running a big risk by going there?"

"I might be, but I want to finish this. One way or the other I want to bring this to an end. If I were you, I wouldn't call that reporter back. I'm not sure that I'd want my name involved with this whole story if I could avoid it."

"That might work for me, but how about you?" Packard was now trying to be helpful, no longer upset about his own situation. "Are you going to be able to stay out of the news on this?"

"I doubt it, Joel, but that may be the least of my problems."

Saturday, November 13, 9:40 a.m. – Washington, DC

The fact that the videotape was in a Beta professional format rather than VHS slowed them down for a few minutes, but the audio visual department at the Bureau was nothing if not well equipped, and they managed to find an old machine and get it set up in one of the small conference rooms within ten minutes of Mr. White's arrival. As he explained to Jay Harris, the tape consisted of 80 minutes of film that had been taken by a local TV station in Jesup, Georgia at the time of the trial. Most of the footage had never seen the light of day on the evening news, but the completed tape had been made available to the various trial participants in accordance with the judge's request.

"I think you'd better bring in a pot of strong coffee before you turn this thing on," Mr. White had told Harris as they were getting started. "If I remember right, what they included on this tape were the opening arguments, a little bit of the witness testimony, then the closing arguments and finally the reading of the jury verdict. It's pretty boring stuff. Even my wife wouldn't sit all the way through it, and that's after I told her I had a starring role." White laughed nervously as he mentioned the starring role, not wanting to overplay his part in the trial, but still proud about his performance in the witness chair some ten years after the fact.

On this Saturday morning Harris was the only agent sitting in the small conference room as they viewed the tape. Stinnett had opted to spend the weekend with the family hoping there would be some fresh perspective on the case when he returned on Monday. After watching the first 20 minutes of the tape, Jay was beginning to wonder if his time might not also have been better spent on something else.

"Is there anything different on the rest of the tape," he asked, "or is it just more of the same?"

"I'm not sure that I remember anything that stood out," White said. He had managed to find an ashtray and was lighting up his second cigarette of the morning. "What is it that you're looking for?"

"That's my problem," Jay said. "I don't really know what I'm looking for. This is pretty much of a long shot, but we don't have a lot of other things going for us at the moment." Harris had finished the one cup of vending machine coffee that he had brought with him into the room, and was wishing that he had taken White's advice about having a full pot available. "Maybe I'll skip ahead of the tape and look at where they read the verdict."

As he fast-forwarded through the tape, pausing for a moment to watch a portion of White's testimony, Jay was starting to think about where he could go next on his search for a person who would fit the second profile. If the "losing trial" theory got shot down, he would be left without an obvious motive to serve as the basis for the next stage in the investigation.

The last segment of the tape was the reading of the verdict, and Harris watched the truck driver's family listen passively as the judge read the jury's decision that there was not sufficient evidence to warrant a finding against the company. "With regard to the charge of strict liability in the death of James Robert Talbot, we find for the defendant, Aortek Incorporated. With regard to the charge of contributory negligence, we also find for the defendant."

Just as Mr. White recalled, the family seemed to accept the verdict with a minimum of emotion, almost a visible affirmation that once again, the system did not bend over backwards to help the little people. Jay got up and started moving towards the tape player as the station credits appeared on the screen. He watched the last few moments as Mr. Talbot's family was starting to leave the courtroom with their attorney, pausing to speak briefly with some of the people who had been seated behind them. As Jay reached for the eject button on the tape deck, he watched as a woman on crutches moved slowly towards the family. The woman seemed to be in pain as she leaned forward to put her arm around Mrs. Talbot, struggling to keep her balance as she shifted the two crutches to her other hand. Harris knew this woman! He had met her somewhere! But where? The woman he had met was not on crutches. Her hair had been a different style, and she was older. He had met her just within the past week or two. It was Martha Laudner!

"Mr. White," Jay said, motioning him over towards the monitor, "who is this woman and what was she doing at the trial?" By the time White had moved closer, the tape had ended, and Harris had to back it up a few minutes to run the key footage again. As Jay pointed to the woman on crutches, White leaned in towards the screen, anxious to be of assistance now that it seemed there might be something of interest on the tape.

"That's the wife of the man who was killed when Talbot's truck hit a car. I don't remember her name, but I know she was at most of the trial. Her husband was killed along with their two children when the truck Talbot was driving ran into them. They were on their way to Florida, as I recall. Tragic situation. She was injured pretty badly herself."

"Did she testify in the case?"

"No, her damages weren't part of the claims. If the jury had come back with a clear ruling that the graft failure caused the accident, which they probably should have, then I imagine that this woman would have filed suit against the company. The fact that the jury ruled the way they did meant that she didn't have a case against the company."

Over the next ten minutes, Harris played the critical portion of the tape several times, asking White each time about different points of law and the possibility that a failure of Talbot's graft actually did cause the accident, regardless of the way the jury ruled. On the third playback, Jay noticed a man holding on to Martha, helping her to balance as she spoke to Mrs. Talbot. The man appeared older than Martha, but he was turned slightly away from the camera and it was difficult to get a clear view of his face.

"Who is that man?" Jay asked. "Do you remember him being at the trial?"

Mr. White stared at the monitor as the tape was played back again. "I'm not sure I recognize him," he said, "but I do remember a man sitting next to the woman during most of her trial. It could be this man, but I can't say for sure. If it was this man, then he was at a couple of the other trials also. There was sort of an unofficial victims group that would attend these trials and then try to help each other out with information on how the company witnesses would testify and what kind of evidence would be introduced. Things like that. This man looks like he was one of those people."

Jay looked at his watch to check the time. He was starting to think of all the action items that should now be initiated. Don Stinnett would have to give up the weekend with the family, but this was an extraordinary break. Martha Laudner had to be a prime suspect! She not only had an unquestionable motive, but she also had access to a database that could be used to track the location of the men who worked at the company.

"Mr. White," Jay said, "you've been of immense help to us with this tape. I'd like to hang on to it for a few days and have some of our technical people see if they can enhance the image of the man we were talking about. Then if it's okay with you, we'd like to run prints of some of the key frames so we can have a hard copy for identification purposes."

"Do you want me to come back to the Bureau to pick it up? My wife thinks this whole exercise is a little on the fringe of reality."

"We'll bring the tape back to you, Mr. White, along with a framed thank you letter. It won't be Hoover's signature on the letter, but it will be signed by the Director of the FBI."

Saturday, November 13, 9:40 a.m. – Washington, DC

This would be the second interview of the day. The first one an hour before had gone smoothly, but five minutes into the session Foster knew that the candidate would not be a fit with the company culture at Remote Monitoring. David Morkin had allocated an hour for each of the interviews, but then gave Tim an extra half hour on the schedule in case he wanted to spend more time with any of the candidates. As was his custom, David put the strongest candidate third on the schedule, knowing that was the best position for purposes of making a strong comparison.

Foster was staying in room number 312 which had been reserved in his name. The interviews, two in the morning and two after lunch, would be taking place in the adjoining suite, number 314. That room had been reserved by David Morkin. In room 534, Joe Sheldon's two children had just helped him brush off his tuxedo as he prepared for the wedding. And on the eighth floor, assistant catering manager Joyce Weidner was directing the placement of the floral arrangements for the reception.

The Regency Park Hotel had opened for business in 1988, one of the new style hotels that offered larger room accommodations for families or business meetings at prices considerably less than comparable first tier properties. The key to making the economics work was a location that was convenient but not exorbitantly priced, and an interior design standard that gave a great deal of attention to the creative use of plastic. The architect for the Regency Park had also borrowed extensively from the style of some of the more prestigious hotels by incorporating a huge central atrium which extended upward the entire height of eight-story building. On the east end of the top floor there was an open area that had originally been a concierge lounge but was now used for private parties and other assorted social gatherings. It was here that the wedding reception and lunch would be held.

"Can I fly a paper airplane off the balcony?" Joe Sheldon's son asked when he and his father had walked through the area earlier in the morning when checking on arrangements for the reception.

"I want you to stay back from that railing," Joe said. "I'm going to have enough on my mind this noon without worrying about you or your sister falling over the edge."

With the open atrium design, all the guest rooms and suites were accessed by corridors and doorways which opened out onto the central core of the building. The railing that bordered each three-foot-wide corridor was at a height sufficient to meet the minimum safety requirements, but not so high as to impair the view for the adventuresome guest who enjoyed peering down into the lobby area below. Tim Foster had a railing outside the entrance to his room, but when it came to heights, he did not fit into the adventuresome category. When he had left his room earlier in the morning to have breakfast in the lobby with David Morkin, Tim had literally hugged the wall as he made his way to the elevator. And when David invited him to visit the wedding reception to say hello to Martha, Tim accepted without knowing that the eighth floor area was even more open, even more of a challenge to the borderline acrophobic.

"Your first afternoon appointment isn't until two o'clock, so why don't you stop in at the reception about one thirty and say hello to Martha."

"You sure it won't be an imposition? I don't want to walk in on somebody else's party."

"No, she'd love to see you. You were always one of her favorites – one of her eagles. It'll be a great surprise."

Saturday, November 13, 11:05 a.m. – Washington, DC

The FBI prides itself on being a '24 hours a day, seven days a week' type of organization. But agencies are staffed by people who, while well intentioned, do have other interests in their lives. Jay Harris was swimming against the tide of those other interests as he attempted to get the investigation shifted back into high speed on a Saturday morning.

"I need to reach Bob Kaufmann and Don Stinnett from headquarters along with Keith Sanford from the Denver office and Mark Brinkman from the Baltimore regional office," Harris informed the message center as soon as Mr. White had left. Agents on standby duty and those involved in active investigations carry pagers for purposes of emergency contact. Other agents are expected to leave telephone numbers where they can be reached in the event they need to be called in for duty on short notice. It is a system that works much of the time, but it is a long way from being perfect. So far Jay was one for four, with one more on hold. Sanford had called in from Denver and Harris had instructed him to reinstate the protection detail on Foster. There had been no contact yet from Kaufmann or Brinkman, and Stinnett was holding as Jay finished the call from Denver.

"Don? Thanks for calling back. We've just had a major break in the case." Harris proceeded to give Stinnett the background on the videotape and the possible involvement of Martha Laudner. This was somewhat of a touchy phone call. Stinnett was the section chief who had prime responsibility for directing and coordinating the investigation, but Harris was the agent who, at that particular moment, was in the best position to affect the short-term decision process.

"Jay, you're going to have to hold the fort for awhile," Stinnett said when Harris finished talking. "I'm in the middle of Virginia visiting my dad and I've got about a two hour drive back to Washington in a car without a phone. I was going to leave at three o'clock to be there for our 6:30 meeting with that reporter from the paper, but now I'll leave in a few minutes and then stop every half hour to call in."

"Okay, I'll talk to you again in a little while. I've got Sanford calling me back again on the other line."

The pace was starting to quicken. Jay had one of the weekend duty agents helping him out on the phones, along with a pool secretary who had immediately been assigned the task of finding some coffee and sandwiches. A technician from the video lab had just brought in the first enhanced photo of the man who had been standing next to Martha Laudner in the courtroom. It was an improved image from the one on the tape, but still somewhat grainy. The technician said the next version would be better. Jay stared at the photo as he took the call from Sanford.

"We haven't been able to reach Foster yet," the Denver agent said. "I called his home and spoke with one of his daughters. She said her dad is out of town on a trip but she didn't know exactly where. She thinks it's out east someplace. I'm at my office now but will be on my way to his house in a few minutes. The girl thinks the mother should be home in a few minutes and she'll know where the dad is."

"Have you started protection again?" Jay asked.

"I've got the process started, but until we know where Foster is, I don't really know where to send anybody. I'll call you back as soon as I find out."

Over the next fifteen minutes, Jay's high point was the arrival of the coffee and sandwiches. The low was a telephone discussion with Robert Kaufmann, whose primary concern was determining who would be the one to call Director Nickoloff and how could the news be presented as a positive breakthrough. Harris was saved from the possibility of a self-inflicted verbal wound by another call from Sanford.

"Where did you tell me this Laudner woman lives?" he asked.

"Baltimore. I was in her apartment last week along with Brinkman from the district office."

"Guess where Foster is today. Baltimore! He flew there yesterday afternoon. His wife says he's supposed to have some meetings there today and then he's scheduled to fly back on Sunday. You'll have to arrange for the protection. I can't do him much good sitting here in Denver."

After Sanford had passed on the hotel information that Mrs. Foster had given him, Harris ended the conversation and began procedures to make contact with the Baltimore office. He could no longer wait for a call back from Agent Brinkman. Although the information concerning Martha Laudner was not sufficient to warrant an arrest, the pattern of past activity indicated that further investigation was certainly warranted. With the assistance of the message center, Jay was able to reach Lloyd Armstrong, the Agent in Charge of the Baltimore office. Armstrong would take action to initiate surveillance and a background check on Laudner and would also send agents directly to the hotel to establish some level of protection for Foster while he was in the city.

"How fast can you get protection in place," Harris asked.

"It'll take at least an hour," Armstrong said. "If you know this guy, why don't you give him a call. Tell him about what you've just found out and that we've got some agents on the way to watch his back until he heads out of town."

This was one of those moments when Jay remembered why he usually spent time in his basement lair studying old files instead of actively working cases. He should have thought to make that call as soon as he had a phone number in Baltimore. He had spoken to Foster in Denver and established some level of rapport and trust. There was no answer in the room! Jay let the phone ring seven or eight times, waiting for the hotel operator to come back on the line.

"No, ma'am," he said, "I don't want to leave a message. It's extremely important that I reach him. Do you know, are there any sort of meetings going on in the hotel today? Medical meetings or business meetings that Mr. Foster might be attending."

"No, sir. Not here in the hotel. The only event we have scheduled today is a wedding reception."

Saturday, November 13, 1:20 p.m. – Baltimore

The clerk at the reception desk was not about the break procedure. "Yes, I can tell you that Tim Foster is registered here at the hotel. No, I can't give out any room numbers. You'll have to call him on the house phone."

Mary Devlin had already called twice on the house phone. She had not left a message, hoping to be able to talk to Foster directly. In her purse she had the picture from the prospectus that Branson had sent. She would keep calling the room and keep looking at faces in the lobby. When she was on the flight from Boston she had been second-guessing her judgment about coming to Baltimore. Now that she was at the hotel, she was certain that it was the right decision. One way or another she needed to make contact with the last name in the report.

Now Jay Harris was also at the hotel, also looking to make contact with Tim Foster. When he had been unable to reach Foster on the phone, he requisitioned a car and driver for the short trip into Baltimore. Of the four FBI agents now in the hotel, Harris was the only one who had met Tim, and it was important that somebody be at the hotel who knew what he looked like. Jay was sitting at a table in the lobby with Armstrong and Brinkman from the Baltimore office. The fourth agent was standing by the railing in the corridor next to room 312. The desk clerk had decided that he could bend the rules for the man with the FBI badge.

The woman with the English accent had just poured herself a cup of coffee from the hospitality table in the lobby, and was now sitting in one of the nearby lounge chairs where she could watch the foot traffic coming into the hotel. She could also see the three men at the round table some 20 feet away, and had already compared their faces against the picture that she had placed in front of her. She was close enough to be certain that none of the three were Foster, but not so close that she could hear their conversation.

"You know, we were sitting in her apartment when she found out that Foster used to work at Aortek. Remember that?" Mark Brinkman was talking to Harris, filling time as they waited for some sign of Tim Foster.

"I remember," Jay said. "She actually recruited him for his present job. Now he flies into Baltimore, and for all we know he's having lunch with her someplace. When are we going to hear from surveillance?"

"We've got two agents over at her appointment building talking to neighbors, and one who's on his way to Morkin's office," Dalhberg said. "We do know that she's not home, but that's about it so far. They'll call me here when there's an update." Armstrong tapped the pocket on his suit jacket, still somewhat pleased with himself over the new generation of portable phones that he had managed to acquire for the senior agents in his region.

Tim Foster did have lunch in the same hotel as Martha Laudner, but some five floors apart. As she was cutting the cake on the eighth floor, Foster was finishing a sandwich in room 314. His 10:30 interview had been with Dave Holberg, a sales manager for another monitoring company, and an individual who was appearing to be an exceptionally strong candidate for the vice president's job at Remote. Tim had ordered a room service lunch so the two men could have more time together.

"I appreciate the fact that you could spend some extra time with me today," Tim was telling Holberg after lunch as they got up to leave the room. "You definitely have a great deal of experience in this area and I'll look forward to talking with some of your references."

As they went out the door, they had to move around the man standing near the entrance to room 312. That man was leaning against the wall, so it was necessary for Foster and Holberg to walk on the outer edge of the corridor, next to the railing.

"I'm going to let you take the outside," Tim said, as he paused to let Holberg go ahead. "I'm not too crazy about heights. I'll walk with you to the elevator, and then I have to go up to the eighth floor for a few minutes to say hello to one of the partners from our search firm."

Mary Devlin was looking at the two men walking along the outside corridor on the third floor. Her eye had been drawn to that area before when she had seen a man standing there. Now she was watching again as the two men walked along the corridor towards the elevator on the west end of the building. It was possible that one of the men could be Foster, but just when she thought she might be able to tell, the other man moved to the side of the corridor by the railing, blocking her view. Mary knew that the elevator in the hotel had a glass exterior wall facing into the open lobby area. As she walked past the nearby table on her way to the elevator, one of the three men she had seen before reached in his coat pocket to pull out a small portable phone.

"Armstrong," he said after the first ring. He listened for a few moments and then responded. "Okay. I want one of you to stay there and watch the apartment and the other to come over here."

"What is it?" Harris asked.

"You won't believe this!" Armstrong was standing up and looking around the lobby area. "Laudner is getting married today. One of the neighbors said that the reception is here at this hotel! The neighbor was invited but couldn't come." Armstrong had put the phone back in his pocket and was looking at his watch. "The

373

reception should still be going on. Brinkman, go over to the desk and see if you can find out where it's being held."

Mary had watched as the elevator went up and stopped at the third floor level. One of the men got in and the elevator started down. As the man turned around to look out the glass wall, Mary could see that he was not Foster. She was tempted to talk to him when the door opened on the first floor, to ask him if he knew Tim Foster. But then the elevator started up again, and as Mary watched, the second man got in when the car stopped at the third floor level. He looked briefly down into the lobby, but then turned and moved away from the glass wall. She thought it might be Foster. She looked at the picture again, but she could not be sure.

When the elevator stopped at the top level, Mary moved farther back in the lobby so she could get a better view as the man walked along the corridor. He was heading towards the open reception area at the east end of the building. Now, even though he was away from the railing, she could get a clear view of his face. This time she was certain. It was Tim Foster.

As she moved around to the front of the elevator, two men were walking rapidly towards her. "I can't believe it's right here in the same hotel," one of the men said. "What are the odds against that?"

"If she's not involved it might make sense," the other said. "You put your guests up at the same place that you're going to have a reception. Makes it easier on everyone who's attending."

They were talking quietly now, as they waited for the elevator along with the other woman who was standing there. When the door opened and the three of them got in, Jay Harris reached forward to push the button for the eighth floor from his side of the elevator as Mary Devlin did the same from her side, smiling ever so slightly at the coincidence.

When they arrived on the top floor, Mary got out first and turned to her left to walk around the corridor towards the east end of the atrium. Harris and Brinkman turned right, and looked across the open area as they kept pace with Mary, step for step.

"What the hell are we going to do when we get there?" Brinkman asked. "We really don't have any official reason to be talking to anyone, especially at somebody's wedding reception."

"I don't know yet," Jay said. "If I see Foster then I'll ask him to come with us down to the lobby to talk for a while. If he's not there, then I'm not sure just what we can do. Tell Laudner we'd like to see her, I guess, and hope she doesn't throw us off the balcony."

Tim Foster was trying to stay away from that balcony as David Morkin shook his hand and started introducing him to some of the other guests. "Martha's there near the railing," David said. "Let's go over and say hello. She'll be surprised that you're here."

Martha was standing near the railing with Joe and two other guests, enjoying the sunshine that was filtering in through the large skylight that covered the central atrium. Joe's two children were leaning over the railing, coming perilously close to a decision as to whether or not one of them might just spit and try to hit the flower pot in the lobby eight floors below. Morkin had taken Tim's elbow, and was moving him over towards Martha. As Tim moved reluctantly forward, he noticed a woman walking towards him from one of the side corridors.

"Mr. Foster," she said, while she was still several feet away. "May I speak with you a minute?"

David Morkin held out his hand as if indicating that he did not want to be interrupted just yet. "Martha," he said, "I want to reintroduce you to one of your old friends and one of our new clients, Tim Foster. He's interviewing in the hotel today and wanted to stop up and say hello."

As Martha turned around, the look on her face seemed to be more than one of surprise. She stared at Foster for a moment without speaking. The man standing next to her was the first to say anything, looking back at Morkin as he asked his question.

"Who did you say this is?"

"This is Tim Foster," David said. "He's the president of Remote Monitoring now, and one of our clients, but he used to be one of Martha's eagles."

And then, suddenly, it happened! Tim was pushed backwards towards the railing – his arms reaching out, trying desperately to grab onto something or someone as he struggled to stay away from the edge of the balcony.

Harris and Brinkman were approaching the reception area when the encounter started. "That's Foster," Jay said, "and he's with Martha Laudner!" Harris was looking at one of the men next to Martha, trying to match the face with the digitized image from the videotape. He was about to reach in his pocket to bring out the picture when Foster yelled for help.

As Tim was pushed back against the railing he shouted and instinctively reach out and grabbed onto another body. It was Jimmy Sheldon, Joe's 16-year-old son.

"Grab Jimmy," Martha screamed, "he's going to fall!"

Now Jay was running into the center of the melee, and as Martha grabbed for Jimmy, Harris pulled Foster back from the railing. It would be another few minutes before Tim could speak, and another hour before he would go back to the elevator, with Harris walking alongside, next to the railing. By then, Armstrong had brought in the Baltimore police who made the arrest for attempted murder, with more charges to be filed later in the day for complicity in the deaths of the 13 other men.

Jay would come back to Baltimore several times over the next week to assist in the questioning of the suspect, but he had already heard enough to be convinced. They had arrested the individual behind the serial murders. They had found the person who fit the second profile!

Saturday, November 13, 7:25 p.m. – Washington, DC

The meeting was almost over, and Karl Bonnert was smiling. He had every reason to do so. Denise Altman had been more than cooperative, and although Jay Harris had arrived late, both he and Don Stinnett had provided enough background and detail to ensure that the *Post* story would be accurate. During the meeting, Michael Montgomery had asked most of the questions, and Stinnett was continually surprised at the amount of information that the young reporter had managed to obtain on the various aspects of the case.

"And how did you know these deaths were a part of a serial murder case?" Stinnett had asked, after Michael had gone through the list of victims.

"That was mostly a guess on our part," Michael said, choosing not to bring up the subject of Stinnett's secretary. "We did talk to a number of the victims' families, so we knew that your office was involved in the investigation."

"Well, Michael," Denise was ready to pass out some accolades now that she saw the direction of the story, "we're sure impressed with the research that you've done on this article. And just so you folks know, we'll be issuing a press release in a couple of hours that will cover the history of this case along with the events that have taken place this week." She was getting ready to leave now, putting her notepad into a small leather bag. "Unfortunately, it will be a little late for the evening news or the other morning papers."

"Yes, that is unfortunate," Karl said, with just the minimum amount of deceit in his voice. "We're running kind of tight on time ourselves. Michael, do you have any last minute questions before we wrap this up?"

"Just one. I wanted to check the correct spelling on Baumgardner. Is it spelled as it sounds?"

"That's right," Jay Harris responded. "Baumgardner – Marcus Baumgardner. B-a-u-m-g-a-r-d-n-e-r."

CHAPTER THIRTY
Day Ten

Sunday, November 14, 10:15 a.m. EST

He had been to the convenience store on the corner near his apartment twice, buying three copies of the paper on his first trip and then returning the second time to buy five more. There would be tear sheets available when he went into the office on Monday, but there was nothing like an original front page for the scrapbook and the relatives.

The *Post* used a six-column layout, and Michael's article had been placed in the top half of the two columns on the right side. Lead articles were sometimes given a box placement on the left half of the front page, but in those situations there was usually a photo tie-in, which was not the case with Michael's story. He and Bonnert had talked about possibly using a shot of Jay Harris to accompany the article, but both agreed that the first story should focus on the intricacies of the case and the arrest of the person behind the 13 murders. As is the practice at most major papers, story headlines at the *Post* are written by someone other than the reporter, but with that exception the article appeared exactly as submitted by Michael. The lead paragraph was now different than the draft he had given Karl on Monday, but it was still four sentences, still 100 words.

During the next week, Michael would write a number of follow-on stories, one of which would cover the FBI's successful use of profiles in serial murder cases. Jay Harris would be the focal point of that story, although he had already served notice that neither he nor the FBI thought it appropriate to single out one individual agent for attention. Later in the day, Michael would draft a list of research questions on prior serial cases, but for now he would concentrate on rereading his story and enjoying his 15 minutes of fame.

There had been five phone calls to the Montgomery apartment so far on this Sunday morning, three from friends at the paper and one from a young female acquaintance whose interest in Michael seemed to be increasing on rather short notice. The other call, and the one that was probably the most gratifying, came from

Denise Altman. Even though she came across as being a little on the obsequious end of the compliment scale, it was clear that Denise now saw Michael as someone who would be a continuing factor in her ever challenging task of creating and maintaining a favorable image at the Federal Bureau of Investigation.

"It was an outstanding piece of investigative reporting, Michael," she purred. "Director Nickoloff called me first thing this morning and wanted to be sure that I passed on his compliments."

"I appreciate that."

"We were wondering, Michael, does this piece mean you'll be the *Post* reporter who'll be on the FBI beat from now on?"

"I really don't know about that. I'm sure Hampton will be involved one way or the other when he gets back. I suppose the assignments will be up to Karl."

"Well, I'd like you to know, Michael, that if you do continue working the FBI material or other related stories where you might need some background, then I'd like you to feel free to give me a call anytime. You can contact me on my direct line. If you've got a pencil handy I'll give you the number."

"That would be helpful," Michael said. And then, with just the least bit of a smile on his face, he finished the conversation. "While you're at it, Denise, give me your home number in case I want to call you after hours."

As satisfying as the exchange was with Denise Altman, the conversation that Michael was really looking forward to was the one he hoped to have shortly with Dr. Harold J. Brown. Michael had heard from one of his old classmates that Dr. Brown had suffered a slight stroke a few months ago and was now on medical leave from the University.

"He's got some problem with his eyesight, but his wife reads all the papers to him each morning," Michael's friend had said. "He's supposed to be just as sharp as ever. Probably spending his time writing a hundred word obit."

As Michael dialed the number, he was surprised to realize that he was starting to get nervous. The confidence that was so evident the past week as he bluffed his way into several important sources was now beginning to fade. The article that had made its way through the labyrinth of editorial review at the *Post*, the article that now had the media relations of the FBI calling to pass on adoring comments – that same article just might not meet the exacting standards of Hundred Word Harry, and if not, then Michael would have not met his own self-imposed yardstick of achievement.

"Hello." The call was answered on the second ring, and Michael's heart rate went up another 20 beats per minute.

"Hello. Mrs. Brown? This is Michael Montgomery calling. I was wondering if Dr. Brown might be available this morning."

"Yes he is, Michael. We were hoping you would call. That was a very nice article you had in the *Post* this morning." Elizabeth Brown was sitting across from her husband at the kitchen table in their small but comfortable Tudor style home near the campus of Howard University. Mrs. Brown was an accomplished writer in her own right, having published numerous short stories and a recent historical treatise on the advancement of black women in the sciences, but she knew that on this morning Michael would be most interested in talking to the other writer in the family.

"Did you want to talk to Harry?"

"Yes, if that's okay. Is he feeling up to talking on the phone?"

"I'm sure he'll want to talk to you." She looked across the table and saw that Harry was smiling now as he listened to his wife's end of the conversation. "You know that he's very proud of you, Michael. We both are."

For the first time since college, Michael had his chance to talk to Hundred Word Harry as one writer to another, reliving the events of the past two weeks and discussing questions of style and emphasis and preferred sequence for the articles that would follow. It was a conversation that the young reporter would remember for the rest of his life, made even more meaningful by Dr. Brown's request.

"You know, Michael, Elizabeth read me your article first thing this morning. But I always like to go over the good stuff a second time. I wonder if you'd mind reading your story to me again."

"It would be my pleasure," Michael said. "It would be my pleasure!"

And so, Michael J. Montgomery, newly promoted staff writer for *The Washington Post*, read his byline story to Hundred Word Harry. In the future, there would be other byline stories for

Michael, but this was the first, and this was the one that Dr. Brown wanted to hear.

FBI Cracks Ten Year Serial Murder Case
By Michael J. Montgomery
Washington Post Staff Writer

At first it was an isolated crime, a hit and run in Boston, a murder in Atlanta. But eventually, the individual cases were identified by the FBI as each being part of a series of thirteen mysterious deaths of business executives from different parts of the country. Deaths separated by geography and time, yet linked by a common motive. Months of intensive investigation involving dozens of agents came to a dramatic conclusion yesterday in Baltimore when the person responsible for this bizarre sequence of events was apprehended only moments before the life of a fourteenth victim would have been claimed.

As Special Agent Don Stinnett explained to the *Post* in an exclusive interview yesterday, "This case has been one of the most complex serial murder investigations ever completed by the FBI, in part because it involved not one, but two key perpetrators.

The FBI's work on this case has been directed by Stinnett and Special Agent Jay Harris, one of the Bureau's leading experts in the arcane art of profiling, the process of determining the likely background and characteristics of the individual who would commit such a crime. It was Harris who developed the premise that this serial murder case involved two people, one who actually committed the murders, and a second person behind the scenes, driven by a desire for revenge and retribution so strong that it could be sustained over a period of ten years and the deaths of thirteen men.

This serial murder case began in May of 1985 with the death of John Levard, a medical company executive from Boston, who was killed while attending an industry meeting in Toronto. Over the next ten years, with almost mathematical regularity, twelve other industry executives were killed, all but one of whom had worked for the same company at some time during their career. (See accompanying article on 'victims'.) Although the firm, Aortek Inc., has been out of business since 1986, it was the trail back to the company that gave the FBI its first insight into a possible motive for the serial killings.

The medical device industry in this country is comprised of thousands of firms of various sizes, most of which are capable of the design and manufacture of products that can dramatically extend or improve the quality of life for patients and their families. A few of these firms, unfortunately, are not so capable. This may well have been the situation with Aortek, a company that, before its demise, was based in Houston, Texas, and was involved with the development of implantable grafts used in the surgical repair of aortic aneurysms.

It was the failure of one of these grafts that allegedly caused the death of a Georgia truck driver in 1982, leading to a fiery crash that subsequently claimed the lives of three other people, two of whom were the only grandchildren of a man from Davenport, Iowa. And it was this man, Marcus Baumgardner, who was arrested yesterday in Baltimore and charged as the person responsible for ordering the murder of the men who had worked in key positions at Aortek.

Although various aspects of the investigation are still in process, it now appears that Baumgardner was so distraught over the death of his grandchildren that he carried out this ten-year mission of revenge with a passion and intensity that has rarely been seen, even by those people within the FBI accustomed to dealing with serial cases. Baumgardner was apparently able to develop his target list from the copy of a report that had been written by a disgruntled ex-employee of the company. One of the people questioned at the scene yesterday, Ms. Mary Devlin, acknowledged that such a report had originally been prepared at her request, and may somehow have fallen into the hands of Mr. Baumgardner as he followed other legal proceedings involving the company.

Officials are still uncertain just how Baumgardner had been able to finance the killings, which were apparently all carried out by a Las Vegas hit man who was killed in a shoot-out with the FBI earlier in the week. Special Agent Stinnett indicated that Mrs. Martha Laudner, the mother of the children who were killed in the accident, received a large insurance settlement which may have been shared with her father. Stinnett stated that, at this time, there is insufficient evidence to suggest that Mrs. Laudner was aware of her father's activities, and accordingly she will not be charged with any criminal action.

During this week, the *Post* will publish a series of articles detailing the history of this investigation and the events surrounding the case. We will also look at the experience that the FBI has had over the years in the handling of serial murder cases. Certainly, the arrest yesterday of the man behind these thirteen murders was a tribute to the Bureau's experience, and in particular, to Special Agent Jay Harris, the man responsible for the origin of the second profile.

Made in the USA
Lexington, KY
29 July 2014

November 6, 2013

Kathie,

Thanks for the loan of your first name and your background. You and Kathie McDonnell have a lot in common.

All the best!

TSJJr